*F*yodor *D*ostoyevsky

Fyodor Dostoyevsky

Selected Works

Fyodor Dostoyevsky

The Karamazov Brothers

A novel
in four parts
with an epilogue

In two volumes

Volume One

Translated by *Julius Katzer*

Raduga Publishers Moscow

Translation from the Russian
Designed by *Vladimir Kireyev*

First published 1981
Second printing 1990
English translation ©Progress Publishers 1981

©Raduga Publishers 1990

Printed in the Union of Soviet Socialist Republics

ISBN 5-05-002803-5
ISBN 5-05-002804-3

CONTENTS

THE KARAMAZOV BROTHERS

Verily, verily, I say unto you, except a corn of wheat fall into the ground and die, it abideth alone: but if it die, it bringeth forth much fruit.

(The Gospel according to St. John, Chapter XII, Verse 24)

FROM THE AUTHOR

I feel somewhat hesitant as I set about writing the lifestory of my hero, Alexei Fyodorovich Karamazov. The reason is: though I do call Alexei Fyodorovich my hero, I am well aware that he is not in any way a great man, which is why I anticipate some inevitable questions, such as: what are the outstanding qualities in him that have led you to choose him for your hero? What has he accomplished? To whom is he known, and for what? Why should I, the reader, spend time learning the facts of his life?

The last question is the most crucial, for the only answer I can give is: "Perhaps you will see for yourself from the novel." But supposing that will not be seen from a reading of the novel, and the reader does not agree that there is something remarkable about my Alexei Fyodorovich? I say so because it is something I anticipate with a little sadness. To me he *is* a remarkable person, but I am most doubtful whether I shall be able to convince the reader of it. The reason is that, though Alexei Fyodorovich may have got things done, the manner of it has been vague and indeterminate. Yet in times like ours, it would be strange to expect clarity in people. One thing, perhaps, is beyond doubt: he *is* a strange kind of man, even an oddity. Strangeness and oddity, however, are more likely to prove detrimental than to justify attention. That is especially so in our times when it is in vogue to reduce individual particulars to some common denominator and to try to discern at least some overall order in the universal welter. In most cases, however, there *is* something individual and particular about an oddity, is there not?

But if you do not see eye to eye with me on the latter score, and reply: "There is not", or "Not always", then I may well take heart regarding the significance of my hero Alexei Fyodorovich. For an oddity is "not always" one who is merely individual and particular; on the contrary, it sometimes happens that it is he who bears within himself the very core of the general, while the rest of his contemporaries—all of

9

them—have for a while been somehow swept from his side by a gust of wind, as it were.

I ought not to have launched into these very jejune and hazy explanations, but should simply have begun without any introduction at all: if the novel is liked, it will be read anyway; the trouble is that what I have to offer is only one lifestory, but two novels. The second novel is the main one: it is about my hero's activities in our own days, namely, at the present and current moment. As for the first novel, it dates back thirteen years, and is even hardly a novel at all but merely a fleeting moment in my hero's youth. Yet it is quite impossible to do without the first novel, because in that case much in the second novel will become incomprehensible. But that complicates my initial difficulty even more: if I, i. e. the biographer himself, consider that even a single novel may perhaps be excessive for so modest and indeterminate a hero, then why appear with two, and how is such uppishness on my part to be accounted for?

Since I am at a loss as to how these questions should be dealt with, I make so bold as to evade them, offering no solution at all. Of course, the discerning reader has been aware of that from the very outset, and has only been galled by my using barren words and taking up precious time. To that I will give a precise answer: I have used barren words and taken up precious time out of civility in the first place, and, in the second, out of wiliness: after all, you have been duly warned. Incidentally, I am even glad that my novel falls into two stories, but "with a substantive unity of the whole": after reading the first story, the reader will make up his own mind whether he should set about reading the second. Of course, no obligation is implied: the book can be laid aside even after two pages of the first story, never to be reopened. But there are readers so tactful that they will certainly wish to read it through to the end so as to escape falling into error in forming an unbiassed judgement: all Russian critics are of such stuff. Well, with such people, I can set my heart at rest: despite all their punctiliousness and assiduity, they have been provided with a legitimate pretext to drop the story after the first episode in the novel. Well, that's the lot as far as an introduction is concerned. I fully agree it is superfluous, but since it has already been penned, let it stand.

And now for the story.

PART ONE

BOOK ONE

The History of a Family of Sorts

1.

Fyodor Pavlovich Karamazov

Alexei Fyodorovich* Karamazov was the third son of Fyodor Pavlovich Karamazov, a landowner in our uyezd**, a man who once acquired some notoriety (and is still remembered in our parts) because of his tragic and mysterious death, which took place exactly thirteen years ago and will be dealt with here in due course. For the time, I shall merely say of this "landowner" (as he was known locally though he hardly ever lived on his estate during his whole life) that he was a strange creature, yet of a kind fairly often to be met, namely, not only an evil and thoroughly reprobate man but, at the same time, a bungler, though of those bunglers who are deft at feathering their own nests, and at nothing else, it would seem. For instance, Fyodor Pavlovich began with practically nothing to his name; actually a petty landowner, he was constantly cadging invitations to dinners and fawning for small favours, yet he was worth a cool hundred thousand when he died. At the same time, he remained throughout his life one of the ultimately most inept cranks in our uyezd. I repeat: it was not simply a matter of obtuseness—most of these cranks are quite intelligent and wily—but of sheer ineptitude, and of a special and national brand at that.

---

*By tradition Russians have only one given name which, prior to the October Revolution, was usually that of the corresponding saint in the Orthodox church calendar, and was bestowed at the christening ceremony. The day was known as the *name-day* or *the day of one's angel*. Another established tradition is that a given name is accompanied by a patronymic, which invariably stands between name and surname. Thus, in *Fyodor Pavlovich Karamazov* the patronymic *Pavlovich* indicates that Fyodor Karamazov's father was called Pavel (Paul). The corresponding feminine form ends in *-na*, e. g. *Pavlovna*. To address a person by his name and patronymic (without the surname) is an expression of courtesy, or of respect for one's elders or superiors.—*Tr.*

**Uyezd*—prior to the Revoluiton, an administrative subdivision of a gubernia (province).—*Tr.*

He was twice married, and had three sons: the eldest, Dmitri, by his first wife, and the other two, Ivan and Alexei, by the second. Fyodor Pavlovich's first wife was of fairly wealthy and distinguished stock — the Miusovs, who were local landowners too. I will not even try to explain how it came to pass that a girl with a dowry, good-looking into the bargain and, on top of that, of the vivacious and intelligent kind not uncommon in the present generation and already emergent in the previous could have married such a paltry "runt" as he was then generally called. Why, I once knew a young lady belonging to the "romantic" generation preceding the last, who, after several years of an inexplicable love for a gentleman she could easily have got married to whenever she wished, thought up some insurmountable obstacles to their union, and ended up by jumping into a fairly deep and swift river from a high and steep bank one stormy night and drowning out of a sheer whim, exclusively because she wanted to resemble Shakespeare's Ophelia; had the precipice she had come upon long before and grown attached to been less picturesque, and had there been in its stead nothing but a flat and ordinary bank, there might perhaps have been no suicide at all. This is a true fact and there is reason to believe that such or similar things have been fairly common in our Russian life during the past two or three generations. In the same way, Adelaida Ivanovna's action was no doubt an echo of extraneous influences as well as of her soul's yearning to escape. Perhaps she wished to display some feminine independence and snap her fingers at social conventions and the tyranny of her kith and kin, her facile imagination persuading her — if only fleetingly — that, despite his hanger-on status, Fyodor Pavlovich was a bold and pungent critic at a time of transition to better things, while he was in fact a spiteful buffoon, and nothing else. What added relish to the affair was that it ended in an elopement, something very much to Adelaida Ivanovna's liking. For his part, Fyodor Pavlovich had been fully prepared for such escapades by his social standing, for he was most eager to get on in the world no matter how, the prospect of worming his way into a good family and getting a dowry being a highly attractive one. As for mutual love, there seemed to be none on either side, even despite the bride's good looks. The event was perhaps unique in the entire lifetime of Fyodor Pavlovich, a lecher ready at any moment to go chasing after any female who would as much as beckon to him; yet his future wife was the only woman who failed to arouse the slightest desire in him.

Right after the elopement, Adelaida Ivanovna discovered that she felt nothing but contempt for her husband. The consequences of the marriage took shape at impetuous speed: husband and wife were soon at loggerheads, and their quarrels were never ending, although the family had even become reconciled to the event before long, and given the runaway bride her marriage portion. The young wife, it was said, displayed far more dignity and high character in this than did Fyodor Pavlovich, who, it came to be known, at once did her out of all her money to the tune of twenty-five thousand as soon as she had got it, so that she never saw the colour of her thousands again. Then for a long time, he bent every effort to achieve the transference to himself, through some deed of conveyance, of the little village and the very decent town house that also formed part of her marriage portion; he would have probably succeeded in this if only because of the contempt and loathing that her husband's barefaced and wheedling pertinacity constantly inspired in her, and because her weariness of spirit would have made her to anything that would induce him to desist. Fortunately, however, her family stepped in and curbed the money-grubber. It is positively known that the two often came to blows, but, according to rumour, it was not Fyodor Pavlovich but Adelaida Ivanovna who did the clouting, for this dark-skinned lady was hot-tempered, mettlesome, reckless, and endowed with remarkable physical strength. She finally left home to make off with an impecunious teacher with a seminary background, abandoning the three-year-old Mitya* to her husband's care. The latter at once turned his home into a regular bawdy-house and a scene of drunken orgies, in between which he would drive all over the gubernia, complaining maudlinly to all and sundry of his hav-

*Diminutive of Dmitri.—*Tr.*

14

ing been deserted by Adelaida Ivanovna, and adding details of his conjugal life too shameful for any husband to go into. The main thing was that he seemed gratified and even flattered to publicly play the ridiculous role of an injured husband and to embellish with lurid details the offence given to him. "One might think you'd been promoted to some rank, Fyodor Pavlovich," his listeners would say chaffingly, "you seem so pleased despite all your troubles." Many even went on to say he actually enjoyed the fresh opportunity of playing the buffoon and that, in pretending to be unaware of his ridiculous situation, he was simply out to provoke even more laughter. But perhaps it was all naivety on his part. Who can tell? He finally got wind of his runaway wife's whereabouts. The poor woman proved to be in St. Petersburg where she had fled with her seminarist and had immersed herself in a life of the most complete emancipation. Fyodor Pavlovich immediately set about preparing for the journey to St. Petersburg, without of course quite knowing the reason why. Indeed, he would probably have gone there but, having made up his mind to do so, he at once decided he would do well to fortify himself for the journey with another bout of bibulous ribaldry. It was just then that the news of his wife's death in St. Petersburg reached her family: she had died suddenly in some garret, of typhus, according to one version, or of starvation, as another version had it. On learning of his wife's demise, some said the inebriated Fyodor Pavlovich dashed out into the street, his hands raised heavenwards in joy, shouting, "Lord, now lettest thou thy servant depart in peace." Others asserted that he had burst into such torrents of tears, just like a little child, that people felt sorry for him, despite all their abhorrence of him. Both versions may well have been true; that is to say, he felt overjoyed at his release while weeping for her who had released him — this at one and the same time. In most cases, people — even the wicked — are far more naive and simple of heart than we usually think. The same goes for us.

2.

He Gets Rid of His First Son

One can, of course, easily imagine the kind of father such a man could make and how he would rear his offspring. What happened to him as a father was exactly what had to happen, that is to say, he fully and completely neglected the child born to him by Adelaida Ivanovna, but did so, not out of any ill-will or sense of conjugal vexation but simply because he had quite forgotten his existence. Whilst he was wearying others with his tearful complaints and turning his house into a sink of iniquity, Grigori, a faithful servant of the house, took the three-year-old Mitya under his wing; but for that care at the time, there would have been nobody even to change the child's shirt. Besides, it so happened that his maternal relatives also seemed to have forgotten him at first. His grandfather, that is, Mr. Miusov himself, was no longer among the living; his widowed spouse, Mitya's grandmother, who had moved to Moscow, was too ailing, while Adelaida's sisters had all got married, so that Mitya had to stay with the servant Grigori for almost a whole year, and live in his hut. Incidentally, even had the fond father recollected him (indeed, he could hardly have been unaware of his existence), he would have sent him back to the hut, for the child would still have hindered his drunken revelries. It so came about, however, that Pyotr Alexandrovich Miusov, a cousin of the late Adelaida Ivanovna, returned from Paris at the time. He was later to spend many years abroad, but he was then a very young man standing out from the other Miusovs in being enlightened, with the polish of one who had lived in St. Petersburg and abroad. All his life long, he was an admirer of everything European, and, in his latter years, harboured the liberal ideas of the forties and the fifties. He met with many most liberal men in the course of his career, both in Russia and abroad, knew both Proudhon and Bakunin personally, and, towards the end of his travels, was particularly fond of recollecting and describing the three days of the Paris revolution of February 1848, intimating that he had practically taken part in it at the barricades – one of the most cherished recollections of his youth. He was a man of independent means who, according to the former reckoning, owned about a thousand serfs. His excellently maintained estate was situated just outside our town and bordered on the lands of our celebrated monastery; in his early years, as soon as he had come into his inheritance, Pyotr Alexandrovich brought an endless lawsuit for certain fishing rights along the river, or woodcutting rights in the forest − I am not certain which − even considering it his civic and enlightened duty to bring a court action against the "clericals". On hearing everything about Adelaida Ivanovna, whom he of course remembered and who had once even caught his eye, and on learning that there was a child of the marriage, he intervened in the matter despite all his youthful indignation and his contempt for Fyodor Pavlovich and forthwith told him that he would like to assume responsibility for the child's upbringing. Long afterwards he would recount as a trait characterising Fyodor Pavlovich that, when he broached the subject, the father seemed at a loss for a while as to which child was being referred to, and even seemed surprised to learn that he had a little son somewhere about the house. Though Pyotr Alexandrovich's account may have contained some exaggeration, there must have been something resembling the truth in it. Indeed, throughout his life, Fyodor Pavlovich was given to dissimulation, to suddenly acting some role one would never have expected of him, moreover, quite unnecessarily and even to his own detriment, as in the present instance, for example. This incidentally, is a feature of a great many people, even highly intelligent ones at that, which Fyodor Pavlovich was not. Pyotr Alexandrovich took the matter up with vigour, and was even awarded co-guardianship of the boy (jointly with Fyodor Pavlovich), since the mother had left some estate − a house and some land. Mitya did, in fact, go to live with his uncle once removed. The latter had no family of his own, and as, after settling his affairs and ensuring the revenues from his landed estates, he hurried off to Paris for a lengthy stay, he entrusted the child to the care of an aunt, a Moscow gentlewoman. It so happened that, after settling down in Paris, he, too, forgot all about the child, especially when the February revolution began, which had so captured his imagination and which he could not forget all the rest of his days. On the death of the Moscow gentlewoman, Mitya passed into the care of one of her married daughters, later to change his home for a fourth time, I think. I shall not go into that at present, the more so because I shall have much more to say later about Fyodor Pavlovich's first-born; for the time being, I shall confine myself to the most essential facts about him, without which I cannot even begin my story.

In the first place, this Dmitri Fyodorovich was the only one of Fyodor Pavlovich's three sons to grow up in the conviction that he enjoyed a competence that would make him independent when he came of age. His boyhood and youth were wild; he did not finish the gymnasium*, got enrolled at a military school, was stationed in the Caucasus where he earned promotion, fought a duel, for which he was degraded to the ranks, won promotion again, led a roisterous life, and spent a good deal of money. He began to receive funds from Fyodor Pavlovich only when he came of age, and until then simply ran up debts. He first met his father and got to know him, if only a little, after attaining his majority, when he arrived in our parts with the sole aim of clearing up matters concerning his property. Even then he did not seem to take to his father. His stay was a brief one and he hastened to get away, after managing to obtain a certain sum from Fyodor Pavlovich and reaching an understanding on future payments from his estate. He quite failed in his efforts to get any account from his father (mark this!) as to the value of his land and the income it could bring in. From the very outset, Fyodor Pavlovich noticed (this too should be remembered) that Mitya had an exaggerated and false notion of his fortune. With his own and particular calculations in view, Fyodor Pavlovich was well pleased by this, meanwhile, drawing the conclusion that the young man was flighty,

*Prior to 1917, a secondary school of the highest grade, which prepared pupils for university entrance.—*Tr.*

18

unruly, hot-headed, impatient and dissolute, and that, were some ready cash come to hand, he would calm down at once, if only for a short while, of course. Fyodor Pavlovich began to turn this to his own advantage, placating him by doling out petty sums, which he remitted at intervals. It so came about in the end that when Mitya, having lost all patience, reappeared in our town four years later, with the purpose of squaring accounts with his parent, it suddenly emerged, much to his amazement, that he had absolutely nothing to his name; that it was quite impossible even to make any reckoning; that the money payments made to him by Fyodor Pavlovich exceeded the total value of his property, so that he was probably in debt to his father; that he was not entitled to demand anything more in view of certain transaction he had voluntarily entered into on various specified dates, and so on and so forth. The young man was dumbfounded, suspicious of falsehood and deceit, and practically beside himself, and seemed to have gone out of his mind. It was this circumstance that led to the calamity, an account of which will form the theme of my first or introductory novel, or rather its outer shell. But before I go over to that novel, I must explain how it came about that Fyodor Pavlovich had another two sons, and Mitya two brothers.

3.

The Second Marriage and Its Children

Shortly after he had disposed of the four-year-old Mitya, Fyodor Pavlovich took a second wife, the marriage lasting some eight years. He brought this second wife, Sofia Ivanovna, also a very young girl, from another gubernia whither he had gone in the company of a Jew to attend to a minor contract. Though he was given to dissipation, tippling and brawling, Fyodor Pavlovich was most assiduous in investing his capital to advantage, for he had a nose for business deals, which were nearly always of a shady kind. The daughter of an obscure deacon, Sofia Ivanovna was orphaned in early childhood, and had no relatives in the world; she

19

had been brought up in the house of a wealthy benefactress who was at the same time her tormentor — an aristocratic old lady, the widow of a General Vorokhov. The details are not known to me, but I only heard that the meek, gentle and inoffensive girl was on one occasion actually taken down in time from a noose when she attempted to hang herself from a nail in a lumber-room—so hard had it been for her to put up with the wilfulness and the never-ending admonitions of the old lady, who apparently was not a malicious person but had grown into a most intolerable and petty tyrant out of sheer idleness. Fyodor Pavlovich presented his suit, but the inquiries made about him led to his being sent about his business. It was then that, just as in his first marriage, he asked the orphan girl to elope with him. It is very, very likely that she would never have accepted him had she learnt more details about him beforehand. However, it all happened in another gubernia; besides, what could a girl of sixteen have understood except that it would be better to drown herself in the river than remain with her benefactress. That was how the poor child replaced a benefactress with a benefactor. This time Fyodor Pavlovich did not get a copeck, for the old lady was infuriated, gave them nothing and, on top of that, called down a curse on them. But he had this time not counted on getting anything at all; he had been greatly taken with the artless girl's remarkable beauty, above all her look of innocence, which had taken his breath away—a lecher who had till then pursued only the coarser brand of female beauty. "Those sweet and innocent eyes cut at my heart like a sharp knife," he would say afterwards, with his slimy snigger. However, this, too, could have meant nothing else but the sensual attraction felt by a depraved man. Having taken her without any marriage portion, Fyodor Pavlovich showed that he set no store by his wife; on the ground of her being, so to say, "at fault" to him and his having practically saved her from the noose and, besides, taking advantage of her phenomenal meekness and submissiveness, he even rode roughshod over the most ordinary decencies of conjugal life. Wanton women would visit the house in the wife's presence and wild drinking parties would be held. I can cite as a typical instance the fact that the servant Grigori, a gloomy, pigheaded moraliser, who had hated the former mistress, Adelaida Ivanovna, took up the cudgels for the new mistress and, because of her, quarrelled with Fyodor Pavlovich in a manner hardly befitting a servant, on one occasion even forcibly breaking up an orgy and chasing the worthless women out of the house. Browbeaten from early childhood, the unfortunate young woman subsequently developed a kind of nervous ailment most usual in common country folk, among women who are known as "wailers" for that reason. The dreadful fits of hysteria brought about by her illness even deprived her of reason at times. However, she bore Fyodor Pavlovich two sons, Ivan and Alexei, the former in the first year of her marriage, and the latter three years later. When she died, the boy Alexei was in his fourth year, yet, strange as it may seem, he had, as I know, a life-long memory of his mother, a dreamlike recollection, of course. What befell the two boys when she died was almost exactly the same as had been the case with the first-born Mitya: they were completely neglected and forgotten by their father, and fell to the care of the selfsame Grigori, and in the same hut. It was there that they were found by the general's self-willed widow, the benefactress who had brought up their mother. She was still alive, and, throughout the eight years, had been unable to forget the affront offered her. All those years she had had the most exact and reliable information about the kind of life her Sofia led and, on learning of her illness and the evil doings about her, she said to her hangers-on: "It serves her right. It's what God has sent down upon her for her ingratitude."

Exactly three months after Sofia Ivanovna's death, the general's widow appeared in our town in person; she drove straight to Fyodor Pavlovich's house, and accomplished a good deal during the half hour she spent there. It was eventide. Fyodor Pavlovich, whom she had not seen all those eight years, was tipsy when he came out to greet her. The story runs that the moment she set eyes on him she at once and without a word of explanation gave him two smart and resounding slaps on the face and then, grabbing a tuft of his hair, gave it three downward tugs, after which, without as much as a word, she made for

21

the hut. When she got there, she saw at a glance that the two boys were unwashed and in dirty linen, at which she promptly slapped Grigori's face and told him she was taking them away. She took them out just as they were, had them wrapped in a rug and placed in her carriage, and ordered the coachman to drive home. Grigori accepted the slap without demur, like the faithful servant he was. He bowed low to the old lady as he saw her to the carriage, and said in an impressive tone that God would reward her for the orphans. "You're a dolt all the same!" she retorted as she drove off. Turning the matter over in his mind, Fyodor Pavlovich saw it in a good light and later gave his full and formal consent on all points regarding his children's upbringing by the general's widow. As for the slaps he had been given, he himself drove all over the town to spread the story.

It so happened that the general's widow died soon afterwards, her will containing the bequest of a thousand roubles each to the boys "for their education, the money to be spent on them without fail but made to last until they come of age, for even such a pittance is more than enough for such children; if others so wish, they can pay up," etc., etc. I have not myself seen the will but have heard that there was something strange about it, couched in most unusual terms. The old lady's principal heir, Yefim Petrovich Polenov, Marshal of the Gubernia Nobility, proved to be a man of integrity. An exchange of letters with Fyodor Pavlovich at once convincing him that no money could be dragged out of the father for his children's upbringing (without ever directly refusing to pay up, Karamazov invariably kept putting off things, even with effusive sentimentality at times), Polenov took the orphans under his wing, becoming particularly fond of Alexei, the younger of the two, so that the latter even grew up in his family. I would like the reader to take note of that from the very outset. If, throughout their lives, the young people were indebted to anyone for their upbringing and education, that man was Yefim Petrovich, a most honourable and humane man, of a kind rarely to be met. He kept intact the thousand roubles each of the boys had been left by the general's widow, so that the increment of interest doubled the sum by the time they came of age. He brought them up at his own expense and of course spent far more than a thousand on each of them. I will not, for the time being, go into a detailed account of their childhood and youth but will only mention the most important circumstances therein. Of the elder, Ivan, I shall, incidentally, only say that he grew up into a somewhat sullen and withdrawn youth, far from timid but keenly aware, even at the age of ten, that they were living with a family of strangers and on charity, and that their father was a kind of man to be ashamed of even mentioning, and so on. At a very early age, almost in his infancy (so it was said, at least), the boy began to display a most extraordinary and brilliant aptitude for learning. I do not know exactly why, but it so came about that he parted with Yefim Petrovich's family when he was barely thirteen, and entered a Moscow Gymnasium, boarding with an experienced pedagogue, who was famous at the time and a childhood friend of Polenov's. Ivan himself would subsequently declare that it was all due to the "ardour for good works" in Yefim Petrovich, who was much taken with the idea that a boy of outstanding abilities should be taught by an outstanding tutor. Incidentally, neither Yefim Petrovich nor the outstanding tutor were alive when, after finishing school, the young man entered the University. As Yefim Petrovich had not made the proper arrangements for payment of the legacy left to the boys by the tyrannical old lady, and as a consequence of the red-tape and delay inevitable in our country, the sum, which had grown from one to two thousand to each through the accumulated interest, was not immediately available, so the young man was hard put to it during his first two years at the University, since he had to maintain himself in food and other upkeep and at the same time attend to his studies. It should be noted that he never even attempted to communicate with his father—out of pride perhaps, or contempt for him, or perhaps out of hard-headed conviction which told him that no tangible assistance would be forthcoming from such a father. However that may have been, the young man did not lose heart but obtained work, first by giving private lessons at twenty copecks an hour and then by making the rounds of newspaper offices and selling them news items on street incidents over the signature of

Onlooker. So catchingly and spicily were these always written that they were readily accepted, this alone showing that, intellectually and practically, the young man stood head and shoulders above the numerous, constantly needy and wretched section of our student youth of both sexes, who pester the offices of various newspapers and journals in the two capitals*, unable to invent anything better than the constant reiteration of one and the same request for translations from the French or doing copying work. After establishing contacts with various editorial offices, Ivan Fyodorovich kept them going and, during his final years at the University, began to publish sparkling reviews of books on a number of specialised subjects, thus even acquiring a reputation in literary circles. It was, however, only later that he was able suddenly and fortuitously, to come to the notice of a far wider readership, so that he became known to and remembered by a great many people. The occasion was quite an interesting one. On graduating, and engaged in preparations for travel abroad on his two thousand roubles, he suddenly published, in a leading newspaper, a strange article which attracted attention even from broader circles, and, most important, it was on a subject he was apparently quite unfamiliar with, since his degree was in natural science. It dealt with the question of ecclesiastical courts, which was very much in the public eye at the time. After analysing several opinions submitted on the matter, he went on to set forth his own views. The main features were the overall tone and the strikingly unexpected conclusion. Strangely enough, many churchmen were highly inclined to number him amongst their own. It came as a surprise when, not only secularists but the very atheists gave him their applause. It all ended in some of the shrewder people deciding that the entire article was an impudent hoax and a piece of mockery. I am making mention of the happening because the article eventually reached our local monastery, which was quite famous at the time, and where a deep interest was evinced in the question of ecclesiastical courts, which had come to the fore. The article created quite a stir. When the name of the

*I. e. St. Petersburg, and Moscow, the ancient capital.—*Tr.*

24

author became known, it was asked whether he came from our town and was the son of "that selfsame Fyodor Pavlovich". It was just at that time when the author himself put in an appearance.

Even then, as I remember, I asked myself, with some unease, what had made Ivan Fyodorovich return to our parts. That fateful visit, which led up to so many consequences, long remained something I could never quite make out. Generally speaking, it was strange for a young man of such learning, who looked so proud and cautious, to suddenly appear in so disreputable a house, and to a father who had ignored him and had no knowledge or remembrance of him, and who would, of course, never, in any circumstances, have given a son of his any money should the latter have asked for some, but was constantly afraid lest his sons Ivan and Alexei might also come one day to ask for money. And now the young man had installed himself in the house of such a father, spending a month and then another under the same roof, the two seeming to be getting on famously with each other. The latter circumstance was a source of particular astonishment, not only to me but to many others as well. Pyotr Alexandrovich Miusov, of whom I have already made mention and who was distantly related to Fyodor Pavlovich by his first marriage, happened to be spending some time in our neighbourhood again, on his estate there, having come on a visit from Paris, where he had taken up permanent residence. He was, I remember, most of all surprised on making the acquaintance of Ivan, who greatly intrigued him and with whom he sometimes engaged in intellectual bouts, much to his own discomfiture. "He has pride," he would say to us about him at the time; "he'll always make a living and even now has enough money to go abroad on—so what is he after by staying here? It's clear to all that he hasn't come here for money, because his father won't ever give him any. He's not given to drink or wenching, yet the old man can't do without him—they've become so thick." It was quite true: the young man even had an obvious influence on the old man, who almost seemed to have begun to obey Ivan at times, though he was often highly and even spitefully wilful. He even began to behave more decently sometimes.

It was only later that it transpired that Ivan Fyodorovich had come partly at the request of his elder brother Dmitri and on his behalf. He had first met and got to know the latter almost at the same time during that very visit, but had previously, before arriving from Moscow, entered into a correspondence with him on an important matter of more concern to Dmitri Fyodorovich, of which matter the reader will learn the full details in due course. Yet, even when I had already come to know of this special circumstance, Ivan still seemed an enigma to me, and his arrival inexplicable.

I shall add that Ivan Fyodorovich produced an impression of mediator and conciliator between the father and his elder brother Dmitri Fyodorovich, who was on the worst of terms with his father and was even taking court action against him.

This strange family, I repeat, were met for the first time in their lives, some of its members seeing each other also for the first time. Only Alexei, the youngest son, had been living in our town for the past year, the first of the three to arrive. It is of this Alexei that I find it hardest to speak in this, my introductory story, before bringing him on to the stage in the novel. Yet I shall have to write an introduction about him too, if only to explain a very strange fact in advance, namely that I am obliged to present the future hero of my novel, from the very first scene, in the habit of a novice. Indeed, he had been living a full year in our monastery and was, apparently, preparing to be cloistered there for the rest of his days.

4.

Alyosha*—the Third Son

He was then only twenty (his brother Ivan being in his twenty-fourth year, and Dmitri, the eldest, in his twenty-eighth). I must announce, first and foremost, that this youth, Alyosha, was in no way a fanatic and, in my opinion at least,

*Diminutive of Alexei.—*Tr.*

neither was he even a mystic. To start with, I shall set forth my full opinion: he was simply one who loved mankind from his early years, and if he did take to the monastic way it was only because it alone had captured his imagination at the time, presenting itself, as it were, as the ideal road for a soul striving to escape from the gloom of worldly malevolence into the light of love. That road had tugged at his heart only because it was along it that he had met with a man who was, in his opinion, an extraordinary being, to wit, Zossima, the celebrated *starets** from our monastery, to whom he had grown attached with all the ardent first love of his overflowing heart. I will not gainsay that he was already a very strange creature, and had been so even from the cradle. By the way, I have already mentioned that, although he was only in his fourth year when he lost his mother, he had a life-long memory of her—her face and her caresses, "just as though she were alive and standing before me." Such recollection, as is common knowledge, may remain from even an earlier age, as early as two years, but only as dots of light against a background of darkness, or like a corner torn off a huge canvas which has faded and lost all its colours except for that tiny corner. It was exactly like that with him. He remembered a quiet summer evening, even the open window, the slanting rays of the setting sun (the most vivid recollection, this), the icon in the corner of the room, lit up by the flickering flame of the tiny lamp burning before it and his mother on bended knees before the icon, sobbing her heart out as though in hysterics, screaming and shrieking; clutching him with both arms, hugging him so tight that it hurt, she prayed to the Moth-

***Starets** (literally: old man, elder): a venerable monk or, sometimes, a layman, i. e. unordained preacher given to a religious life of prayer, asceticism and solitude, who offered counsel and guidance to anyone in need of spiritual comfort at moments of suffering or turmoil. A *starets* might attach himself to a monastery or might also be a *strannik* (literally: wanderer), a pilgrim, walking from village to village, living on alms from peasants or monasteries. Such *stranniki* would preach religion and sometimes laid claim to the power of faith-healing. When their teaching ran counter to the tenets of the established Church, they went to prison, but they often seemed better and holier to the peasants than the *batyushka*, the local priest. Even the better educated would consult the *startsi*.

er of God, raising him on arms outstretched to the holy image as though asking for the Virgin's protection ... suddenly the nurse came running in and snatched the child away in fright. Imagine the picture! Alyosha also remembered his mother's face at the moment: he said it was distraught but beautiful, as he could recollect. However, he rarely cared to speak of this recollection to anybody. He was not very demonstrative in his childhood and youth, and even sparing of words, but not from mistrust, or timidity, or morose aloofness; quite the reverse, it sprang from something else, some kind of inner concern, quite personal and with no bearing on other people, but of such importance to him that it seemed to make him forgetful of others. Yet he loved people; he seemed to be living his whole life with a complete trust in them, but no one ever regarded him as simple-minded or naive. There was a something in him that told you and impressed upon you (and did so throughout his life) that he had no wish to pass judgement on people, that he was not one to condemn others, and would never do so. It even seemed that he was tolerant of all things, without the least aspersion, though he was often bitterly sad. This was so much so, moreover, that no one could surprise or frighten him, even in his earliest youth. On arriving at the age of twenty at his father's house, which was a sink of iniquity, he, chaste and pure, merely drew back in silence when it became intolerable to view the scene, but did so without the least sign of contempt or condemnation. His father, that former sponger and therefore so quick to take offence, who had at first met him with sullen mistrust ("He's silent most of the time, so who can tell the workings of his mind?") very soon, before a fortnight had elasped, took to embracing and kissing him terribly often, true, with maudlin tears, and sentimentality. Yet it was obvious that he had grown sincerely and deeply attached to him, in a way such a man had never before been able to.

Indeed, from his early childhood the young man had been a general favourite wherever he went. When he entered the household of Yefim Petrovich Polenov, the benefactor who brought him up, he won all hearts to such a degree that he was treated as a member of the family. Yet he joined the family at an age so tender as to preclude any suspicion of calculating design, intrusiveness or the art of fawning on others. This immediate and unconscious gift of inspiring deep affection was something artlessly inherent in his very nature. It was the same at school, though he might have seemed the kind of boy to arouse distrust, sometimes ridicule or even hatred in his schoolmates. For instance, he was often wrapped in thought, and withdrawn. From his earliest years, he would retire into some quiet corner and engage in reading, yet he could well have been considered a general favourite throughout his school years. He was rarely frolicsome or in the least high-spirited, but one could see at first glance that this was not out of any moroseness in him; on the contrary, he was even-tempered and serene. He never pushed himself forward. Perhaps that was why he was never afraid of anybody, yet his schoolmates at once realised that he took no pride in his intrepidity and seemed quite unaware that he was courageous and without fear. He never harboured resentment: it might happen that, within an hour of an insult, he would reply to the offender or address him with so trustful and serene an air that one would have thought nothing out of the ordinary had taken place between them. It was not that he seemed to have forgotten the affront or consciously forgiven it; he simply did not regard it as such, and this quite won the other children's hearts. There was only one trait in him which, throughout his Gymnasium years, from the lowest to the top form, aroused in his schoolmates a constant desire to make fun of him, not out of any malice but because it afforded them amusement. That feature was a boundless and frenzied sense of retiring modesty, of chasteness. He simply could not tolerate certain words and certain talk about women. Such "certain" words and talk are regrettably ineradicable at schools. Boys who are pure of soul and heart, almost children, often like to talk among themselves, and even aloud, of things, pictures and scenes that even soldiers will not always dare to speak of; moreover, soldiers do not know or understand much of what is already familiar to quite young children of our educated and upper classes. That is not yet moral depravity, nor is it real, vicious and inner cynicism, but only its husk, which is often regarded as something refined, bold, dashing and worthy of imitation. When they saw that Alyosha Karamazov would at once stop his ears with his fingers when they began to speak about "that", they would sometimes crowd around him and, dragging his hands away from his ears, shout obscenities into both ears, while he attempted to free himself, slipped down on to the floor, hid his face, without uttering a word of abuse, and enduring their taunts in silence. Towards the end, however, they desisted and gave up teasing him for being a milksop; moreover, they regarded him as deserving of pity in this respect. Incidentally, he was always among the best pupils in his studies, but never top boy.

After Yefim Petrovich's death, Alyosha stayed on for another two years at the gubernia Gymnasium. Polenov's inconsolable wife left almost immediately for a long stay in Italy, taking with her all her family, which consisted entirely of females, Alyosha going to live at the home of two ladies he had never seen before, who were distantly related to Yefim Petrovich; he had no knowledge of the terms he was to stay there on. Characteristically enough, he was never concerned over who was paying for his upkeep. In this respect he was a complete contrast to his elder brother, Ivan Fyodorovich, who had undergone such distress during his first two years at the University, having to support himself, and who, from his childhood, had eaten the bitter bread of charity from a benefactor. This strange feature in Alyosha's make-up could not, I think, be criticised too severely, for anyone who got to know him even a little could easily see for himself, should the question have arisen, that Alexei was one of those young men who are saintly fools in a way; if such a one came into possession of a fortune, he would not hesitate to give it away for the asking, either for some good works or perhaps even to some adroit trickster who happened to ask for it. In general, he did not seem to know the value of money, though not literally speaking, of course. When he was given some pocket money, which he never asked for, he did not know for weeks what to do with it, or else just spent it at once, without a thought. Pyotr Alexandrovich Miusov, a man who was scrupulous in respect of money matters and of bourgeois honesty, pronounced the following dictum on Alexei when he had subsequently got to know him better: "Here is perhaps the only person in the world who, left to his own resources and with no money, in a public square of an unfamiliar city with a million inhabitants, will not perish, will not starve or freeze to death, because he will instantly be given food and instantly be taken care of. If he isn't taken care of by others, he will at once see to that himself, and all without the least effort or humiliation. Neither will it be a burden on anyone who takes care of him; on the contrary, it will perhaps be accounted a pleasure."

He did not complete his gymnasium course. A year before he was due to finish his schooling, he suddenly informed his ladies that he would be going to see his father on a matter that had come into his head. They felt sorry and were reluctant to let him go. The travelling expenses were very slight, and the ladies would not allow him to pawn his watch—a gift from his benefactor's family before they left for foreign parts—and provided him with a handsome sum, and even with new clothes and underwear. However, he returned half of the money, saying he had made up his mind to go third class. When he arrived in our town, he did not give any direct reply to his father's first question: "Why have you come here before completing your studies?", but was said to be unusually pensive. It soon transpired that he wanted to find his mother's grave. He practically admitted at the time that he had come with that express purpose. But that could hardly have been the sole reason for his coming there. It is more probable that he himself did not realise, and could not have explained, what it was that seemed to have welled up in his soul and had irresistibly led him on to a new, unfamiliar but already unavoidable path. His father was unable to say where his second wife had been buried since he had never visited her grave after the coffin had been consigned to earth; after all those years, he had completely forgotten where it was located.

Apropos of Fyodor Pavlovich, who had been away from our town for quite a long time. Some three or four years after the death of his second wife, he had gone off to the south of Russia, ending up in Odessa, where he lived for several years. At first he got acquainted with, as he put it, "many Jews, Jew-boys, Ikeys and Sheenies", later to be received, not only by "lousy Jews" but even by "worthy Hebrews". It was presumably at that time that he developed within himself the knack of making money and squeezing it out of others. He returned to our town for good about three years prior to Alyosha's arrival. Those who had known him in the past found that he had aged terribly though he was not so old actually. It was not exactly with more dignity that he now comported himself, but somehow with even greater effrontery. Thus, the former buffoon now revealed a liking for making others play the fool. His behaviour with the women was no less obscene than it had been in the past, but was now even more revolting. He soon opened a chain of taverns in the area, and it was clear that he was now worth a hundred thousand, perhaps somewhat less. Many residents of the town and the surrounding uyezd were soon in his debt, on the very best security of course. He had run to a kind of paunchy flabbiness of late, somehow begun to lose his complacency and self-control, and had even fallen into a kind of eccentricity, beginning one thing and ending up with another, wool-gathering as it were, and ever more frequently in his cups; had it not been for the selfsame servant Grigori, who had also aged considerably and sometimes looked after him almost like a valet, Fyodor Pavlovich might not have been able to live such an unruffled life. Alyosha's arrival seemed to have affected him even in the moral sense, as though something had awakened in this prematurely old man which had long lain dormant in his soul. "Do you know," he would say, his eyes resting on Alyosha, "that you resemble her—I mean the wailer?" That was the way he would refer to his late wife and Alyosha's mother. It was the servant Grigori who at last showed Alyosha his mother's grave, taking him to the town cemetery where, in a far-off corner, he saw a gravestone of cheap workmanship but decently kept, and bearing the name, social status, age and the date of death of the deceased, below which were engraved four lines of old-fashioned burial verse of the kind usually to be seen on the graves of folk of the middling station in life. Surprisingly enough, all this proved the doing of Grigori, who had himself put up the gravestone over the poor woman's grave, all at his own expense, after Fyodor Pavlovich, whom he had so often pestered with reminders of the grave, finally made off for Odessa, dismissing from his mind all such things as graves and memories. Alyosha did not display any particular emotion at his mother's graveside, merely listening to Grigori's measured and sober account of how he had put up the gravestone; he stood there for a while, with bowed head, and then walked off without a word. After that, he did not, perhaps for a whole year, revisit the cemetery. This minor episode also had an effect—a most original one—on Fyodor Pavlovich: he suddenly paid a thousand roubles to our monastery for prayers to be said for the repose of his wife's soul—not the second one, Alyosha's mother, but for Adelaida, the one who used to drub him. That same evening he got drunk, and reviled the monks to Alyosha. He was not a religious man, and had probably never placed even a five-copeck candle in front of an icon. Such people sometimes do have the strangest impulses of thought and sentiment.

As I have already mentioned, he had run to puffiness, his face testifying in no uncertain way to the kind of life he had always led. Besides the fleshy bags under the little eyes, which were always suspicious, sardonic and full of effrontery; besides the numerous deep wrinkles on the fat little face, there protruded from below his pointed chin a big Adam's apple, longish and fleshy, in the manner of a pouch, this giving him a repulsively gross appearance. Add to all this a long and vulpine mouth, which revealed the stumps of black and decayed teeth. Saliva would sputter from his mouth whenever he opened it to speak. Incidentally, he liked to poke fun at his own face, although he seemed quite pleased with it, particularly the nose, which was not very big but thin and aquiline. "A real Roman nose," he would say, "which goes with my Adam's apple to make the face of an ancient Roman patrician of the period of decline." It was something he seemed to take pride in.

Shortly after the discovery of his mother's grave, Alyosha suddenly informed his father of his desire to enter the monastic life, the local monks having agreed to accept him as a novice.

33

He went on to explain that this was his fondest wish and that he was asking his father for his formal consent. The old man already knew that the *starets* Zossima, who had found refuge in the monastery hermitage, had produced a deep impression on his "gentle" boy.

"That particular *starets* is, of course, the most honest monk of the lot," he remarked, after listening in thoughtful silence to Alyosha and evincing not the least surprise at his request. "H'm, so that's where you want to go, my gentle boy!" He was somewhat primed, and suddenly smiled his slow, tipsy smile, which was not without a sly cunning. "H'm, just imagine, I did have a presentiment you'd end up in something like this. It's something you've always set your heart on. Well, why not? You have your couple of thousand, so you have a portion, and as for me, you can be sure I'll never let you down, my dear boy. Why, I'll pay in for you right away whatever sum is needed, if they ask for it. If they don't—well, why insist, eh? After all, you spend money the way a canary pecks at its feed—a couple of grains a week. H'm. D'you know there's a convent in the outskirts of a certain town, with a group of buildings housing only what they call 'monastery wives'—thirty in all, I think. I've been there— an interesting place in its own way, of course, just in the sense of variety. What is bad about it is the terrible Russianism— not a single Frenchwoman among them, and they could well afford that, for they're wallowing in money. Well, they'll turn up alright as soon as they find out. There's nothing of the kind hereabouts, no "monastery wives", but only monks—two hundred of them. Everything on the square. They're rigorous and strait-laced—I'll admit that. H'm. So you want to join the monks? I do feel sorry for you, Alyosha, indeed I do; believe me, I've grown very fond of you— Incidentally, it's all most opportune: you will pray for us sinners, who have committed so many trespasses down here. The thought has always been with me: who is it that will ever pray for me? Is there such a person in the world? I'm terribly stupid on that score, my dear boy. Perhaps you don't believe me? Indeed, terribly stupid. You see, however stupid I may be, I keep on thinking and thinking— at intervals of course; you can't expect me to be doing that all the time, after all. The devils, I think to myself, can't possibly forget to drag me down with hooks to their regions when I die. With hooks? I ask myself. Where do they get them from? What are they made of? Iron? Where are they forged? Have they got some kind of smithy down there? I suppose the monks over there at the monastery are of the opinion that in Hell, for instance, there must be some kind of ceiling. Now I'm quite prepared to believe in Hell, only without the ceiling. That will make it more gracious and more enlightened, more Lutheran, that is to say. After all, what difference does it make whether there is a ceiling there, or not? Yet the whole accursed question hinges on that. You see, if there's no ceiling, there can't be any hooks. And if there are no hooks, the whole thing goes by the board, which is again unlikely for who will there be to drag me down with hooks? And if a man like me is not to be dragged down, then what will it all come to, and where is justice to be found on earth? *Il faudrait les inventer,* those hooks, which are meant for me, for me alone: if only you knew, Alyosha, if only you knew what a man of shame I am!"

"But there are no hooks there," said Alyosha in a low and grave voice, with a look at his father.

"Of course, of course, merely the shadows of hooks. I know, I know that. It's just how a Frenchman described Hell: *"J'ai vu l'ombre d'un cocher, qui avec l'ombre d'une brosse frottait l'ombre d'une carrosse."* How do you know that the hooks don't exist? You'll think differently after you've been with the monks. Well, go there and get at the truth, and then come and let me know: it will be easier to enter the world to come if you know for sure what is to be found there. Besides, it will be more proper for you to live there with the monks than with me, an old toper, with all those wenches about the place—though nothing can besmirch you, for you are like an angel. Well, I suppose nothing will affect you over there either, so I'm giving you my permission because I am counting on that. You have a good head on your shoulders. Your flame will burn and then go out; then you'll get cured and come back. I'll be expecting you, for, my dear boy, I feel you're the only person on earth who has not condemned me; I feel that, and I can't but feel it!"

He even burst into snivelling tears. He was sentimental—evil and sentimental.

5.

The Startsi*

Some of my readers may have thought that my young friend was of a morbid, rapture-prone and ill-developed nature, a pallid dreamer, a stunted and puny creature. The reverse was true: he was at the time a well-built, red-cheeked, clear-eyed lad of nineteen, the very picture of health. He was even very good-looking, straight-limbed, of medium height, his hair light-brown, the features regular on his oval-shaped, somewhat elongated face, his dark-grey eyes shining and wide-set, and he himself very thoughtful and obviously most even-tempered. It may, perhaps, be said that red cheeks are no impediment to fanaticism or mysticism; for my part, I have a feeling that Alyosha was more of a realist than most. Oh, of course, he firmly believed in miracles while at the monastery, but as I see it, miracles will never nonplus the realist. It is not miracles that incline the realist towards faith. If he is a non-believer, the true realist will always find within himself the strength and the ability not to believe even a miracle; if a miracle confronts him as an irrefutable fact, he will sooner disbelieve the evidence of his senses than admit the fact. Even if he does so, he will admit it merely as a natural fact hitherto unfamiliar to him. With the realist, it is not a faith that is born of a miracle, but a miracle that is born of faith. If he has believed but once, he must, without fail, admit even a miracle because of his very realism. The Apostle Thomas once said he would not believe until he saw, but when he did see, he said, "My Lord and my God!" Was it a miracle that made him believe? Most probably not, but he did believe solely be-

*Plural of *starets*. — *Tr.*

cause he wished to, and, in his heart of hearts, may have already believed even when he said, "Except I shall see ... I will not believe."

It will perhaps be said that Alyosha was obtuse and undeveloped, that he failed to complete his studies, and the like. It is true that he did not complete his schooling, but it would be grossly unjust to say he was obtuse. I shall just repeat what I said above: he took to this road solely because it was the only one to grip his imagination and offer him instantaneously an ideal way for a soul yearning to escape out of the darkness into the light. Add to all this that he was, in some degree, already a young man of our recent times, namely, upright by nature, demanding the truth, seeking it and believing in it; once he had gained that belief, he demanded an immediate participation in it with all the might of his soul, striving towards a supreme act of faith, and eager to sacrifice anything, even life itself, for that act. It is, however, to be regretted that such young men do not seem to realise that, in a multitude of such cases, the sacrifice of one's life is perhaps the easiest of all sacrifices, and that to devote five or six years of youthful fervour to the arduous and taxing matter of studies, of knowledge, if only to multiply tenfold their ability to serve that truth and the act of faith they have chosen and dedicated themselves to performing—that is a sacrifice which is only too often almost beyond the capacity of many of them. Alyosha merely chose a road running opposite to all the others, being led on by the same thirst for an early feat of faith. When, after serious thought, he was overwhelmed by a realisation of the existence of immortality and God, he naturally said to himself at once, "I want to live for the sake of immortality, and will accept no half-way compromise." In exactly the same way, had he decided that there was no immortality or God, he would have at once become an atheist and a Socialist (since socialism is not only a labour question or one of the so-called fourth estate, but, in the main, a question of atheism, of the present-day embodiment of atheism, a question of a Tower of Babel, one being built deliberately without God, not in order to reach unto heaven but to bring down heaven to earth). To Alyosha it seemed even strange and impossible to go on living in the old way. For it is written: "If thou wilt be perfect, go and sell that thou hast and give to the poor ... and come and follow me." So Alyosha said to himself, "I can't just give two roubles instead of selling whatsoever I have, or merely attend morning mass instead of 'follow me'."

Perhaps, of his childhood memories, something remained in his mind of the monastery near our town, where his mother may have taken him to mass. Or then, it may have been the effect on his imagination of the slanting beams of the setting sun before the icon his poor mother had held him up to in outstretched arms. He had looked very thoughtful when he had arrived in our parts, perhaps merely to see whether it was a matter of "whatsoever thou hast", or only of a couple of roubles, when—he had met this *starets* at the monastery.

As I have already mentioned, this was the *starets* Zossima; however, a few words would be in place here on what *startsi* at our monasteries are in general. I am sorry to say I do not feel competent or knowledgeable enough for that, but shall at least try to explain things, if only briefly and superficially. In the first place, the authorities on the subject assert that *startsi* and the *starets* institution appeared at our Russian monasteries quite recently, less than a hundred years ago, whereas they have existed for well over a thousand years in the Orthodox East, especially at Sinai and on Mount Athos. The *starets* institution, it is claimed, existed and could not but have existed in old times in Russia too, but fell into decay, with the *startsi* dying out as a consequence of the disasters that befell our country: the Tartar yoke, the Troubled Times, and the rupture of the former ties with the East after the conquest of Constantinople. It was revived with us at the close of the last century by one of our greatest ascetics (as he has been called) Paissi Velichkovsky and his followers, but till now, even almost a hundred years later, it exists at far from many monasteries and has even been persecuted at times as an innovation unheard of in Russia. It flourished especially at the celebrated Kozelski Optin monastery. I am unable to say when and by whom it was introduced at our local monastery, but it was considered in its third succession there, the *starets* Zossima being the last, but he was practically dying of weakness and illness, and nobody even knew who was to take his place. This was an important matter for our monastery, for it had never been previously distinguished for anything in particular: it had neither relics of saints nor thaumaturgical icons; there were not even glorious traditions linked with our history, or any record of historical exploits or services to the country. It has flourished and won renown all over Russia only for its *startsi*, to see and to listen to whom crowds of pilgrims have flocked to us from thousands of versts away, from all parts of our country. And so, what is a *starets*? A *starets* is one who takes your soul, your will, into his own soul and will. When you have chosen a *starets*, you forego your own will and surrender it to him in complete submission and complete humility. This ordeal, this awesome school of life, is accepted voluntarily by the assenter in the hope that, after a lengthy period of trial, he will subdue his self and achieve such control over himself that, after his novitiate, he will ultimately win absolute freedom, that is to say, freedom from himself, and thus escape the fate of those who have lived out their lives without finding themselves in themselves. This *starets* institution is not grounded in any theory, but was evolved from an Eastern practice dating back a thousand years. The obligations towards a *starets* are not the same as the novitiate discipline usual at our Russian monasteries as well. Here confession to the *starets* is never ending on the part of those who have placed themselves under him, and the bond between the binder and the bound is indissoluble. There is the story, for instance, that once, in the most distant days of Christianity, a novice who had failed to carry out an act of obedience imposed on him by his *starets*, departed from the monastery and went to another land, leaving Syria for Egypt. After many outstanding deeds of piety, he was granted the grace of suffering an agonising martyrdom for his faith. When, honoured for his saintliness, his body lay in church in preparation for burial, and the deacon called out the words, "Leave this place, ye unbaptised!", the coffin with the martyr's body was suddenly levitated from its place and was cast forth from the church. This happened three times. It transpired only later that, since the saintly man had once broken his vow of obedience and abandoned his *starets*, he could not win forgiveness without permission from the latter, even if he had suffered so much for the faith. It was only when the *starets*, who had been summoned to the place, absolved him from his oath of obedience that the body could be committed to earth. All this is, of course, nothing more than a legend, but here is a recent occurrence: a Russian monk of our own days, who was seeking salvation on Mount Athos, was unexpectedly told by his *starets* to leave the Mount, which he had come to love deeply as a shrine and peaceful haven, and go first to Jerusalem to pay homage to the holy places and then back to Russia, northwards to Siberia. "Your place is there, not here," he said. The amazed and sorrow-stricken monk went to Constantinople, where he begged the Oecumenical Patriarch to absolve him from his vow of obedience. His Holiness replied that he could not do so; moreover, there was not, neither could there be, any power on earth that could grant absolution from the obedience due to his *starets*, with the sole exception of the authority of him who had imposed it on the monk. Thus, *startsi* are invested with an authority which is, in certain cases, boundless and beyond understanding. That was why the *starets* institution was at first met at many of our monasteries with something bordering on persecution, yet came in for immediate and high esteem among the people. For instance, both common folk and the most distinguished people would come flocking to our monastery for obeisance to its *startsi,* to whom they would confess their doubts, sins and vexations, and ask for counsel and guidance. This led to those opposed to the *startsi* complaining that, apart from other infractions, the sacrament of confession was being arbitrarily and frivolously degraded, though in fact the constant laying bare of the soul to the *starets* by his novice or any layman has nothing of the character of a sacrament. The outcome, however, was that the *starets* institution has survived and gradually become established at Russia's monasteries. It is also probably true that this tested instrument for man's regeneration from bondage to freedom and moral improvement, an instrument dating back already a thousand years, may work in reverse, leading some, not to humility and full mastery over one's self but, on the contrary, to the most satanic pride, namely to enchainment, not freedom.

The *starets* Zossima, who was about sixty-five, came of a landowning family. He had been in the army in his early youth, and had served in the Caucasus in the rank of company officer. Alyosha must have been profoundly impressed by some special quality in his soul. He lived in Zossima's cell, for the old man had grown very fond of him and gave him constant access to himself. It should be noted that though Alyosha lived in the monastery he was under no particular discipline: he was free to leave whenever he so wished, even for days on end; if he did wear a cassock, he did so of his own free will so as not to look different from the rest of the inmates. But this was something to his own liking. It may have been the influence on his youthful imagination of the authority and renown that constantly accompanied the *starets* Zossima. Many people said of the latter that, by having received, in the course of many years, all those who had come to open up their hearts to him and thirsted after his counsel and words of healing, he had taken into his soul such a store of revelations, sorrows and avowals that he ultimately came to possess so keen an insight that a first glance at the face of a stranger who had come to see him would allow him to intuit what he had come for, what he wanted, and even what anguish it was that was tormenting his conscience, and would astonish, confound and sometimes almost alarm the visitor by his knowledge of his secret even before he uttered a word. At the same time, Alyosha could invariably observe that many, almost all, of those who had come to see the *starets* for a private talk entered his cell in fear and trepidation but emerged almost always looking joyful and comforted, even the gloomiest face becoming a happy one. Alyosha was particularly struck by the *starets* being in no way a severe man; on the contrary, he was always almost blithe in manner. The monks said of him that he showed greater attachment to the more sinful, and the more a man had sinned, the greater his love for him. Even towards the end of the *starets*'s life, there were among the monks such that hated and envied him, but they were already becoming few in number and now kept silent, though there were among them several who were well known and of great dignity in the monastery, like, for instance, one of the aged monks, who strictly observed his vow of silence and the practice of austerity. For all that, the vast majority were unequivocally on the side of the *starets*, many even loving him with all their hearts, fervently and sincerely. Some were almost fanatically devoted to him. These said quite openly, though not too audibly, that he was beyond any doubt already a saint and, since his death was at hand, they looked forward even to immediate miracles and great renown in the very near future for the monastery after his decease. Alyosha, too, had unquestioning faith in the thaumaturgical powers of the *starets*, just as he absolutely believed the story of the coffin that had been ejected from the church. He saw many, who had come with their ailing children or grown-up relatives and implored the *starets* to lay hands on them and pray for them, return shortly afterwards—some on the following day—to fall in tears on their knees before him to thank him for having healed their sick. Whether it had really been a cure or else only some natural improvement in their condition did not worry Alyosha in the least, so great was his faith in the spiritual powers of his teacher, whose renown he felt as his own triumph. But his heart was dilated and he looked positively radiant when the *starets* emerged through the hermitage gateway to mix with the awaiting throng of pilgrims, ordinary folk who had come from all parts of Russia expressly to see him and get his blessing. On bended knees and with tears in their eyes, they kissed his feet and the very ground he trod, moaning and sobbing; the women held up their babes to him and led their physically and mentally sick up to him. The old man spoke to them, offering a short prayer and dismissing them after a blessing. His recent attacks of illness left him so weak at times that he lacked the strength to leave his cell, so that the pilgrims sometimes had to wait at the monastery for several days on end for him to come out. Alyosha never even asked himself why they loved the old man so, or why they stood on their knees before him, reduced to tears at the sight of his face. Indeed, he was well aware that for the meek souls of humble Russian folk, ground down by toil and suffering, and most of all by the everlasting injustice and sinfulness—their own and the world's—there was no greater need and consolation than acquiring some shrine or saintly man, falling down at his feet and bowing down to him. "Even if there is sinfulness, injustice and temptation among us, there is somewhere in the world one who is so saintly and exalted; he possesses and knows the truth, so truth is not dead in the world and will therefore reach us too one day, and will reign all over the earth as has been promised." Alyosha knew that such were the sentiments and even the thinking of the people. That was something he could understand. But he did not harbour the least doubt that the *starets* was that very saintly man such folk yearned for, that custodian of God's own truth; he shared the faith of the weeping peasants and their ailing womenfolk as they held out their children to the *starets*. Moreover, he was convinced in soul, even more profoundly than anyone else in the monastery, that when Zossima passed on he would confer extraordinary grace on it. Indeed, the flame of some inner ecstasy had been burning ever more strongly in his heart of late. He was nothing abashed by the uniqueness of the example set by the *starets*. "Nevertheless, he is a saintly man who carries in his heart the secret of spiritual rebirth for all, a power that will ultimately establish truth on earth, so that all will be sanctified and all people will love one another, and there will be neither rich nor poor, neither exalted nor humiliated; all men will be God's own children and the true kingdom of Christ will come." That was what Alyosha's heart thirsted after.

A most powerful impression seemed to have been produced on Alyosha by the arrival of his two brothers, whom he had never before met. He took to his half-brother Dmitri sooner and more closely, than to his uterine brother Ivan, though the former was the later arrival. He was terribly eager to get to know Ivan better but they had not yet become intimate, though they had met quite frequently during the two months Ivan had been living there: Alyosha himself was of a reticent disposition and was apparently in a state of anticipation and somewhat ashamed of something, while his brother Ivan—though Alyosha had at first noticed his intent and curious glances at him—seemed to have stopped giving him even the least thought, something that Alyosha noted with some disconcertment. He attributed his brother's coolness to the difference in their ages and particularly in their education. But there was another thought that Alyosha harboured: Ivan's lack of interest and sympathy might have sprung from something Alyosha had not the slightest knowledge of. He had a feeling that Ivan was engrossed in something very personal and important, and was straining towards some goal perhaps difficult of attainment, which was the only reason why he was so inattentive towards Alyosha. The latter could not help wondering whether this expressed some kind of contempt on the part of a learned atheist for a silly novice. He knew for certain that his brother was an atheist. This contempt, if it did exist, could not be offensive, but it was with a sense of uneasy and, to him, incomprehensible embarrassment that he awaited the time his brother would wish to draw closer to him. Brother Dmitri Fyodorovich would express the deepest respect for Ivan, speaking of him with a particular warmth. It was from him that Alyosha learnt in detail of the important piece of business which had more recently established so strong and remarkable a tie between the two elder brothers. Dmitri's admiration for his brother Ivan struck Alyosha all the more for Dmitri being almost quite uneducated in comparison with Ivan; taken together, they presented such a contrast in personality and character that one could hardly imagine any two men more unlike each other.

It was at that time that a meeting or rather a gathering of all the members of this motley family took place in the cell of the *starets*, an event which was to have so extraordinary an influence on Alyosha. The pretext for this gathering was in fact a trumped up one. It was a time when the conflict between Dmitri and his father over the inheritance and property questions seemed to have come to a head, the relations between them having reached breaking point and become intolerable. It must have been Fyodor Pavlovich himself who first suggested, probably in jest, that they should all get together in Zossima's cell and, without resorting to his direct mediation, try to reach some decent understanding, the presence and person of the *starets* lending the scene dignity and making for reconciliation. Of course, it occurred to Dmitri, who had never visited the *starets* and had never even seen him, that the entire arrangement was designated to overawe him, as it were, but as he secretly blamed himself for many outbursts of temper in recent arguments with his father, he took up the challenge. It should be noted, incidentally, that he was not staying with his father, as Ivan was, but at another end of the town. It so happened that Pyotr Alexandrovich Miusov, who was living near our town at the time, grasped eagerly at this idea of Fyodor Pavlovich's. A liberal of the forties and fifties, free-thinker and atheist, he took up the matter with the keenest interest, perhaps out of boredom or else for the sake of amusement. He felt a sudden desire to see the monastery and the "saint". As his long-standing quarrel with the monastery had not been patched up and his lawsuit with it over land boundaries and certain woodcutting and fishing rights and the like was still dragging on, he hastened to avail himself of the opportunity, on the pretext of wishing to see the Father Superior so as to resolve their differences amicably. A visitor with such laudable intentions would of course be received at the monastery with more consideration and courtesy than one who came out of mere curiosity. All these facts could have led to a definite influence within the monastery being exerted on the ailing *starets*, who had almost never left his cell of late and, because of his illness, given up receiving even his ordinary visitors. However, everything ended in his giving his consent and the day being appointed. "Who made me a judge or a divider over them?" was all he said with a smile to Alyosha.

Alyosha was much put out when he learnt of this meeting. His brother Dmitri was the only one of the contending and litigating parties who would view the interview seriously; he realised that the others would be coming out of motives that were frivolous, and perhaps offensive to the *starets*. Brother Ivan and Miusov would be motivated by curiosity, perhaps of the crudest brand, and his father perhaps by a desire to stage some scene of buffoonery. Indeed, Alyosha knew his father only too well, though he kept silent on that score: the lad, I repeat, was not the simpleton all took him for. It was with a heavy heart that he awaited the appointed day. He was undoubtedly most anxious for all the family differences to end in some way, but his main concern was for the *starets*: he trembled for him and his renown, and was afraid of any vexation being caused him, especially by Miusov's refined and courteous ridicule and the learned Ivan's supercilious innuendoes; that, at least, was the light he saw things in. He even wanted to run the risk of warning the *starets* about his possible visitors, but on second thought he refrained. He only sent word, on the eve of the event, to his brother Dmitri, this through an acquaintance, that he loved him and expected him to live up to his promise. This gave Dmitri pause, for he could not remember making any promises; he merely replied by letter that he would make every effort to maintain his self-control "in the face of vileness" and, with all respect for the *starets* and brother Ivan, he felt sure that some snare had been set, or some low farce being staged. "Nevertheless, I would sooner bridle my tongue than be lacking in respect for the holy man you hold in such high esteem," Dmitri wrote in conclusion. The letter gave Alyosha little comfort.

BOOK TWO

An Incongruous Gathering

1.

They Come to the Monastery

The weather was wonderful, warm and bright on that day in late August when the meeting with the *starets* was to take place immediately after late mass, at about half past eleven. However, our visitors did not turn up for the church service, arriving when it was practically over. They arrived in two carriages: one was a smart turn-out, with two fine horses in harness; in it was Pyotr Alexandrovich Miusov accompanied by a young man of about twenty, Pyotr Fomich Kalganov, a distant relative of his, who was preparing to enter a University. Miusov, who was staying with him for some reason, was trying to induce him to go abroad with him to Zurich or Jena where he could read for a degree, but the young man had not yet made up his mind. He seemed wrapped in thought and preoccupied. His face was pleasant, his build sturdy, and his stature quite tall, but at times his gaze was a strangely fixed one: like all absent-minded people, he would stare at you for quite a while without actually seeing you. He was sparing of words and a little awkward, but at times—and only when he was alone with somebody—he would suddenly burst into impetuous speech and become prone to laughter, sometimes at nothing in particular. However, such outbursts of animation would pass off just as rapidly as they had suddenly set in. Invariably well and even immaculately dressed, he was already of independent means, with prospect of much more to come. He was on friendly terms with Alyosha.

Fyodor Pavlovich Karamazov, in the company of his son Ivan, drove up in an ancient, rickety but spacious hired carriage drawn by a pair of pinkish-grey jades, which had fallen well behind Miusov's carriage. Dmitri was late, though he had been informed of the appointed time on the previous day. The visitors left their carriages at the inn, by the monastery wall, and

proceeded on foot through the gateway. Except for Fyodor Pavlovich, the other three had apparently never even seen a monastery, while Miusov had not attended a church service for perhaps thirty years. He looked about himself with some curiosity
that was not without an admixture of an assumed ease of manner. To his observant mind, the monastery grounds presented
nothing of interest, except perhaps for the church and ancillary
buildings, which were ordinary enough. The last of the wor-
shippers were coming out of the church, bare-headed and
crossing themselves. Among the humble folk were several people
of quality—two or three gentlewomen and a very old general,
who had all put up at the inn. The beggars at once surrounded
our visitors, but got nothing for their pains. Only young Kalganov took a ten-copeck coin out of his purse and, embarrassed,
goodness knows why, hurriedly gave it to an old woman. "Share
this out," he said quickly. None of his companions made any
remark on the matter, so there was no cause for embarrassment,
but when he noticed this, he felt even more embarrassed.

The situation was a strange one, however; their arrival should
actually have been expected, and even with some show of honour: one of them had recently made a donation of a thousand
roubles, while another was a very wealthy landowner, a most
highly educated man, so to say, on whom the monks were
partly dependent in respect of fishing rights in the river, in consequence of the possible outcome of the lawsuit. Yet no official person was there to meet them. Miusov glanced abstractedly
at the tombstones near the church, and was on the verge of ob-
serving that burial in so "holy" a place must have cost the relatives a pretty penny, but held his counsel: the simple irony in
this liberal was turning almost into anger.

"Who the devil is there to ask in this absurd place?" he suddenly said, as though speaking to himself. "We have to make up
our minds because time is running short."

They were suddenly approached by an elderly and balding
gentleman with ingratiating little eyes, who wore a roomy
summer overcoat. Raising his hat, he introduced himself with a
honeyed lisp as Maximov, a Tula landowner, and immediately made their concern his own.

"The *starets* Zossima," he said, "lives in a hermitage—a hermitage, sirs, in complete seclusion, about four hundred paces away from the monastery—the way's through the wood—the wood—"

"I know it's through the wood," Fyodor Pavlovich said to him in reply, "but we don't quite remember the way. We haven't been here for a long time."

"You go through this gateway and straight through the wood—through the wood. Come along with me, if you please—I'm going there myself—yes, myself. This way, sirs, this way—"

They passed through the gateway and made for the wood. The landowner Maximov, a man of about sixty, ran rather than walked alongside, staring at them with convulsive and almost incredible curiosity, his eyes seeming to start out of their sockets.

"You see," Miusov observed in a severe voice, "we've come to see the *starets* on some private business of ours. We have, so to speak, been granted an audience by this 'personage' and so, while we are grateful to you for showing the way, we shall not ask you to go in with us."

"But I've been there—been there already— *Un chevalier parfait*!" and the landowner snapped his fingers in the air.

"Who is a *chevalier*?" Miusov asked.

"Why, the *starets*, sir, that magnificent *starets* Zossima, the monastery's fame and glory. What a *starets*—"

His disconnected speech was cut short, however, when they were overtaken by a monk, short of stature, very pale and hollow-cheeked. Fyodor Pavlovich and Miusov came to a standstill. The monk addressed them with a low and most deferential bow.

"The Father Superior requests the pleasure of the company of all you gentlemen after you have been to the hermitage. In his apartments at one o'clock, not later. You, too, are invited," he added, addressing Maximov.

"I'll be there without fail," exclaimed Fyodor Pavlovich, terribly gladdened by the invitation, "without fail! Mind you, we've all promised to be on our best behaviour— What about you, Pyotr Alexandrovich? Are you coming?"

"Most certainly! What have I come here for if not to see all the customs here. The only thing that bothers me is that I'm in your company, Fyodor Pavlovich—"

"Well, Dmitri Fyodorovich hasn't shown up yet."

"It would be excellent if he didn't put in an appearance. Do you imagine I enjoy this messy business of yours, with you here for good measure? So we'll be there for dinner," he said to the monk. "Please thank the Father Superior for us."

"No, sir, I've been instructed to conduct you to the *starets*," the monk replied.

"In that case, I'll go straight to the Father Superior—meanwhile straight there," Maximov twittered.

"The Father Superior is engaged at present, but do as you please—" said the monk hesitantly.

"What an importunate old fellow," Miusov observed aloud when Maximov had trotted off back to the monastery.

"He resembles von Sohn*," Fyodor Pavlovich said suddenly.

"That's all you can think of—why should he resemble von Sohn? Have you ever seen von Sohn?"

"I've seen his photograph. It isn't the features, but something hard to define. The very spit of von Sohn. I can always tell from the face alone."

"I daresay so! You're a connoisseur of such things. Now look here, Fyodor Pavlovich, you said just now that we'd promised to be on our best behaviour. You haven't forgotten, I suppose. Keep yourself in check, I tell you. I have no intention of being classed together with you if you start your clowning— You see the kind of man he is," he went on, addressing the monk. "I'm afraid to call on decent people in his company."

On the monk's pale and bloodless lips there flickered a thin and quiet little smile, which was not without a kind of slyness, but he said nothing in reply; it was only too clear that he did so out of a sense of dignity. Miusov frowned more than ever.

"The deuce take them all, with the outward show they've developed through the centuries. In fact, it's all hocus-pocus and rubbish!" was the thought that flashed through his mind.

*The case of the brutal murder of a certain von Sohn in a low tavern came up at the St. Petersburg District Court on March 28-29, 1870.—*Tr.*

"Here's the hermitage. We've reached it!" Fyodor Pavlovich exclaimed. "But the gate's locked."

He repeatedly made sweeping signs of the cross before the saints depicted over the gateway and on either side of it.

"Do at Rome as the Romans do," he remarked. "In all, twenty-five holy men are seeking salvation at this hermitage. They look at one another and live on cabbage leaves. What's most singular is that no woman can pass through this gateway. That is actually the case. But why is it I've heard the *starets* does receive ladies?" he said, suddenly addressing the monk.

"There are several women of the common folk out there, sitting on the ground and waiting near the veranda. As for ladies of quality, two little rooms have been built adjoining the veranda but outside the walls. You can see the windows over there. When the *starets* feels strong enough, he comes out to see them by an inner passageway, so you see it's outside the grounds. There's a lady waiting there now, a Kharkov landowner, Madame Khokhlakov, with her ailing daughter. He's probably promised to see them though he's been feeling so weak of late that he hardly ever appears to the common people."

"So there is a loop-hole from the hermitage towards the ladies. Oh, no, holy father, don't think I'm being suggestive. It's just in a manner of speaking. You must know that on Mount Athos—you must have heard of it—not only is the presence of women out of order, but even of all creatures of the female sex—no hens or turkey hens, no heifers—"

"Fyodor Pavlovich, I'll go away and leave you here alone, and after I'm gone they'll turn you out—I'm telling you that in advance."

"Am I a hindrance to you, Pyotr Alexandrovich? Look," he exclaimed suddenly, stepping inside the ground, "what a vale of roses they live in!"

Indeed, though there were no roses, there was a multitude of rare and beautiful autumn flowers wherever they could be planted. There were flower beds around the church buildings and between the tombs. The one-storied wooden little house, fronted by a veranda on the entrance side, which contained Zossima's cell, also had flowers growing all about it.

"But was it like this under the previous *starets* Varsonofius? He had no use for ornature, they say, and could jump to his feet at times and lay about with his stick, lamming even the ladies," Fyodor Pavlovich remarked as he mounted the steps.

"The *starets* Varsonofius did really seem to be somewhat eccentric at times, but a good deal that's told about him is nonsense. He never beat anyone at all with a stick," replied the monk. "And now, gentlemen, just wait for a moment and I'll announce you."

"I set you the condition for the last time, Fyodor Pavlovich. D'you hear? Behave properly, for else I'll settle scores with you," Miusov had time to repeat in an undertone.

"I can't make out what has put you in such a twitter," Fyodor Pavlovich sneered. "Are your sins worrying you? I'm told he can tell by one's eyes what the visit is all about. What store you set by their opinion—you, such a Parisian and so progressive a gentleman. You do surprise me, indeed you do!"

Before Miusov had time for a retort to this sarcasm, they were asked to come in. He felt somewhat irritated as he walked inside—

"I know in advance that I'll feel annoyed and start arguing. I'll get worked up—and only discredit myself and my ideas," was the thought that flashed through his mind.

2.

The Old Buffoon

They entered the room almost simultaneously with the *starets*, who came out of his bedroom the moment they appeared. Already awaiting the *starets* in the cell were two hermitage hieromonachs*—one of them the Father Librarian, and the other—Father Paissi, a sickly though not yet elderly man, reputedly a great scholar. Besides them there stood waiting in a corner (and remaining standing throughout the interview) a lad in ci-

---

*In the Eastern Church: a monk who is also ordained as a priest.—*Tr.*

vilian clothes, who looked about twenty-two. He was a seminarist and future theologian, who for some reason enjoyed the patronage of the monastery and its fraternity. He was fairly tall, fresh-complexioned, his cheekbones prominent, and his narrow and observant brown eyes expressive of intelligence. His air of profound deference bore no visible trace of servility and had a certain dignity. He did not even bow to the callers, thereby intimating that he was not their social equal, but, on the contrary, inferior and subordinate in standing.

When the *starets* Zossima entered, accompanied by a novice and Alyosha, the two hieromonachs rose to greet him with profound bows, their fingers touching the floor, and kissed his hand after receiving his blessing. The *starets* replied with just as low a bow to each of them after giving his blessing, and then asked them in turn for a blessing. The entire ceremony was conducted very solemnly, not like some ordinary rite but almost with a kind of warmth. To Miusov, however, it all seemed designed to produce an impression. He was standing in front of his fellow-visitors. Despite his convictions, he had even given thought, on the previous evening, to the propriety of approaching the *starets* and receiving his blessing, at least that, even if he did not kiss his hand—all this out of ordinary civility (since such was the custom there). He instantly changed his mind, however, on witnessing all the bowing and kissing on the part of the monks; with grave dignity, he made a deep but conventional bow and went back to take a seat. Fyodor Pavlovich followed suit, sedulously aping Miusov. Ivan Karamazov's bow was grave and polite, if somewhat stiff, while Kalganov felt so embarrassed that he did not bow at all. The *starets* lowered the hand he had raised for a blessing, and, bowing again to them, asked them all to be seated. A sense of shame made the blood suffuse Alyosha's cheeks. His worst forebodings were coming true.

The *starets* seated himself on a leather-upholstered mahogany settee of old-fashioned construction, meanwhile inviting the visitors, with the exception of the two hieromonachs, to sit down on four mahogany chairs covered with badly worn black leather, all standing in a row along the opposite wall. The hieromonachs took seats on either side of the room, one by the door, the other at the window. The seminarist, the novice and Alyosha remained standing. The cell was far from spacious and looked drab, the furniture and the other things in it—the barest essentials—being crude and cheap. There were two pots of flowers on the window-sill, and a large number of icons in a corner, one of them of the Virgin, of vast size and probably painted long before the Schism. Before it an icon-lamp was burning. It was flanked by two icons in refulgent setting, beside which were carved cherubims, china eggs, a Catholic crucifix of ivory, with a Mater Dolorosa embracing it, and several foreign etchings of paintings by great Italian artists of past centuries. Next to these fine and expensive etchings were several very crude Russian lithographs of saints, martyrs, holy men and the like, of the kind on sale for a few copecks at fairs. There were also several lithographed portraits of Russian hierarchs past and present, but these hung on the other walls. Miusov's glance travelled cursorily over all this "official stuff" and rested intently on the *starets*. He had a high regard for his own judgement, a weakness excusable at least, since he had already turned fifty, an age at which an intelligent and well-to-do man of the world always rises in his own esteem, sometimes despite himself.

From the outset, he did not like the *starets*. Indeed, there was something in the latter's face that would not be to the liking of many people besides Miusov. He was a slight, bent-backed little man with very weak legs, and, though he was only sixty-five, illness made him look far older, at least by ten years. His shrunken face was covered with a network of fine wrinkles, especially about his eyes, which were small, light-coloured, alert and bright, like two brilliant points. The sparse hair covered only his temples; his pointed beard was short and scanty, and the mouth, with its frequent ironical smile, was thin-lipped. His nose was not long but sharp, like the beak of a bird.

"By all appearances, a malicious and mean little man, full of petty pride," was the thought that flashed through Miusov's mind. In general, he felt thoroughly displeased with himself.

The cheap little wall clock with its two weights hurriedly struck the hour of twelve, this helping to get the conversation started.

"We are punctual to the minute," Fyodor Pavlovich exclaimed, "but my son Dmitri Fyodorovich has not turned up yet. I apologise for him, holy *starets*!" (the appellation actually made Alyosha start). "As for myself, I'm always punctual to the minute, remembering that punctuality is the politeness of princes—"

"But you at least are not royalty," Miusov murmured, at once losing his self-control.

"That's very true. I'm not royalty. Just imagine, Pyotr Alexandrovich, I'm well aware of that, I assure you, but I'm always saying the wrong thing! Your reverence!" he cried with sudden feeling. "You see before you a buffoon, yes, verily a buffoon! That's what I call myself. An old habit, alas! And if I sometimes do speak absurdities, I do so on purpose, with the idea of being amusing and agreeable. One has to be agreeable, don't you think? Some seven years ago, I had some business dealings in an obscure little town. I wanted to set up a company with some merchants there. So off we went to the district police inspector, the *ispravnik**, because we had to ask him to do something for us and then invite him to dinner. When he came out to see us, we saw a tall, stout, fair-haired and gloomy-looking man—such men are dangerous in these situations: they're liverish, sir, liverish. So up I went to him with the free-and-easy air of a man of the world. 'Mr. *Ispravnik*, will you be, so to say, our Napravnik?' I said. 'What do you mean by Napravnik?' he asked. I at once saw that the thing was a flop, for he stood there glum and pigheaded. 'I only wanted to make a joke to amuse the company, as Mr. Napravnik is our well-known Russian orchestral conductor, the kind of man we need for harmony in our enterprise—' My explanation and comparison were reasonable, weren't they? 'Excuse me,' he said, 'I'm a police officer, and

*A play on words: *ispravnik*—a district police officer prior to 1917; Eduard Napravnik (1839-1916)—Russian composer and operatic conductor.—*Tr.*

will permit no punning on my rank.' He then turned on his heel and walked off. I followed him, shouting, 'Yes, yes, you're the *Ispravnik*, and not Napravnik!' 'No,' he said, 'since you've said so, I *am* Napravnik.' And imagine, our business deal fell through! It's always like that with me, always. I'm sure to cause harm to myself because I'm affable! Once, many years ago, I said to a person of consequence, 'Your wife's a ticklish lady', meaning honorable, of high morals, so to say, to which he suddenly replied, 'How do you know? Have you tickled her?' I failed to restrain myself, deciding to be complaisant. 'Indeed, I have,' I said, at which he once gave me a fine tickling– Only it all took place long ago so I don't feel ashamed to tell the story; that's the way I'm always doing myself harm!"

"That's exactly what you're doing now," Miusov muttered in disgust.

The *starets* studied them both without a word.

"Am I? Just imagine, I realised that too, Pyotr Alexandrovich, and let me tell you, I knew in advance that I'd be doing that as soon as I opened my mouth, and even foresaw that you'd be the first to remark on it. The moment I see that my joke isn't coming off, your reverence, my cheeks begin to cleave to my lower gums; it's almost like a spasm. It's been like that since my youth when I had to sponge on the nobility and make a living that way. I've been an inveterate buffoon since birth, your reverence, just like some fool for Christ's sake. It may be that there is an evil spirit within me, if only one of small calibre, for a more important one would have chosen another abode, only not yours, Pyotr Alexandrovich, for you're not much of an abode. But then, I possess faith—I believe in God. Only I've had my doubts of late, but now I stand awaiting great truths. I'm just like the philosopher Diderot, your reverence. You probably know, my holy father, that during the reign of the Empress Catherine the philosopher Diderot called on Metropolitan Platon. When he entered, he began to declare, 'There is no God', at which the great hierarch raised a forefinger and replied, 'The fool hath said in his heart, there is no God.' The man fell at the Metropolitan's feet: 'I believe, ' he cried, 'and accept baptism!' He was baptised then and there, with Princess

Dashkova as sponsor, and Prince Potemkin as godfather—"

"This is intolerable, Fyodor Pavlovich! You know very well you're inventing nonsense and that the stupid anecdote is untrue, so why are you playing the fool?" said Miusov, his voice trembling, and he no longer able to check himself.

"All my life I've had a feeling it's untrue!" Fyodor Pavlovich exclaimed with warmth. "But I'll tell you the whole truth, gentlemen. Distinguished *starets*, I crave forgiveness: I thought up the last part, the one about Diderot's baptism, on the spur of the moment; it never occurred to me before. I invented it just for fun. I play such pranks, Pyotr Alexandrovich, to make myself more agreeable, though at times I hardly know why I do so. As for Diderot, I heard of 'The fool hath said' incident at least twenty times in my early years from local landowners I was staying with; incidentally, I also heard it from your aunt Mavra Fominishna, Pyotr Alexandrovich. To this day, they're still sure that 'the atheist Diderot' did call on Metropolitan Platon to dispute about God—"

Miusov rose to his feet, not only losing all patience, but seemingly unaware of what he was doing. He was furious and realised that it made him look ridiculous. Indeed, something quite inconceivable was taking place in the cell. For some forty or fifty years, even under the preceding *startsi*, visitors had gathered in the cell invariably with a feeling of the most profound awe. Almost all those allowed into the cell entered in the awareness that a rare privilege was being conferred on them. Many fell down on their knees and did not rise throughout the entire visit. Many people even of "quality" and outstanding scholarship, and, moreover, even free-thinkers, who had come out of curiosity or some other motive, considered it their prime duty—all of them, without exception—to display the most profound respect and tact throughout the reception, the more so for there being no question of money but exclusively of loving-kindness, on the one hand, and, on the other, of contrition and a thirst to find a solution for a difficult problem of the soul or some perplexity in the life of their own hearts. That was why the onset of buffoonery on the part of Fyodor Pavlovich, which revealed such irreverence for the place he found himself in, evoked in those present, or at least in some of them, a sense of amazement and bewilderment. The two hieromonachs, whose features, however, showed no change of expression, waited in earnest expectancy to hear what the *starets* would say, but seemed on the point of rising to their feet as Miusov had. Alyosha, on the verge of tears, stood with hanging head. He found it most strange that his brother Ivan Fyodorovich, the only person he had placed reliance on, and who alone had influence enough on his father to check him, was sitting quite motionless on his chair, his eyes lowered, and apparently waiting even with a kind of curious interest to see how it would all end up, just as though he were a complete stranger there. Alyosha could not even bring himself to cast a glance at Rakitin (the seminarist), who was almost a close friend of his: he knew his thinking (and was the only one at the monastery to do so).

"Forgive me—" Miusov began, addressing the *starets*, "if I may seem to you another participant in this disgraceful levity. I was mistaken in believing that even a man like Fyodor Pavlovich would wish to understand what was due of him when visiting so venerable a person— I never thought I would have to apologise simply for having entered in his company—"

Pyotr Alexandrovich could not go on and, quite embarrassed, was on the point of leaving the room.

"Pray, do not feel any distress," the *starets* said, rising suddenly on his feeble legs and, taking Pyotr Alexandrovich by both hands, making him sit down in his armchair. "Please calm yourself; I ask you most insistently to be my guest." With a bow, he turned back and resumed his seat on the sofa.

"Great *starets*, say whether my vivacity is offensive to you, or not!" Fyodor Pavlovich cried out, clutching the arms of his chair with both hands and prepared, as it were, to jump up according to the reply he got.

"I earnestly request you too to feel no distress or embarrassment," the *starets* said to him in impressive tones. "Feel no embarrassment and make yourself quite at home. Above all, do not feel ashamed of your own self, for that is the sole cause of it all."

"Quite at home? Show my true colours, you mean to say? Oh, that's a lot, far too much but—I accept with grateful humility! You should know, blessed father, that you should not challenge me to show my true colours—it's too risky; but then, I wouldn't let myself go that far. I'm warning you for your own protection. As for the rest, it's all wrapped in dark obscurity, though there are some who'd be only too glad to show me up. I'm referring to you, Pyotr Alexandrovich; as for you, most holy being, I must give vent to my admiration!" He rose and, raising both hands aloft, proclaimed: "Blessed is the womb that bare thee, and the paps which thou has sucked, especially the paps! Your remark 'do not feel ashamed of your own self, for that is the sole cause of it all'—that remark has pierced me to the heart and revealed what lies within me. That is what I feel whenever I meet with people—namely, that I am more despicable than anybody else and am generally taken for a buffoon, so I say, 'Very well then, I shall indeed play the buffoon; I am not afraid of what you may think of me because you are all, down to the last man, more despicable than I am!' That's why I'm a buffoon, great *starets*—out of a sense of shame, yes, of shame, I play the rowdy only to cover up my sense of inferiority. If only I could be certain that, whenever I put in an appearance, I would be accepted as the most pleasant and clever of men—good Lord, what a good man I'd be! Master!" and he dropped on his knees—"what shall I do to inherit eternal life?" Even then, it was hard to decide whether he was speaking in jest or was really moved.

Raising his eyes at him, the *starets* said with a smile:

"What you should do is something you've known for a long time—you're intelligent enough: do not engage in drunkenness and stupid prattle; do not yield to prurience and particularly to avarice, and, besides, close down your taverns—if not all of them, then two or three at least. Above all, above all—do not lie."

"Is it Diderot you're referring to?"

"Not particularly. Above all, don't lie to yourself. One who lies to himself and gives ear to his own lies ends up by being unable to distinguish the truth either within or without himself, and consequently loses all respect for himself and for others. With his respect for none, he has no capacity for love and, to occupy and distract himself in the absence of love, he yields to passions and engages in dissipation, his vices dragging him into the bestial and all that out of constant lying to others and himself. One who lies to himself is the first to take offence, and taking offence is sometimes a source of pleasure, isn't it? A man knows very well that nobody has offended him, and that he has clutched the offence out of thin air, lied for his own delectation; he has hyperbolised to create some kind of picture; he has grasped at a phrase and made a mountain out of a molehill—he is aware of all this and yet is the very first to take offence; he does so for the delight of it, to achieve a sense of keen pleasure, thereby reaching the point of genuine hostility— But rise, and now be seated, I beg of you—this, too, is false posturing—"

"Blessed man, give me your hand to kiss!" cried Fyodor Pavlovich, jumping up to press his lips on the old man's thin hand. "Indeed, indeed, taking offence does give one pleasure. You've put it better than I've ever heard before. Indeed, all my life long, I have been taking offence to please myself and for my sense of beauty, since there are times when it is not only pleasant but even picturesque to be offended—that's something you've forgotten to mention, great *starets*: the beauty of it! I must remember to make a note of that! I have lied and lied all my life long, every day and hour; verily, I am a liar and the father of a lie. But perhaps not the father of a lie—I get texts all mixed up; well, the son of a lie—that will suffice. Only, dear angel, may I lie about Diderot sometimes? Diderot will cause no harm, but there *are* words that do that. Great *starets*, I almost forgot that I'd decided the year before last to find out something here—yes, to come here expressly to ask and find out—only please tell Pyotr Alexandrovich not to interrupt. Here's what I want to ask: is it true that the *Lives of the Saints* somewhere tells the story of a holy miracle-worker who suffered torture for his faith, and when his head was at last cut off he arose, picked up the head, 'kissed it lovingly', and walked a long way, carrying it in his hand and kissing it lovingly. Is that true or not, revered Fathers?"

"No, it is not true," said the *starets*.

"There's nothing of the kind in any of the *Lives of the Saints*. Which saint do you say it's been written about?" asked the Father Librarian.

"I don't know which saint. I don't know and can't say. Somebody spoke of it and led me into error. I heard it, and do you know who from? It was from Pyotr Alexandrovich Miusov here, who grew so angry over Diderot. It was he who told the story."

"I've never said it to you, and I never speak to you at all."

"True, you did not tell it to me but you did tell it to a social gathering I was present at a little over three years ago. I mentioned the fact because you shook my faith with your amusing story, Pyotr Alexandrovich. You weren't aware of it and had no knowledge that I returned home with my faith shaken and that the damage has been growing since then. Indeed, Pyotr Alexandrovich, you've been the cause of a great downfall! That's more than merely Diderot!"

Fyodor Pavlovich was getting more and more worked up, though it was already perfectly clear to all present that he was play-acting again. However, Miusov felt mortified.

"What nonsense! It's all nonsense," he muttered. "I may have really said something of the kind at one time or another—but not to you: I heard it from somebody in Paris—from a Frenchman who said it was read out from the *Lives of the Saints* at our morning masses— He was a most learned man who made a special study of Russian statistics—he had lived in Russia for quite a while—I haven't read the *Lives of the Saints* myself—and have no intention of doing so. All kinds of things are told at the dinner table— We were dining at the time—"

"Well, you were having dinner while I lost my faith!" said Fyodor Pavlovich with a snigger.

"What's your faith to do with me!" Miusov was on the verge of exclaiming, but suddenly curbed himself and said contemptuously, "you actually besmirch whatever you touch."

The *starets* suddenly rose from his seat.

"You will excuse me, gentlemen, for leaving you for several

61

minutes," he said, addressing all his visitors, "but there are people waiting for me who came before you did. Yet you should stop your story-telling," he added good-humouredly, turning to Fyodor Pavlovich.

He made to leave the cell, with Alyosha and the novice dashing after him to help him down the stairs. Alyosha felt choked; he was glad to get away, but he also felt glad that the *starets* had not taken offence and was in a good humour. The latter wished to go to the veranda to give his blessing to people who were awaiting him, but Fyodor Pavlovich intercepted him in the doorway.

"Most blessed man," he exclaimed with feeling. "Permit me to kiss your hand again! Indeed, you're a man one can speak to and get along with! D'you think I'm always thinking up things and playing the buffoon like that? You should know that I behaved like that on purpose, just to test you. I was feeling you out all the time to find out whether one can get on with you, and whether there is room for my humility alongside of your pride. I can issue you with a certificate of honour: one *can* get on with you! I shall now fall silent and not utter another word. I'll sit down in my arm-chair and stay silent. It's your turn to speak now, Pyotr Alexandrovich; you're the most important person remaining—for some ten minutes."

3.

Peasant Women with Faith

This time a crowd of about twenty peasant women had gathered downstairs at the wooden veranda attached to the wall surrounding the monastery grounds. They had been informed that the *starets* would be coming out at last and they had got together in expectation. Also there were Madame Khokhlakov and her daughter, but they had come out into the veranda from premises set aside for gentlewomen. Madame Khokhlakov, a wealthy lady whose clothes always displayed taste, was still young and very good-looking, somewhat pale and with sparkling eyes that were almost quite black. She was not over thirty-three and had been a widow for five years. Her daughter, who was fourteen, suffered from paralysis of the legs. The poor girl had been unable to walk for the past six months and was taken about in a long and comfortable wheel-chair. She had a winsome little face, somewhat thin from illness but full of gaiety. There was a roguish gleam in her big dark eyes with their long lashes. Ever since the spring, her mother had intended to take her abroad but they had been delayed all summer by the affairs of their estate. They had been staying in our town for a week, more on business than for devotion, but had already visited the *starets* three days before. Though they knew he was hardly to see anyone, they had unexpectedly returned begging to be granted once again "the happiness of seeing the great healer".

In expectation of his appearance, the mother was sitting on a chair by her daughter's wheel-chair; two paces from her stood an old monk, who was not of the local monastery but had come from remote and obscure cloister in the North. He, too, sought Father Zossima's blessing. But when he appeared, the *starets* first went straight towards the crowd, who had gathered at the front steps to the veranda. He paused on the top step, put on his stole and began to give his blessing to the women, who pressed towards him. A woman prone to hysteria was led up to him by the hand; as soon as she saw him, she began to shriek in an absurd fashion, hiccuping and writhing as though in a fit of convulsions. Covering her head with his stole, the *starets* pronounced a short prayer over her, at which she fell silent and calmed down. I do not know how the matter stands nowadays, but in my childhood I often had occasion to see and hear such hysterical women in the villages. They would be brought to morning mass, where they would shriek and bark like dogs, so that they could be heard all over the church, but when the Host was brought in and they were led up to it, their "possession" ended at once and the sick women quieted down for a while. I was always struck and astonished by this when I was a child, but, in reply to my questions at the time, I was told by some landowners and especially by my teachers in the town that it was all a sham designed to dodge working, and could always be eradicated by the appropriate severity. Various instances would be cited to bear that out. It was later that I learnt to my surprise from medical specialists that there was no shamming about it: it was a terrible ailment afflicting women, mostly in Russia, evidently as a result of the hard lot of our peasant women. It was an illness brought about by backbreaking toil too soon after difficult and abnormal childbirth, with no medical aid during labour, and also by hopeless misery, beatings and the like, which some women cannot endure, though others can. The strange and immediate healing of a raving and struggling woman as soon as she was led to the Host, something that had been explained to me as shamming and, moreover, as some trickery practised by the "clericals", probably derived from quite natural causes: those who led the sick woman up to the Host, and, in the first place, the woman herself implicitly believed as an established truth that the evil spirit that had possessed her could not hold out if she was administered the sacrament and made to bow down before it. That was why it always happened (and could not but happen) that the nervous and, of course, mentally sick woman always experienced a kind of convulsion in her body when she bowed down to the Host, a shock caused by the expectation that a miracle of healing would surely take place and the firm conviction that it would come about. And that it did, if only momentarily. That was exactly what happened hardly had the *starets* covered the sick woman with the stole.

Many of the woman crowding about him were moved to tears of deep emotion and rapture by the impact of the moment; others tried to kiss at least the hem of his garment, while yet others began to wail in singsong tones. He gave all of them his blessing and spoke to some of them. He already knew the woman he had soothed, for she had been brought from nearby, from a village only six versts away, and had been brought to him before.

"And here's somebody from afar!" he said, addressing a woman who was not at all old as yet but very thin and hollow-cheeked, her face not so much weather-beaten as dark almost to blackness. She was on her knees, her eyes fixed on the *starets*, with something like frenzy in their gaze.

"From afar, from afar, Father, some three hundred versts from here. From afar, Father, a long way from here," she said in a singsong voice, her head swaying from side to side, a hand supporting her cheek. Her words came in a moan. A mute and long-suffering sorrow is to be met among peasants, something withdrawn and wordless. But there is another kind of sorrow that is past endurance and finds vent in a flood of tears, after which it gives way to moaning complaint, especially so with women. This kind of grief is just as crushing as the silent kind, the lament bringing relief only by still more embittering and rending the heart beyond consolation and being fed by a sense of desolation, the constant plaints springing from a constant need to keep the wound bleeding.

"I suppose you're of the townspeople," the *starets* went on, looking at her with curiosity.

"Indeed we are, Father, we're country folk who've become townspeople. It's to see you that I've come here, Father. I've heard of you, Father, heard of you. I've just buried my little son, and have set out to pray to the Lord. I've been to three monasteries, where they said to me, 'Go, Nastasia, and see him', meaning you, dear friend, so here I am. I was at church yesterday, and I've come here to see you today."

"Why are you weeping?"

"I'm grieving for my little son, Father. He was only three— he'd have been three in another three months. My heart bleeds for my little son, Father, my little son. He was the last of the four we had, Nikita and I, and now they're all gone. Our children don't seem to hold on, Father. I buried the first three without grieving overmuch, but now that I've buried the last one I can't forget him. He stands before my eyes and never leaves me. It sears my heart whenever I look at his linen, his little shirt or his boots, and I wail. I lay out whatever is left after him, every little thing, and I weep as I look at them. I say to my husband Nikita: 'Let me go, husband, let me set out on a pilgrimage.' He's a carter. We're not poor, Father, not poor. We have our carting business and we're our own masters. We own the horses and the van. But what good is it all to us? He's taken to drink, has my Nikita, in my absence. He's sure to, just as in the past. As soon as I'm away, he gives way to it. But he's not on my mind now. It's over two months since I've been away from home. I've forgotten it all, quite forgotten, and don't want to call it to mind. How can I go on with him? I'm through with him, quite through, and done with it all. I don't want to look upon my house and property again. I hope I'll never see them again!"

"Listen to me, woman," said the *starets*. "Once, long, long ago, a very saintly man saw a woman just like you, in a church. She was weeping, and also for her infant child, her only one, whom the Lord had taken to himself. 'Don't you know,' said the saintly man to her, 'how audacious such infants are before the throne of God. There are none bolder in the Kingdom of Heaven. "Thou hast granted us life, O Lord," they say to God, "and didst take it away when we had scarcely seen it." They ask and request so boldly, that the Lord at once confers the rank of angels upon them. Therefore,' said the holy man, 'be of good heart, woman, and do not weep, for your child is with the Lord, in his host of angels.' Those were the words spoken of old to the weeping woman by the holy man. He was of great sanctity and could not have told her a falsehood. Therefore, know you too, woman, that your child is standing for sure before the throne of the Lord, happy and rejoicing, and praying to God for you. That's why you should rejoice, and not weep."

The woman listened to him with bowed head, her cheek resting on the palm of a hand, and then heaved a heavy sigh.

"That's exactly how my Nikita would comfort me, in the same words as yours. 'You're so unreasonable,' he would say, 'why are you crying? Our son is surely singing before the Lord, together with His angels.' He would say that to me, but would be in tears himself. I could see him crying just like me. 'I know, dear Nikita,' I say to him; 'where else could he be if not with the Lord, only he's not down here with us, Nikita, near us as he used to be!' If only I could just have a look at him, only one look. I wouldn't even go up to him, or say a word, I would just sit quiet in a corner just to see him for a single minute, and hear him at play in the yard, calling out, as he used to, in his little voice, 'Mum, where are you?' If only once, going pat-a-pat, just as he used to. I remember, when he would come running up, shouting and laughing. If only I could hear it once more—I would recognise it. But no, Father, he's gone and I'll never hear him again! Look, here's his little sash, but he's gone, and I'll never see him again, or hear him!"

She pulled out from her bosom a little embroidered sash her boy had worn, and burst into sobs as she looked at it, hiding her eyes with her fingers, through which the tears were streaming.

"This," said the *starets*, "is the Rachel of old, weeping for her children, refusing to be comforted for her children, because they were not. Such is the earthly lot of you mothers. And do not seek consolation, for that is not what you need. Don't be comforted, but weep, only whenever you weep be sure to remember that your little son is one of God's angels, looking down on you, seeing you, and rejoicing at your tears, which he points out to the Lord. Your maternal grief will long be with you, but in the end it will turn into quiet joy, and your bitter tears will be only tears of quiet and tender joy, tears that cleanse the heart and save you from sin. As for your boy, I shall pray for the repose of his soul. What was his name?"

"Alexei, Father."

"A sweet name. After Alexei, man of God."

"Yes, Father, after Alexei, man of God."

"What a saintly man he was! In my prayers I shall remember your child, and your sorrow. I shall pray for your husband's well-being. Only it's sinful for you to have left him. Go back to your husband and take care of him. Your boy will see from on high that you've forsaken his father and will shed tears: why should you upset his bliss? He lives on; he's alive, for the soul lives for ever. Though he's not in the house, he's by you, unseen. How can he enter your house if you say it's hateful to you? Who can he come to if he doesn't find you, his father and mother, together? You have dreams about him and you are in torment, but if you return home he will send you gentle dreams. Go back to your husband, woman, go back this very day."

"I shall, Father, I'll go at your bidding. You've touched me to the heart. Nikita, dear Nikita, you're waiting for me, waiting!" The woman began in her singsong voice, but the *starets* had already turned away towards a very old woman, dressed like a townswoman, not a pilgrim. Her eyes showed that she had come with some aim in view and that she had something to say. She said she was a NCO's widow from close by, in fact from our town. Her son Vassili, who was in the commissariat service, had gone to Irkutsk in Siberia. He had written twice from there, but a whole year had gone by since his last letter. She had made inquiries about him, but she really did not know the right quarters for inquiries.

"Only the other day, Stepanida Bedriagina—she's a merchant's wife and very wealthy—was telling me to go to the priest and have it put down for mention in his prayers at the service for the repose of his soul, as though he were departed. He'll be troubled in his soul, she said, and write to you. 'It's a sure thing,' she said, 'which has been tested many a time.' But I have my doubts, Father. You are our light; tell me if that's true or not, and if it would be right thing to do."

"Drive it out of your thoughts. Even asking is something you should be ashamed of! Is it possible to offer prayer for the repose of the soul of somebody who's alive? And his own mother, too. It's most sinful, just like witchcraft and can be forgiven only because of your ignorance. Better pray to the Queen of Heaven, for speedy intercession and defence, for his health and for you to be forgiven for your wrong thinking. Let me tell you this: your son will come to see you soon or else will surely write. I want you to know that. Now go and stop worrying. Your son is alive, I say to you."

"May God reward you, our good father and benefactor, who prays for us and our sins—"

But the *starets* had already noticed, in the crowd, two burning eyes fixed on him. A young peasant woman with a wasted face, who looked consumptive, was gazing at him in silence; her eyes were beseeching him for something but she seemed apprehensive of approaching him.

"What is it, my child?"

"Cleanse my soul, Father," she said in a low and unhurried voice and, falling on her knees, she bowed down at his feet.

"I have sinned, dear Father, and I'm afraid of my sin."

He sat down on the lower step, and the woman, still on her knees, drew closer to him.

"I've been a widow for over two years," she began in a half-whisper, with a shudder. "I had a hard time in my marriage. My husband was an old man who used to beat me cruelly. As he lay ill, I couldn't help thinking, looking at him, what would happen to me if he got well and got up again. It was then that the idea came to me that—"

"Stay," said the *starets* putting an ear close to her lips. The woman went on in a low whisper so that nothing could be made out. She soon concluded her story.

"Over two years ago?" the *starets* asked.

"Yes, over two years. I gave no thought to it at first, but now I've taken sick. I'm having a bad time of it from misery."

"Have you come from afar?"

"Five hundred versts from here."

"Have you spoken of it at confession?"

"I have. Twice."

"Have you been admitted to Holy Communion?"

"I have. Yet I'm afraid. Afraid to die."

"Have no fear of anything. Cast out all fear and all worry. If only your penitence does not fail, God will forgive you everything. There is no sin on earth, there can be no sin that the Lord will not forgive the truly repentant. Man cannot commit a sin so great as to tax God's boundless love. Can there be any such sin that will exceed God's love? Only give constant thought to repentance and cast out all fear. Believe that God loves you in a way you simply can't imagine, loves you even with your sin and in your sin. There is greater rejoicing in Heaven over one repentant sinner, it was said long ago, than over ten just men. Go and have no fear. Don't get upset because of others, and don't feel anger if others offend you. Forgive in heart your dead husband for the way he treated you, and become truly reconciled with him. Penitence means love, and if you love, then you are of God— Love atones for everything and brings salvation to everything. If I, a sinner just like you are, have been moved by your words and have felt sorry for you, God will do so far more.

Love is so priceless a treasure that you can win the whole world with it and atone, not only for your own sins but for those of others. Go, and fear not."

He thrice made the sign of the cross over her, took a little icon off his neck and put it on her. She wordlessly bowed down to the ground. He rose to his feet, looking cheerfully at a buxom peasant woman with a babe in her arms.

"I'm from Vyshegorye, dear Father."

"You've actually trudged here six versts with your baby. What is it you want?"

"I've come just to look at you. I've been to see you before, or have you forgotten? Your memory isn't so good if you have. They were saying in our parts that you were ailing, so I thought to myself that I should go and see for myself. I see you now: what kind of sick man are you? You have another twenty years of life before you (God keep you!), indeed you have! How can you ail if there are so many people praying for you?"

"Thank you for everything, my dear."

"Yes, there's something I'd like to ask you to do—a small thing. Here's sixty copecks I want you to give to others poorer than me. As I was coming here, I thought I should do that through you. You'd know who to give it to."

"Thank you, my dear, thank you for your goodness. I love you. I'll do so without fail. Is your baby a girl?"

"Yes, Father, Lizaveta by name."

"The Lord bless you both, you and the babe Lizaveta. You've gladdened my heart, woman. Good-bye, dear one, good-bye."

Bowing low, he blessed them all.

4.

A Lady of Little Faith

As she watched the scene of Father Zossima's meeting with the common folk and his blessing of them, Mme Khokhlakov's eyes filled with tears, which she wiped away with a handkerchief. She was a society woman of some sentimentality, and with propensities that were genuinely kindly in many respects. She was enraptured when the *starets* finally went up to her.

"I was so deeply moved as I watched the heart-moving scene—" she could not go on for emotion. "Oh, I understand how the people love you; I love them too. I want to love them—indeed, one cannot but love them—our wonderful Russian people, so simple in their grandeur!"

"How is your daughter's health? You wanted to talk to me about her again?"

"Oh, I've been pressing for it, and prayed for the opportunity. I was ready to fall on my knees and remain kneeling at your windows for three days until you let me in. We have come to see you, great healer, to express our heartfelt gratitude for healing Lise, healing her completely—and how? By praying over her last Thursday, and laying your hands on her. We've hurried here to kiss those hands, and give vent to our feelings and our veneration."

"How can I have healed her? Isn't she still lying in her chair?"

"But her night fevers have gone completely these last two days—since Thursday," the lady went on hurriedly and nervously. "Moreover, her legs are stronger. She awoke this morning feeling quite well after a good night's sleep. Look at those rosy cheeks and bright eyes! She would be crying all the time, but now she's full of laughter, happy and cheerful. Today she insisted on being allowed to stand up, and she stood without any support for a whole minute. She's laid a wager with me that she'll be doing a square dance in a fortnight's time. I called Doctor Herzenstube, the local physician, who shrugged his shoulders and said he was simply amazed and puzzled at the improvement. And you would prefer us not to trouble you and hasten here to thank you. Lise, thank him, thank him!"

Lise's pretty and laughing little face grew suddenly grave. She raised herself in her chair as much as she could. Her eyes fixed on the *starets*, she clasped her hands before him but, unable to restrain herself, burst into sudden laughter.

"It's him, him I'm laughing at!" she exclaimed, pointing at

Alyosha, in childish vexation for having been unable to repress her laughter. Anyone looking at Alyosha, who was standing a pace behind the *starets*, would have seen the flush that suffused his cheeks. He dropped his eyes to conceal the flash in them.

"She has a message for you, Alexei Fyodorovich, a message— How are you?" the mother went on, extending an exquisitely gloved hand. The *starets* turned round to cast a sudden and keen glance at Alyosha, who went up to Lise and, with a strange and awkward smile, held out a hand to her. Lise tried to look important.

"Katerina Ivanovna has sent this through me," she said, handing him a little note. "She particularly asks you to call on her as soon as you can, and not to disappoint her but be sure to come."

"Asks me to call? Me? What for?" Alyosha muttered in astonishment. His face expressed sudden concern.

"Oh, it's all about Dmitri Fyodorovich and—all these recent happenings," the mother hastened to explain. "Katerina Ivanovna has arrived at a certain decision—but for that she's simply got to see you— Why? I don't know, of course, but she asks you to come as soon as possible. You'll do so for sure. It's something your Christian feelings will prompt you to do."

"But I've met her only once," Alyosha continued in perplexity.

"Oh, what a noble-minded and peerless creature she is! Think what she has gone through, what she is enduring just now, and imagine what lies ahead for her—it's all simply terrible, terrible!"

"Very well, I'll go," Alyosha decided, after glancing through the short and cryptic note which, except for an earnest request that he was to come at once, gave no reason why he should do so.

"Oh, how sweet and splendid of you that will be!" Lise exclaimed with sudden animation. "I told Mama you wouldn't go for anything, because you are seeking salvation. How good you are! I've always thought you are a good man and I'm glad to tell you so now!"

"Lise!" the mother said chidingly, her smile at once returning after the admonition.

"You've forgotten us as well, Alexei Fyodorovich; you never come to see us. Yet Lise has told me on two occasions she feels good only with you." Alyosha looked up, suddenly blushed again, and then, just as suddenly, smiled without knowing why. Incidentally, the *starets* was no longer watching him. He had entered into conversation with the visiting monk, who, as we have already said, had been standing by Lise's wheel-chair, waiting for the *starets* to come out. He was evidently of humble origin, that is to say, of the common classes, with narrow-minded and inflexible religious views but firm in his faith and stubborn in his own way. He explained he had come from Obdorsk, somewhere in the Far North, from the monastery of St. Sylvester, a poor community of only nine monks. The *starets* gave him his blessing, inviting him to visit his cell whenever he wished.

"How can you make so bold as to do such deeds?" the monk suddenly asked, pointing significantly and solemnly at Lise, a reference to the act of "healing".

"It's too soon, of course, to speak of that. Relief is not yet a complete cure and could have been brought about by other causes. But if anything has taken place it has been by no other power but the Divine will. Everything comes of God. Come and see me, Father," he went on, "for I'm afraid I can't see people at all times. I'm ailing and know that my days are numbered."

"Oh, no, no!" the mother cried out. "God will not take you away from us. You'll live a long, long life. What are you ill with? You look so well, cheerful and happy!"

"I feel extremely well today, but I'm quite aware that it's only for a while. I have a thorough understanding of my ailment. If I seem so cheerful to you, you couldn't have said anything to please me more: man has been created for happiness, and one who feels quite happy has been granted the right to say to himself, 'I have kept God's commandment on earth'. All the righteous, all the saints, all the holy martyrs were happy people."

"Oh, what bold and lofty words you say!" the mother exclaimed. "When you speak, the words seem to pierce one.

73

And yet—happiness, happiness—where is it to be found? Who can say of himself that he's happy? Oh, if you've been so kind as to have allowed us to see you again, then listen to what I did not say last time, what I dared not say—about everything that has caused me so much suffering for such a long, long time! Forgive me but I'm suffering, I am indeed—" She clasped hands before him in a flood of uncontrollable emotion.

"What from in particular?"

"From—disbelief."

"Disbelief in God?"

"Oh, no, no! I dare not even think of that, but the after-life—it's all such a mystery! And there's no one—literally no one—to give an answer! Listen, you're a healer, with insight into the human soul; I dare not expect you to believe me entirely, but I solemnly assure you that I'm not speaking lightly: the thought of an afterlife brings up a feeling of anguish in me—fear and horrors—and I don't know who to turn to—I've never dared to— And now I've made so bold as to turn to you. Dear God, what will you think of me now?" she went on, her hands clasped.

"Don't worry about what I may think," the *starets* replied. "I quite believe that your anguish is sincere."

"Oh, how grateful I am to you. Look, I close my eyes and think to myself: since everyone has faith, where does all my lack of faith spring from? And here people assert that it all springs from a fear of the awesome phenomena in Nature, and has no existence in reality. Well, I think, and I've believed all my life long: when I die, it all comes to a sudden end, and there will be nothing but 'weeds growing on my grave', as a writer has put it. It's something awful! How, how am I to regain my faith? I had faith when I was a little child, but it was something mechanical and unthinking. But how, how can the existence of faith be proved? I've come here to throw myself at your feet and ask you for an answer. If I let this opportunity slip by, nobody will ever answer me. How is it to be proved? What can bring conviction? Woe is me! As I stand and look about myself, I see that people are so indifferent, almost all of them; nobody cares, and I alone can't put up with it. It's dreadful, dreadful!"

"It's dreadful, no doubt. But here nothing can be proved, though one can achieve conviction!"

"How? In what way?"

"By an experience of active love. Try to love your neighbours actively and tirelessly. And the more progress you have made in love, the firmer your belief will be in the existence of God and the immortality of your soul. If you achieve complete forgetfulness of self in love of your fellow-creatures, you will certainly gain faith, and doubt will never be able to enter your soul. That has been tested and proved."

"Active love? That's another problem—and what a problem, what a problem! You see, I have such a love of mankind that, believe me, I sometimes dream of giving up everything I possess, leaving Lise and becoming a sister of mercy. I close my eyes, think and day-dream, and at such moments I feel a surge of unconquerable strength. No wounds, no running sores could deter me then. I could cleanse and bind them with my own hands. I would attend to the afflicted and be ready to kiss their sores."

"That of itself is very much, and it's good that your mind is bent on such things and no others. There's no knowing: you may indeed perform some good deed."

"Yes, but could I put up with that kind of life for long?" the lady continued vehemently and almost frantically. "That's the crucial question, my most agonising problem. I close my eyes and ask myself: 'Could you endure for long along that road? What if the sick man whose sores you are cleansing fails to feel immediate gratitude to you, but, on the contrary, begins to harass you with his whims, without appreciating or taking note of your humane service, becomes rude in his demands, and even complains to the authorities (as is often the case with acute sufferers)— what then? Will your love endure or not?' And, just fancy, I am horrified to have arrived at the conclusion that if anything does exist which can at once diminish my 'active' love of mankind, it is that ingratitude, and nothing else. In a word, I can work only for pay: I demand immediate payment, that is to say, praise for myself and requital of love with love. Otherwise, I'm incapable of loving anybody!"

She spoke in the throes of the most sincere self-castigation;

as she concluded, she looked at the *starets* in resolute defiance.

"That's exactly the same sort of thing I was once told by a doctor a long time ago," the *starets* observed. "He was an elderly man, and undoubtedly a clever one. What he said was just as outspoken, though it was in jest, a sad kind of jest. 'I love mankind,' he said, 'though I'm amazed at myself: the greater my love of mankind in general, the less I love people in particular, that is to say, separately, as individuals. In my mind's eye,' he said, 'I've often arrived at impassioned ideas of service to mankind, and I might very well make the supreme sacrifice for others, were that suddenly necessary for some reason; yet I can't put up with living in the same room with anybody else for even a couple of days. I know that from experience. If somebody comes near me, his personality begins to oppress my self-esteem and constrains my freedom. I can even come to hate the finest of men in a matter of twenty-four hours; one for the sole reason that he dawdles over his dinner, and another for constantly blowing his nose because of a cold in the head. I grow hostile to people, as soon as I feel their least touch. But then it has always happened that the more I have hated people as individuals, the more ardent my love of mankind as a whole has grown.'"

"But what is to be done? What should one do in such a situation? Should one yield to despair?"

"No. Suffice it that it causes you distress. Do what you can and it shall be reckoned unto you. You've done much since you've been able to know yourself so deeply and sincerely! But if you've spoken to me in such sincerity merely for me to commend you for being truthful, then you will, of course, achieve nothing in your striving for active love. It will all remain a dream, and your whole life will slip by like an apparition. In that case, you will of course give up all thought of the future life, and in the end calm down after a fashion."

"What crushing words! It is only now, at the instant you were speaking, that I realised what I was actually expecting—your commendation of my sincerity in telling you I could not put up with ingratitude. You've shown me the kind of person I am, gained an insight into me, and explained me to myself!"

"Are you speaking in earnest? Well, now that you have unburdened your mind, I believe in your sincerity and goodness of heart. Even if you do not achieve happiness, you should always remember you're on the right road and try not to depart from it. Above all, eschew falsehood, all falsehood, especially towards yourself. Keep watch over your own falsehood and scrutinise it hourly and at every minute. Eschew contumely both for others and for yourself. What seems to you evil in yourself is cleaned by the very fact that you've discerned it in yourself. Cast out fear too, for fear is merely an effect of any falsehood. Never fear your own faintness of heart in your striving towards love; neither should you be too much afraid even of your evil actions. I'm sorry I can't say anything more comforting to you, for, compared with the stuff that dreams are made on, active love is something rigorous and formidable. Romantic love yearns for exploits that can be performed without the least delay and is open to the public view. In fact, it can reach a dimension in which life itself is sacrificed provided the ordeal is brief and soon over, just like on the stage, with an audience looking on and applauding. Active love, on the other hand, calls for hard work and patience, and for some people it is even perhaps a science. However, I predict that, at the very moment you will see with horror that— despite all your efforts— you are receding from your goal instead of approaching it, at that very moment, I predict, you will suddenly attain that goal and will clearly see the wonder-working power of God, who has loved and guided you all the time. Forgive me, but I can't stay with you any longer. There are people waiting for me. Goodbye."

The lady was in tears.

"Lise, Lise—please give her your blessing!" she cried, all of a flutter.

"But she doesn't deserve to be loved," the *starets* said jokingly. "She's been naughty all the time, as I've seen. Why have you been poking fun at Alexei?"

Indeed, that was exatcly what Lise had been doing all the time. She had long ago noticed, in fact at their previous meeting, that she made Alyosha feel bashful and that he kept his eyes away from her, which amused her immensely. She waited persistently to catch his glance: unable to endure her gaze, Alyosha would involuntarily cast a swift glance at her as though drawn by an irresistible force, at which she would give him a triumphant smile. This disconcerted and abashed Alyosha even more, so he finally turned away from her and took refuge behind the *starets*. Attracted by the same irresistible force, however, he again turned to see whether she was looking or not and saw Lise practically hanging out of her wheel-chair and watching him closely out of the corner of an eye in eager expectation of his look. On catching his glance she burst into such laughter that the *starets* could not help remarking:

"Why are you teasing him, you naughty girl?"

Lise blushed suddenly and unexpectedly. Her eyes flashed, and her face turned grave.

"Then why has he forgotten everything?" she asked, speaking in a nervously rapid and indignant tone of complaint. "He used to carry me around in his arms when I was a little girl, and play with me. Didn't you know he used to come to us to teach me how to read? When he was saying good-bye to us two years ago, he said he would never forget we were friends for always, always! And now he's afraid of me, as though I'll eat him up. Why doesn't he want to come up to me? Why doesn't he speak to me? Why won't he come to see us? Don't you let him? We know he goes wherever he wants to. I can't very well invite him to come, can I? That wouldn't be proper. He should be the first to remember, if he hasn't forgotten. Oh, no, he's out to save his soul! Why have you made him wear that long cassock of his? It will trip him up if he starts to run—"

Unable to control herself, she covered her face with a hand and broke into a prolonged fit of nervous and silent laughter, which shook her whole body. The *starets* listened with a smile and tenderly gave her his blessing. As she kissed his hand, she suddenly pressed it to her eyes and began to cry.

"You aren't cross with me, are you? I'm a silly girl, who's worth nothing at all—and Alyosha may be right, quite right, in not wanting to come to see such a ridiculous girl!"

"I will certainly send him along," the *starets* decided.

5.

It Shall Surely Come to Pass!

The *starets* had been away from his cell for about twenty-five minutes. Though the time was more than half past twelve, Dmitri Fyodorovich, on whose account they had all gathered, had not yet put in an appearance. But he almost seemed forgotten, and when the *starets* returned to his cell he found his visitors engaged in almost animated conversation, in which Ivan Fyodorovich and the two hieromonachs were very active. Miusov, too, seemed eager to have his say, but was meeting with little success. He was evidently in the background and his remarks seemed almost ignored, so that this new circumstance merely exacerbated his mounting irritation. Even previously, he had had some sharp exchanges in the field of knowledge with Ivan Fyodorovich, whose somewhat disdainful attitude he could not put up with. "In the past, at least," he thought to himself, "I stood on a par with whatever was progressive in Europe, but this new generation gives us the cold shoulder." As for Fyodor Pavlovich, who had promised to sit still and keep silent, he had indeed been quiet for a time while, watching his neighbour Pyotr Alexandrovich with a sardonic grin, obviously enjoying his dudgeon. He had some old scores to settle with him and was loth to let the opportunity slip by. Finally, losing all patience, he leaned towards his neighbour and again set about twitting him in an undertone.

"Why was it you didn't leave after the 'loving kiss'? Why did you consent to stay on in such an unseemly company? Simply because you felt humiliated and insulted and remained behind so as to hit back by displaying your intellect. You won't leave now until you've shown off your intelligence."

"So you're at it again! On the contrary, I'll leave at once."

"You'll go after the rest have!" Fyodor Pavlovich said stingingly, almost at the moment the *starets* returned to his cell.

The argument died down momentarily; the *starets*, resuming his seat, cast an amiable glance at the company as though intimating they might continue. Alyosha, who understood almost any expression fleeting across his face, could clearly see he was terribly tired and making an effort to carry on. His illness had brought on fainting fits of late because of his exhausted condition. The pallor spreading over his face was of the kind that preceded an attack of fainting, and his lips had gone white, but he seemed unwilling to dismiss his visitors. There seemed to be some purpose to that, but what could it be? Alyosha kept an attentive eye on him.

"We've been discussing a highly interesting article by this gentleman," said the librarian, the hieromonach Iosif, addressing the *starets* and pointing at Ivan Fyodorovich. "In it, he has drawn some new conclusions, but the underlying idea seems to cut both ways. In connection with the question of the powers of ecclesiastical courts in respect of public matters, he has published an article in a journal in reply to a book on the subject, written by a member of the clergy—"

"I'm sorry to say I haven't read your article, but I've heard of it," the *starets* replied, looking keenly and intently at Ivan Fyodorovich.

"He's taken a most interesting stand," the Father Librarian went on, "one that would reject the separation of Church and State in the matter of such courts."

"That's interesting," the *starets* observed to Ivan Fyodorovich, "but in what particular sense?"

The latter replied after a pause, but did so, not with haughty courtesy, as Alyosha, on the day before, had feared he might, but with modest restraint and obvious goodwill, and, it would seem, with no mental reservations.

"I proceed from the proposition that this mixing of elements, that is to say, the hypostases of Church and State, taken separately, will, of course, be perpetual, though it is impossible and cannot ever be brought, not only into some normal relationship but even into one that is in some way compatible. That is because the entire matter is founded on falsehood. In absolute and pure essence, no compromise is, in my opinion, possible between Church and State in such matters as jurisdiction. My ecclesiastic opponent affirmed that the Church has an exact and definite place in the State. In reply, I voiced the objection that, on the contrary, the Church should incorporate the entire State and not occupy only a nook in it: should that prove impossible at present, it should, in the essence of things, be made the direct and principal aim of the entire future development of Christian society."

"Very true!" Father Paissi, the taciturn and learned hieromonach, said in a firm but nervous voice.

"But that's sheer Ultramontanism!"* cried Miusov, crossing and recrossing his legs impatiently.

"Well, we have no mountains here!" Father Iosif exclaimed; then, addressing the *starets*, he went on: "He is replying, incidentally, to the following 'fundamental and essential propositions' advanced by his opponent, who, you will note, is an ecclesiastic. First: 'no social association can or should appropriate the authority to exercise control over its members' civil and political rights'; second: 'the Church should not possess criminal and civil jurisdiction, since that is incompatible with its nature both as a divinely ordained institution and as an association of people for religious ends'; third: 'the Church is a kingdom not of this world'—"

"For an ecclesiastic, that is a most unworthy play upon words," said Father Paissi again, unable to check himself. "I've read the book you've objected to," he went on, addressing Ivan Fyodorovich, "and been amazed by its author asserting that 'the Church is a kingdom not of this world'. If it is not of this world, then it can't exist on earth at all. Holy Writ does not use the words 'not of this world' in that sense. Such words are not to be trifled with. It was to set up the Church on earth that our Lord Jesus Christ descended here. Of course, the Kingdom of Heaven is not of this world but in Heaven, but it is entered only through the Church, which has been founded and established on earth. That is why laymen's puns in such a context are unworthy and improper. The Church is verily a kingdom and ordained to rule; it will ultimately and undoubtedly become a

---

*Ultramontane: literally, one living beyond the mountains, specifically north or south of the Alps; here, a member of the Ultramontane party in the Roman Catholic Church.—*Tr.*

kingdom on earth—that has been promised—"

He suddenly fell silent, as though curbing himself. After listening to him with respectful attention, Ivan Fyodorovich now addressed the *starets* with the utmost composure, and with all his previous frankness and goodwill.

"The crux of my article," he said, "consists in Christianity having existed on earth in olden times—during the first three centuries of Christianity—only in the Church and only as the Church. But when the pagan Roman State wished to become Christian, it inevitably came about that, when it did so, it merely absorbed the Church, while still remaining a pagan State in very many of its practices. In essence, that was bound to happen. But, as a State, Rome retained too much of its pagan civilisation and wisdom, as, for instance, the very aims and fundamentals of the State. As for the Church of Christ, it doubtlessly could not, when it entered the State, surrender any of its fundamentals, the rock it stood on; it could pursue only its own aims as ordained and revealed by the Lord, and among them that of converting the whole world—and consequently the entire ancient pagan State—into a Church. Thus (that is to say, in respect of the future), it is not the Church that should seek for itself a definite place in the world like 'any social association' or like 'an association of people for religious ends' (as the author I am objecting to has put it) but, on the contrary, any earthly State should eventually turn completely into a Church and become nothing else but a Church rejecting all aims that are not in harmony with those of the Church. All this will in no way detract from its honour or glory as a great State, or from the glory of its rulers; it will only divert it from the false and still pagan road, and place it on the right and true road, which alone leads to eternal aims. That is why the author of *The Fundamentals of Ecclesiastical Courts* would have formed a correct judgement if, in seeking out and proposing those fundamentals, he would have looked upon them as nothing more than a temporary compromise still necessary in our sinful and imperfect times. But as soon as the author makes so bold as to announce that the fundamentals he has brought forward, and part of which has just been enumerated by Father

Iosif, are unshakable, elemental and eternal, then he is running full tilt against the Church and its holy, eternal and unshakable vocation. That is what my article boils down to, its full summary."

"Which, in brief," Father Paissi continued, with emphasis on every word, "says that, according to certain theories only too manifest in our nineteenth century, the Church should be regenerated into a State, thus ascending from a lower form to a higher one, so as to disappear in it, yielding place to science, the spirit of the times, and civilisation. If it is unwilling to do so and offers resistance, it will be allotted a kind of nook in the State, and that under surveillance—that is the case everywhere in our time and in all the European lands of today. But the Russian understanding and hope call, not for the Church to be regenerated into the State, thereby ascending from a lower type to a superior one but, on the contrary, for the State to end up by being deemed worthy to become exclusively a Church, and nothing more. That will surely come to pass!"

"Well," said Miusov with a grin, and again crossing his legs, "I must admit you've given me some comfort. As far as I can make out, all this is, consequently, the achievement of an ideal that is infinitely remote, at the second coming of Christ. That may be so: a beautiful utopian dream of the disappearance of wars, diplomatists, banks and the like—something even smacking of socialism. Yet I thought all this was being said in earnest, and that the Church would, for instance, *immediately* set about trying cases of crime and sentencing criminals to flogging, penal servitude, and even death."

"But even if ecclesiastical courts were the only ones to exist," said Ivan Fyodorovich imperturbably, without batting an eyelid, "the Church would even now refrain from condemning people to penal servitude or death. In that case, crime and the way it's looked upon would be bound to change, of course by degrees, not suddenly or at once but fairly rapidly."

"Are you speaking in earnest?" asked Miusov, eyeing him closely.

"If the Church embraced everything," Ivan Fyodorovich continued, "it would cast out all disobedient and criminal elements, and would not engage in cutting off heads. But in that case, I ask you, where would the outcast go? He would have to cut himself off, not only from people, as at present, but from Christ as well: his crime would make him rise up, not only against men but also against the Church of Christ. That is how, strictly speaking, the matter stands at present, though that has not been announced, and the criminal's conscience very, very often enters into compromise with itself: 'I have stolen, but I've not gone against the Church, and I'm no enemy of Christ'—that is what the criminal of today very often asserts. But when the Church takes the place of the State, it will be hard for him to say—unless he denies the Church all over the earth: 'All men are in error; all have strayed; the entire Church is false. I alone—murderer and thief that I am—comprise the true Christian church.' That is something very hard to say to oneself; it calls for vast conditions, circumstances that do not often exist. And now, on the other hand, take the way the Church itself views crime: should that not change as against its present and almost pagan view, which, from the mechanical amputation of the infected limb as practised today for the protection of society, should develop—this time fully and honestly—into the idea of man's moral regeneration, his resurrection and salvation—"

"But what does that mean?" Miusov broke in. "I again fail to understand you: that is another kind of dream, something without shape and beyond comprehension. What kind of exclusion, what kind of excommunication, do you mean? I suspect you're simply making fun of us, Ivan Fyodorovich."

"But that is how the matter actually stands at present," the *starets* suddenly said, and all present at once turned to him. "Were there no Church of Christ today, there would be no curb on the criminal's evil deeds, and ensuing punishment, that is to say, genuine punishment, not the mechanical kind which has just been mentioned, and, in most cases, merely hardens the heart; I am referring to genuine punishment, the only efficacious kind, the only punishment that deters and brings peace of mind, and consists in an awareness of one's own conscience."

84

"How can that be, may I ask?" asked Miusov with the keenest curiosity.

"It's like this," the *starets* began. "All this hard labour and the former floggings have corrected nobody; what is more important, they hardly intimidate the criminal, and, far from decreasing, the number of crimes is continually on the rise. That's something you cannot but agree with. What follows is that society is not protected at all, since though an offending member is mechanically amputated and exiled to some remote and out-of-the-way place, his place is immediately taken by another criminal, perhaps by a couple. If anything does protect society even today, and even reforms the criminal himself, turning him into another man, then that is again nothing but the law of Christ working through his conscience. It is only by an awareness of his guilt as a son of Christian society, that is to say, of the Church, that he also recognises his guilt in respect of society itself, that is, the Church. Thus, it is only towards the Church, and not towards society, that the criminal is capable of being aware of his guilt. Thus, if jurisdiction were exercised by society as a Church, then that society would know whom to return from excommunication, and restore to fellowship with it. As things stand at present, the Church, which has no actual powers of jurisdiction, but can only express moral condemnation, has of its own accord eschewed all active punishment of the criminal. It does not excommunicate him, but merely does not deny him its paternal admonition. Moreover, it even endeavours to maintain Christian communion with the criminal: it allows him to attend Church services, partake of the Eucharist, and receive its aid; it treats him more as a captive than as a culprit. Good Lord! What would become of the criminal if even Christian society, that is to say, the Church, were to reject him in the way the civil law has rejected him and cut him off? What would be if the Church punished him with excommunication immediately and each time after his punishment by the civil law. Why, no despair could be more bitter, at least to the Russian criminal, because Russian criminals have kept their faith. Perhaps—who can tell?—a terrible thing might happen then: the criminal's despairing heart might lose its faith, and then what?

But the Church, like a loving and tender mother, stands aloof from all active punishment, because a man found guilty and punished by a State court has been chastised enough, and there must be somebody to take pity on him. The main reason for that holding aloof is that its judgement is the only one that contains the truth and for that reason cannot participate either in substance or morally in any other passing of judgement, even as a temporary compromise. No deal can be entered into on that score. The criminal in other lands is seldom repentant, they say, because even the most up-to-date doctrines bolster his conviction that a crime is no crime but only an act of rebellion against an unjust and oppressive force. He has been cut off from society by a force that triumphs over him, in an absolutely mechanical way; that exclusion is accompanied by a manifestation of hatred (that, at least, has been acknowledged in Europe itself)— hatred, and complete indifference and oblivion in respect of his further fate as an erring brother. Thus, all this takes place without the least compassion on the part of the Church, since, in many cases, there are no churches left at all there but only churchmen themselves and magnificent church edifices; the churches themselves have long been striving to rise from their inferior status as a Church to a superior status as a State, so as to disappear completely within it. That, at least seems to be the situation in the Lutheran countries. As for Rome, a State has been proclaimed in the place of the Church during the last thousand years; that is why the criminal himself is no longer conscious of membership of a Church and, having been cut off, sinks into despair. If he does return to society, it is often with such hatred that the latter itself rejects him, as it were. You can judge for yourselves what the outcome will be. In many cases, it would seem, things are the same with us, but the point is that, apart from the established courts of law, we have the Church too, which never loses touch with the criminal as with a dear and still prized son; besides, there is still preserved, if only in the mind, the judgement passed by the Church, which, though inactive, still lives for the future, at least as a dream; it is undoubtedly recognised at heart by the criminal himself. Also true is what has just been said here, namely, that were ecclesiastical courts really to be instituted in full force—in other words, if all society were to turn into a Church—then not only would the latter's judgement exert an influence in reforming the criminal in a way it can never do today, but the number of crimes would decrease dramatically. Nor can there be any doubt that, in many cases, the Church would understand the future criminal and the potential crime quite differently from what is the case today; it would be able to rewin the outcast, prevent his evil-doing and regenerate the backslider. True," the *starets* said with a smile, "Christian society is not ready yet, and rests only on the seven righteous men, but since their number never diminishes it will stand unshaken in anticipation of its complete transmutation from society as a community that is still almost pagan, into a single, oecumenical and sovereign Church. That shall surely come to pass if only at the end of time, for that alone has been preordained. And there is no need to be concerned with the times or the seasons, since the secret of the times and the seasons lies in the wisdom of God, in His foresight and love, and what may still seem very far off according to human reckoning may, at the Lord's preordination, be near, even at the doors. That latter shall surely come to pass."

"It surely shall!" Father Paissi echoed with severe reverence.

"That is strange, most strange!" said Miusov, not so much with vehemence as with a kind of repressed indignation.

"What is it that seems so strange to you?" Father Iosif inquired cautiously.

"But what's the meaning of all this?" exclaimed Miusov, evidently losing his self-control. "The State is to be eliminated on earth, with the Church being elevated to the degree of a State! That is more than Ultramontanism, it's super-Ultramontanism. It's more than could have entered the mind of Pope Gregory VII!"

"You understand it the wrong way round, sir," said Father Paissi with severity. "It is not the Church that is transmuted into a State. Please realise that, for it smacks of Rome and its ambition. It is the third temptation of the devil! On the contrary, it is the State that is transmuted into a Church, rises to that level and becomes a world-wide Church, something that is quite the reverse of Ultramontanism and Rome, as well as of your interpretation; it is the glorious destiny of Orthodoxy on earth. That star will shine from the East."

Miusov's silence was eloquent, his entire figure expressive of extraordinary dignity, a supercilious and condescending smile playing on his lips. As for Alyosha, his heart throbbed as he looked on the scene, for the entire conversation had moved him most profoundly. He happened to glance in the direction of Rakitin, who was standing motionless at the same place by the door, listening and watching intently, though his eyes were lowered. From the high colour of his cheeks Alyosha could tell that Rakitin was no less agitated than he was. Alyosha knew the reason why.

"I'd like to tell you a short anecdote, gentlemen," Miusov suddenly said in an impressive tone and looking especially dignified. "When I was in Paris some years ago, soon after the December revolution, I had occasion to meet a highly interesting gentleman during a call at the home of a leading member of the government, an acquaintance of mine. The gentleman was not exactly an ordinary detective but something like the chief of a special detail of state security agents, quite an influential post in its way. I availed myself of the opportunity to enter into conversation with him with a view to gratifying my avid curiosity; since he was there, not socially but in his subordinate capacity (he had come to submit some kind of official report), and, seeing how I had been received by his superior, he spoke to me with a certain frankness—of course, up to a certain point— he was more courteous than outspoken, in the way the French know how to display courtesy, the more so for my being a foreigner. However, the drift of his argument was perfectly clear: he was referring to the socialist revolutionaries, who were being persecuted at the time. I shall omit the central theme of our talk, and limit myself to a most interesting remark dropped by this individual. 'We,' he said, 'are not particularly worried over all these socialists proper: the anarchists, the atheists and the revolutionaries; they are under surveillance and their moves are known to us. But among their number are a few that stand

out—those that believe in God and are Christians, and Socialists at the same time. These are the people we fear most for they
are formidable. The Christian Socialist is far more to be dread-
ed than his atheistic counterpart.' I was struck by his words
even then, and they have suddenly come to mind here, gentlemen—"

"Do you mean that they can be applied to us, and that you
see us as Socialists?" asked Father Paissi point-blank, but before
Pyotr Alexandrovich could think of a reply, the door opened,
and Dmitri Fyodorovich, the long-awaited visitor, entered. True,
he was already no longer expected, so that his sudden appearance even evoked momentary surprise.

6.

Why Should Such a Man Live?

Dmitri Fyodorovich, a young man of twenty-eight, of medium height and with an agreeable face, looked much older than
his years. He was of sturdy build and one could surmise that he
possessed considerable physical strength, yet there was something
unhealthy about his face, which was gaunt and hollow-cheeked,
its complexion sallow. His fairly large and protuberant dark
eyes seemed expressive of an unyielding obduracy, albeit with
some vagueness in them. Even when he was agitated and spoke
with irritation, his gaze seemed quite out of keeping with
his inner state, and expressing something unrelated to what was
happening. "It's hard to guess what he's thinking of," many
who spoke to him would sometimes say. Others, who discerned
something pensive and morose in his eyes, would be startled by
his sudden outbursts of laughter, which spoke of gay and play-
ful thoughts, just while he looked so sullen. Incidentally, his
somewhat sickly face now spoke for itself: his extremely roisterous and dissolute way of life of late was common knowledge,
as was the violent anger he displayed in his quarrels with his
father over certain disputed sums. A number of stories about
that were circulating in the town. True, he was short-tempered

by nature, his mind "abrupt and ill-balanced", as Semyon Iva-
novich Kachalnikov, our justice of the peace, so aptly described
him. He was impeccably and elegantly dressed, his frock-coat
all buttoned up, in black gloves, and carrying a top hat. As a
recently retired army officer, he wore a moustache but no beard
as yet. His dark-brown hair was cut short and somehow combed
forward on his temples. He had the long and firm stride of
the professional soldier. He stopped short on the threshold,
cast a rapid glance at the company, and walked straight up to
the *starets*, sensing that he was the host. He bowed low to him
and asked for his blessing; the *starets*, rising from his seat,
blessed him. Dmitri Fyodorovich kissed his hand respectfully,
and said with great agitation, almost in anger:

"I crave your forgiveness for having kept you waiting, but
Smerdyakov, our servant, who had been sent by Father, emphatically told me twice, in reply to my insistent question, that
the appointment was for one o'clock. I now suddenly learn—"

"Please don't worry," said the *starets*, interrupting him. "It
really doesn't matter—you're just a bit late, and it's of no consequence—"

"I'm most grateful to you: no less could be expected of your
goodness of heart." After rapping out these words, Dmitri Fyodorovich made another bow, then, turning abruptly towards his
father, he bowed to him just as low and respectfully. He had
obviously decided beforehand to do so, sincerely considering
it almost his duty to thereby express his respect and good
intentions. Though taken by surprise, Fyodor Pavlovich proved
equal to the occasion in his own fashion: in reply to his son's
gesture, he jumped up from his arm-chair and made just as
low a bow. His expression suddenly grew solemn and impressive, which, however, made him look positively malicious.
Then, after bowing silently to all the others, Dmitri Fyodorovich strode to the window, sat down on the only vacant chair,
close to Father Paissi, and, leaning forward, at once made ready
to listen to the conversation he had interrupted.

His appearance had not taken up more than a couple of minutes, so the conversation could not but be resumed, but Pyotr
Alexandrovich no longer thought it necessary to reply to Fath-

her Paissi's insistent and almost irascible question.

"Permit me to drop the subject," he said with a certain urbane indifference. "It's a bit too abstruse. I see Ivan Fyodorovich is smiling; it must be because he has something interesting to say for this occasion too. Just ask him."

"I've nothing particular to say," Ivan Fyodorovich replied at once, "except for a brief remark: European liberalism in general and even our Russian liberal dilettantism have often and for a long time past confused the ultimate outcome of Socialism with that of Christianity. This wild conclusion is a characteristic feature in them. It has emerged, incidentally, that Socialism and Christianity are confused not by the liberals and the dilettanti alone; in many cases, the same is done by the political police—in other countries, of course. Your Paris anecdote is highly characteristic, Pyotr Alexandrovich."

"I would again request that the subject be dropped in general," Pyotr Alexandrovich repeated. "Instead, I shall tell you another anecdote, a most interesting and characteristic one, about Ivan Fyodorovich himself. As recently as some five days ago, he solemnly stated, during an argument at a social gathering here consisting mostly of ladies, that there exists nothing at all in the world to make men love their fellow-creatures; that there is no natural law that man should love all mankind; that, if love has hitherto existed on earth, it has not been because of some natural law but solely because men have had a faith in their immortality. Ivan Fyodorovich added parenthetically that natural law consists of nothing more than that: were you to destroy mankind's faith in its immortality, that would immediately destroy in it, not only love but every vital force designed to continue life on earth. Moreover, nothing would be considered immoral: everything would be permissible, even anthropophagy. As though that were not enough, he ended with the assertion that, for any individual, for instance, of the kind we now are, who believes neither in God nor in his own immortality, the moral law of Nature should be immediately changed into the full opposite of the previous law, that of religion, and that self-centredness, even to the extent of crime, should not only be permitted to man but should even be considered the most essential, reasonable and almost the most honourable outcome in his condition. From that paradox, gentlemen, you can infer all the other views our amiable eccentric and paradoxer, Ivan Fyodorovich, has deigned to air and perhaps intends to express in the future."

"Just a moment!" Dmitri Fyodorovich exclaimed suddenly. "I want to make sure that I've heard correctly. Did you say, 'crime should not only be permitted to man but should even be considered the most essential, reasonable and almost the most honourable outcome from the condition of any atheist?' Did you, or didn't you?"

"Those were the words," said Father Paissi.

"I'll remember that."

After these words he fell silent just as suddenly as he had burst into the conversation. All looked at him with curiosity.

"Is that really your conviction as to the consequences of people losing their faith in the immortality of their souls?" the *starets* asked Ivan Fyodorovich suddenly.

"Yes, that was my contention. Without immortality there can be no virtue."

"You are a happy man if that is what you believe, or else you are most unhappy!"

"Why unhappy?" Ivan Fyodorovich asked, smiling.

"Because in all probability you yourself believe neither in your soul's immortality nor even in what you've written about the Church and the church question."

"You may be right—yet I wasn't quite joking—" Ivan Fyodorovich suddenly and strangely admitted, with a rapid flush.

"That you weren't quite joking is true enough. That's an idea as yet unresolved in your heart, and tormenting it. But even one who is undergoing torment sometimes finds diversion in his despair, out of sheer despair, it would seem. It is out of despair that you too find diversion in journalistic articles and social small talk, without yourself believing in your dialectic, and make mock of that dialectic to yourself, albeit with an ache in your heart— That question has not been solved within yourself: therein lies your great sorrow, for it is crying out for a solution—"

"But can it be solved within me, and solved in a positive sense?" Ivan Fyodorovich continued with his strange questioning, regarding the *starets* with the same inexplicable smile.

"If it cannot be solved in a positive sense, it will never be solved in the negative either. You are yourself well aware of that property of your heart, and all your torment lies in that. But you may thank your Creator for having given you a superior heart capable of that torment, 'seeking those things which are above and setting your affections on things above, for our conversation is in Heaven'. God grant that your heart's solution will reach you whilst your are still on earth, and may God bless your path!"

Raising his hand, the *starets* was about to make the sign of the cross over Ivan Fyodorovich from where he was seated, but Ivan Fyodorovich suddenly rose from his chair, went up to him to receive his blessing, and, after kissing his hand, went back in silence to his seat. His mien was firm and earnest. This act, as indeed the entire conversation with the *starets*, so unexpected of Ivan Fyodorovich, somehow so amazed them all with its air of strangeness and even solemnity that they all fell silent for a time. Alyosha's face was expressive almost of fright. Miusov suddenly hunched his shoulders, but at that same moment Fyodor Pavlovich jumped up from his chair.

"Most divine and holy *starets*," he exclaimed, pointing a finger at Ivan Fyodorovich. "This is my son, flesh of my flesh, the most beloved of my flesh! This is my most deferential, so to say Karl Moor, while that son, Dmitri Fyodorovich, who has just entered and against whom I am seeking justice from you, is the most undutiful Franz Moor, both of them out of Schiller's *Robbers*. In that case, I'm the *Regierender Graf von Moor**. Pass judgement and save us! We need not only your prayers but also your prophecies."

"Speak without tomfoolery, and don't begin by insulting members of your family," the *starets* replied in a faint and exhausted voice. He was obviously growing more and more tired, and his strength was perceptibly running out.

*The reigning Count von Moor (German).—*Tr.*

"This is the disgraceful farce which I anticipated when I was coming here!" cried Dmitri Fyodorovich indignantly, and he too jumped up from his seat. "Forgive me, reverend Father," he went on, addressing the *starets*. "I'm a man of little education and don't even know what to call you, but you've been deceived and been too kind in allowing us to gather here. My father wanted a scene, he alone knows for what reason. He always has some motive. But now I think I do know the reason."

"They all put the blame on me, all of them!" Fyodor Pavlovich cried in his turn. "Here's Pyotr Alexandrovich chipping in too. You *are* doing that, Pyotr Alexandrovich, you are," he went on, turning to Miusov, though the latter had no intention of interrupting him. "I'm accused of appropriating my children's money and making a handsome profit on it! But tell me: aren't there courts of law? They'll make the proper reckoning, Dmitri Fyodorovich, from your receipts, letters and agreements, and let you know how much you possessed, how much you have squandered, and how much is left to you! Why does Pyotr Alexandrovich refuse to pronounce his judgement? After all, Dmitri Fyodorovich is no stranger to him. It's because you're all against me, while Dmitri Fyodorovich in fact owes me money—not some paltry sum, but several thousand roubles. I've got all the documents to bear that out! His riotous living is the talk of the town! And at the place he used to serve, he had to pay out now a thousand, now two for having seduced respectable girls. It's all known to us, Dmitri Fyodorovich, in the most intimate details, and I can prove it all— Would you believe it, most holy Father: he has won the heart of a most honourable young lady, of a good family and with a substantial fortune, the daughter of his former officer, a colonel who has served his country well and been decorated with the Order of St. Anne with crossed swords. He compromised her reputation by a promise of marriage. She is here now, an orphan and engaged to him, and yet, before her very eyes, he's dallying with a local charmer. And though this temptress has lived, so to speak, in a common-law marriage with a most worthy gentleman, she is of an independent nature and like an impregnable fortress to all men, just as if she were a lawful wife, for she's a woman of virtue—yes, holy fathers, of virtue. And Dmitri Fyodorovich would unlock that fortress with a key of gold, which is why he's trying to victimise me and pluck me of my money. Meanwhile, he has wasted thousands on this charmer, and keeps on borrowing money for the purpose—and do you know who from? Shall I tell them, Mitya?"

"Hold your tongue!" cried Dmitri. "Wait till I'm gone, and don't dare to besmirch in my presence the good name of a most honourable young lady. Your effrontery in mentioning her name would disgrace her— I won't allow it!"

He was choking with anger.

"Mitya! Mitya!" cried Fyodor Pavlovich hysterically, squeezing out some tears from his eyes. "Does a father's blessing mean nothing to you? What if I call a curse down on you? What then?"

"You brazen dissembler!" bellowed the furious Dmitri.

"He says that of his father, his own father! How will he speak of others? Gentlemen, just imagine: there's a poor but respectable man living here, a retired army captain burdened with a large family, who ran into some trouble and was discharged from the service, but without any scandal or court-martial, and with an unblemished character. Our Dmitri Fyodorovich grabbed him by the beard in a tavern some three weeks ago, dragged him into the street by that very beard, and gave him a public thrashing, and all because the poor man is a confidential agent in some little business of mine."

"It's all untrue! True on the surface, but false at bottom!" cried Dmitri Fyodorovich, trembling with anger. "Father! I don't justify what I did. Yes, I admit that in public: I behaved like a brute to the captain. I regret it now and I feel disgusted with myself for my savage rage. But this captain, this agent of yours, actually called on the lady you've called a charmer and suggested to her, on your behalf, that she should take my promissory notes that are in your possession and sue me for the money, so as to get me into a debtor's prison should I keep pestering you with property claims. And now you're blaming me for being attracted to a lady you yourself induced to ensnare me! She told me the whole story herself, while making mock of you! You would put me behind bars only because you were jealous of me and had begun to importune her with your love. I know all about that, too. She made mock of you—d'you hear?—made mock of you as she told me everything. So here, holy fathers, you have before you this man, this father, who rebukes his profligate son. You, gentlemen, who have witnessed this scene: forgive my anger, but I knew in advance that this treacherous old man would bring all of you together here to create a squabble. Yet I came with forgiveness in my heart, prepared to forgive and ask forgiveness if he stretched out his hand. But as he has, this very minute, insulted not only me but a most honourable young lady whose name I dare not mention in vain out of a sense of reverence for her, I've decided to publicly expose all his scheming, even if he is my father!"

He was unable to continue speaking. His eyes were glittering and his breathing laboured. The company in the cell were deeply disturbed too and, with the exception of the *starets*, had started up from their seats. The hieromonachs looked severe, but awaited guidance from the *starets*, who remained seated, looking very pale, but not from agitation but because he felt too ill and weak. A smile of entreaty played on his lips, and he raised his hand at times as if to stop the two raving men. Of course, a single gesture from him would have sufficed to put an end to the scene, but he seemed to be expecting something and watching them intently, as if wishing to understand something still unclear to him. Pyotr Alexandrovich Miusov finally felt quite humiliated and disgraced.

"We are all to blame for this ugly scene," he said heatedly, "but I could not have anticipated it all when I set out for this place, although I did know who I was dealing with... We must put an end to it at once. Believe me, your reverence, I had no exact knowledge of the details of what has transpired here and was unwilling to give them credence; they've come to my knowledge for the first time— A father is jealous of his son over a woman of loose morals, and himself intrigues with that creature to get his son put behind bars— It is in such company that I've been forced to come here. I've been deceived; I declare to you all that I've been as much deceived as the rest—"

"Dmitri Fyodorovich!" Fyodor Pavlovich suddenly yelled in a voice that did not sound like his own. "If only you weren't my son, I'd challenge you this instant to a duel—with pistols, at three paces ... through a handkerchief—a handkerchief," he concluded, stamping with both feet.

There are moments in the lives of inveterate liars who have play-acted all their lives, when they enter so thoroughly into their assumed roles that they actually tremble and shed tears of emotion, though at that very moment (or only a second later) they could whisper to themselves: "You know you're lying, you man without shame, for you're acting a part even now, despite all your 'sacred' ire and the 'sacred' moment of that wrath."

Dmitri Fyodorovich frowned bleakly and regarded his father with withering contempt.

"I thought—I thought," he said in a low and restrained voice, "that I'd return to my native parts with the angel of my soul, my future wife, so as to cherish him in his old age, and what do I see? Nothing but a depraved debauchee, a vile buffoon!"

"A duel!" the old wretch yelled out again, gasping for breath and sputtering with each word he uttered. "And you, Pyotr Alexandrovich, should know, sir, that there has perhaps never been in all your family a woman more high-minded and of greater integrity—d'you hear me, sir?—of greater integrity than she you've had the effrontery to call a 'creature'. As for you, Dmitri Fyodorovich, you've given up your fiancée for that 'creature', so you've decided for yourself that your fiancée is not fit to hold a candle to her. That's the kind of 'creature' she is!"

"For shame!" exclaimed Father Iosif.

"It's a shame and a disgrace!" Kalganov, who had hitherto been silent, suddenly cried in his boyish voice which was trembling with agitation. He had flushed crimson.

"Why should such a man live?" Dmitri Fyodorovich growled in hollow tones, almost beside himself with rage and raising his shoulders so high that he looked almost hunch-backed. "No, tell me if he can be allowed to go on defiling the earth?" he went on, eyeing each of them in turn and pointing at the old man. He spoke in a slow and measured tone.

"D'you hear, d'you hear this patricide, you monks?" cried Fyodor Pavlovich, addressing Father Iosif. "That's how he's replied to your 'for shame'. What is shameful here? That 'creature', that 'woman of loose morals', may well be holier than you are, you hieromonachs who seek salvation! She may have fallen in her youth, a victim of her environment, but she 'loved much', and Christ himself forgave a woman who had 'loved much'–"

"It was not that kind of love that Christ forgave," the gentle Father Iosif put in impatiently.

"Yes, it was for that kind, monks, for that very kind! You are saving your souls on a diet of cabbage, and consider yourselves righteous! You feed on gudgeons, one a day, and think you can bribe God with gudgeons!"

"This is intolerable, intolerable!" was to be heard from all sides of the cell.

The scandalous scene was cut short most unexpectedly. The *starets* suddenly rose to his feet. Alyosha, almost beside himself with anxiety for him and the rest, hastened to support him by an arm. The *starets* took a step towards Dmitri Fyodorovich and, on reaching him, sank on his knees before him. At first, Alyosha thought that it was caused by weakness, but he was mistaken. On his knees, the *starets* bowed low to Dmitri Fyodorovich, even touching the floor with his forehead–a full, distinct and deliberate move. So astonished was Alyosha that he even failed to support the *starets* when he rose to his feet, a faint smile on his lips.

"Forgive me! Forgive me, all of you!" he said, bowing in farewell to all his visitors.

Dmitri Fyodorovich stood dumbfounded for a few moments. What did it mean–that bowing down to the ground? "Good God!" he cried out suddenly, covering his face with hands, and then rushed out of the room. He was followed in a crowd by the visitors, who, in their confusion did not even say good-bye or bow to their host. Only the hieromonachs went up to the *starets* for his blessing.

"What did he mean by kneeling at his feet? Was it symbolical of something?" asked Fyodor Pavlovich, in an attempt to resume the conversation. He had suddenly grown very quiet for some reason, and did not make so bold as to address his words to anyone in particular. They were all leaving the hermitage at the moment.

"I'm not responsible for a madhouse or for madmen," Miusov at once replied angrily, "but I shall get rid of your society and, believe me, for good. Where's that monk?"

"That monk"—the one who had invited them to dinner with the Father Superior—did not keep them waiting, but met them as soon as they had descended the steps from the cell, as though he had been waiting for them the whole time.

"Will you do me the favour, Father, of conveying my profound respects to the Father Superior and apologising personally for me, Miusov, to his Reverence. Please tell him that unforeseen circumstances have arisen that prevent me from having the honour of being present at his table, greatly as I would like to," Pyotr Alexandrovich said irritably to the monk.

"I am that unforeseen circumstance, of course!" Fyodor Pavlovich at once put in. "You see, Father, Pyotr Alexandrovich does not wish to remain in my company, or else he'd go there at once. And go you will, Pyotr Alexandrovich; pray go to the Father Superior, and I hope you'll enjoy the meal! I'm doing the declining, not you. And now for home, home; I'll eat at home, for I don't feel equal to eating here, Pyotr Alexandrovich, my most amiable relative."

"I'm no relative of yours, and never have been, you contemptible fellow."

"I said that on purpose just to stir your bile because you disclaim any relationship, though we are related as I can prove from the church calendar. I'll send the carriage for you later, Ivan Fyodorovich. You may stay on if you like, Pyotr Alexandrovich; even propriety demands that you should go to the Father Superior. An apology is due for the commotion we created—"

"But are you really leaving? You're not lying, are you?"

"Pyotr Alexandrovich, how could I dare to do that after what's happened? Forgive me, gentlemen, I was simply carried away, yes, carried away! Besides, I feel shocked, and ashamed into the bargain. Gentlemen, one man may have the heart of an Alexander of Macedon, and another that of Fido, the lap-dog. Mine is like Fido's. I feel quite abashed. Really, how can I go to dinner after such an escapade, and gobble down the monastery gravy? Forgive me, but I can't do that!"

"The deuce only knows whether he's deceiving us!" Miusov thought, coming to a halt in hesitation as he watched the retreating buffoon with a look of perplexity. The latter turned round and, on noticing that Miusov was watching him, blew him a kiss.

"Are you, too, coming to the Father Superior's?" Miusov asked Ivan Fyodorovich abruptly.

"Why not? Besides, I was especially invited by him yesterday."

"Unfortunately, I do feel almost obliged to attend this confounded dinner," Miusov continued in the same tone of bitter irritation, totally disregarding the fact that the little monk was listening. "We should at least apologise for the commotion we've raised, and explain it was none of our doing— What do you think?"

"Yes, we should explain it wasn't our doing. Besides, Father won't be there," Ivan Fyodorovich remarked.

"I should hope not! Oh, confound the dinner!"

Yet they all walked on, the monk listening in silence. Only once, as they were passing through the wood, did he remark that the Father Superior had been kept waiting and that they were over half an hour late. There was no reply. Miusov looked at Ivan Fyodorovich in hatred.

"Here he is, going to the dinner as if nothing had happened!" he thought. "A brazen face and the conscience of a Karamazov."

7.

A Seminarist Bent on Getting On in the World

Alyosha helped the *starets* to his bedroom and made him sit down on the bed. It was a tiny room with the barest necessities: a narrow iron bedstead with a strip of felt for a mattress.

In a corner, below the icons, was a lectern with a crucifix and a Gospel lying on it. The *starets* sank in exhaustion on the bed, his eyes glittering and his breathing laboured. After sitting down he looked intently at Alyosha as though he was turning something over in his mind.

"You'd better go, my dear boy. Porfiri will attend to me. Hurry, you're needed there. Go to the Father Superior and wait at table."

"Pray, let me stay on here," Alyosha entreated.

"They need you more over there. There's no peace there. You'll wait and be useful. Say a prayer if evil spirits arise. And remember, son, (the *starets* liked to call him thus) that this is not the place for you in the future. Remember, that, young man. Leave the monastery as soon as the Lord calls me to himself. Leave it for good."

Alyosha gave a start.

"What's the matter? I tell you this is not the place for you for the time being. I give you my blessing for the great service you will perform in the world. There is a long road ahead of you. And you must take a wife, too. You will have to put up with much before you retrace your steps. There will be much for you to do. But I have no doubts about you, which is why I'm sending you forth. Christ is with you. Preserve Him in your heart, and He will preserve you. You will see much sorrow and find happiness in that sorrow. This is my behest to you: seek happiness in sorrow. Work, and keep on working. Remember my words from now on, for though I shall speak to you again, my hours, not only my days, are numbered."

Alyosha's face betrayed his emotion, the corners of his mouth quivering.

"What's wrong with you again?" the *starets* said with a gentle smile. "Let lay people shed tears as they part with their dead; here we rejoice for the departing father. We rejoice, and pray for him. And now leave me. I must say my prayers. Go in haste. Be near your brother, the two of them, not only one."

The *starets* raised a hand in blessing. It was no use protesting, though Alyosha longed to stay on. He was also eager to ask the *starets*—indeed, the question was on the tip of his tongue: "What was the significance of the profound bow to brother Dmitri?", but he dared not. He knew the *starets* would have told him unasked, had he thought it fit. Consequently, he did not wish to do so. But the bow had amazed Alyosha terribly: he blindly believed it contained some hidden significance—hidden and perhaps awesome. As he left the hermitage to reach the monastery in time for the dinner (only to wait at table, of course), his heart suddenly contracted painfully and he came to a halt: he again seemed to hear the words spoken by the *starets*, foretelling the rapid approach of his death. What he had foretold with such certitude would surely come to pass. That was something Alyosha believed implicitly. But how could he remain without him, no longer see him or hear his voice? Whither should he go? Good Lord!! He had told Alyosha to shed no tears and to leave the monastery. Alyosha had never felt such anguish before. He hastened through the wood between the hermitage and the monastery and, unable to cope with his heavy thoughts, he began to look at the ancient pines bordering the pathway. He did not have far to go—some five hundred paces, no more. He did not expect to walk into anyone at that hour, yet at the first bend in the path he suddenly noticed Rakitin, who was waiting for somebody.

"Is it me you're waiting for?" asked Alyosha as he drew level with him.

"Yes, it is," said Rakitin with a grin. "I see you're hurrying to get to the Father Superior. I know he's giving a dinner. There hasn't been such dinner since he entertained the Bishop and General Pakhatov, d'you remember? I shan't be there but you go along and serve the gravy and dressings. Just tell me one thing, Alexei: what did that vision mean? That's what I'm asking you."

"What vision d'you mean?"

"That bowing down to the ground to your brother Dmitri Fyodorovich. He actually knocked his forehead on the floor."

"You mean Father Zossima?"

"Yes, Father Zossima."

"His forehead?"

"I see I've expressed myself disrespectfully. Well, that

may be so! Anyway, what did the vision mean?"

"I don't know what it means, Misha."

"I felt sure he wouldn't tell you the reason why. Of course, there's nothing out of the ordinary about it—just the run-of-the-mill and usual benign nonsense. But there was a purpose behind the trick: all those sanctimonious people will start talking about it and spread the story all over the gubernia, asking each other what it all means. To my thinking, the old man has a keen nose indeed: he sniffed out a crime. Your place reeks of it."

"What do you mean by crime?"

Rakitin was evidently eager to tell him something.

"It will take place in your family—this crime. Between your brothers and your wealthy daddy. So Father Zossima knocked his forehead against the floor in case something comes about in the future. If that does happen, people will say, 'That's just what the holy *starets* foretold and prophesied', though I can't for the life of me see any prophesying in a man banging his forehead against the floor. No, there was something symbolical about it, allegorical, and the devil knows what else! The report will pass from mouth to mouth and be remembered: he predicted a crime and indicated the criminal. It's always like that with fools for Christ's sake: they cross themselves at the sight of a tavern and throw stones at a church. Your *starets* is the same: he drives a just man away with a stick, and bows down at a murderer's feet."

"What crime? What murderer? What do you mean?" Alyosha stopped in his tracks; Rakitin halted, too.

"What murderer, you ask? As though you don't know. I'm willing to wager that you've thought of it yourself. Now here's something curious. Look here, Alyosha, you always speak the truth, though you're always sitting between two stools. Tell me: has it ever occurred to you, or hasn't it?"

"It has," Alyosha replied in a low voice. Even Rakitin was taken aback.

"Has it? Has it really occurred to you, too?" he cried.

"I—I haven't exactly given it thought," he muttered, "but as soon as you began to speak of it just now in such a strange way, I had a feeling that I'd thought of it myself."

"You see (and how clearly you've expressed it), you see? The idea of a crime occurred to you as you were looking at your daddy and your dear brother Mitya, didn't it? So I'm not mistaken, eh?"

"Hold on, hold on for a moment," Alyosha interrupted him in alarm. "What has made you think so? Why does it interest you so much? That's the prime question."

"These are two separate questions, but quite natural ones. I'll reply to them in turn. Why have I seen it? I wouldn't have noticed anything if I hadn't suddenly seen through your brother Dmitri Fyodorovich today, seen him through and through at one go. I realised his entire nature from a single feature of his. With these most honest but voluptuous people there is a line they must never be driven across. If he is, he'll make a dash at your daddy with a knife. But your daddy is a bibulous and intemperate loose-liver, who never knows where to draw the line—so they'll be unable to keep themselves in check and they both end up in the ditch—"

"No, Misha, if it's only that, you've reassured me. It won't come to that."

"Then why are you trembling all over? D'you know what? Mitya may be an honest man (stupid but honest) but he's a lecher. That's his definition and all his inner make-up. His low sensuality comes from his father. I can't help marvelling, Alyosha, at your virgin-like purity. After all, you're a Karamazov, and sensuality runs in your family like a raging fever. So these three lechers are watching one another with knives held behind their backs. The three have locked horns, and you may well become the fourth."

"You're wrong about that woman. Dmitri—despises her," Alyosha said with a shudder.

"D'you mean Grushenka? No, my boy, he doesn't. How can he despise her if he's openly jilted his fiancée for her. That ... that's something beyond your ken as yet. When a man falls in love with a beauty, a woman's body, or even just one part of her body (that's something a sensualist will understand), he'll sacrifice his own children for her, betray his father and his mother, Russia and his fatherland; though he's honest, he will steal though he's gentle, he'll commit murder; though he's faithful, he'll stoop to deceit. Pushkin, that bard of lady's legs, sang their praise in verse. Others do not do that, but feel a thrill whenever they view such legs. But then, it's not merely their legs. Contempt will get him nowhere in this matter, even if he does despise Grushenka. He does, yet can't tear himself away from her."

"I realise that," Alyosha blurted out.

"Really? Well, I suppose you do if you blurt it out like that," said Rakitin spitefully. "It just escaped from you—you couldn't help it! Well, the admission is all the more valuable: so the subject is familiar to you, and you've given thought to it—I mean, lechery. You innocent one! You're a modest chap, Alyosha; I agree you're a saint, but you're secretive, and the devil alone knows what thoughts have come into your head, and what you know already! Though innocent, you've peered into such depths—I've been watching you for a long time. You're a Karamazov, a Karamazov through and through—so breed and natural selection do mean something: a lecher after your father, and a fool for Christ's sake after your mother. But why are you shivering? I'm telling the truth, am I not? Do you know what Grushenka asked me to do? She said, 'Bring him here (meaning you); I'll pull his cassock off him.' She was most insistent about it: she kept on asking me to bring you along. I couldn't help wondering why she should take such an interest in you. She's quite an extraordinary woman, too, you know!"

"Give her my regards but tell her I won't be coming," said Alyosha with a wry smile. "Complete what you have to say, Mikhail, and then later I'll tell you what I think."

"There's nothing to add; it's all clear. It's the same old story, my dear chap. If there's a lecher within *you*, then what is there to say of your uterine brother Ivan? He's a Karamazov, too. Therein lies the entire Karamazov question: you're lechers, money-grubbers and fools for Christ's sake! Your brother Ivan publishes theological articles for some unknown and ridiculous reason, though he's an atheist and has admitted that it's a despicable business—this brother Ivan of yours. Besides, he's out to win Mitya's fiancée for himself, and he seems to be getting his way. Very much so; he'll do that with Mitya's consent, because

Mitya himself is letting him get her just to be rid of her, and get to Grushenka as soon as possible. And mark this: he is doing all this despite his high-mindedness and selflessness. It's people like that who are most of all fated to create evil. I'll be damned if one can know what to make of you after all this: he admits that he's acting despicably, and continues doing so. And now listen further: the old man is getting in Mitya's way. The old man has suddenly gone crazy over Grushenka: he simply drools the moment he looks at her. It was because of her alone that he created such a scene in the cell—simply because Miusov dared to call her a loose creature. He's just like an amorous tomcat. At first, he employed her at a salary in some shady deals, but he's suddenly grown aware of her looks and quite lost his head; he keeps pestering her with all kinds of suggestions, none of them honourable, of course. Well, the precious father and son are bound to collide along that path. But Grushenka does not care for either of them; she's playing a waiting game, goading them on, and weighing which of the two will be to her profit, because while the father can be plucked of a lot of money, he'll never marry her and may very well end up by turning stingy and shutting his purse. That's where Mitya comes into the picture: he has no money but he can marry her. Yes, marry her! He'll give up his fiancée, that peerless beauty Katerina Ivanovna, a wealthy girl of the nobility and a colonel's daughter, and marry Grushenka, a woman once kept by an elderly tradesman named Samsonov, a dissolute lout and the local mayor. Something criminal may very well develop out of this collision. That's exactly what your brother Ivan is looking forward to, for then he'll be in clover: he'll get Katerina, a girl he's been pining for, and pocket a dowry of sixty thousand into the bargain. To a man of small consequence and with no money, that's a most attractive prospect to start with. Mind you, far from wronging Dmitri, he'll be conferring a tremendous favour on him. I know for certain that last week, when Mitya was on a drunken spree with some Gipsy wenches in a tavern, he yelled that he was unworthy of a fiancée like Katerina but that brother Ivan was the one that deserved her. In the end, Katerina Ivanovna will not, of course, turn down so fascinating a man as Ivan Fyodorovich; even now she's hesitating between them. I can't make out how this Ivan has won you all over and why you should all be so taken with him. He's making mock of you; he's in clover and enjoying life at your expense."

"How do you know all this? What makes you speak with such confidence?" the frowning Alyosha asked with sudden sharpness.

"And why are you asking me now, and are afraid of my answer in advance? It shows you agree that I'm speaking the truth."

"You dislike Ivan. Money won't tempt him."

"Won't it? And what about Katerina Ivanovna's looks? It isn't only the money, though sixty thousand is quite an attractive sum."

"Ivan's above that. He wouldn't be tempted by any amount of money. It's not money or security he's after. Perhaps it's suffering that he seeks."

"What new blether is this? How just like you members of the nobility!"

"Oh, Misha, his is a tempestuous soul! His mind is involved. He is in the grip of a mighty and unresolved thought. He's not one of those who seek millions, but is among those who seek solutions to their thoughts."

"That's a piece of literary theft, Alyosha. You're just rephrasing your *starets*. Well, Ivan *has* set you a riddle," cried Rakitin with undisguised malice. His expression had changed completely and his lips were wrinkled in a sneer. "The riddle itself is a stupid one, and there's nothing to unravel. Use your brains and you'll understand. His article is ridiculous and absurd. You must have heard his silly theory: 'If there's no immortality of the soul, there can be no virtue, which means that everything is permissible.' (You remember how brother Mitya exclaimed, 'I'll remember that!') It's a theory that will be attractive to scoundrels. How silly of me to be abusive—well, not to scoundrels but to schoolboy braggarts with the 'irresolvable profundity of their thought'. He's a small-time boaster, and it all boils down to: 'On the one hand, it must be admitted, but on the other, one cannot but recognise!' His entire theory is a piece of low chicanery. Mankind will find within

107

itself the strength to live for virtue even without a belief in the immortality of the soul; it will find it in a love of liberty, equality and fraternity—"

Rakitin had got so worked up that he could scarcely restrain himself. But suddenly he stopped, as though recalling something.

"Well, that will do," he said, his smile even wryer than before. "What are you laughing at? D'you think I'm being vulgar?"

"No, I never even thought of thinking that. You're clever—but never mind, it was silly of me to laugh. I can understand your getting all worked up over it, Misha. Your agitation told me that you are attracted to Katerina Ivanovna yourself; I suspected that long ago, and it's why you dislike my brother Ivan. Are you jealous of him?"

"I suppose you think I'm jealous of her money, too. Why don't you say so?"

"No, I'll say nothing about the money. Why should I offend you?"

"I believe it since you say so, but the devil take you together with your brother Ivan. You can't understand that he is quite dislikable, even apart from Katerina Ivanovna. What on earth should I like him for? After all, he does do me the honour of running me down. Why, then, shouldn't I be entitled to reply in kind?"

"I've never heard him say anything about you, good or bad. He doesn't speak about you at all."

"But I've learnt that he gave my person a thorough dressing down at Katerina Ivanovna's the day before yesterday—that's how much he's interested in yours truly. Well, after that I can't say who is jealous of whom, old man. He deigned to voice the idea that if I didn't take up an archimandrite's career in the not so distant future and didn't become a monk, I would most certainly move to St. Petersburg and join the staff of some leading journal in the department of literary criticism, of course, where I would contribute for a matter of ten years, ultimately acquiring the ownership of the periodical. Then I'd continue its publication, giving it a definite liberal and atheistic trend, with a Socialist hue, even with a slight gloss of Socialism, but keeping my ears pricked, in other words, running with the hare and hunting with the hounds and misleading the simpletons. Your brother holds that it is the aim of my career to avoid letting the tinge of Socialism prevent me from channelling my subscribers' money into my bank account and then investing it at the earnest opportunity, with advice from some Jew, until I'm able to build a big house in St. Petersburg, move my editorial office into it, and let out the other storeys to tenants. He's even picked the location: at the Novo-Kamenny Bridge which, they say, is being planned across the Neva, to link Liteiny Prospekt with the Vyborg suburb—"

"But Misha, that's exactly what will happen, down to the last word!" Alyosha suddenly exclaimed, unable to restrain a merry laugh.

"You're waxing sarcastic, Alexei Fyodorovich."

"Oh, no, I said that in jest. I'm sorry. There's something quite different on my mind. But who could have supplied you with all those details, and who could you have heard them from? You couldn't have been at Katerina Ivanovna's in person when he was speaking about you, could you?"

"I wasn't there, but Dmitri Fyodorovich was, and I heard it all from him with my own ears. As a matter of fact, you should know he did not actually say it to me, but I happened to overhear his words, of course, against my will, because I was sitting in Grushenka's bedroom at the time, and could not get out while he was in the next room."

"Oh, yes, I'd forgotten she's a relative of yours—"

"A relative? Grushenka—a relative of mine?" Rakitin exploded, turning crimson. "Have you gone mad? Is there something wrong with your brains?"

"Why, isn't she related to you? I've heard she is—"

"Where could you have heard it? Oh, you Karamazovs, who preen yourselves on your noble and ancient descent, yet your father used to play the buffoon at other people's tables and was allowed into their kitchens only in charity. Of course, I'm only a priest's son and a worm in the eyes of you noblemen, but you shouldn't insult me with such wanton light-heartedness. I, too, have a sense of honour, Alexei Fyodorovich. I can't be related to that whore of a Grushenka, please understand that!"

Rakitin was extremely exasperated.

"Do forgive me; I had no idea—and, besides, how can you call her a whore? Is she—that kind of woman?" asked Alyosha, flushing suddenly. "I repeat that I heard she was a relative of yours. You often call on her, and you've told me yourself you're no lover of hers—I never thought that you, of all people, held her in such contempt! Does she really deserve it?"

"If I do call on her, I have my own reasons. It's none of your business. As to being related to her, I daresay your brother or even your father is far more likely to make her your relative than mine. Well, here we are. You'd better make for the kitchen. Hullo, what's going on over there? Can we have come too late? Dinner couldn't possibly be over so soon! Or have the Karamazovs been at it again? They probably have. There's your father, with Ivan Fyodorovich following him. They've dashed out of the Father Superior's quarters. And there's Father Isidor shouting something to them from the steps. Your father's shouting too, and waving his arms—probably using bad language, I suppose. But there goes Miusov, driving off in his carriage. And there's that Maximov trotting along. There must have been quite a row, and no dinner! Surely they haven't given the Father Superior a drubbing! Or perhaps they've been given one! That would have served them right."

There were grounds for Rakitin's excitement. There had indeed been a scene, disgraceful and unexpected, a kind of spontaneous eruption.

8.

A Disgraceful Scene

As a man of sincere delicacy and good breeding, Miusov went through a kind of highly delicate process as he entered the Father Superior's room in the company of Ivan Fyodorovich; he felt ashamed of having yielded to anger. He felt that his disrespect for that despicable Fyodor Pavlovich should not

110

have made him lose his temper in Father Zossima's cell and lose his self-control as he had done. "At least, the monks were not at fault in anything," he suddenly decided, mounting the steps to his destination, "and if the people here are decent (Nikolai, the Father Superior, is himself of the nobility), why shouldn't I be courteous and affable to them? I won't enter into any argument, I'll even agree with whatever they say and win them over with honeyed words—and—after all, show them that I've nothing in common with that Aesop, that buffoon, that Pierrot, and was caught off my guard, just like all of them were—"

As for the disputed woodcutting and fishing rights (he had no exact idea where the places in question were located) he had decided to relinquish them that very day once and for all, the more so because they were not particularly valuable, and drop all court action against the monastery.

All these good intentions were fortified when they entered the Father Superior's dining-room. It was not actually a dining-room, because his quarters consisted only of two rooms. Though these were much larger and more comfortable than Father Zossima's rooms, the furnishings were not marked by any particular luxury: the furniture was of mahogany, upholstered in leather, and in the old-fashioned style of the eighteen-twenties; the floors were even unstained but everything was spick and span, and on the window-sills were many choice flowers. At the moment, however, the highlight of the scene was the sumptuously laid table, albeit in a relative sense: the table-cloth was spotlessly clean and the dinner service sparkling; there were three kinds of excellently baked bread, two bottles of wine, two of excellent monastery mead, and a big glass jug of monastery kvass famous in the neighbourhood. There was no vodka at all. Rakitin later described it as a five-course dinner, to wit, sterlet soup served with fish patties, then excellent fish boiled after a special recipe, followed by salmon croquettes, ice-cream and compote. Besides, there was a fruit jelly. Rakitin, who had a nose for such things, learnt all this in the kitchen, where he had connections. Indeed, his sources of information were universal. Restless and envious by nature, he was well aware of his considerable abilities, which he nervously exaggerated in his overweening opinion of himself. He knew for a certainty that he would become a public figure of some kind, but Alyosha, who was quite fond of him, was distressed to see that his friend Rakitin was dishonest, without being in the least sensible of being so. On the contrary, his awareness that he would not steal money left lying on a table led Rakitin to consider himself a man of the highest integrity. That was something that nobody, let alone Alyosha, could make him understand.

As somebody insignificant, Rakitin could not be invited to dinner, but Father Iosif and Father Paissi were, as was another hieromonach. They were already in the Father Superior's dining-room when Miusov, Kalganov and Ivan Karamazov arrived. The landowner Maximov was there too, standing somewhat aside. The Father Superior stepped forward into the middle of the room to welcome the visitors. He was a tall old man, thin but still hale, with black hair streaked with grey, and a long, glum and solemn face. In silence he bowed to his visitors, who this time all went up to him for his blessing. Miusov even went so far as to try to kiss his hand but the Father Superior somehow snatched it away in time, so that the kiss did not materialise. On the other hand, Ivan Fyodorovich and Kalganov went through the full ritual, that is to say, gave the Father Superior's hand the smacking kiss usual with simple-hearted peasants.

"We must offer you our whole-hearted apologies, most reverend Father," Pyotr Alexandrovich began, with a broad and courteous smile, but still in a dignified and respectful tone, "for arriving without Fyodor Pavlovich, who was invited by you and accompanied us here. He has been obliged to decline attending your dinner, and not without reason. Carried away by his unfortunate quarrel with his son, he let fall certain words in the reverend Father Zossima's cell, words that were utterly out of keeping—in fact, quite unseemly—as, I believe (he cast a glance at the hieromonach) your high reverence is already aware. Therefore, realising that he had been at fault, he felt sincere regret and shame, and, unable to overcome that sense of shame, he asked us—his son Ivan Fyodorovich and myself—to convey to you his deep-felt regret, contrition and repentance—in short, he hopes and desires to make amends for everything later, and now asks for your blessing and begs you to forget that has taken place—"

He fell silent. As he pronounced the final words of his tirade, he was so pleased with himself that no trace of his former irritation remained in his soul. He again felt a full and sincere love of mankind. The Father Superior, who had listened with dignity, said in reply, with a slight inclination of the head: "I sincerely regret his absence. Perhaps, at our table, he might come to love us, and we him. Pray be seated, gentlemen."

But he first turned to the icon and began to say grace. All those present bowed their heads reverently, Maximov even stepping forward, his palms pressed together with particular fervour.

It was at that very moment that Fyodor Pavlovich played his final prank. It should be noted that he had really meant to leave, realising how impossible it was for him to dine with the Father Superior as though nothing had happened, after his disgraceful behaviour in Father Zossima's cell. It was not that he felt so very much ashamed of himself, or blamed himself; quite the contrary, perhaps; still he felt it would be unseemly. Yet hardly had his creaking carriage driven up to the steps of the inn and he was getting into it when he suddenly stopped short: he recalled what he had himself said at Father Zossima's, "I feel, whenever I meet with people, that I am more despicable than anybody else and generally taken for a buffoon, so I say, very well then, I shall indeed play the buffoon, because you are all, down to the last man, more despicable than I am." He felt a wish to revenge himself on others for his own vile acts. He suddenly remembered once having been asked: "Why do you hate so-and-so with such bitterness?" He had answered, in an outburst of his brazen buffoonery, "I'll tell you why: true, he has done me no harm, but I once played a shameless trick on him, and scarcely had I done so when I at once felt that I hated him." The recollection made him give a quiet and malicious chuckle at a moment of thoughtfulness. His eyes flashed and his lips even began to quiver. "Once I've begun, I might as well carry it through," he decided suddenly. His innermost feeling at the moment might be expressed in the fol-

113

lowing words: "Since I can't now rehabilitate myself, I'll be as shamelessly caddish to them as I can. I don't give a damn for what you may think of me, so there!" He ordered the driver to wait, and rapidly retraced his steps to the monastery, where he made straight for the Father Superior's. He had no clear idea of what he would do, but knew that could no longer control himself, so that the least thing could impel him to the utmost limit of some abominable behaviour, but no farther; he would commit no crime or any act punishable by law. In the last resort, he was always able to curb himself and often felt surprised at his ability to do so. He appeared on the scene precisely at the instant grace ended and the company were preparing to seat themselves at the table. Stopping in the doorway, he scanned them with a glance and gave a long, impudent and malicious chuckle, looking them all boldly in the face.

"They all thought I'd left, but here I am again!" he cried in a loud voice.

For a moment, they all looked straight at him in silence with a sudden presentiment that something revolting, ridiculous and positively disgraceful was about to happen. Pyotr Alexandrovich's mood changed from one of even temper into savage fury. Everything that had subsided and died down in his heart now flared up again.

"No, I can't put up with this!" he cried. "I simply can't and—I certainly won't!"

The blood rushed to his head. His speech even became impeded but he was beyond thinking of such things, and grabbed his hat.

"What is it he can't put up with?" cried Fyodor Pavlovich. "'He simply and certainly can't?' Shall I come in or not, your reverence? Am I welcome at your table?"

"With all my heart," the Father Superior replied. "Gentlemen!" he suddenly went on, "may I request you most earnestly to set your chance differences aside, unite in love and harmony, with a prayer to the Lord at our humble meal—"

"No, no, it's impossible!" Miusov exclaimed, quite beside himself.

"Well, if Pyotr Alexandrovich finds it impossible, so do

I, and I shan't stay on. That's why I'm here. From now on, I shall stick by his side: if you leave, Pyotr Alexandrovich, I'll follow suit; if you stay on, so shall I. Your words on harmony among relatives have stung him to the quick, your reverence, for he refuses to recognise our kinship. That's so, isn't it, von Sohn? That's von Sohn standing over there. Hullo, von Sohn."

"D'you—mean me?" muttered the amazed Maximov.

"Of course, I do," cried Fyodor Pavlovich, "Whom else? I couldn't mean the Father Superior, could I?"

"But I can't be von Sohn; I'm Maximov."

"No, you're von Sohn! Do you know who von Sohn was, your reverence? He was the victim in a case of murder. He was done in at a bawdy-house—I think you'd call it a house of ill-fame. He was murdered and robbed and, despite his advanced years, he was shoved into a packing-case, nailed down and forwarded in a goods train, all nicely labelled, from St. Petersburg to Moscow. While he was being nailed down, the scarlet women were singing songs and playing the psaltery, I mean the piano. So this is the selfsame von Sohn, only risen from the dead, eh, von Sohn?"

"How disgraceful! What's happening?" voices were asking from the group of hieromonachs.

"Come on, let's go!" cried Pyotr Alexandrovich, addressing Kalganov.

"No, no, permit me!" shrilled Fyodor Pavlovich, interrupting him and taking another step into the room. "Permit me to complete matters. There, over at the cell, you vilified me for my gudgeons. Pyotr Alexandrovich Miusov, my relative, likes his words to contain *plus de noblesse que de sincérité;* for my part, I, on the contrary, like mine to have *plus de sincérité que de noblesse,* and I snap my fingers at *noblesse.* Right, von Sohn? Excuse me, your reverence, I may be a buffoon and act the buffoon, but I'm the soul of honour and wish to speak my mind. Indeed, I'm the soul of honour, while nothing but wounded vanity speaks in Pyotr Alexandrovich. I've come here today perhaps to have a look round and speak my mind. My son Alexei is seeking salvation for his soul here; I happen to be his father, and I am and have to be involved in his welfare. I've been listening and playing a part, but I've been watching things on the quiet, and I now want to give you the final act of the performance.   How do matters stand with us? Whatever falls to the ground remains there for all time. But I won't remain lying there for all time. I wish to rise to my feet. Holy fathers, you've aroused my indignation. Confession is a great sacrament, one that I revere and am prepared to prostrate myself to, but over there in the cell they all go down on their knees and confess aloud. Is confession in public permitted? The Fathers of the Church established that confession should be whispered in the priest's ear. Only then will confession become a sacrament, and it has been so since olden times. How can I confess in public that I've done this or that, for instance—you know, this or that—understand? It may be improper even to mention such things. It's a disgrace. No, Fathers, such things here may lead up to sectarianism. I shall write to the Synod at the first opportunity, and take my son Alexei home from here—"

It should be noted, at this point, that Fyodor Pavlovich had the knack of picking up whatever evil reports were in circulation. There had been malicious gossip, which had even reached the Bishop's ears, regarding not only our monastery but others as well where the *starets* institution was established, to the effect that the *startsi* were held in excessive esteem, even to the detriment to the Fathers Superior; that the *startsi*, incidentally, were making wrong use of the sacrament of confession, and so on and so forth. These were absurd charges which had died out of themselves, both in our town and elsewhere. But the foolish spirit of evil which had taken hold of Fyodor Pavlovich and his nerves and was hurling him ever deeper into the depths of vileness prompted him to bring up the old imputation, of which he had not the slightest understanding. He had been even unable to express it intelligently, the more so for nobody having been kneeling and confessing to the *starets* in his cell this time, so that he could not have witnessed anything of the kind and was merely repeating the old rumours and gossip, which he remembered but poorly. But, having given voice to his stupid charges, he at once realised that he had been speaking sheer

116

nonsense and felt an urge to prove to his listeners and above all to himself that what he had said was not in the least absurd. Though he was well aware that whatever he would say would only pile up the absurdity, he was incapable of curbing himself and plunged on.

"How abominable!" cried Pyotr Alexandrovich.

"Pardon me," said the Father Superior, "But as was said long ago: many here have begun to speak against me, even saying certain evil things. Hearing it all, I have said to myself: 'This is correction from Jesus,' and sent to heal my vain soul. We, therefore, humbly thank you, our honoured guest."

And he bowed low to Fyodor Pavlovich.

"Tut-tut! Nothing but sanctimony and threadbare phrases. The old phrases and the old gestures! The old lies and the official show of formal obeisances! We know their worth! 'A kiss on the lips and a dagger in the heart,' just as in Schiller's *Robbers*. I have no use for hypocrisy, Fathers; I want the truth! But the truth does not lie in the eating of gudgeons, and that is something I have proclaimed! Fathers and monks, wherefore do you observe the fasts? Why do you expect to be rewarded in Heaven for that? Why, I'm prepared to observe the fasts myself in this life; be useful to society without shutting yourself up in a monastery with all victuals found, and without expecting any reward up on high—that'll be much harder. I, too, can engage in smooth talk, Father Superior. Now let's see what they have served here," he went on, going up to the table. "Old port, claret bottled by the Yeliseyev Brothers, well, Fathers, you do yourselves proud! That's quite an improvement on gudgeon, isn't it? And what excellent wines the fathers have served to them, tee-hee, tee-hee! And where does it all come from? From the Russian muzhik who brings you in his calloused hands part of his miserable earnings which he has taken away from his family needs and his tax payments. Why, holy fathers, you are bloodsuckers of the people!"

"Your words are disgraceful," said Father Iosif, while Father Paissi did not utter a sound. Miusov rushed out of the room, followed by Kalganov.

"Well, Fathers, I'm off with Pyotr Alexandrovich! I'll never again set foot here, even if I'm asked to on bended knees. I sent you a thousand roubles, so there's a glint of expectancy in your eyes, tee-hee! No, there is no more money coming from me. I am taking revenge for my young years, for all the humiliation I had to endure!" he cried, banging on the table with a fist, with a pretence of strong feeling. "This monastery has meant a lot to me. It has made me shed many a bitter tear. It was you who set my crazy wife against me, invoking a curse on me with bell, book and candle, and you spread the story all over the neighbourhood. Enough, Fathers, this is an age of liberalism, an age of steamships and railways. Neither a thousand nor a hundred roubles, not even a hundred copecks will you get from me!"

Again, it should be noted that our monastery had never meant anything in particular to him and that he had never shed a bitter tear over it. But he was so carried away by his own eloquence that he almost believed in it himself for a moment. His emotion brought him even to the verge of tears, but at that moment he felt it was time to turn back. In reply to his malicious falsehood, the Father Superior bowed his head, and said impressively, "Again, it is written, 'Suffer with circumspection and with joy the dishonour that falleth upon thee, and be not confounded or feel hatred for him who hath dishonoured thee.' That is how we shall act."

"Tut-tut! Suffer with joy—and all that rigmarole! Pause and consider, Fathers; I'll be off. Invoking my parental authority, I'm taking my son Alexei away from here for good. Ivan Fyodorovich, my most dutiful son, permit me to order you to follow me! And why should *you* stay on, von Sohn? Come along to town with me. I can offer you a jolly time. It's only a short verst from here. Instead of lenten fare, I'll give you sucking-pig with stuffing. We'll have dinner, with brandy and liqueurs. Hi, von Sohn, don't you know what's good for you?"

He left, shouting and gesticulating. It was at that very moment that Rakitin caught sight of him, and drew Alyosha's attention to him.

"Alexei," his father shouted to him from a distance, as soon as he saw him, "come home for good this very day. Bring your pillow and mattress with you, and never set foot here any more."

Alyosha stood rooted to the spot, watching the scene intently and in silence. Meanwhile Fyodor Pavlovich got into his carriage; Ivan Fyodorovich was about to follow suit in gloomy silence, without even turning round to say good-bye to Alyosha, when a grotesque and almost incredible scene took place which put the finishing touches on the entire episode. Rakitin and Alyosha saw the landowner Maximov suddenly dash up to the carriage step, quite out of breath, afraid to be late. He was in such a hurry that, in his impatience, he put a foot on the carriage step on which Ivan Fyodorovich's left foot still rested, and, clutching at the box, made ready to jump in.

"I'm going with you, too! I'm with you, too!" he cried jumping up and down, ready for anything, giggling and with an expression of eager glee on his face. "Take me along with you!"

"Well, didn't I tell you he's von Sohn!" cried the delighted Fyodor Pavlovich. "He's a real von Sohn risen from the dead! But how did you manage to escape from there? What von Sohnian antics did you perpetrate there, and what has made you give up that dinner? You must be a brazen-faced fellow! I'm one myself, but you've outdone me, left me far behind. Jump in, jump in quickly. Let him in, Ivan. It'll be fun. He can make do with lying on the floor. You can, can't you, von Sohn? Or he can sit next to the coachman! Do that, von Sohn!"

But Ivan, who was already seated in the carriage, silently gave Maximov a violent shove in the chest, which sent him flying several yards away. It was only by chance that he did not fall to the ground.

"Drive off!" Ivan shouted angrily to the coachman.

"What's up? Why did you do that?" Fyodor Pavlovich exclaimed in protest, but the carriage had started off. Ivan Fyodorovich made no reply.

"You're a fine one!" Fyodor Pavlovich continued after two minutes of silence, looking askance at his son. "It was you who brought up the idea of visiting the monastery; you egged me on, and gave your approval. Why are you angry now?"

"Enough of your nonsense," Ivan said severely, cutting him short. "Give yourself some respite."

Fyodor Pavlovich said nothing for another couple of minutes.

"I wouldn't say no to a glass of brandy now," he observed sententiously.

Ivan Fyodorovich said nothing in reply.

"You'll have some too when we get home."

Ivan Fyodorovich remained silent.

Fyodor Pavlovich waited for another couple of minutes.

"I'll take Alyosha away from the monastery all the same, however little it may be to your liking, most respectful Karl von Moor."

Ivan Fyodorovich shrugged his shoulders contemptuously and, turning away, kept his gaze fixed on the road. They said no more all the way home.

BOOK THREE

The Lechers

1.

In the Servants' Quarters

Fyodor Pavlovich's house was located at some considerable distance from the town centre, but not quite in its outskirts. It was fairly old but quite attractive in appearance: on a single floor with a mezzanine, painted grey and with a sheet-iron roof painted red. Incidentally, it could well last for a long time, and was spacious and snug, with numerous closets, all sorts of nooks, and unexpected staircases. It was inhabited by rats, but Fyodor Pavlovich did not mind them too much. "At least, they provide some company when you're alone in the house," he would say. Indeed, it was his wont to send the servants away to the outbuilding for the night, and lock himself in alone. This lodge stood in the yard; and was roomy and solidly built. Fyodor Pavlovich had the cooking done in it, though there was a kitchen in the house itself: he disliked the smell of cooking, and had the meals brought in across the yard, irrespective of the season of the year. In general, the house had been built for a large family, and could accommodate five times as many people, masters and servants, as were actually living in it. At the time of our story, however, it was occupied only by Fyodor Pavlovich and Ivan Fyodorovich, with three servants in the outbuilding: old Grigori, his old wife Marfa, and a young servant, Smerdyakov by name. A few words of detail will have to be said here about the three. We have already made sufficient mention of old Grigori Kutuzov. His was a firm and unbending nature, stubborn and undeviating in achieving any aim he had set himself, if only he saw that aim (often most illogically) as an unshakable truth. On the whole, he was a man of incorruptible integrity. Though she had given him unquestioning obedience all her life, his wife, Marfa Ignatievna, nagged him terribly; thus, after the abolition of peasant serfdom, she kept pestering him to leave Karamazov's service, settle in Moscow and start a little shop there (they had some savings put by). Grigori, however, decided once and for all that she was talking nonsense, since "all women are dishonest", and that he should not leave their former master, no matter what kind of man he was, because that was their "duty".

"Now do you realise what duty means?" he asked, addressing Marfa.

"I do, Grigori Vassilievich, but I'll never understand why it is our duty to stay on here," she replied with firmness.

"Well, you don't have to understand, but that's how it's going to be. So hold your tongue in future."

And that was how it was: they did not leave, and Fyodor Pavlovich paid them a small wage, which they received regularly. Besides, Grigori was well aware that he had a definite influence over his master. He felt it, and was not mistaken. That wily and obstinate buffoon Fyodor Pavlovich, who was firm enough when it came to "certain things in life", as he put it, was, to his own surprise, extremely weak-natured when it came to other "things of life". He was aware of that, knew which ones he could not cope with and was even afraid of many of them. He had to be most circumspect in certain matters, which was difficult without someone who could be trusted, and Grigori was a most trustworthy person. There had even been many an occasion in the course of his career when Fyodor Pavlovich had stood in danger of getting a drubbing, and a sound one at that, and it had always been Grigori who had extricated him from his predicament, though he invariably gave him a piece of his mind afterwards. But blows alone would not have intimidated Fyodor Pavlovich: there had been outstanding instances, even very delicate and complicated ones, when he himself could not have accounted for the acute realisation which would suddenly overcome him that he stood in need of somebody faithful and devoted. There was something almost morbid about such instances: licentious and often viciously insect-like in his sadistic lust, Fyodor Pavlovich would at times, during his bouts of drunkenness, experience a spiritual fear and a moral convulsion which even caused him physical anguish.

"My heart flutters in my throat at such moments," he would sometimes say. It was at such moments that he liked to have close at hand, though not in the same room but at the lodge, somebody faithful and firm, quite unlike him, one who was not lecherous, a man who, though he had seen all his bawdy goings-on and knew all his secrets, put up with them all without any objection, out of a sense of loyalty, and above all, never rebuked him, or heaped coals of fire on his head either as regards this world or the next, one who would defend him in case of need—but from whom? From somebody unknown, but dreadful and dangerous. It was a matter of there being *another* man close at hand, long known to him and friendly, to be summoned at bad moments, if only to look into his face and perhaps exchange a word or two, even if quite irrelevant; if the man was not averse and displayed no anger, he experienced a sense of relief, but if the man was angry, it made him feel even more dejected. There were occasions (though quite rarely) when Fyodor Pavlovich would go to the lodge even at night and wake Grigori to ask him to come over to the house for a while. The latter would do so, and Fyodor Pavlovich would start to speak about the most trivial subjects, but would soon let him go, sometimes even with a gibe or a jest, and then, casting off all cares, he would go to bed and sink into restful slumber. Something of the kind also came to pass after Alyosha's arrival. Alyosha "pierced his heart" by living under the same roof, seeing everything and condemning nothing. Moreover, Alyosha brought with him something extraordinary: a total absence of contempt for the old man; on the contrary, he treated him with invariable kindness and a perfectly natural and unaffected attachment he so little deserved. All this came as a complete surprise to the lone old lecher, who had till then had room only for what was "filthy". After Alyosha had gone, he acknowledged to himself that he had realised something he had not previously wished to understand.

I already mentioned, at the beginning of my narrative, that Grigori detested Adelaida Ivanovna, Fyodor Pavlovich's first wife and mother of his first-born son Dmitri, and that he, Grigori, had, on the contrary, protected his second wife, the hysterical Sofia Ivanovna, against his master and anybody who took it into his mind to speak ill or disrespectfully of her. His liking for the unfortunate woman had grown into something sacred to him, so that, twenty years later, he would not tolerate even any slighting allusion to her from anyone and would at once challenge the offender. In appearance, Grigori was cold and dignified; he was sparing of speech, but when he did speak, his words were weighty and sober. In just the same way, it was impossible to tell at first glance whether he loved his meek and submissive wife or not; yet he did love her, and she knew it, of course. This Marfa Ignatievna was not only a far from unintelligent woman but perhaps with greater discernment than her husband, or at least shrewder in practical matters. Yet, from the very outset, she submitted to him with unquestioning meekness, respecting him absolutely for his spiritual superiority. Remarkably enough, they had extraordinarily little to say to each other throughout their married life, and that only on the most essential daily matters. The dignified and impressive Grigori invariably turned his affairs and cares over in his mind quite on his own, so Marfa Ignatievna had long ago understood once and for all that he stood in no need of advice from her. She felt that her husband appreciated her reticence, considering it a sign of her good sense. He had never struck her except on one occasion, and then only lightly. Once, in the first year of Fyodor Pavlovich's marriage to Adelaida Ivanovna, the village women and girls, who were then still serfs, were told to gather in the courtyard of their master's house for songs and dances. They had begun with *How Green Is the Meadow* when Marfa Ignatievna, who was still a young woman, dashed in front of the chorus and did a Russian folk dance in an unusual way—not in the country style practised by the peasant women, but in the manner she had learnt as a house servant with the wealthy Miusovs: she had performed at their private theatre, where the actors had been taught to dance by a dancing master from Moscow. Grigori had watched his wife dancing her steps, and when they returned home to their hut an hour later he had taught her a lesson by pulling at her hair a little. Matters ended at that and the punishment was never repeated, for Marfa Ignatievna decided that her dancing days were over.

God had not blessed them with children. In fact, a child had been born to them but soon died. Grigori seemed to be fond of children, and never concealed his liking, that is to say, did not feel ashamed to show it. When Adelaida Ivanovna ran away from home, he took Dmitri, who was three at the time, into his care for almost a year, combing his hair and even himself washing the boy in a tub. Then he had looked after Ivan and Alyosha, for which he had had his face slapped, as I have already related. His own child had gladdened him in anticipation while his wife was still pregnant, but its birth had filled his heart with grief and horror: it had six fingers. Grigori felt so crushed when he saw it that he did not utter a word until the baptism, even staying out in the garden for his vigil of silence. It was springtime, and during all those three days he was digging the beds in the kitchen-garden. The child was to be christened on the third day; by that time, Grigori's mind was made up. On entering the hut where the priest and the visitors had gathered—last to appear was Fyodor Pavlovich himself, who was to stand godfather—he suddenly declared that the babe "should not be baptised at all". He did so in a low voice, tersely, and bringing out each word with difficulty, his blank stare fixed on the priest.

"Why not?" the priest asked in good-humoured surprise.

"Because it's ... a deformity," Grigori muttered.

"A deformity? What do you mean by a deformity?"

Grigori was silent for a while.

"A mistake of nature has taken place," he muttered, though most vaguely but with conviction, evidently loth to dwell on the matter.

The remark evoked laughter and the poor babe was christened, of course. Grigori prayed fervently at the font, but did not change his opinion of the new-born babe. Incidentally, he raised no obstacles, but during the two weeks the sickly infant lived he hardly looked at it, was even unwilling to notice it, and kept away from the lodge most of the time. But when the boy died of thrush two weeks later, he laid it in the coffin himself, gazing at him in grief; when the shallow little grave was being filled in, he fell on his knees and bowed, his forehead touching the earth. He never mentioned the child afterwards, and Marfa Ignatievna never spoke of it in his presence. If she had occasion to speak to anybody about her "little babe", she never raised her voice above a whisper even if Grigori Vassilievich was not there. As she observed, he "took to religion" after the burial, read *The Lives of the Saints*, mostly in solitary silence, invariably donning his big, round, silver-rimmed spectacles. He rarely read aloud, except perhaps during Lent. He was fond of the Book of Job, and somehow got hold of a copy of the sayings and sermons of our "Divinely inspired Father Issac the Syrian"*, which he read assiduously for many years, without understanding a single word in it but perhaps prizing and loving it all the more for that reason. Of late, he had become interested in the flagellant practices, of which an instant had appeared in the neighbourhood. He seemed to have been deeply impressed but did not consider it necessary to go over to the new faith. His immersion in "divine" reading, of course, enhanced the gravity of his expression.

He was perhaps given to mysticism, so that the birth of his six-fingered child and its death coincided with another strange, unexpected and most unusual event which, as he himself later said, left an "imprint" on his soul. It so came about that on the very night following the funeral of the six-fingered child, Marfa Ignatievna was awakened by what seemed to her the wail of a new-born babe. In her alarm, she woke her husband, who, after listening, remarked that it sounded more like somebody groaning, "a woman perhaps". He got up and got dressed; it was a fairly warm night in May. When he went out on the porch, he could clearly hear groans coming from the garden, which was locked up for the night from the courtyard, so that it could be entered only by that entrance, went back to the lodge, lit a lantern and took the key to the garden. Paying no heed to the hysterical horror of his wife, who kept on assuring him that she had heard a baby crying and that it was her own child calling her, he went back into the garden without a word. There

*A Father of the Church, who lived in the 7th century.—*Tr.*

126

he immediately understood that the groaning came from the bath-house in the garden near the wicket, and that the groans came from a woman. On opening the bath-house, he saw a sight that dumbfounded him: the idiot girl, who was constantly straying the town's streets and went by the name of Smelly Lizaveta,* had got into the bath-house where she had just given birth to a baby. She lay dying, with the child next to her. She could say nothing for she had always been dumb. But all this calls for a special explanation.

2.

Smelly Lizaveta

There was a particular circumstance here which came as a profound shock to Grigori and fully strengthened in him an unpleasant and even revolting suspicion he had harboured for some time. This Smelly Lizaveta was a dwarfish girl, "just a little under five foot in height", as many of the pious old women in our town so touchingly recollected after her death. Her twenty-year-old face, healthy-looking, broad and rosy-cheeked, was blankly idiotic, the fixed stare in her eyes being unpleasant, though it was mild enough. All her life long, summer and winter alike, she walked about barefooted, wearing nothing but a hempen smock. Her very thick and almost black hair, curly like sheep-wool, formed a kind of huge hat on her head. Besides, it was always caked in mud, with leaves, bits of wood and shavings clinging to it, for she always slept on the ground or in the dirt. Her father Ilya had been a sickly and homeless townsman, who had lost his all, taken to drink and been hired as a kind of handyman many years ago in a well-to-do lower-middle class family in our town. Lizaveta's mother had died long before. Always sickly and spiteful, Ilya used to beat Lizaveta black-and-blue whenever she came home, which she rarely did,

*See Chapter II. In the Russian, Lizaveta is nicknamed *smerdyaschaya*—"stinking, evil-smelling", which I have rendered as *smelly.—Tr.*

for she was pitied and fed throughout the town as a fool in God's name. Ilya's master, he himself, and even many compassionate people in the town, mostly of the merchant class, made many attempts to get her clad more decently than in a single smock, and would provide her with a sheepskin coat and high boots for the winter. Though she would unprotestingly let herself to be clothed in this fashion, she would then make off, preferably to the main entrance to the cathedral, remove everything she had been given—kerchief, skirt, sheepskin and boots—leave it there and go away in her smock, barefooted just as before. It once so happened that, on his tour of inspection of our town, the new governor felt hurt in his best feelings when he caught sight of Lizaveta, and though he realised that she was simply a "saintly fool", as he had been informed, he pointed out that it was a breach of public decency for a young girl to wander about in nothing but a smock, and that it should be put an end to. But the governor departed, and Lizaveta was left alone. Finally her father died, which endeared her even more to all the God-fearing folk in the town. In fact, she seemed to be even liked; even the boys did not tease or hurt her, and our boys, particularly from school, are a lively lot. The girl would enter houses she did not know, whence she was never driven out; on the contrary, she was treated with kindness and given some small coin. She would take the coin and at once go to the church and drop it in the alms-box. If she was given a bagel or a bun at the market-place, she would not fail to give it to the first child she met, or else stop one of the wealthiest ladies in our town and give it to her, and the lady would be only too pleased to accept it. She herself never tasted anything but black bread and water. She would enter some expensive shop and sit down there, with costly goods or money lying about, but the shopkeepers never kept an eye on her for they knew that she would never take a copeck even if thousands of roubles were placed in front of her. She scarcely ever went to church, but slept either at the church door or would climb over a wattle fence (even today we have a lot of fences made of wattle instead of wooden boards) into somebody's kitchen-garden. She used to turn up once a week at home, or rather at the house of her late father's former employer, but did so every night during the winter, sleeping either in the passageway or the cowshed. Her ability to stand up to that kind of life was a source of amazement, but she was hardened to it: though she was so short of stature, she was sturdily built. Some of our townsfolk declared that she did all this out of a sense of pride, but that hardly made any sense: she could not utter a single word, and it was only at times that she would give an inarticulate grunt, so what kind of pride could she have? Now it so happened on one clear and warm September night (this was quite some time ago) that a drunken company from our town—some five or six young men—were on their way home from the club at full moon, which is very late in our parts. They were proceeding along the back alleys, between the wattle fences beyond which stretched the kitchen-gardens of the nearby houses. The alley led to a foot-bridge across the long and stinking pool that went by the name of our river. The tipsy gentlemen saw Lizaveta asleep at a wattle fence, among the nettles and burdocks, and halted over her, laughing uproariously and cracking most indecent jokes. It came into one young buck's mind to ask an absolutely eccentric question on a most impossible subject: "Could anyone at all regard such an animal as a woman, just now, for instance—and so on." With proud distaste they all decided it was out of the question. However, Fyodor Pavlovich, who happened to be of the company, at once came to the fore with the opinion that she could be considered a woman, even very much so; there was something particularly spicy about it, and so on and so forth. At that time, it is true, he seemed to be going out of his way to play the buffoon; he was given to thrusting himself forward to amuse the gentry, of course, with a show of equality, though he was nothing but a complete upstart in their eyes. This was just at the time when the news of the death of his first wife Adelaida Ivanovna reached him, and, his hat in crape, he was toping and behaving in a most unseemly fashion, so much so as to shock even the most dissolute at the sight of him. Of course, the band turned this unexpected opinion into a joke, one of them even trying to provoke him to action. The others, however, gave vent to their

129

disgust in even stronger terms, though still with the utmost levity, and finally made off. Fyodor Pavlovich later averred most emphatically that he had left with all the others. That may have been so—nobody knew for certain, but some five or six months later all the town were speaking with sincere and intense indignation of Lizaveta having been made pregnant, and asking who the sinner, the culprit, could have been. It was then that a strange rumour began suddenly to spread all over the town that no other than Fyodor Pavlovich was the offender. Whence the rumour? By that time, only one of the tipsy band was still living in our town: an elderly and esteemed civil councillor, a family man and father of grown-up daughters, one who would certainly have never spread the tale whatever may have actually happened. The other five had already left the town. The rumour, however, pointed straight at Fyodor Pavlovich and did so with persistence. Of course, he was not excessively put out by such talk, and would never have bothered to make reply to such folk as petty tradesmen and the like. He was stiffnecked in those days and never spoke to anyone outside his own circle of officials and members of the nobility whom he was out to entertain. It was then that Grigori stood up for his master with might and main, and not only defended him most vigorously against all such insinuations, but was even abusive and quarrelsome in doing so, thus making many people change their minds. "The hussy has herself to blame," he would assert emphatically, claiming that the culprit was none other than Slippery Karp, a notoriously dangerous convict, who had broken out of prison and was in hiding in our town. The conjecture sounded plausible, for Karp was still in people's minds; they recollected that he had been loitering about the town during those nights in early autumn and had committed three robberies. This incident, however, far from diminishing the liking generally felt for the poor idiot girl, even made her an object of greater care and concern. Mrs. Kondratyev, a well-to-do merchant's widow, even had the girl brought to her house late in April and took steps to ensure that she should not be allowed to leave until after her delivery. A constant watch was kept over her, but despite all the vigilance Lizaveta managed to get away from the Kondratyev house on the very last day and found her way into Fyodor Pavlovich's garden. How she had been able, in her condition, to climb over a high and strong fence remained a mystery in its way. Some asserted that someone had helped her over, others that it had been done by some supernatural agency. It had most probably happened in some complex if natural way: Lizaveta, who was used to clambering over low fences into other people's kitchen-gardens to spend the night there, had somehow or other managed to mount Fyodor Pavlovich's fence and, despite her condition, jump down into the garden, though not without some harm to herself. Grigori rushed to Marfa Ignatievna, whom he sent to attend to Lizaveta, while he himself ran off to fetch an old midwife, who happened to live close by. The baby's life was saved, but Lizaveta was dead by the break of day. Grigori took the baby, brought it home, told his wife to be seated, and laid it on her lap: "An orphan-child of God is everybody's kin, and yours and mine all the more so. This one has been sent to us by our dead child, but it is the offspring of a devil's son and a righteous girl. Nurse it and shed no more tears." So Marfa Ignatievna reared the child, which was christened and given the name of Pavel, to which by common consent the patronymic of Fyodorovich was added. To this, Fyodor Pavlovich raised no objections, even finding it amusing, though he continued to vehemently disclaim any responsibility. The townspeople were pleased at his having taken the foundling in. Fyodor Pavlovich later invented a surname for the child: Smerdyakov, after its mother's nickname. It was this Smerdyakov who subsequently became Fyodor Pavlovich's second servant, and, at the time our story begins, was living in the lodge, together with Grigori and Marfa. He was employed as cook. I should really add something about this Smerdyakov, but I find it awkward to distract my reader's attention for long with such ordinary matters as servants, so I shall take up the thread of my narrative, in the hope that Smerdyakov will find his place in the story in due course.

3.

An Ardent Heart's Confession, in Verse

For a while, Alyosha stood, greatly perplexed by his father's command shouted to him from the carriage as it was leaving the monastery. Not that he stood rooted to the spot, for that was not his wont. Despite his uneasiness, he at once went in to the Father Superior's kitchen to discover what his father had been up to upstairs. He then set off, trusting that, on his way to the town, he would be able to find a solution to a problem that was very much on his mind. I shall say in advance that he was not in the least put out by his father's shouting at him or ordering him to return home "with pillows and mattress". He realised only too well that an order uttered in such a loud and theatrical tone had been given in the heat of moment, just to make a jaunting display—much in the same way as a local tradesman, who was recently celebrating his own name-day with a group of friends, went on the rampage because he was not given any more vodka; he got so worked up that he began to smash up his own china, tear his own clothes and his wife's, and ended up by wrecking his own furniture and breaking all the windows in the house, and all this just to make a display. Something of the kind had, of course, now taken place with his father. On the following day, the drunken tradesman, now sober, of course, regretted the smashed crockery. Alyosha knew that the old man would certainly let him return to the monastery on the next day, even perhaps that very day. Besides, he was quite sure that his father was capable of hurting anybody's feelings but would not wish to wound his, Alyosha's. He was also convinced that there was no one anywhere who would ever wish to hurt him; moreover, no one could ever do that to him. That was axiomatic, something given once and for all and to be unquestionably accepted; in that sense, he pursued his way without the least hesitation.

At that moment, however, another kind of fear, one of a quite different kind, was stirring within him; it was the more agonising for his being unable to define it, to wit, the fear of a woman, of Katerina Ivanovna, to be more explicit. It was she who, in the note handed to him a short while before by Madame Khokhlakov, had beseechingly asked him to call on her about something. This demand and the necessity of going there without fail at once filled his heart with an aching pain which had grown ever more intense all the morning, despite all the happenings that had ensued at the monastery, then at the Father Superior's, and so on and so forth. He was afraid, not because he did not know what she would be speaking of, or what he would have to say in reply. In general, it was not the woman in her that he feared: of course, he had little knowledge of women, yet he had spent all his life, from early childhood until his monastery days, exclusively among women. It was this particular woman—namely Katerina Ivanovna—that he was afraid of. He had felt afraid of her ever since he had first seen her. In all, he had seen her only once or twice, perhaps three times, and had on one occasion even exchanged a few chance remarks with her. He recollected her as a beautiful, proud and imperious girl, but it was not her beauty that troubled him, but something else. It was the inexplicability of his fear that now enhanced that fear itself. The girl's aims were the most honourable—that he knew: she was out to save his brother Dmitri, though the latter's behaviour towards her had been reprehensible; in this, she was guided by magnanimity alone. Despite this awareness and the justice he could not but render to all these excellent and magnanimous sentiments, a chill ran down his spine the nearer he drew to her house.

He realised that he would not find his brother Ivan Fyodorovich, who was a close friend of hers, at her house since he was most probably with his father. It was even more certain he would not find Dmitri there either, and he had a presentiment why. And so his talk with her would be tête-à-tête. He wanted so much to go and see his brother Dmitri before the fateful talk took place. Without showing him the letter, he could have a few words with him. But Dmitri lived quite a long way off and was probably out. After a minute's hesitation, he made up his mind. Crossing himself with habitual rapidity and smiling for some reason, he set out with firm steps towards the formidable young lady's house.

Its location was known to him, but it would take a long time to get there if he went along Bolshoi Street, then crossed the town square and went that way. Ours is a small but straggling town and the distances in it are quite considerable. Besides, his father was expecting him: he might not have had time to forget his command and might be testy, which was why Alyosha had to make haste to see the girl and then get home in time. In view of these considerations, he decided to take a short cut and go along the byways and back alleys, for he knew every inch of the ground. That meant by-passing the streets, walking between deserted fences, even climbing over some of them, and crossing other people's back-yards, but that was alright for he was known to everybody. Taking that route would enable him to reach Bolshoi Street in half the time. At one place, he had to pass very close by his father's house, past a garden adjoining his father's and attached to a ramshackle little four-windowed house. It belonged, as Alyosha knew, to a bedridden old woman who lived with her daughter, a city-bred lady's maid who had until recently been in service at generals' homes in St. Petersburg but had joined her sick mother a year before to take care of her; the daughter was fond of showing off her smart dresses. The two, mother and daughter, had sunk into dire poverty, and, as neighbours, even went to the Karamazov kitchen every day for the soup and bread Marfa Ignatievna so readily supplied them with. Yet, though she came for the soup, the daughter never sold a single one of her dresses, one of which even had a very long train. It was from his friend Rakitin, who knew whatever was going on in the town, that this latter circumstance became known to Alyosha, quite by chance, of course, and had naturally been immediately forgotten. But on drawing level with their neighbour's garden, he suddenly remembered the long train and, as he raised his downcast and thought-bowed head, he met with the last person he had expected to see.

Standing perched on something in the neighbour's garden and leaning over the wattle fence stood his brother Dmitri Fyodorovich, violently gesticulating and beckoning to attract his attention and apparently afraid, not only to call out but even to utter a single word for fear of being overheard. Alyosha at once ran up to the fence.

"It's a good thing you looked up, for I was on the verge of shouting to you," Dmitri Fyodorovich said in a joyful but hurried whisper. "Climb up here! Quick! Oh, what piece of luck you're here. I was just thinking of you—"

Alyosha was glad, too, but did not know how to get over the fence. Mitya put a powerful hand under his elbow and helped him jump over. Catching up his cassock, Alyosha got across with the agility of a barefooted street arab.

"Good for you! And now come along!" Mitya exclaimed in delighted undertones.

"Where to?" asked Alyosha also in a whisper, looking about and finding himself in a deserted garden, with no one in the vicinity. It was a small garden, yet the house was at least fifty paces away from them. "Why are you whispering if there's no one about?"

"Why am I whispering? Oh, damn it all!" Dmitri suddenly cried out in a loud voice. "Indeed, why am I whispering? Well, you can see what pranks nature can play. I'm on secret watch here, and guarding a secret. I'll explain matters later, but, realising it's a secret, I suddenly began to speak in a hushed voice, just like a fool, when there's no need to. Come on! Right over there. Not a word for a while. I'd just like to hug you!

Glory to God in the Highest
Glory to the God in me!—

"I was repeating that just now, before you came—"

The garden was about a dessiatine in area, perhaps a little more, but planted with trees only along the borders, the four fenced sides: apple-trees, maples, limes, and birch-trees. The middle was a lawn producing several poods of hay in the summer, and let out in the spring for a rent of several roubles. There was also a shrubbery of raspberries, gooseberries and currants along the fences and the recently planted vegetable-beds were close to the house itself. Dmitri Fyodorovich led his visitor to a furthermost corner of the garden, where, among the closely growing limes and long-standing currant, elder, guelder rose and lilac bushes there appeared a green and dilapidated pergola, its latticed sides blackened and crooked with age, but the roof still offering shelter from rain. Nobody knew when pergola had been built, but it must have been put up some fifty years before by the then proprietor of the house, Alexander Karlovich von Schmidt, a retired lieutenant-colonel. But it was now in a state of decay, the floor was rotting, its planks all loose, and the woodwork smelled musty. Inside was a green wooden table dug into the ground; around it stood green wooden benches which were still usable. Alyosha had immediately noticed his brother's elevated state; on entering the pergola he saw a half-bottle of brandy and a glass on the table.

"Brandy!" Dmitri laughed. "I can see from your glance that you're thinking 'He's drinking again!' Don't believe the Phantom.

> *Distrust the false and lying mob*
> *And cast aside your gnawing doubt—*

"I'm not toping but just 'indulging' as your swine of a Rakitin would say. He's certain to become a civil councillor and will keep on saying, 'I'm indulging'. Sit down. I would like to take you, Alyosha, and press you to my bosom till I could crush you, because you're the only person in the wide, wide world I really—re-ally—(mark that!) love!"

He uttered the last words in a kind of frenzy.

"No one but you, and, besides, a 'hussy' I've fallen in love with, to my undoing. But falling in love does not mean loving. One can fall in love and, at the same time, feel hate. Remember that! I say so whilst I'm still cheerful! Sit down here at the table. I'll be here at your side and look at you, and keep on talking. You'll keep mum and I'll go on talking because the time is ripe. On second thought, you know, I'd better keep my voice down because—because here you can never tell who may be eavesdropping. I've said I'll explain everything: 'to be continued', as they say. Why have I been simply dying to see you all these days, and still feel that way? (I dropped anchor at this place five days ago.) Yes, all these days. Because it's only to you I can tell everything, because I've got to; because I need you; because tomorrow I'll fall headlong from the clouds; because tomorrow life will end and begin. Have you ever felt, ever dreamt what it's like to fall into a pit from a mountain top? Well, I'm doing that now, and not in a dream. I feel no fear and neither should you. I *am* in fear, but it's pleasurable. I mean, it's not pleasurable but rapturous— Well, to hell with it! Come what may. It makes no difference: strong spirit, weak spirit, womanish spirit—come what may! Let us now praise Nature: see how bright the sunshine, how clear the sky, how green the leaves; it's still summery and placid, and the time is past three in the afternoon! Where were you going?"

"I was going to see Father, but first I meant to call on Katerina Ivanovna—"

"Going to see her and Father! You don't say so! What a coincidence! Why d'you think I was expecting you and calling you? What was I yearning, hungering and thirsting for in all the convolutions of my soul and even in my ribs? It was to send you to Father with a message from me, then to Katerina Ivanovna, and thereby have done with them both. An angel had to be sent. I could have sent anybody, but I wanted to send an angel. And there you were on your way to see her and Father."

"Did you really want to send me?" cried Alyosha, looking very distressed.

"But you knew it! I see you realised that at once. But not a word—not a word for a while. I want to see neither your pity nor your tears!"

Dmitri stood up, thought for a while, and put a finger to his forehead: "She asked you herself to call, didn't she? She sent you a note or something, and that's why you were going to her. Otherwise, you wouldn't do that, would you?"

"Here's her note," said Alyosha, taking it out of his pocket. Mitya scanned it.

"So you going by the backway! Ye gods, I thank you for sending him that way, and I got hold of him just like that old fool

137

of a fisherman in the fairy-tale caught the golden fish*. Listen, Alyosha, listen to me, my dear brother: I have decided to tell you everything now. For I simply have to tell somebody. I've already told an angel in heaven, but I've also got to tell it to an angel on earth. You are that angel on earth. You will hear me out, pass judgement, and forgive— And I stand in need of somebody higher forgiving me. Listen: if two creatures suddenly part company with everything earthly and fly off into the extraordinary, or at least one of them does and, before taking off or perishing, he comes to the other and says, 'Do this or that for me—something that no one is ever asked to do and may only be asked on one's death-bed,' can that other person refuse—if he is a friend or a brother?"

"I'll do so, but tell me what it is, and do it quickly," said Alyosha.

"Quickly— H'm. Don't be in such a hurry. You hurry and aggravate yourself. There's no need for haste now. The world has taken to a new road. Oh, Alyosha, it's a pity you've no idea of what being enraptured means! But what am I saying to you? As if you have no idea of that! What do I, booby that I am, say:

> *Display nobility, O man!*

Who wrote that line of verse?"

Alyosha decided to bide his time, realising that it was, perhaps, only here that his duty really lay. Dmitri sank into thought for a moment, an elbow propped on the table and his chin cupped in his palm. They were both silent.

"Alyosha," said Mitya, "you're the only person who won't laugh at me! I'd like to begin—my confession—with Schiller's *Ode to Joy*, his *An die Freude*. But I don't know German. All I know is *An die Freude*. Don't think this is just drunken babbling. I'm not in the least drunk. Brandy's brandy, but it takes two bottles to make me drunk—

---

*See: *The Tale of the Fisherman and the Fish* by Alexander Pushkin, Russia's great national poet (1799-1837).—*Tr.*

> *And Silenus, with his ruddy mug,*
> *Seated on a stumbling moke—*

but I haven't downed even a quarter of a bottle. You see, I'm not Silenus. Not Silenus but *silen**. I am strong, for I've made up my mind for good now. Forgive the pun; there's so much you've got to forgive me today, let alone a pun. Don't get disturbed. I'm not being long-winded; I'm talking sense, and I'll come to the point right away. I'm not going to keep you in suspense. Hold on: how does it go?—"

Raising his head, he paused in thought, and burst into verse:

> *Timid, naked, savage hid*
> *Troglodyte in mountain cleft;*
> *Nomad scourged the plain and did*
> *Leave the fields of fruits bereft;*
> *Mighty Hunter through the wood*
> *Prowled with bow and spear to hand;*
> *Hapless Sailor mournful stood,*
> *Cast upon the callous strand.*
>
> *Down from Mount Olympus keening,*
> *Ceres seeks her ravished child.*
> *Nature knowing aught of greening,*
> *Spreads a welcome bleak and wild:*
> *Neither hut nor hearth whereby her*
> *Weary wanderer's soul to rest;*
> *Not a temple to inspire*
> *Fear of God in mortal breast.*
>
> *Ear of wheat and dark sweet grape—*
> *None to grace the harvest feast.*
> *Altars heaped with bloody bait—*

*A play on words. The Russian form of *Silenus*, is *Silen*, which coincides with the short form of the adjective *silny*—strong, i. e. *silén*.—Tr.

> *Smoking flesh of human beast.*
> *All that greets her grieving eye,*
> *Misery's withering blight has kissed,*
> *All in sight doth testify:*
> *Far the fall of man from bliss!**

Mitya suddenly broke into tears; he seized Alyosha by the hand.

"Alyosha, my dear friend, I'm humiliated, humiliated even now. Man has to put up with so much on earth; he faces so many trials! Don't think I'm just a boor of officer rank who does nothing but guzzle brandy and indulge in lechery. I hardly think of anything else but this humiliated man—if only I'm not lying. I hope to God I'm not lying this time or assuming merit for myself. I'm thinking of that man because I am myself that kind of man.

> *Would he lift his soul immortal*
> *From the foulest wretched depths;*
> *Swear then man an oath eternal*
> *To his ancient Mother Earth.***

The problem is: how am I to swear an oath eternal to Mother earth? I don't kiss it or cut its bosom open, so should I become a peasant or shepherd? I go on forward and don't know whether I'll find myself amidst stench and shame, or amidst joy and light. There's the rub, for everything in the world is a riddle! And every time I happened to sink into the depths of the vilest depravity (and it's always been that way), I've always read out that poem about Ceres and Man. Has it corrected me? Never! For I'm a Karamazov. Because if I do go plunging into the bottomless pit, I do that head foremost, heels uppermost, and I even feel pleased to be falling in so humiliating a fashion and find that it becomes me. It is at that very moment of degradation that I suddenly begin that ode. Even if I'm accused, even if

*Friedrich Schiller, *An die Freude*, translated by Laura Beraha.
**From the poems of Friedrich Schiller, translated by Laura Beraha.

I'm vile and base, let me kiss the hem of the vestment enveloping my God; even if I'm following the devil at the moment, yet I'm your son, O Lord, and I love thee and feel the joy without which the world cannot be or exist.

> *Joy eternal rains from heaven,*
> *Slakes the soul of all below,*
> *Sets the cup of life fermenting,*
> *Fires the brew with mystery's glow.*
> *Joy mystery's lured the seedling lightward*
> *Carved the chaos into stars;*
> *And with wisdom undeciphered*
> *Scattered suns through realms afar.*

> *From the breast of bounteous nature*
> *All that breathes imbibes of Joy,*
> *Drenched in Joy her every creature,*
> *One and all in Joy conjoined.*
> *Joy that banished woe with friendship*
> *Raised the poet, milked the grape.*
> *Lust's the lot of lowly insects—*
> *Angels bow before God's grace.* *

"But enough of verse! I've shed my tears, so let me weep. Let it be fatuous, something that will be generally laughed at, but you won't do that. There, your eyes are flashing. Yes, enough of verse. I now want to tell you about 'insects', those God had endowed with lust:

> *Lust's the lot of lowly insects!*

That insect is me, Alyosha, and whatever has been said refers to me. All we Karamazovs are made that way, and even in an angel like you that insect is alive and will stir up tempests in your blood. Tempests, for lust *is* a tempest—more than a tempest! Beauty is something awesome and terrifying! Awesome because

---

*Friedrich Schiller, *An die Freude*, translated by Laura Beraha.

141

it can't be defined, and it can't be defined because God has set us nothing but riddles. Here the shores meet, and all contradictions live cheek by jowl. I've had little schooling, Alyosha, but I've given the matter a lot of thought. There are an awful lot of mysteries! There are too many riddles bearing down on man on earth. Solve them as best you can, and get out of trouble unscathed. Beauty! I can't stand the idea that a man of lofty heart and high intelligence should start out with the Madonna ideal, and end up with the Sodom ideal. What's still worse is that, with the Sodom ideal already in his soul, he does not deny the Madonna ideal, which sets his heart afire, really truly afire, just as in the years of his youthful purity. No, man is all-encompassing, even too much so, and I'd like to cut him down to size. The devil alone knows what to make of it all! What seems shameful to the mind presents itself to the heart as beauty—sheer beauty. Can there be any beauty in a Sodom? Yet, believe me, Sodom is where the vast majority of people *do* find beauty—did you know that? What is horrible is that beauty is not only an awesome but a mysterious thing. It is where the Devil and God are locked in struggle, with man's heart as the battlefield. Incidentally, it is of one's own aches and pains that one usually speaks. And now for the facts themselves.

4.

An Ardent Heart's Confession, in Anecdote

"I was leading a wild life there. Father asserted a short while ago that I spent several thousand roubles on seducing the fillies. That's a filthy invention; nothing of the kind ever took place, and whatever *did* take place did not call for money. To me, money is merely an accessory, an ebullition from the heart, a setting. It would be a lady one day; a street wench on the next. I would give both a good time and spend money like water, with music, uproar and Gypsy singers. If necessary, I would pay the lady too, because they all accept it, and eagerly too, it must be admitted, and they're both pleased and grateful. Well-born ladies have been fond of me—not all of them, but quite a few. Yet I've always liked the back alleys, the deserted and dark lanes beyond the town square—it's there that you run into adventure and the unexpected, and find gold nuggets in the mud. I'm speaking figuratively, of course: such back streets did not exist literally in that town, but they were there in the moral sense. If you were what I am, you would understand what such things mean. I loved the lewd and the shame of lewdness. I loved cruelty, for am I not a bug, a vicious insect? In a word, a Karamazov! On one occasion there was a picnic for practically the whole town. We were travelling in seven troikas. It was in the dark of a winter night, and I began squeezing the hand of a young girl sitting next to me in the sleigh and got her to kiss me. She was the daughter of a civil servant, a poor, sweet, gentle and meek creature. She permitted very, very much in the dark. She thought, poor child, that I'd call the next day and ask for her hand (I was appreciated, in the main, as a highly eligible young man), but I never exchanged a single word with her the next five months. I could see her eyes following me from a corner of the room whenever there were dances (and we were often having them); I saw them glowing with gentle indignation. But this game merely titillated the insect lust I nurtured within myself. Five months later, she married an official and left the town —angry and perhaps still in love with me. They are living quite happily now. Note that I haven't told a soul of that or said anything to injure her reputation. I may be base in my desires, and love what's low, but I'm not dishonourable. But you're blushing and your eyes are flashing. Well, you've heard enough of this filth. But all this has been merely the prelude, something in the style of Paul de Kock, though the vicious insect was growing, and was filling my soul. My memories of women could fill a volume. God keep them, the sweet things. I never liked to quarrel, whenever I broke off a relationship. I never let any one of them down through loose talk, and never injured a reputation. But enough of that. You don't suppose I've called you here simply to hear such balderdash, do you? No, I'm going to tell you something more interesting, but don't be taken aback by my revealing no sense of shame to you. I'm even glad to be frank with you."

"It's because I blushed that you're saying that," Alyosha suddenly remarked. "But it was not your words or your deeds that made me blush, but the realisation that I'm just like you."

"You? Aren't you drawing the long-bow?"

"No, I'm not," said Alyosha with some ardour. (The idea had obviously arisen in his mind long before.) "The rungs are one and the same, only I'm standing on the bottom rung and you're somewhere up there—on the thirteenth. That's how I see it, but it's one and the same thing, absolutely the same. Anyone who sets foot on the bottom rung is bound to reach the top one."

"So it's better not to set foot there at all, isn't it?"

"Anyone who can do so, should avoid doing that."

"And you? Can you avoid it?"

"I don't think I can."

"Not another word, Alyosha, not another word, my dear fellow. I'd like to kiss your hand, just like that, because you move me so. That minx of a Grushenka—and she has a knowledge of human nature—once said to me that she'd eat you up one day. Alright, alright, not another word on that score. From such abomination, from this fly-blown field, let's go on to my own tragedy, which is another fly-blown field, I mean, full of vileness of every kind. The point is that, though the old man was lying when he spoke of my seduction of innocent girls, the matter stood that way in my tragedy, though it happened only once, and even then didn't actually come off. The old man, who cast aspersions on me in his cock-and-bull story, knows nothing of this happening—I've never told anybody about it; you'll be the first to hear it now, with the exception of Ivan, of course. Ivan knows it all. He learnt of it long before you did. But he knows how to keep a secret."

"Does he?"

"He does."

Alyosha was all ears now.

"I was serving in that border battalion, and though I held the rank of ensign I felt under constant surveillance, as though I were a convict of some kind. But I was extremely well received in the little town. I spent my money very liberally, so they thought I was wealthy: I thought so too. But I must have been to their liking for some other reason. Though some heads were shaken, I was quite popular. But my lieutenant-colonel—an elderly man– took a sudden dislike to me, and was constantly picking on me. However, I had some backing, and, besides, the whole town was on my side, so there wasn't much he could do about it. It was all my own fault, for I failed to pay him the respect due to him. My pride was to blame. The obstinate old man, who was really a good sort, kind-hearted and hospitable, had been married twice, but both wives were dead. The first wife, who had been of humble origin, had left him a daughter just as unpretentious as herself. When I came there, she was a spinster of about twenty-four, who was living at her father's together with an aunt, her late mother's sister. The aunt was an embodiment of meek simplicity, and the niece–the lieutenant-colonel's elder daughter–of pert simplicity. I like to be kindly when I reminisce, and I must say she was the best-natured woman I've ever met–Agafya her name was; just imagine: Agafya Ivanovna. She was not so bad-looking after all–to the Russian taste: tall, buxom, with a full figure; she had fine eyes, though her features were somewhat coarse. She was not eager to marry, and had turned down two proposals; yet she remained invariably cheerful. We became intimate friends–no, not in that way; everything was quite pure; we were just good friends. I've often been intimate with women in a quite sinless fashion–just friendship. I would say the most shockingly outspoken things to her, and, just imagine, she only laughed. Many women enjoy such 'frank' talk–mark that!–and she was a spinster, which very entertaining. Besides, she was no society girl. Her aunt and she lived at her father's with a kind of self-imposed humility, placing themselves on a lower footing than the rest of society. She was generally liked and her help sought, because she was an excellent dressmaker; indeed, she had a gift for it and never demanded payment for her services, which she rendered out of the goodness of her heart, but whenever some gift was offered, she did not turn it down. As for the lieutenant-colonel–well, he was quite different matter! He was one of the leading person-alities in our parts, who lived on a liberal scale, kept open house, and gave suppers and dances. When I got there and joined my battalion, the whole town was talking of the expected arrival of his second daughter, really a beauty, from the capital, where she was at an aristocratic finishing school. This second daughter was that selfsame Katerina Ivanovna and the child of the lieutenant-colonel's second wife—already deceased—who came of the distinguished family of some important general, though I know for a certainty that she had brought the lieutenant-colonel no dowry. Of course, she had important connections but that was all, with the exception of some expectations; money there was none. However, when the daughter turned up (on a visit, not for good), the entire town seemed to come to life. Our most distinguished ladies (two wives of Excellences, one Mrs. Colonel and all the rest after them) at once displayed a keen interest in her; she was in great demand at entertainments arranged for her, and was the belle of the balls, the picnics, and the *tableaux vivants* given to aid some needy governesses. I did not pay her the least attention, but carried on as wildly as before, and one of my pranks at the time became the talk of the town. One evening, at the battery commander's, I intercepted her glance as she was looking me over, but even then I did not go up to her, evincing no desire to make her acquaintance. It was some time later, also at a party, that I did go up to her to say a few words. She scarcely gave me a look, and compressed her lips in scorn. 'Just you wait!' I thought to myself, 'I'll get my own back.' I was a most awful boor in most cases at the time, and I realised it. The chief thing was that I felt that Katenka* was not some simpering boarding-school miss but a person of character, proud and genuinely high-principled; above all, she had intellect and education, while I possessed neither. D'you think I meant to propose to her? Not at all; I just wanted revenge for her failure to realise what a fine fellow I was. Meanwhile, I went on with my life of drinking and violence, so that in the end the lieutenant-colonel placed me under arrest for three days. It was just at that time that Father sent me six thousand, after I had sent him a disclaimer on his property that is to say, a statement that we were "quits" and that I would demand nothing more of him. I didn't understand the least thing at the time: until I came here and right up to the

*Diminutive of Katerina.—*Tr.*

last few days, perhaps until this very day, I haven't been able to make head or tail of my money squabbles with Father. Well, to hell with that! I'll return to it. Well, just at the time I received the six thousand, a highly interesting piece of reliable information reached me in a letter from a friend of mine: it seemed that displeasure with our lieutenant-colonel had been evinced; he was suspected of 'certain irregularities', and, in a word, a nasty surprise was being cooked for him by his ill-wishers. Indeed, the divisional commander arrived and gave him a thorough dressing-down. Shortly afterwards, he was told to retire. I shan't go into the details of how it all came about; of course, he had had his enemies, but a marked coolness now arose in the town towards him and his family, and all backs were turned on him. That was when I played my first card. On meeting Agafya Ivanovna, with whom I had always maintained a friendship, I said to her: 'D'you know your father's short of 4,500 roubles of battalion money?' 'What do you mean? Why are you saying such things? The general was here a short while ago and the money was all there.' 'It was there all right, but now it isn't.' She got terribly scared. 'Don't frighten me like that please,' she said. 'Who told you that?' 'There's no cause for worry,' I said. 'I won't breathe a word to anyone. I can keep my mouth shut in such matters. Only I'd like to add, just in case, so to say, that if your father is asked to produce the four thousand five hundred and can't do so, then, to avoid his being court-martialled and reduced to the ranks at his age, you'd better send your sister along to me on the quiet. I've just been sent some money, so I can let her have the four thousand, and keep the whole matter a dead secret.' 'Oh, what a despicable fellow you are!' (Her very words!) 'How horribly despicable you are! How dare you!' When she was leaving in high dudgeon, I called out after her that it would be a dead secret with me. I may as well tell you in advance that the two females—Agafya and her aunt—behaved like perfect angels throughout the entire business. They simply adored that haughty girl of a Katya, humbled themselves before her and waited on her as if they were her maids— Only Agafya told her all about the business—I mean our talk. It was later that I learnt of it for certain. She held nothing back, which, of course, was exactly what I wanted.

"The new major suddenly arrived to take over the battalion, which he did. The old lieutenant-colonel suddenly took ill, was laid up, kept indoors for a couple of days and did not hand over the battalion money. Our Dr. Kravchenko averred that he was really ill. But I had known for a certainty and for a long time that over the past four years the money would disappear for a while soon after every auditing of the lieutenant-colonel's accounts. He used to lend it to a local merchant, an old widower, Trifonov by name, a bearded man in gold-rimmed spectacles, whom he trusted implicitly. The latter would go off to the fair, put his money to good use, and, on getting back home, he would return the money intact, together with some gift and the interest. But this time (I learnt all about it quite by chance from Trifonov's snotty-nosed son and heir, a most dissolute whelp), this time, I say, Trifonov returned nothing when he came back from the fair. The lieutenant-colonel rushed to his house, but all the reply he was given was: 'I've never received any money from you, and couldn't have.' So there was our lieutenant-colonel languishing at home, a wet towel about his head, the three women putting ice on his crown. Suddenly an orderly arrived with instructions that the money was to be turned in at once, within two hours. The lieutenant-colonel signed the book (I saw his signature there later), got up and said he was going to don his uniform. He dashed into his bedroom, took a double-barrelled shot-gun, primed it, rammed home a service bullet, took the boot off his right foot, pressed the muzzle against his chest, and began to feel for the trigger with his big toe. Meanwhile, Agafya, whose suspicions had been aroused following my warning, stole up to his bedroom just in time to see what was going on. She rushed in, flung herself on him from behind and threw her arms about him; the gun went off, the bullet harmlessly hitting the ceiling. The others came rushing in, took hold of him, and took the gun away—I learnt all the details afterwards. I was at home at the time; it was getting dark and I was making ready to go out. I had got dressed, combed my hair, scented my handkerchief and taken my cap when the door flew open and before me, in my apartment, stood Katerina Ivanovna.

"The strangest things happen: no one had seen her in the street or entering my place so it all passed off unnoticed. My apartment had been let to me by two ancient ladies, the widows of civil servants, who attended to me. They held me in deep respect, obeyed me in all things and did what I'd ordered them to—they kept mum about the whole affair. I caught on at once, of course. She walked in, looking straight at me, her dark eyes fixed on me in resolve and even defiance, but I could discern indecision on her lips and about them.

"'My sister told me you'd let me have four thousand five hundred roubles if I came for it myself: So here I am—give me the money!' she gasped in fright, her voice failing her and the corners of her mouth and the lines around her lips quivering— But Alyosha, are you listening or are you asleep?"

"Mitya, I know you'll tell me the whole truth," said Alyosha in agitation.

"That's exactly what I'll tell you. If you want the whole truth, then here it is. I won't spare myself. My first thought was Karamazovian. I was once bitten by a centipede and laid up for a fortnight with a high temperature; in just the same way, I now felt a centipede, a venomous insect, sting me in the heart, understand? I looked at her from head to foot. You've seen her, haven't you? She *is* beautiful, but she was beautiful in a different way then. At that moment, she was made beautiful because of her nobility while I was despicable, because she stood there in the grandeur of her greatness of heart and her sacrifice for her father; I was merely a bug. And, cad and bug as I was, she was *wholly* dependent on me, through and through, body and soul. She stood within a circle. I'll tell you quite frankly: the thought, that venomous centipede thought, possessed my heart with such force that the suspense almost stopped it from beating. It seemed there could be no resisting the urge: I could act only like a bug, a venomous tarantula, without the least pity. I could hardly breathe. Listen: on the very next morning, I would, of course, have gone to ask for her hand to complete the matter in a most honourable way, so that no one should or could have the least inkling of what had happened. Though I'm a man of

149

base desires, I have my integrity. But at that very moment a voice whispered in my ear, 'But when you come tomorrow with your proposal of marriage, she won't be at home and will order the coachman to send you packing. Hold me up to shame all over the town—I have no fear of you, she will say." I looked at the girl: the voice had not deceived me; that was how it would be, of course. I'd be thrown out on my ear—her face told me that. I felt the spite mounting in me, and I felt an urge to play a most caddish, swinish and utterly vulgar trick on her: I'd look at her with a sneer and as she stood there before me, I would bowl her over in a tone of voice that only a cheap shopkeeper could use, and say:

" 'You mean the four thousand! Why, I was speaking in jest, really! You couldn't have been so credulous, could you! I'd be most willing to let you have a couple of hundred, but four thousand! That's not a sum to be flung away on such folly. You've gone to all this trouble for nothing, I'm afraid.'

"But I would have lost out, of course: she would have run off, but it would have been so infernally vengeful and made all the rest worthwhile, while I knew I'd howl with remorse the rest of my life, but I felt I had to go through with it all! Believe me, that kind of thing had never happened to me with any woman: I mean looking with hatred at a woman at such a moment. But I swear to you that I glared at her with utter hatred for a full three or five seconds—a hatred that is a hair's breadth removed from the maddest love! I went to the window and pressed my brow to the ice-covered pane; I remembered that the ice seemed to burn my forehead like a flame. I didn't detain her for long— don't worry. I turned round, went to the desk, opened a drawer and took out an unendorsed letter of credit carrying 5 per cent interest, to the value of five thousand roubles (it was lying in my French dictionary). I showed it to her in silence, folded it and handed it over to her, myself opened the door into the passageway, stepped back a pace, made a low and most respectful and impressive bow—you may believe me! She gave a violent start, gazed at me for a second, turned terribly pale— well, as white as a sheet, and then suddenly, without a word, not impulsively but very gently, as it were, she bowed low and went down at my feet, her brow touching the floor—not the kind of curtsey you'd expect from a girl from a finishing school but in the old Russian tradition! Then she sprang to her feet and ran off. I was wearing my sword when she ran away; I drew it, wishing to fall upon it, I don't know why—damn silly, of course, but it must have been at a moment of uplift. You must realise that one can kill oneself at such a moment. However, I did not kill myself, but only kissed the sword and sheathed it—something I should not have mentioned perhaps. I even can't help thinking that I have somewhat spun out the story of the strife within me so as to pat myself on the back. Well, let it be as it is, and to the devil with all this prying into the human heart! So much for the 'incident' with Katerina Ivanovna. So now only brother Ivan and you are in the know—and nobody else!"

Dmitri Fyodorovich rose to his feet, took a step or two in agitation, produced a handkerchief, mopped his brow, and then sat down again, only not where he had been before but on the bench opposite, at the other wall, so that Alyosha had to turn round to be facing him.

5.

An Ardent Heart's Confession, "Heels Uppermost"

"Now, I know the first half of the matter," said Alyosha.

"You understand the first half: it was a drama, and took place over there. The second half is a tragedy, and will take place here."

"I still don't understand anything of the second part," said Alyosha.

"What about me? D'you think I do?"

"Just a moment, Dmitri; here's a crucial question: tell me, are you still her fiancé?"

"I became engaged to her, not right away but only three months after that happening. The very next day it all took place, I said to myself that the matter was ended and done with, without any sequel. I considered it despicable to propose to her after that. For her part, she never communicated with me for the rest of the six weeks she stayed on in our town. With a single exception though. On the day after her visit, their maid slipped into my quarters and, without a word, handed an envelope to me. It was addressed to so-and-so. I tore it open, and found in it the change from the letter of credit for the five thousand roubles. She had needed only four thousand five hundred, but there had been a loss of two hundred odd roubles when it was cashed. She returned about two hundred and sixty roubles I think; I don't remember exactly. Besides the money, there was nothing in the envelope, no note, no word, no explanation. I looked for some pencil mark on the envelope, but there was n-nothing! So I went on a spree on the remainder of the money, so that the new major had to reprimand me in the end. Well, the lieutenant-colonel turned in the battalion funds with no delay and to everybody's surprise, because nobody thought the money was intact. Scarcely had he done so when he fell ill, took to his bed, where he spent some three weeks. Softening of the brain set in suddenly, and he died five days later. He was buried with military honours for he had not yet retired from the service. Some ten days after his funeral, Katerina Ivanovna, her sister and her aunt set out for Moscow. Just before they left, in fact on the very day of their departure (I had not seen them and did not see them off), I received a tiny note on fine blue paper, with a single pencilled line: 'I'll write to you. Wait. K.' That was all.

"I'll explain things to you very briefly. In Moscow their fortunes changed at lightning speed and the unexpectedness of a tale from the Arabian Nights. The relative, the general's widow, suddenly lost two nieces who were her next of kin and heiresses; they both died of smallpox in a single week. The grief-stricken old lady welcomed Katerina Ivanovna as though she were her own daughter, her star of salvation; she clung to her and had her will changed at once in her favour. But that was all to come; for the time being, she gave her a dowry of eighty thousand roubles to be used as she thought fit. She was an hysterical woman. I saw something of her later in Moscow. Well, I suddenly received a remittance of four thousand five hundred roubles. Of course, I was completely at a loss and struck dumb with amazement. The promised letter arrived three days later. I have it with me now; it's always with me, and will be till my dying day. I'll show it to you if you wish, you simply must read it: she offered herself to me as my fiancée, did so herself. 'I love you to distraction,' she wrote. 'What if you don't love—it makes no difference; only be my husband. Have no fear; I shan't hamper you in any way: I'll be like a piece of your furniture, the carpet you walk on— I want to love you for ever; I want to save you from yourself'— I'm unworthy, Alyosha, to even retell those lines in my vulgar words and my detestable tone of voice, my invariably detestable tone of voice, which I've never been able to cast off! The letter stabbed me to the heart, even as it does to-day. D'you think I find things easy now? Do I feel at ease today? I wrote in reply at once (I was unable to go to Moscow at the moment). I wrote that reply with my tears, but there's only one thing I shall always feel ashamed of: I mentioned that she was now wealthy and with a dowry, while I was merely an ignorant churl—I spoke of the difference the money had made. I should have borne that in silence but it somehow slipped off the nib. I at once wrote to Ivan in Moscow and, in the letter, I explained everything as best I could—on six pages of writing—and I sent Ivan to her. Why are you looking at me like that? All right, so Ivan fell in love with her and is still in love with her! I know that, in your opinion, in the opinion of the world, I acted foolishly but perhaps it is that foolish act that will now save us all! Oh, can't you see how highly she thinks of him, and what esteem she holds him in? When she compares the two of us, can she possibly love a man like me, especially after everything that took place here?"

"But I'm sure she loves a man like you, and not a man like him."

"It is her own virtue she loves, and not me," Dmitri Fyodorovich ejaculated involuntarily and almost spitefully. He laughed, but at the next moment his eyes flashed, he turned red and struck the table emphatically with a fist.

"I swear, Alyosha," he exclaimed in intense and sincere anger at himself, "believe me or not, but as surely as God is holy, and Christ is the Lord, I swear that though I only just now scoffed at her finer feelings, I know I'm a million times more shoddy in spirit than she is, and that those finer feelings of her are as sincere as a heavenly angel's! The tragedy of it is that I know it for certain. What's wrong in a fellow being just a little rhetorical? Aren't I doing just that? But I'm speaking in earnest, in dead earnest. As for Ivan, I can understand how he must be cursing nature now—he with a mind like his! Who has been preferred? A blackguard who, even here, when he's already engaged and the cynosure of all eyes, has been unable to curb his vile urges—and that in the sight of his fiancée, his own fiancée! And such a man as I am has been preferred, while he's been rejected. And why? Because a girl wishes to violate her life and her future out of a sense of gratitude! How absurd! Mind you, I've never said a word to Ivan in this connection. Neither has Ivan ever breathed a word to me about it, not even the slightest hint; but fate will judge aright, and the worthy man will win out, while he who is unworthy will vanish for good into his back alley—his squalid back alley, the place he loves so well and is at home in. There, amidst the mud and stench, he'll joyfully perish of his own free will and choice. My speech has been all rambling and my words are withered and sere as though uttered quite at random, but my mind is made up. I'll go under in my back alley, and she'll marry Ivan."

"Just a moment, Mitya," Alyosha again broke in with great disquiet. "There's one thing you haven't made clear to me yet: you're still engaged to her, aren't you? Aren't you? How can you break it off if she, your fiancée, doesn't want to?"

"Yes, I'm formally and solemnly engaged to her. It all took place when I came to Moscow, with the proper ceremony, complete with icons, and in grand style. The general's widow gave us her blessing and—would you believe it?—even congratulated Katya: 'Your's is a good choice,' she said, 'I can see him through and through.' And imagine, she took a dislike to Ivan, and had no words of congratulation for him. In Moscow I had a long talk with Katya, telling her all about myself, in all honesty, exactitude and sincerity. She listened to everything I had to say.

There was bashfulness so sweet,
And words of tenderness—

"Well, there were proud words, too. It was then that she extracted from me a solemn promise to reform. I gave it, and now—"

"And now what?

"And now I've called you and dragged you over here, on this very day—remember the date!—with the purpose of sending you, again on this very day, to Katerina Ivanovna, and—"

"What?"

"To tell her that I shall never come to see her again, and that I sent you to say good-bye for me."

"But can that be possible?"

"Why, it's just because that's impossible that I'm sending you in my stead, for how can I tell her that myself?"

"But where will you be going?"

"Into the back alley."

"So it'll be to Grushenka after all!" Alyosha exclaimed sorrowfully, throwing up his hands. "So Rakitin has really been speaking the truth? I thought you'd been to see her several times, and that was all."

"Can a fiancé make such calls? Can that be possible when I'm betrothed to such a girl and stand in full view of the crowd? I still have some sense of honour left. The moment I began to call on Grushenka, I ceased from being a fiancé and an honest man—I realise that. Why are you looking at me like that? You see, I first went to her place with the intention of giving her a drubbing. That was because I had learnt and now know for a fact that Father's agent, that captain, had handed my promissory note over to Grushenka, for her to get the money from me, the purpose being to stop me from pestering Father. They were out to scare me. So I went there to thrash her. I had had some glimpses of her before. She does not catch the eye. I knew about her old merchant, who's ill and bedridden now, but will leave her a handsome sum. I also knew that she likes to make money and does so by lending it out at exorbitant interest—she's merciless, a shyster and full of tricks. I'd come to give her a thrashing but I stayed on with her. The thunderstorm broke, the blow fell, and I was floored. I still am, and know I'm done for, and there's no other road for me. The circuit of time

155

is complete. That's my present condition. It so happened at the time that I, a pauper, suddenly had three thousand in my possession. I took Grushenka to Mokroye, a place some twenty-five versts from here, where I got hold of some Gypsy dancers and singers, and lots of champagne. I spent my thousands on getting all the folk drunk there—the men and the women. Three days later I was stripped bare, but felt on top of the world. D'you think that got me anywhere? She never gave me a chance. It's her being so curvaceous that really got me, I tell you. That spitfire of a Grushenka has a curve on her body, which reaches right down to her foot, even to the little toe of her left foot. I saw it and even kissed it, but that was as far as I got—I swear it! 'I'll marry you if you wish,' she said to me, 'after all, you're as poor as poor can be. Promise not to beat me, but to let me do whatever I feel like doing, and then I may marry you,' she continued laughingly, and she's laughing still!"

Dmitri Fyodorovich rose from his seat almost with a kind of fury, seeming all at once to be quite drunk. His eyes were suddenly bloodshot.

"Do you really want to marry her?"

"I'll marry her like a shot if she'll take me; if not, I'll stay on even as a menial, to sweep her yard. Look here, Alyosha—" he cried, stopping short in front of his brother and, grabbing him by a shoulder, he began suddenly to shake him violently, "Do you realise, you innocent boy, that this is all something crazy, out of this world, for there's tragedy in it! I want you to know, Alexei, that I may be a base man with low and degrading passions, but Dmitri Karamazov can never become a thief or a pickpocket, or a filcher! Yet you should now learn that I've become a thief—a pickpocket and sneak thief! The very morning I set out to deal with Grushenka, Katerina Ivanovna sent for me and, telling me to keep it a dead secret from everybody (I don't know why, but there must have been a reason), asked me to go to the gubernia central town and send three thousand roubles by post to Agafya Ivanovna in Moscow; the money was to be sent off from there so that nobody in our town should have any inkling of the matter. Well, it was with the three thousand in my pocket that I found myself at Grushenka's, and it was on

156

that money that we went to Mokroye. Afterwards I pretended to have hastened off to town but I did not give her the post-office receipt, telling her that the money had been sent and that I'd let her have the receipt but I haven't done so till now—it has simply escaped my memory, in a way. What d'you think may happen now? Supposing you call on her today and say to her, 'He's sent me to say good-bye to you for him', and she asks you, 'What about the money?' You might as well say to her, 'He's a low rake, a vile creature, saddled with unbridled passions. He didn't send off your money but squandered it because he couldn't curb himself, just like a beast'; yet you could add, 'He is no thief though, for here's your three thousand which he is returning to you; send it to Agafya Ivanovna yourself. He's asked me to say good-bye to you for him.' And now, she has only to ask, 'Where's the money?' "

"Mitya, you're in a fix, indeed, but not as much as you think; don't sink into despair, don't!"

"D'you really think I'll shoot myself if I don't get the three thousand to pay back! I'll do nothing of the kind—that's the trouble. I can't bring myself to do that now, but perhaps I'll do it later. And now I'm off to Grushenka—my goose is cooked!"

"And what will you do there?"

"I'll be her husband; I may have that honour, and if her lover calls, I'll just go into the next room. I'll clean her young men's galoshes for them, get the samovar going, and run the errands—"

"Katerina Ivanovna will understand everything," Alyosha suddenly proclaimed. "She'll understand the depth of all this misfortune and make it up with you. She has a lofty mind: she'll see for herself that your unhappiness is boundless."

"She won't be reconciled to it all," said Dmitri with a grin. "You see, there are things no woman can tolerate. D'you know what the best thing to do is?"

"What is it?"

"Return the three thousand."

"Where can it be obtained? Look here, I've got two thousand, and Ivan will give another thousand—that makes three. Take the money and pay it back."

"But when will your three thousand arrive? Besides, you're not of age yet, and it's essential, absolutely essential that you should bid farewell for me this very day, with or without the money, for I can't carry on any longer—I've reached that point. Tomorrow will be too late, too late. I'll send you to Father."

"To Father?"

"Yes, to him before you go to her. Ask him for the three thousand."

"But, Mitya, he won't let you have it."

"As though he would! I'm sure he won't. D'you know the meaning of despair, Alexei?"

"I do."

"Listen: legally speaking, he owes me nothing. I've received my share already—all of it, I know. But morally, he owes me something—does he or doesn't he? After all, he started with Mother's twenty-eight thousand, and turned it into a hundred thousand. Let him give me only three thousand out of that twenty-eight, only three, and he'll bring up my life from the pit and many sins shall be forgiven him for it! For the three thousand, I'll close the matter—I give you my solemn promise, and he won't ever hear anything more about me. I'm giving him his last chance to be a father. Tell him that the chance is being sent to him by God Himself."

"Mitya, he won't do it for anything."

"I know he won't, I know it for certain. Especially now. Moreover, there's something else I know: it was only some days ago, perhaps only yesterday, that he first learnt *for sure* (mark that: for sure!) that Grushenka may indeed not be joking and means to get hitched with me. He knows the kind of woman she is—he knows that moll. Do you expect him to let me have the money in addition, and so help to get us hitched when he's crazy about her himself? But that's not all. I can tell you something more. I know that some five days ago he drew three thousand roubles from the bank in hundred-rouble notes and put them in a large envelope with five seals and tied crosswise with red tape. I know all the details, as you see! Written on the envelope are the words: 'To my angel Grushenka, should she wish to come'. He scrawled the words himself, furtively and in dead secrecy; nobody knows that he has the money except his servant Smerdyakov, whose honesty he trusts implicitly. So he's been expecting Grushenka during the last three or four days, hoping she'll come for the envelope. He's let her know it, and she's sent word she may turn up. Well, if she does come to the old man, I can't very well marry her, can I? You will now be understanding why I'm hiding in ambush here, and what I'm watching for!"

"For her?"

"Yes, for her. Foma, a local man who used to serve in my regiment, rents a cubicle from one of the landlady sluts here. He's a kind of servant and night watchman, and goes grouse-shooting in the daytime. That's how he makes a living. I've taken up my quarters at his place; neither he nor the mistresses of the house are in the know, that is to say that I'm keeping watch here."

"Is Smerdyakov the only one who knows?"

"He alone does, and he'll let me know if she comes to the old man."

"Was it he who told you of the envelope?"

"It was. It's a dead secret. Even Ivan knows nothing about the money, nothing at all. Father is sending him off to Chermashnya for two or three days: a prospective buyer has turned up, who's offering eight thousand for the stand of timber there, so the old man has been asking Ivan to help him by going there for two or three days to attend to the deal. He wants Ivan to be away when Grushenka comes."

"So he's expecting Grushenka today?"

"No, there are no signs she'll be coming today. She won't be coming!" Mitya exclaimed suddenly. "Smerdyakov thinks so too. Father's in his cups at the moment, sitting at table with brother Ivan. Go there, Alexei, and ask him for the three thousand—"

"Mitya, dear, what's the matter with you?" cried Alyosha, springing up and gazing at the frenzied Dmitri Fyodorovich. For a moment he thought the latter had gone out of his mind.

"Oh no, I'm not mad," said Dmitri Fyodorovich, gazing intently and even solemnly at his brother. "After all, I know why I'm sending you to Father and what I'm saying: I believe in a miracle."

"A miracle?"

"A miracle of Divine Providence. God knows my heart, and sees all my despair. He sees the whole situation. Surely He won't allow such a horrible thing to come about. Alyosha, I believe in a miracle. Go!"

"I shall. Tell me: will you wait for me here?"

"I will. I understand it won't be soon, and that you can't come barging in and springing the question. He's tipsy now. I shall wait for three hours, four, five, six, or seven, but remember that, this very day, even if it's midnight, you will call on Katerina Ivanovna, *with or without the money* and say to her, 'He's told me to say good-bye to you for him.' Use those very words: 'He's told me to bid you good-bye!' "

"Mitya! But what if Grushenka does come today—or, if not today, then tomorrow or the day after?"

"Grushenka? I'll be on the look-out, rush into the house and upset things—"

"But if—?"

"If there's an if, I'll commit a murder. I couldn't tolerate it."

"*Who will you murder?*"

"The old man. I shan't kill her."

"Mitya, what's this you're saying?"

"I don't know—I don't know— Perhaps I won't, and perhaps I will. I'm afraid he'll suddenly become hateful to me at that very moment, with that face of his. I hate his Adam's apple, that nose of his, those eyes, and his brazen snigger. I loathe the sight of him. That's what I'm afraid of. It may be too much for me to withstand—"

"I'll be off, Mitya. I hope God will order things as He knows best, so that nothing horrible will happen—"

"And I'll stay on and wait for a miracle to take place. But if it doesn't—"

Alyosha, deep in thought made for his father's house.

6.

Smerdyakov

Alyosha did in fact find his father still at table. As usual, the table was laid in the drawing-room, though there was a dining-room in the house. The drawing-room, the most spacious in the house, was furnished with a kind of outdated ostentation. The furniture, white and extremely old, was covered with silken upholstery of faded red, and in the piers stood mirrors in carved white-and-gilt frames of old-fashioned and pretentiously fanciful workmanship. On the white-papered walls, which were cracked in places, two large portraits, met the eye: one of some prince who had been governor-general of the province some thirty years previously, and another of a prelate, also long dead. In the right-hand corner hung several icons, before which an icon-lamp was lit at night, not so much out of piety as to provide some light. Fyodor Pavlovich went to bed very late, at three or four in the morning; before doing so, he would pace the room, or sit in an arm-chair, sunk in thought. It was a habit he had developed. He usually slept quite alone in the house sending his servants to their own quarters, but his servant Smerdyakov would often stay behind for the night, sleeping on a long chest in the ante-chamber. Dinner was over when Alyosha came in, but coffee and the sweet had been served; Fyodor Pavlovich liked to have something sweet with his brandy after dinner. Ivan, too, was at the table, sipping his coffee. The servants Grigori and Smerdyakov were in attendance. Masters and servants obviously seemed in extraordinarily high spirits. Fyodor Pavlovich was roaring with laughter; from the hall Alyosha could hear his long-familiar squeaky laugh and could at once tell from its sound that his father was far from drunk, but, for the time being, merely elevated.

"Here he comes! Here he comes!" Fyodor Pavlovich screeched in sudden high delight. "Join us and sit down here! Have some coffee; it's lenten fare but lovely and hot! I won't offer you brandy because you're an abstainer—but perhaps you'd like some? No, I'd better let you have some liqueur—we

161

have some excellent stuff! Smerdyakov, go and fetch it from the cupboard, the second shelf on the right. Here are the keys. Look sharp about it!"

Alyosha protested—he didn't want any liqueur.

"It'll be served all the same, if not for you, then for us," Fyodor Pavlovich said beamingly. "But stay—have you had dinner?"

"I have," said Alyosha, who had in fact had only a slice of bread and a glass of kvass in the Father Superior's kitchen. "But I would like some hot coffee."

"Capital, my dear boy! Coffee he shall have. Shall I have it warmed up? No, it's still boiling. It's first-class coffee, made by Smerdyakov. He's an artist when it comes to coffee and fish or meat pies, yes and fish-soup, too. You must come one day and sample some of it. Let me know in advance—but just a moment! Didn't I tell you to come back home this very day, with your mattress and pillows? You've brought the mattress, haven't you? He-he-he!"

"No, I haven't," Alyosha replied, grinning too.

"Oh, but I did give you a fright, didn't I? My dear boy, could I do anything to offend you? Of course, not! D'you know, Ivan, I can't have him look me in the eye like that, and just laugh! I simply can't! When he does that, I start laughing in my innards! I just love that boy! Alyosha, I want to give you my parental blessing."

Alyosha rose to his feet, but Fyodor Pavlovich had already changed his mind.

"No, no, I'll make the sign of the cross over you for the time being, so sit down. Well, I have a treat in store for you, something up your street. You'll enjoy it. Balaam's ass has begun speaking here, and what things he says!"

It emerged that the reference was to the servant Smerdyakov. A young man of twenty-four, he was very tight-lipped and kept himself very much to himself. It was not that he was shy or shamefaced; on the contrary, he was supercilious by nature, and seemed to look down his nose at others. It is now high time for a few words to be said about him. He had been brought up by Marfa Ignatievna and Grigori Vassilievich, but the boy had grown "without the least gratitude", as Grigori once put it; he was morose and looked upon the world with furtive suspicion. In his boyhood he had been given to hanging cats and burying them ceremoniously, dressing up in a bedsheet for the purpose, as a kind of surplice, and chanting and swinging something over the dead cat to serve as a censer. All this had been done on the sly, in the greatest secrecy. Grigori had once caught him at this exercise and given him a sound thrashing, which had made the boy shrink into a corner and sulk there for a week. "The wretch doesn't care the least for either of us," Grigori said to Marfa Ignatievna, "or for anyone else, for that matter. Are you at all human?" he went on, suddenly addressing the boy. "No, you're not. You were spawned by the mould in the bath-house—that's what you were." As later emerged, Smerdyakov never forgave him those words. It was Grigori who taught him to read and write and, when the boy turned twelve, began to teach him the Scriptures. It all came to naught almost immediately. At the second or third lesson, a sudden grin appeared on the boy's face.

"What's the matter?" Grigori asked, looking at him severely from under his spectacles.

"Oh, nothing much. If God created light on the first day, and the sun, the moon and the stars on the fourth day, where did light shine from on the first day?"

This simply flabbergasted Grigori, the boy meanwhile eyeing him with a sneer. There was something even supercilious in the glance. Grigori lost all self-control. "I'll show you where from!" he cried, slapping his pupil's face in his fury. The boy took the blow in silence, but again retreated into his corner for several days. It so happened, a week later, that he had his first fit of the falling sickness, a disease that never left him till the end of his days. On learning of this, Fyodor Pavlovich at once seemed to change his attitude towards the boy. Until then he had regarded him with some indifference, though he had never scolded him and always gave him a copeck whenever he met him. If he was in a good humour, he would send the boy something sweet from his table. But, on learning of Smerdyakov's illness, he began to display concern in him: he had a doctor called in to see what could be done, but the illness proved incurable. The fits occurred, on the average, about once a month and at varying intervals. They also differed in violence, some being light, others extremely severe. Fyodor Pavlovich gave the strictest orders to Grigori that he was never to punish the boy corporally, and began allowing him to come upstairs to see him. He also forbade teaching him anything for the time being. One day, when the boy was about fifteen, Fyodor Pavlovich saw him lingering at the bookcase and reading the titles through the glass door. Fyodor Pavlovich had quite a number of books, a hundred odd volumes actually, but he had never been seen reading any of them. He at once gave Smerdyakov the key to the bookcase. "Do some reading. Better be the librarian than gad about the courtyard. Sit down at these books. Here, read this one," he added, taking off the shelf Gogol's *Evenings on a Grange Near Dikanka*.

It did not prove to his liking. He read it without as much as smiling, and finished it with a frown on his face.

"Well, didn't you find it funny?" Fyodor Pavlovich asked.

Smerdyakov made no reply.

"Answer me, you fool!"

"It describes things that are untrue," Smerdyakov mumbled, grinning.

"Be off with you; you have the soul of a lackey. Stay, here's Smaragdov's *World History*. It contains nothing but the truth. Read it."

But Smerdyakov could not get through even ten pages, finding the book dull. So the bookcase was again locked. Shortly afterwards, Marfa and Grigori informed Fyodor Pavlovich that Smerdyakov had suddenly begun to display signs of an extraordinary squeamishness in his food: before beginning his soup, he would bend over his plate, fiddle about in it with his spoon in search of something, and taking a spoonful as a sample, hold the spoon up to the light.

"What's that—a cockroach?" Grigori would ask.

"A fly, perhaps," Marfa would remark.

The squeamish youth never answered, but acted in the same way with his bread, meat or whatever he was given to eat: he would hold up a piece on his fork, examine it as through a microscope and, after lengthy consideration, despatch it into his mouth. "What airs he gives himself!" Grigori would mutter, as he looked at him. On learning of this new trait in Smerdyakov, Fyodor Pavlovich decided he should be trained as a cook and, to that end, sent him off to Moscow where his apprenticeship lasted several years. He returned greatly changed in appearance. He had suddenly become extremely old-looking for his age, prematurely wrinkled and pasty-complexioned, even resembling a eunuch. In the moral sense he had changed but little since he had set off for Moscow: he was just as unsociable and felt not the slightest need for the company of others. He had not been given to speech in Moscow either, as we later learnt; he had shown extremely little interest in that city, learning just a little about it and paying no heed at all to the rest. He had been to the theatre on one occasion, whence he had returned silent and displeased. On the other hand, he returned home in good attire, a well-brushed frock-coat and spotless linen, keeping his costume spick and span by brushing it thoroughly twice a day, and he liked to black his smart box-calf top-boots with a special brand of English boot polish and then give them the finishing touches until they had a mirror-like gloss. He proved an excellent cook. Fyodor Pavlovich paid him a regular wage, which Smerdyakov spent almost entirely on clothing, pomades, scents and the like. He seemed to hold the female sex in the same contempt as the male, conducting himself with them with a cold dignity and almost aloofness. Fyodor Pavlovich now saw him in a somewhat different light, the reason being that his fits of epilepsy were becoming more frequent. When that took place, the meals were cooked by Marfa Ignatievna, which did not suit Fyodor Pavlovich at all.

"Why is it your fits have become more frequent?" he would sometimes ask, looking askance at his new cook. "You should get married. I'll find you a wife if you wish."

Such words would only make Smerdyakov turn pale with vexation but he would say nothing in reply, after which Fyodor Pavlovich would leave him alone, realising that he was past hope. What was really important was that his honesty could be fully relied on and that he would never take or steal anything. It so happened on one occasion that, when he was quite tipsy, Fyodor Pavlovich dropped in the mud three hundred-rouble bank-notes he had just received, while he was crossing his own courtyard. He missed the money only on the following day; he had scarcely begun to go through his pockets when he suddenly saw three bank-notes lying on the table. How had they got there? Smerdyakov had picked them up and brought them the day before. "I've never seen the likes of you, I must say," Fyodor Pavlovich said, giving him ten roubles in reward. It should be added that he was not only certain of Smerdyakov's honesty, but even had a liking for him for some reason, though the young man regarded him with the same scowling moroseness as he did the rest of the world, and was always silent. If he ever spoke, it was very rarely indeed. Had it ever occurred to anybody at the time to ask himself, as he looked at Smerdyakov, what interests the latter had, and what was in his mind, it would really have been impossible to tell just by looking at him. Yet it would sometimes happen that he would come to a standstill in the house, or in the yard or the street, wrapped in thought, and remain thus for as long as ten minutes or so. A physiognomist who happened to study his face at close quarters would have said that it expressed neither thought nor reflection, but simply a kind of contemplation. The artist Kramskoi has painted a remarkable canvas entitled *The Contemplator*, which depicts a winter forest scene: on the roadway, clad in a shabby caftan and bast-shoes, stands a solitary muzhik, who seems to have strayed there quite by chance. He looks deep in thought but he is not thinking but *contemplating*. Were he to be nudged he would start and look at you in bewilderment, as though awakened from slumber. True, he would come to himself at once, but, if asked to say what he was thinking of while standing there, he would probably be unable to recall anything. Yet he would most certainly keep hidden within himself the impression he was under while he was deep in contemplation. He holds such impressions dear and they no doubt accumulate within him without his being aware of them; neither does he not know, of course, why and for what purpose he does so. Perhaps, the accumulation of such impressions over many years will suddenly make him abandon everything and set out on wanderings towards Jerusalem in search of salvation; but then, he may suddenly set his native village ablaze, or perhaps he may do both things. There are many such "contemplators" among the common people. Smerdyakov must have been one of them and amassed his impressions with eagerness, hardly realising the reason why.

7.

The Disputation

But Balaam's ass did suddenly begin to speak, and on a strange subject. While making his morning purchases at the merchant Lukianov's shop, Grigori had heard from him the story of a Russian soldier who had been serving at some distant border post and made prisoner by some   Asiatics. Threatened with immediate and cruel death if he did not abjure his Christian faith and embrace Islam, he refused to deny his religion and was flayed alive, dying the death of a martyr and praising and glorifying Christ. The exploit had been reported in a newspaper received that very morning. Grigori had spoken of it while waiting at table. As was his wont, Fyodor Pavlovich enjoyed joking and engaging in small talk over the dessert after dinner, if only with Grigori. He was in a mellow and expansive humour this time. Sipping his brandy and listening to the story, he remarked that such a soldier deserved to be canonised at once and that his flayed skin should be sent to some monastery: "It would attract crowds and lots of money." Grigori frowned his displeasure at this light-hearted treatment of the matter and his master's habitual impiety. A sudden grin appeared on the face of Smerdyakov, who was standing at the door. He had often been allowed to wait at table, though only towards the end of dinner. But after Ivan Fyodorovich's arrival he had begun to do so of his own free will every day.

"What are you grinning at?" asked Fyodor Pavlovich, at once intercepting the grin and of course realising that it was meant for Grigori.

"You see, sir," Smerdyakov suddenly and unexpectedly began in a loud voice, "even if that praiseworthy soldier's exploit was so very great, I think it would be no sin if, in a fix like that, he were to deny the name of Christ and his own baptism, so as to preserve his own life for good works, so that he could through the years atone for his faint-heartedness."

"What d'you mean by no sin? Rubbish! That will land you right in Hell, where you'll roast like mutton," Fyodor Pavlovich went on.

It was at this juncture that Alyosha came in, to Fyodor Pavlovich's great delight, as we have seen.

"That's something up your street—up your street!" he tittered gleefully, making Alyosha sit down and listen.

"That can't be so about the mutton, sir, and nothing will happen there for such things, and there oughtn't to be either, in all fairness," Smerdyakov observed importantly.

"What d'you mean: in all fairness?" Fyodor Pavlovich exclaimed even more gleefully, jogging Alyosha with his knee.

"He's a scamp, that's what he is!" cried Grigori, looking Smerdyakov wrathfully in the eye.

"Don't be in such haste to call me a scamp, Grigori Vassilievich," Smerdyakov objected with perfect composure, "and rather give the matter better thought: once I've been captured by tormentors of Christians, who demand that I should curse God's name and renounce holy baptism, my own reasoning entitles me to do so, since there's nothing sinful in that."

"You've said that already! Prove it, and don't beat about the bush!" Fyodor Pavlovich roared.

"Broth-cook!" Grigori muttered contemptuously under his breath.

"Don't be in such haste to call me a broth-cook either, and, without using hard words, give the matter better thought again, Grigori Vassilievich. For at the moment I say to my tormentors, 'No, I'm no Christian and curse my true God', I at once become anathema by Divine and special judgement and am completely cut off from the Holy Church as though I were a heathen, not only after I've said those words but even when I think of saying them, so that I'm excommunicated even before a quarter of a second has passed. Is that so, Grigori Vassilievich, or isn't it?"

He addressed Grigori with obvious satisfaction, though he was actually replying to Fyodor Pavlovich's questions; he was well aware of that, but deliberately pretended that the questions had been put by Grigori.

"Ivan," Fyodor Pavlovich suddenly exclaimed, "bend down and give me your ear. It's for your benefit he's staging all this, because he wants you to praise him. Do so."

Ivan Fyodorovich gave his father's excited communication his utmost attention.

"Stay, Smerdyakov, hold your tongue for a while," Fyodor Pavlovich again exclaimed. "Ivan, give me your ear again."

Again Ivan Fyodorovich bent down with grave attention.

"I love you as much as I do Alyosha. Don't think I don't love you. Would you like some brandy?"

"I would," Ivan Fyodorovich replied. "You seem quite well primed," he thought to himself, giving his father an intent look. He had been watching Smerdyakov with extreme curiosity.

"Anathema! You're accursed, as it is!" Grigori burst out. "How dare you carry on this argument, you rascal, if—"

"Hold your tongue, Grigori, hold your tongue!" said Fyodor Pavlovich, cutting him short.

"Hold on, Grigori Vassilievich, for just a moment, and listen to what I've got to say, for I'm not through yet. You see, at the very moment I'm accursed by God, at that supreme moment I've already become what amounts to a heathen, and my baptism is cancelled and imposes no duty on me—isn't that so?"

"Wind up, my lad, and make it snappy," said Fyodor Pavlovich, sipping his brandy with relish.

"And if I'm no longer a Christian, I haven't lied to my tormentors when asked, 'Are you a Christian or not?', since God Himself has stripped me of Christianity by virtue of my very intent, even before I've said a word to my enemies. Since I've been cast out, then on what grounds and with what justice can I be called to book as a Christian, in the world to come, for having denied Christ, when, through that thought alone, even before that denial, my baptism has become null and void? If I'm no longer a Christian, I can't deny Christ, for there's nothing for me to deny. Who will hold a heathen Tartar responsible, Grigori Vassilievich, even in heaven, for not having been born a Christian? Who'll think of punishing him for that, arguing that you can't flay an ox of two hides! Even the Almighty, should he call that Tartar to account on his death, will let him off with the lightest punishment (for some punishment he must be given) on the grounds that he's not to blame for having been brought into the world a heathen, and born of heathen parents. The Lord can't forcibly take that Tartar and say he also was a Christian, can he? That would mean the Almighty was telling a lie. And can the Lord, the Almighty Ruler, of heaven and earth, tell a lie, even in a single word?"

The dumbfounded Grigori stared at the speaker with goggling eyes. Though he did not quite understand what was being said, he did make out the drift of all that hotch-potch of nonsense, and stood stock-still like one who has suddenly run his head into a wall. Emptying his glass, Fyodor Pavlovich burst into shrill laughter.

"What do you say to that, Alyosha? What a casuist he is! He must have been with the Jesuits, Ivan. Well, you evil-smelling Jesuit, who has been giving you learned instruction? But you're talking nonsense, you casuist, sheer, utter and arrant nonsense! Dry your tears, Grigori, we won't leave him a leg to stand on, this very minute. Now tell me this, you Balaam's ass: even if you are right in respect of your tormentors, yet you've renounced your faith in your own heart, and become anathema; that's something you won't be patted on the head in hell for. What will you say to that, my excellent Jesuit?"

"Of course, I've denied my faith in my own heart—there's no doubt on that score, sir. Yet there's no particular sin in that, and even if there has been a sin, it's of the most ordinary kind, if I may say so."

"What d'you mean: of the most ordinary kind?"

"You're an accursed liar," Grigori hissed.

"Give the matter some thought, Grigori Vassilievich," Smerdyakov continued in a staid and unruffled tone, aware of his victory but putting on a show of magnanimity to a vanquished foe. "Give the matter some thought. Is it not said in

Holy Writ that if you have faith as a grain of mustard seed and say to this mountain that it should be removed and cast into the sea it will do so at once, without delay, at your first bidding? And so, Grigori Vassilievich, if I'm without faith and you have so much that you keep on rebuking me, why don't you try and tell this mountain to be cast, no, not into the sea (for it's so far off) but at least into our stinking little stream, the one which runs at the bottom of our garden; you will at that moment see for yourself that nothing will move and everything will remain just where it is, no matter how you shout at it. And that means, Grigori Vassilievich, that you lack proper faith, but keep on abusing others for lacking it. Again, as no one in our times—not you alone, but absolutely no one at all, from the highest persons down to the humblest muzhik—can cast mountains into the sea, with the possible exception of one man in the whole world, two at most, engaged in seeking salvation in solitude somewhere in the Egyptian wilderness, so that they can't be found at all—then, if that is so and all the rest seem to have no faith, can it be that all the rest—all the inhabitants of the whole world, except those two anchorites, will be cursed by God? Will He, in His well-known mercy, forgive none of them? Therefore, I hope and believe that, though I have doubted, I shall be forgiven when I shed tears of repentance."

"Hold on!" Fyodor Pavlovich screeched in a transport of delight. "So you think that there do exist two men who can move mountains, eh! Mark that, Ivan, and record it: there you have the Russian all over, as large as life!"

"You're absolutely right when you call that a feature of the people's faith," Ivan Fyodorovich agreed with a smile of approval.

"So you do agree! If that is so, then it must be true! It's true, Alyosha, isn't it? That's exactly what Russian faith is like, isn't it?"

"No, Smerdyakov's faith is not Russian at all," said Alyosha in a grave and firm voice.

"It isn't his faith I'm referring to, but this particular feature—those two hermits, and nothing but that trait. It's quite Russian, isn't it?"

"Oh, yes," Alyosha smiled, "it's quite Russian."

"Your words have won you a ten-rouble gold coin, you Balaam's ass, and I'll let you have it this very day. As for the rest, it's all stuff and nonsense, sheer stuff and nonsense. You should realise, you dolt, that nothing but thoughtlessness is the reason for our lack of faith, because we're always in a hurry: in the first place, our affairs keep us too busy; in the second, the Lord hasn't provided us with enough time—only twenty-four hours in the day, so we don't get enough sleep, let alone find time for repentance. But you renounced your faith in the face of your tormentors when you had nothing else but your faith to think of, and you should have shown your faith! That adds up to sin, I believe, doesn't it?"

"It does, indeed, but just consider, Grigori Vassilievich, it is just that which makes things easier. You see, if I believed in God's truth as I should have, it would really have been a sin for me not to agree to torment for my faith and to embrace the heathen religion of Mahomet. But then there would have been no torment in store for me, for all I would have had to do would have been to say to the mountain: move and crush my tormentor, and it would have moved at that very instant and crushed him as if he were a cockroach, and I would have gone off unscathed, praising and glorifying the Lord. But had I tried it all out at that instant and called upon the mountain to crush my tormentors and it didn't do so, how could I have helped feeling doubt at the time and at such a fearful hour of mortal terror? I know even as it is that I shall never enter the kingdom of Heaven in full (for since the mountain did not move at my command, that means that my faith is not thought highly of up there and no particular reward awaits me in the world to come) so why should I let myself be flayed and all to no good purpose? For even had half the skin on my back been flayed off, the mountain would not have moved at my call or my cry. Why, at a moment like that, one can feel not only doubt but even go out of one's mind, so that it will become quite impossible to think straight. Consequently, how can I be held particularly to blame if I keep a whole skin, because I can see no prospect of advantage or reward either down here or up there?

Therefore, putting all trust in the Divine mercy, I harbour the hope that full forgiveness will be mine—"

8.

Over the Brandy

The argument came to an end but, strange as it may seem, Fyodor Pavlovich, who had been in such good spirits, began suddenly to frown. Pulling a long face, he gulped down some brandy, which was already a glass too much.

"And now get out of here, you Jesuits," he cried to the servants. "Off with you, Smerdyakov. I'll let you have the promised ten-rouble gold coin this very day, but now off with you! Wipe those tears of yours, Grigori; run along to Marfa. She'll comfort you and put you to bed. The rascals won't let us sit here in peace after dinner," he snarled in vexation when the servants had at once withdrawn at his command. "Smerdyakov has got into the habit of showing up at dinner," he added turning to Ivan Fyodorovich. "You've aroused his curiosity. What have you done to win his liking?"

"Nothing whatsoever," the latter replied. "For some reason, he's decided to think highly of me, that lackey and lout. Suitable human material, incidentally, when the time is ripe."

"Suitable in what sense?"

"There'll be others and better ones, but there'll also be the same kind. That kind will come first; the better ones will follow."

"And when will the time be ripe?"

"The signal rocket will start to burn, but may fizzle out. People are not given to listening to these broth-cooks."

"That may be so, but a Balaam's ass like him thinks and thinks, and the devil alone knows what all that thinking will lead to."

"To the amassing of ideas," said Ivan with a grin.

"You see, I know very well that he can't stand the sight of me any more than all the rest. He has just as little liking for you, though you may think he's decided 'to think highly of you'. All the more so, he has the same feeling for Alyosha, whom he simply despises. But he's not light-fingered, for one thing; he doesn't gossip either, keeps his mouth shut, doesn't engage in scandal, and makes excellent fish and meat pies into the bargain. But enough of him! Why should we dwell on him so?"

"Indeed. Why should we?"

"As for the ideas he may be hatching in his mind, I must say that, generally speaking, the Russian muzhik has to be birched. I've always said so. Our muzhiks are full of deceit and deserve no pity, so it's good that they sometimes get the birch even nowadays. The Russian land is strong because of its wealth of birch forests. If those are destroyed, it will spell the end of the Russian land. I'm all for the clever ones. We've stopped flogging the peasants because we've grown too clever, but they still go on flogging themselves. And a good thing too. For with the same measure that ye mete withal, it shall be measured to you again, or how does the passage run? In short, it shall be measured. But Russia is a pigsty. My dear fellow, if you only knew how much I hate Russia—well, not exactly Russia, but all these vices—but perhaps Russia too. *Tout cela c'est de la cochonnerie.* But d'you know what I do like? It's wit."

"You've just downed another glass. Shouldn't you stop?"

"Wait, I'll have one more, and then another, and I'll stop at that. Just a moment: you interrupted me. I was talking to an old man while passing through Mokroye, and he said to me, 'There's nothing we like more than sentencing wenches to be birched, and we always let the lads do the flogging. A lad will tomorrow marry the girl he has flogged today, so it quite suits the girls.' How do you like these Marquis de Sades? Whatever you may think of it, it has its points. Shouldn't we go along and get a view of it, eh? Are you actually blushing, Alyosha? There's nothing to be ashamed of, my child. What a pity I didn't stay for dinner at the Father Superior's and didn't tell the monks about the Mokroye girls! Don't be annoyed with me, Alyosha, for my having offended your Father Superior. There are things that rouse my choler. If God does exist, then I shall be held to

174

account, of course, and bear the consequences; if there's no God at all, then they should be shown up even more, your Fathers? In that case, cutting off their heads isn't enough, because they've held up progress. Believe me, Ivan, that idea chafes my sentiments. No, I can see from your eyes that you don't believe me. You agree with the others that I'm only a buffoon. Alyosha, do you believe that I'm nothing more than a buffoon?"

"I believe that you're not merely a buffoon."

"I believe that you believe me, and that you're speaking in all sincerity. Your glance is sincere and so are your words. With Ivan it's different. He's arrogant. Yet I would clamp down on your monastery. I'd make away with all that mysticism through-out the Russian land at one fell swoop, so as to bring all the dolts to their senses. And how much gold and silver the Mint would be getting!"

"But why make away with it?" Ivan asked.

"For the truth to shine forth in radiance, that's why."

"But if that truth does shine forth in radiance, you'll be the first to be stripped to start with and then—made away with."

"Bah, you may be right! Oh, what an ass I've made of my-self!" Fyodor Pavlovich exclaimed, slapping his forehead. "If that's so, let your monastery remain standing, Alyosha, and we, intelligent folk, will feel snug in our warm homes and sip our brandy. D'you know, Ivan, I suppose it's all been pur-posely pre-arranged that way by that very God? Now tell me, Ivan: is there a God, or not? Stay: speak with certitude, speak in dead earnest! Why are you laughing again?"

"It's that witty remark of yours that has made me laugh—about Smerdyakov's faith in the existence of those two ancients who could move mountains."

"Do I resemble him now?"

"Very much so."

"Well, that goes to show that I'm a Russian too, with that very Russian trait. And you, too, philosopher that you are, can be caught tripping over some trait of the same kind in you. I'll catch you, if you like, I'll wager I'll do that tomorrow. Yet you must tell me: is there a God, or not? Only speak in earnest! I want you to be serious about it."

"No, there's no God."

"Alyosha, is there a God?"

"There is a God."

"Ivan, does immortality exist, well, some kind of, just a teeny-weeny kind?"

"Neither is there any immortality."

"None at all?"

"None at all."

"That's to say, a most absolute nothingness? But perhaps there is a something. After all, that's better than nothing at all."

"Almost absolute nothingness, I say."

"Alyosha, does immortality exist?"

"It does."

"Both God and immortality?"

"Yes, both God and immortality. Immortality lies in God."

"H'm. Ivan's more probably right. Good Lord, only to think how much faith and drive man has wasted on that dream, for so many thousands of years! Who's been making mock of man? Ivan, now tell me once and for all: is there a God, or not? This is the last time I'm asking you!"

"I'm telling you for the last time that there isn't."

"Then who's making mock of man, Ivan?"

"The devil, I suppose," Ivan Fyodorovich replied with a wry smile.

"But does he exist?"

"No, there's no devil either."

"The more's the pity. The devil take it; what wouldn't I do with him who was the first to think up a God! Being hanged on an aspen-tree is less than he deserves."

"There would have been no civilisation at all if God hadn't been thought up."

"Wouldn't there? Without God, you mean to say?"

"There wouldn't. And no brandy either. I think I'll have to take the brandy away from you."

"Hold on, hold on, my dear boy, just another glass. I've hurt Alyosha's feelings. You're not resentful, are you, Alexei. My dear, dear little Alyosha!"

"Not at all. And I know what you think. Your heart is kinder than your mind."

"My heart kinder than my mind? Good Lord, and that coming from you? D'you love Alyosha, Ivan?"

"I do."

"Do love him. (Fyodor Pavlovich was getting very drunk.) Listen, Alyosha, I was rude to your *starets*, but I was all worked up. But there's a lot of wit in him, don't you think so, Ivan?"

"I suppose there is."

"Of course, there is, *il y a du Piron là-dedans*. He's a Jesuit, of the Russian brand, that is to say. As in a creature with a noble mind, there's a concealed indignation seething in him because he has to play a part—don the garb of holiness."

"But he does believe in God."

"Not one jot or tittle. Didn't you know that? Why, he says that to all and sundry, well, not exactly to them all, but to the intelligent kind who call on him. He actually said forthright to Governor Schulz: *'Credo*, but what in I don't know!'"

"Really?"

"He certainly did. But I have respect for him. There's something Mephistophelean about him, or, rather, something from *A Hero of Our Time*—Arbenin,* or whatever—You see, he's a lecher so much so that I'd fear for my daughter or my wife if they went to him for the confession. When he starts talking, you know— Well, the year before last he invited us to tea, with liqueurs thrown in (the good ladies keep him supplied with liqueurs). The way he set about describing the old days made us burst our sides with laughing—especially his story of how he cured a woman paralytic. 'If I didn't have bad legs, I'd perform a dance for you,' he said. What do you say to that, eh? 'I've had my share of pranks,' he said. He actually did merchant De- midov out of a cool sixty thousand."

"What do you mean? Did he steal the money?"

"Well, Demidov, who trusted in his honesty, brought him the

*Fyodor Pavlovich is confusing Pechorin, the main character in the poet Lermontov's prose classic *A Hero of Our Time* (1840), and Arbe- nin, who figures in his drama *The Masquerade* (1842).—*Tr.*

money for safe keeping. 'Take care of it, my friend. I'm expecting a police search tomorrow.' So he kept it very safe. 'It's your donation to the church,' he declared. 'You're a rascal,' I said to him. 'No,' he replied, 'I'm no rascal, but merely broad-minded—' Incidentally, it wasn't him at all—it was somebody else. I've got him mixed up with another man—quite unawares. I'll have another glass, and I'll call it a day: take the bottle away, Ivan. I've been drawing the long bow—why didn't you stop me, Ivan? You should have told me I was talking nonsense."

"I knew you'd stop of your own accord."

"That's not true. You acted out of spite—sheer spite. You look down on me. You've come here to live under my roof, and yet you look down on me in my own house."

"Very well, I'll go away. The brandy has gone to your head."

"I've begged you on bended knees to go to Chermashnya—for a couple of days, and yet you haven't gone there."

"I'll go there tomorrow if you really insist."

"You won't do it. You want to keep tabs on me, that's what you want. It's out of sheer spite that you won't go there."

The old man had got quite worked up, reaching that stage of intoxication at which the drinker, hitherto quiet in behaviour, flies off the handle out of an urge to assert himself.

"Why are you staring at me? That look in your eyes! Their expression says to me, 'What a sot you are!' They're full of suspicion and contempt— You've come here with some design at the back of your mind. Take Alyosha: his eyes are clear and candid. He doesn't despise me. Alexei, you must have no love for Ivan—"

"Don't be angry with my brother! Stop offending him," Alyosha broke in with sudden insistence.

"Well, I can do that. Oh, what a splitting headache I have. Take the brandy away, Ivan. This is the third time I'm asking you." As he fell into thought, a sly smirk suddenly came over his face. "Don't be angry with an enfeebled and useless old man, Ivan. I know you have no love for me, but don't be angry with me all the same. There's nothing to love me for. You'll set out for Chermashnya, where I'll join you and bring you a present.

I'll show you a choice little wench I've had my eye on for quite a while. She's still a tomboy but you don't have to give such girls a wide berth—they're little gems."

And he gave his hand a smacking kiss.

"To me," he went on with sudden animation, seeming to grow sober for an instant as soon as he mounted his hobby-horse. "For me—oh, you kids, you young innocents—for me no woman has ever been unattractive—that's been my creed! Is that something you can understand? No, it isn't, for you have milk flowing in your veins instead of red blood; you're still un-hatched! To my thinking, something greatly interesting can be discovered in any woman, a something no other woman has. Only you have to know how it's to be found—that's the key. It calls for talent. I've never found any woman ugly: her being a woman is in itself half the attraction—but that's something over your heads! Even in old maids you can come across things that leave you simply amazed by the fools who have let such women fade without bringing them to light! The first thing to do with the barefoot wenches and the plain-looking ladies is to bowl them over. That's the right way! Didn't you know that? They must be bowled over by making them enraptured, transfixed and overcome by shame at having a fine gentleman fall in love with such a sloven. It's so glorious that there have always been lowly folk and their masters, so there'll always be a scullery-maid and her master—and what more is needed to be pleased with life! Just a moment—Alyosha, I was always taking your dead mother by surprise, but it was in a different way. I would refrain from caressing her, but then, all of a sudden, when the moment was right, I suddenly set about fawning on her, crawling on my knees, kissing her feet, and would always, always—I can recall it as if it were today—bring her to burst into a sweet little laugh, a bubbling, rippling and subdued laugh, nervous and peculiar. She was the only woman with that kind of laugh. I knew that it was a prelude to one of her fits and that she would begin her shrieking the very next day, and also that such laughter did not signify any delight; it was a kind of deceptive emotion, but no worse for being so. So now you realise what is meant by an ability to hit the mark in all things! On one occasion, a certain Belyavsky, a handsome fellow and rich into the bargain, who had taken to her and was a frequent caller, suddenly gave me a slap in the face one day, and in front of her too. And she—that lamb-like creature—why, I thought she would give me a thrashing for permitting the blow. How she fell upon me. 'You've been slapped, slapped!' she cried. 'He struck you in the face! You were trying to sell me to him,' she went on. 'How dared he strike you in front of me! Never dare ever to approach me again! Run along and challenge him to a duel—' To get some humility driven into her, I took her to a monastery, where the holy fathers read prayers over her. Alyosha, I swear to God that I never did anything to hurt the poor creature! Except on a single occasion during our first year of marriage. She was much given to prayer, and observed all the festivals of the Holy Virgin with particular piety. On such occasions, she would invariably drive me away to my study. Well, I decided I'd knock all that mystic stuff out of her head, so one day I said to her, 'You see that icon of yours, don't you? Well, I'll take it down from its place. You think it can work miracles, but I'll spit on it in your presence and nothing at all will happen to me!' When she saw me do so, good God, I thought she was going to kill me then and there, but she only jumped to her feet, threw up her hands, then hid her face in them, trembled all over and collapsed—all of a heap— But Alyosha, Alyosha, what's wrong, what's wrong with you?''

The old man, thoroughly alarmed, jumped up from his seat. As soon as he had begun to speak of his mother, a gradual change had come over Alyosha's face. It turned crimson, his eyes blazed, and his lips quivered— The tipsy old man had spluttered on, without noticing anything until something very strange happened to Alyosha: he was overcome in exactly the same way as had been said of his mother. He suddenly jumped up from his seat at the table, threw up his hands and then hid his face in them just as his mother was said to have done, and fell back in his chair, shaken by an hysterical fit of violent but silent sobbing. The old man was taken aback by the extraordinary similarity.

"Ivan, Ivan! Some water quick! It's just like her—exactly

the same! Spurt some water on his face from your mouth—
that's what I used to do to her. It's because of his mother—his
mother," he mumbled to Ivan.

"But his mother was mine too, wasn't she?" Ivan suddenly
snarled in uncontrollable anger and contempt. His blazing
eyes gave the old man a start. Something exceedingly strange
had taken place at this point, if only momentarily: it had completely slipped his memory that Alyosha's mother was Ivan's
too.

"What d'you mean—your mother?" he muttered uncompre-
hendingly. "Why are you saying that? Whose mother do you
mean?—Could she—why, damnation take it, so she was! Damnation! Forgive me, Ivan, my memory has never blanked out
like that before—and I thought—hee-hee-hee," he tittered, and
stopped short. A broad grin, drunken and meaningless, spread
over his face. At that very moment a terrific commotion
broke out in the hall, furious shouting could be heard, the
door flew open and Dmitri Fyodorovich burst into the room.
The terror-stricken old man took refuge behind Ivan Fyodorovich.

"He'll murder me, murder me! Don't let him! Keep him
away!" he cried, clutching at the skirt of Ivan Fyodorovich's
frock-coat.

9.

The Lechers

Grigori and Smerdyakov came running into the room, hard
upon Dmitri Fyodorovich. They had been struggling with him
in the passageway in an attempt to keep him out, as Fyodor
Pavlovich had ordered some days before. When Dmitri Fyodorovich halted for a moment to look about himself, Grigori
dashed round the table to close the double doors on the opposite side leading to the inner apartments, and backed up against
them, his arms outstretched, prepared to block any entry to the
last gasp, so to speak. On noticing that, Dmitri screamed rather

than cried, as he made a dash at Grigori.

"So that's where she is! She's hidden there! Out of my way, you rogue!" He tried to grab at Grigori, who pushed him back. Beside himself with fury, Dmitri swung a fist and hit Grigori with all his might. The old man fell prone on the floor; Dmitri jumped over him and broke in the doors. Pale and trembling, Smerdyakov stood at the other end of the room, huddling close to Fyodor Pavlovich.

"She's here," Dmitri Fyodorovich yelled, "I've just seen her myself, turning towards the house, but couldn't catch up with her. Where is she? Where is she?"

The shout "She's here!" had an amazing effect on Fyodor Pavlovich. His terror vanished.

"Hold him! Hold him!" he screamed as he dashed after Dmitri Fyodorovich. Meanwhile, Grigori got up from the floor, looking quite dazed. Ivan Fyodorovich and Alyosha ran after their father. From the third room came the sudden sounds of something crashing on the floor: it was a large glass vase (not of the expensive kind) standing on a marble pedestal, which Dmitri Fyodorovich had knocked against as he ran past it.

"Grab him!" the old man shouted. "Help!"

Ivan Fyodorovich and Alyosha managed to catch up with the old man, and dragged him back into the drawing-room.

"Why are you chasing after him? He'll really murder you!" Ivan Fyodorovich cried angrily at his father.

"Ivan, Alyosha, she must be here then. Grushenka's here. He says he saw her running past him—"

He was gasping for breath: he had not been expecting Grushenka at the time, so that the sudden news that she was there immediately sent him off his head. Trembling all over he seemed like one bereft of reason.

"But you've seen for yourself that she hasn't come!" Ivan shouted.

"She may have entered by the other entrance."

"But it's locked, and you've got the key—"

At this point, Dmitri reappeared on the scene. He had, of course, found the back entrance locked, and the key to the locked door was in Fyodor Pavlovich's pocket. The windows in all the rooms were closed too, so that Grushenka could not have possibly got in or out.

"Hold him!" Fyodor Pavlovich shrieked on seeing Dmitri again. "He's stolen the money in the bedroom!"— Breaking loose from Ivan's grip, he again made a dash at Dmitri, who, raising both hands, suddenly clutched the two tufts of hair remaining on the old man's temples, gave them a pull, sending him crashing to the floor. For good measure, he kicked the prone figure in the face two or three times with his heel. The old man groaned agonisingly. Though not so strong as his brother Dmitri, Ivan Fyodorovich threw his arms about him and dragged him away with all his might from the old man. Alyosha, too, did what he could to help with his puny strength by clasping his brother from the front.

"You madman, you've killed him!" Ivan cried.

"He's got his deserts!" Dmitri exclaimed, gasping for breath. "If I haven't done him in now, I'll do it another time. You won't be able to protect him!"

"Dmitri! Get out of here right away!" Alyosha exclaimed commandingly.

"Alexei! You alone can tell me, and you're the only one I can believe: has she been here or not? Only a short while ago I saw her stealing along the wattle fence towards the house. She ran off when I called to her—"

"I swear she hasn't been here and wasn't at all expected to come!"

"But I saw her— Consequently, she— I'll go at once to find out where she is— Good-bye, Alexei! Not a word to the babbling old crank about the money, but go to Katerina Ivanovna without fail, and say to her, 'He told me to say good-bye to you for him—say good-bye to you. Yes, to wish you well and say good-bye!' You can describe this scene to her."

Meanwhile, Ivan and Grigori had raised the old man from the floor and seated him in an arm-chair. His face was covered with blood but he was fully conscious and listened eagerly to Dmitri's shouting. He was still under the impression that Grushenka was really somewhere in the house. Dmitri glared at him with hatred as he departed.

"I feel no regret for the blood-letting!" he exclaimed. "Beware, old man, and cherish your dream, just as I cherish mine! I curse you and disown you completely—"

And he ran out of the room.

"She's here, she must be here! Smerdyakov, Smerdyakov!" the old man wheezed in a scarcely audible voice, beckoning to Smerdyakov with a forefinger.

"She isn't here, she isn't, you mad old man!" Ivan shouted at him angrily. "Here, he's fainted! Water! A towel! Be quick about it, Smerdyakov!"

The latter rushed to get some water. At last they got the old man undressed, took him to his bedroom and put him to bed. A moistened towel was wrapped about his head. Weakened by the brandy, the violence of his emotions and the blows he had been given, he closed his eyes as soon as his head touched the pillow, and fell asleep. Ivan Fyodorovich and Alyosha returned to the drawing-room. Smerdyakov was removing the broken pieces of the vase, while Grigori was standing at the table, his eyes downcast.

"Shouldn't you wrap something moistened round your head and lie down too?" said Alyosha, addressing Grigori. "We'll keep an eye on him. My brother must have struck you a terrible blow—on the head."

"He had the nerve to hit me!" Grigori said gloomily, bringing out each word.

"He had the 'nerve' to hit his father, and not only you!" Ivan Fyodorovich remarked with a grimace.

"I used to wash him in a tub—and now he's had the nerve to hit me!" Grigori repeated.

"Damn it all, he'd probably have committed murder if I hadn't dragged him away. It wouldn't have taken much to finish off the old crank," Ivan Fyodorovich said to Alyosha in an undertone.

"God forfend!" Alyosha exclaimed.

"But why 'forfend'?" Ivan continued in the same undertone, with a wry face. "One viper will devour the other, and good riddance to both!"

Alyosha gave a start.

"Of course, I won't allow a murder to be committed, just as I didn't only now. Stay here for a while, Alyosha. I'll go out for a breath of fresh air. My head's begun to ache."

Alyosha went into his father's bedroom and sat for about an hour behind the screen at the head of the bed. The old man suddenly opened his eyes and gave him a long and silent look, evidently recalling things and musing over them. All at once an expression of extraordinary agitation came over his face.

"Alyosha," he whispered apprehensively. "Where's Ivan?"

"In the courtyard, with a headache. He's on the look-out."

"Let me have the looking-glass, the one over there!"

Alyosha handed the little round-shaped folding mirror that stood on a chest of drawers. The old man scrutinised his face in it: his nose was badly swollen and there was a sizable purple bruise over his left eyebrow.

"What does Ivan say? Alyosha, my dear and only son, I fear Ivan; I fear him more than the other one. You're the only one I'm not afraid of—"

"Have no fear of Ivan either. He's angry with you, but he'll protect you."

"Alyosha, but what about the other one? I suppose he's run off to Grushenka! Tell me the truth, my dear boy: was she here just now, or not?"

"Nobody saw her, so it can't be true. She wasn't here."

"Mitya wants to marry her, you know, marry her!"

"But she won't marry him."

"She won't, won't, won't. That's the last thing she'll do!" the old man exclaimed joyfully, as though he had heard the best news in the world. He clasped Alyosha's hand in his delight and pressed it warmly to his heart. There were even tears in his eyes. "That icon of the Mother of God, the one I spoke to you of—I want you to keep it and take it away with you. And you may return to the monastery—I was joking, so don't be angry with me. My head aches, Alyosha— Alyosha, soothe my heart: be an angel and tell me the truth!"

"You mean the same thing: whether she was here or not?" said Alyosha bitterly.

"No, no, no, I believe you. But here's what I want you to do: call on Grushenka yourself, or try to see her somehow. Get to know from her, as soon as you can and using your own judgement, which one of us two she means to have. Well, what? Can you do that, or can't you!"

"I'll be sure to ask her if I see her," murmured the embarrassed Alyosha.

"No, she won't tell you," the old man broke in, "she's a flighty piece. She'll start to kiss you and say it's you she's after. She's a cheat and a brazen hussy. No, you shouldn't call on her, you shouldn't!"

"Indeed, it wouldn't be right, Father, not right at all."

"Where did he tell you to go when he shouted 'Go there' as he ran off?"

"To Katerina Ivanovna."

"For money? To ask for money?"

"No, not for money."

"He's got no money at all; he's penniless. Listen, Alyosha, I'll turn things over in my mind in bed tonight, and you go for the time being. You may be seeing her— Only be sure to come to see me in the morning. Do that without fail. I'll tell you something tomorrow. Will you come?"

"I will."

"When you come, try to make it appear you've come of your own accord to see me. Not a word to anybody that I've asked you to come. Say nothing to Ivan."

"Very well."

"Good-bye, my dear boy. I shall never forget how you stood up for me. I'll have something to tell you tomorrow—only I must do some more thinking—"

"And how are you feeling now?"

"I'll be up and about tomorrow, quite well, quite well!"

As he was crossing the courtyard, Alyosha found his brother Ivan sitting on the bench at the entrance gate and pencilling down something in his notebook. Alyosha told him their father was conscious and awake and had sent him back to the monastery to spend the night there.

"Alyosha, I'd be very glad to see you tomorrow morning,"

said Ivan Fyodorovich amiably, rising from his seat. His affability came as a complete surprise to Alyosha.

"I'll be at the Khokhlakovs' tomorrow," Alyosha replied. "I may be calling on Katerina Ivanovna tomorrow, too, if I don't find her at home just now—"

"So you are indeed going to Katerina Ivanovna's right away! To 'bid her good-bye', as he put it?" said Ivan with a sudden smile, making Alyosha feel embarrassed.

"I think I now understand everything his exclamation meant and something of what came before that. Dmitri has probably asked you to call on her and tell her that—er—er, in short that he 'bids her good-bye', eh?"

"Ivan, what will the awful animosity between Father and Dmitri end up in?" Alyosha exclaimed.

"It's hard to say. The matter may end in nothing at all—it may just fade away. That woman is a man-eater. At all events, the old man must be kept indoors and Dmitri kept out."

"May I ask you another question, Ivan? Is any man, as he regards all the rest, entitled to decide which of them deserve to live, and which are more undeserving?"

"But why should you bring in a decision according to merit? That question is most frequently decided in men's hearts, not on grounds of merit but on other and far more natural grounds. As for being entitled, who hasn't the right to have wishes?"

"But surely not such things as another man's death?"

"Why not even another man's death? Why lie to oneself when all men live in that fashion and are hardly capable of living otherwise? Are you referring to what I said about 'one viper devouring the other'? In that case, may I, in my turn, ask you something: do you consider me capable, like Dmitri, of spilling the crazy old man's blood, in fact, murdering him?"

"How can you say that, Ivan? The idea never even occurred to me! Besides, neither do I consider Dmitri—"

"Thanks for that, at least," Ivan retorted. "I want you to know I'll always protect him. But as for my own wishes on that score, I shall give myself full freedom. I'll be seeing you tomorrow. Don't condemn me or regard me as a villain," he added with a smile.

They shook hands with unwonted warmth. Alyosha felt that his brother had taken the first step towards him, and had done so with some purpose in view.

10.

The Two Meet

Alyosha left his father's house feeling even more crushed and dejected in spirit than when he had come there. His mind, too, seemed fragmented and scattered, yet at the same time he felt apprehensive of trying to piece the fragments together and draw some general conclusion from all the agonising contradictions he had lived through during the day. His state bordered on despair, a feeling that had never before visited Alyosha's heart. Towering over everything else, like a mountain, stood the main question, dreadful and irresolvable: how would matters end between his father and his brother Dmitri, with regard to that dreadful woman? He had witnessed the scene: he had been there himself and seen them confronting each other. Yet it was his brother Dmitri alone who could turn out to be unfortunate, wholly and terribly unfortunate: disaster loomed ahead of him. Others were also involved, perhaps even more than might have seemed to Alyosha previously. There was something even mysterious in the matter. His brother Ivan had taken a step towards him, which Alyosha had long wished for, but for some reason that step towards a better mutual understanding frightened him now. And what about those two women? Strange to say, he had felt extremely embarrassed when he had started out for Katerina Ivanovna's house earlier, but he felt nothing of the kind now. On the contrary, he was hastening there as though expecting to get some guidance from her. However, it was now obviously more difficult than before to convey the message: the question of the three thousand had been decided once and for all, and his brother Dmitri, now feeling dishonoured and forlorn, would, of course, be undeterred by any downfall. Moreover, he had instructed Alyosha to describe the scene at his father's house to Katerina Ivanovna.

It was seven o'clock already and dusk was falling when Alyosha came up to Katerina Ivanovna's commodious and comfortable house in Bolshoi Street. He knew that she had two aunts living with her. Incidentally, one of them was related not to her but to her half-sister Agafya Ivanovna; she was the meek lady who had looked after her and her sister at her father's home when she had returned from her finishing school. The other aunt was a more refined and impressive Moscow lady, though moneyless. They were rumoured to be quite subservient to Katerina Ivanovna and kept merely as chaperons. The only person Katerina Ivanovna obeyed was her benefactress, the general's widow, who was tied down to Moscow by illness and to whom it was her duty to write twice weekly with full details of her doings.

When Alyosha entered the hall and asked the maid to announce him, the inmates were obviously aware of his arrival (having probably seen him through the window), for he suddenly heard some noise, and the sound of hurrying footsteps and rustling skirts; it may have been two or three women running out of the room. Alyosha found it strange that his coming could have created such a flutter. However, he was at once shown into a drawing-room, spacious and elegantly and substantially furnished in a style that was not in the least provincial. It contained many sofas and settees, as well as tables large and small; there were pictures on the walls, vases and lamps on the tables, lots of flowers and even an aquarium at a window. Though it was somewhat dark in the room because of the twilight, Alyosha could make out a small silk cape left on a sofa that had evidently just been vacated; on the table in front of the sofa were a couple of cups of chocolate, some sponge-cakes, a cut-glass salver with blue raisins, and another with sweets, this showing that some visitor was being entertained. He realised that he had interrupted a call, and he pulled a long face. At that very instant, the door curtains were parted and Katerina Ivanovna entered with rapid and hurried footsteps, her hands outstretched and a radiant smile of delight playing on her face. She was followed by a maid with two lighted candles, who placed the candlesticks on a table.

"You're here at last, thank goodness! I've been simply praying to God all day long for you alone to come! Pray be seated."

He had found her beauty breath-taking even before, when, some three weeks earlier, his brother Dmitri had brought him to the house for the first time to present him to Katerina Ivanovna, at her express request. There had been practically no conversation between them during that call: thinking that Alyosha felt very bashful, Katerina Ivanovna had seemed anxious to spare his feelings and had chatted with Dmitri Fyodorovich all the time. Alyosha had been silent but he had been most observant. He had been struck by the haughty girl's imperious air, her proud ease of manner and her self-assurance. All that was beyond doubt, and he had felt he was not in any way exaggerating. He had found her great blazing dark eyes most beautiful, especially with her pale and somewhat sallow complexion and her elongated face. But in those eyes as well as in the shape of those exquisite lips there was a something that might well have aroused an ardent love in his brother, though not for long perhaps. He had been on the verge of voicing this thought almost outspokenly to Dmitri, when, after their call, the latter begged Alyosha not to hold back the impression he had brought away after meeting his fiancée.

"You will be happy with her, but perhaps—it will be an unquiet happiness."

"Indeed, such women remain what they are: they do not bow to fate. So you think I won't love her for ever and ever, don't you?"

"I don't. Perhaps you will love her for ever, but you won't always be happy with her—"

Alyosha had voiced his opinion, blushing and vexed with himself for having yielded to his brother's insistence and given vent to such "foolish" thoughts: his opinion had seemed terribly foolish to him the moment it had escaped his lips. Besides, he had felt ashamed of having expressed an opinion of a woman in terms so unequivocal. It was with the greater amazement that he now felt, at first glance at Katerina Ivanovna, as she came running into the room, that he may have been badly mistaken on that occasion. This time her face shone with artless kindliness and warm-hearted sincerity. Instead of her former "pride and haughtiness", which had then struck Alyosha with such force, one could now discern nothing but a bold and noble energy and a clear-eyed and unshakable faith in herself. At his first glance and from the first words spoken, Alyosha realised that she was fully aware of all the tragicalness of her relationship with a man she loved so dearly and that she probably knew everything, positively everything. Notwithstanding, there was so much refulgence in her gaze and such faith in the future that an awareness of guilt came suddenly over Alyosha. She had at once conquered him and won him over to her side. He also noticed, from the first words she spoke, that she was in a state of intense excitement, to a degree perhaps exceptional in her—a condition almost resembling even some ecstasy.

"I've been expecting you with such impatience because it's from you alone, and from nobody else, that I can learn the whole truth!"

"I've come—" Alyosha mumbled in confusion, "I've—he's sent me—"

"Oh, I had a feeling he'd send you. I know everything now, everything!" Katerina Ivanovna exclaimed, her eyes suddenly flashing. "Just a moment, Alexei Fyodorovich, I'll tell you beforehand why I've been expecting you. You see, I may know far more than even you do; it's not news that I need from you. What I need is to learn your own and personal last impression of him. I want you to tell me in the most outspoken, unadorned and even unsparing terms (oh, be as unsparing as you wish!) how you see him and his position at present, after you met him today. That will perhaps be better than my speaking to him personally, since he does not wish to see me any more. Do you understand what I want of you? What is the message he's sent you with (I knew he'd send you to me!). Tell me frankly, down to the very last word!"

"He told me to say—good-bye to you for him—that he'd never, never come again—to say good-bye to you—"

"Good-bye? Is that exactly what he said?"

"It was."

"Perhaps he made some kind of slip—chose the wrong words—didn't use the words he meant to?"

"No, those were the very words he told me to pass on to you: 'good-bye'. He told me three times not to forget to convey his message."

Katerina Ivanovna flushed.

"And now, Alexei Fyodorovich, help me. It is at this point that I shall be needing your help. I'll tell you just what I think, and you must simply tell me whether I'm mistaken or not. Now listen: if he'd sent you to say good-bye to me in passing, as it were, without insisting on the exact wording and with no particular emphasis, that would have been all—the end of everything. But if he insisted on that particular wording and tried to impress on you that you shouldn't forget to say *good-bye* to me—then he must have been all worked up, perhaps besides himself? He'd made up his mind and was terrified by having done so! He wasn't leaving me with firm step, but had tumbled downhill headlong. The emphasis on the wording may have been sheer bravado—"

"Yes, indeed!" Alyosha agreed eagerly. "That's what I now believe."

"If that's so, he's not altogether lost! He's merely in despair, but I can save him yet. But wait: has he told you anything about some money—three thousand roubles?"

"Not only has he spoken of it but it has done more than anything else to crush him. He said he has forfeited his honour and that nothing matters now," Alyosha replied with some vehemence, feeling a gush of fresh hope in his heart: perhaps there was a solution and a way of salvation for his brother. "But—do you know about the money," he went on, and suddenly stopped short.

"I've known for a long time and for certain. I sent a telegram to Moscow and I've known for some time that the money did not arrive. He did not send the money off, but I said nothing of the matter. During the past week, I've learnt how much he needs the money— I have set myself a single purpose in all this: I want him to know who to turn to, and who is a true friend to him. But no, he doesn't want to believe I'm his truest friend;

he doesn't want to find out what kind of person I am, and regards me only as a woman. I've been trying so hard all week to find some way to make him realise he needn't feel ashamed for having squandered the three thousand roubles. I mean he may feel shame for himself or of what others may think but he should not feel that way with me. After all, he opens his heart to God without feeling any shame. Why doesn't he realise how much I'm prepared to put up with for his sake? Why is it that he knows me so little, how dare he know me so little after everything that has happened? I want to save him for ever. Let him forget that I'm engaged to him! He fears me because his honour is in question! Yet he wasn't afraid to speak freely to you, Alexei Fyodorovich? Don't I deserve the same?"

She was in tears as she spoke the concluding words; the tears were running down her face.

"I must let you know," Alyosha said, his voice trembling too, "what took place between him and our father only a short while ago—" And he went on to describe the entire scene to her: he told her how he had been sent to get the money and how Dmitri had burst into the room and fallen upon his father, after which he had asked Alyosha with special emphasis to go and convey his "message".

"He's gone to that woman," Alyosha added in a low voice.

"And do you think I won't put up with that woman? Does he think I won't? But he won't marry her," she said, with a sudden and nervous laugh. "Can a Karamazov burn with such a passion for ever? This is passion, not love. He won't marry her because she won't become his wife—" and Katerina Ivanovna gave a strange smile.

"But perhaps he will marry her," said Alyosha sadly, lowering his eyes.

"He won't, I tell you! The girl is an angel—d'you know that? Do you?" Katerina Ivanovna exclaimed with sudden vehemence. "She's the most fantastic of fantastic creatures. I know how seductive she is, but I know, too, how kind-hearted, firm-minded and noble she is. Why are you looking at me like that, Alexei Fyodorovich? Perhaps my words have surprised you; per-

193

13-721

haps you don't believe me? Agrafena Alexandrovna,* "she cried out suddenly to someone, looking towards the next room. "Come and join us. This is Alyosha here, a fine man. He knows everything about our affairs. I want you to meet him!"

"I've only been behind the curtain for you to call me," said a sweet and even somewhat sugary woman's voice.

The door curtains were parted and who else but Grushenka, laughing in delight, walked up to the table. Alyosha felt as if some new and powerful sensation had come over him. He fixed his gaze on her, unable to look away. So this was that horrible woman—the "man-eater", as his brother Ivan had blurted out half an hour before. Yet before him stood, it would seem, a most ordinary and uncomplicated human being—a good-natured and attractive woman, certainly good-looking but how resemblant to all other good-looking but "ordinary" women! True, she was very, even very good-looking, with a kind of Russian beauty so loved by many even to the point of passion! She was well above medium height, but somewhat shorter than Katerina Ivanovna (who was quite tall), full of figure with feline and even flowing movements of her body, cloyingly languorous, just like her voice. She did not enter as Katerina Ivanovna had, with firm and vigorous step, but, on the contrary, noiselessly. Her feet made not the slightest sound on the floor. She sank into an arm-chair with a soft swishing of her gorgeous black silk dress, and languidly arranged about her milky white neck and opulent shoulders her costly black cashmere shawl. She was twenty-two, and looked exactly her age. She had a creamy complexion, the cheeks tinted a pale pink. Her face might have been considered too broad, the lower jaw even a little protrusive. The upper lip was thin, the somewhat prominent lower lip being twice as full, and pouting. But her masses of magnificent light-brown hair, her perfect sable-black eyebrows and her superb grey-blue eyes with their silky lashes would have made even the most blasé of men who chanced to see her in a crowd or among strollers in the street come to a sudden standstill at the sight of her face and remember it long afterwards. What struck Alyosha

*Agrafena: the full form of the diminutive *Grushenka.—Tr.*

most in that face was its expression of childlike trustfulness. Her gaze was that of a child; she expressed delight as a child would; she walked up to the table with a delighted look as though in expectation of something with the impatience and trustful curiosity of a child. Her glance gladdened the heart—Alyosha could feel that. There was also something else about her which he could not and would not know how to explain to himself, but which perhaps affected him without his being aware of it, namely the selfsame flowing voluptuousness of her movements, their feline noiselessness. Yet hers was a strong and opulent body. Under the shawl one could sense the well-rounded broad shoulders and the high and still quite girlish bosom. The body perhaps held out the promise of a Venus of Milo, though already on a somewhat exaggerated scale—that could be surmised. Connoisseurs of beauty in Russian women could have unerringly predicted, as they looked at Grushenka, that such fresh and still vernal beauty would lose its harmony by the age of thirty: the body would thicken, the face would grow saggy, with crow's feet rapidly appearing about the eyes and wrinkles on the forehead, and the creamy complexion would perhaps become coarsened and blowsy—in short, the fleeting and short-lived beauty so often to be seen in Russian women. Alyosha, of course, gave no thought to such things; though she fascinated him, he asked himself, with an unpleasant sensation and somehow regretfully, why she affected that drawling lisp and could not speak in a natural way. She evidently did so because she found something attractive in that drawling and sugary delivery of sounds and syllables. It was, of course, merely a bad habit born of ill breeding and testifying to a lack of a proper upbringing and to a vulgar understanding, acquired in childhood, of good manners. Yet this intonation and manner of speech impressed Alyosha as something totally out of keeping with the childlike ingenuousness and joyous expression of her face and the candid radiance of her eyes! Katerina Ivanovna at once made her sit down in an arm-chair facing Alyosha and impetuously kissed her laughing lips several times. She seemed quite in love with Grushenka.

"This is the first time we've met, Alexei Fyodorovich," she said rapturously. "I wished to see her and get to know her, and wanted to call on her but she came here herself at my first intimation. I felt sure we'd settle everything between us, everything! I felt it in my heart— I was implored to give up the idea but I felt it would work out, and I haven't been mistaken. Grushenka has explained everything to me and told me of all her plans. She flew into this place like an angel, bringing peace and joy with her—"

"You didn't turn up your nose at me, my good and sweet young lady," Grushenka drawled in her crooning voice and with the same fetching and joyous smile.

"Don't dare to say such things to me, you charmer, you sorceress! Turn my nose up at you, forsooth! I'll just kiss that lower lip of yours again. It looks a wee bit swollen so I'll make it swell up just a bit more, and again more— Listen to the way she laughs, Alexei Fyodorovich. It does one's heart good to see such an angel—"

Alyosha flushed, a faint shiver running down his spine.

"You pamper me, my dear young lady, but I may not be deserving of your kindness."

"Undeserving? Did you say undeserving?" Katerina Ivanovna exclaimed just as warmly. "Do you know, Alexei Fyodorovich, what a fantastic little head she has on her shoulders, and what a wilful and proud little heart beats in her breast! She's noble-hearted and magnanimous, Alexei Fyodorovich—do you know that? Only she had a run of bad luck. She was too ready to make any sacrifice for a man who was unworthy of her, or perhaps wayward. There was a man, also an army officer, she fell in love with and gave him everything—that was quite a while ago, some five years—but he forgot her and married another. He has been widowed and has written to say he's coming here—and it's him alone that she loves; she's loved him all her life! He'll come for her, and Grushenka will be happy again, for she's been miserable all these five years. Who can reproach her! Who can boast of her favour! Only that merchant, a legless old man—but he was more of a father, friend and protector. He found her in despair and torment, abandoned by one she had

196

loved so much—she was even ready to drown herself, but that old man saved her, saved her!"

"How staunchly you are defending me, dear young lady. You're a little too hasty in all things," Grushenka again drawled.

"Defending you? Is it for me to defend you? Can I make so bold as to defend you? Grushenka, my angel, give me your little hand. Look at it, so soft and charming. You see it, Alexei Fyodorovich, a hand that has brought me happiness and given me a new lease of life. I'll kiss that hand—on the back and on the palm—there, there and there!" and she did rapturously kissed the really charming but perhaps excessively plump hand three times. Stretching out her hand with a nervous and charming giggle, Grushenka watched the "dear young lady" kiss it, which seemed to please her. "Perhaps it's somewhat too effusive," was the thought that flashed through Alyosha's mind. He flushed and a sense of unease gripped his heart.

"Won't you be putting me to shame, dear young lady, by kissing my hand like that in front of Alexei Fyodorovich?"

"Do you really think I did that to put you to shame?" said Katerina Ivanovna, somewhat surprised. "Why should you give such a bad meaning to my action, my dear?"

"But perhaps you don't quite understand me either, dear young lady; perhaps I'm far worse than you think I am. I'm wicked at heart, and headstrong. I turned poor Dmitri Fyodorovich's head just in mockery."

"But now you intend to save him, don't you? You've promised to. You'll bring him to his senses and reveal to him that for a long time you've loved another man, who is now offering you his hand—"

"Oh, no, I never made any such promise. It was you who spoke of that all. There was no such promise from me."

"Then I must have misunderstood you," said Katerina Ivanovna in a low voice, and seeming to turn a little pale. "You promised—"

"Oh, no, my angelic young lady, I didn't promise you anything," Grushenka put in, speaking in a low and even tone, and still with the same blithe and innocent expression. "You can now see, most worthy young lady, what a wicked and wilful creature I am as against you. If I feel like doing anything, I do it. I may have promised something a little while ago, but I again ask myself: supposing he suddenly catches my fancy again? You see, I took a liking to him on one occasion—I liked him for close on an hour even. So perhaps I'll go right-away and tell him to stay on with me this very day—that's how fickle I am—"

"But only a short while ago you were telling me—something quite different," Katerina Ivanovna was scarcely able to bring out.

"Oh, but that was a short while ago! I'm so soft-hearted and silly, you see. Imagine what he's been through because of me! And if I suddenly return home, change my mind and feel sorry for him—what then?"

"I never expected—"

"Oh, my dear young lady, how kind-hearted you are compared to me, how noble. Perhaps, you'll stop liking such a silly creature as I am, now that you learnt what kind of person I am. Give me your dear hand, my angelic young lady," she said tenderly, and took Katerina Ivanovna's hand with a show of reverence. "And now, my dear young lady, I'll take your little hand and kiss it just as you did mine. You kissed my hand three times so I ought to kiss yours three hundred times for that, so as to make it all square. Let it be that way and then let it be as God wills: perhaps I shall become your complete slave and want to slavishly please you in all things. Let it be as God decides, without any pledges or promises. What a charming little hand you have, my dear and overwhelmingly beautiful young lady!"

She slowly raised the hand to her lips, true, with the strange intention of making it all square with kisses. Katerina Ivanovna did not take her hand away: she was listening with timid hope to Grushenka's concluding and rather strangely expressed promise to "slavishly" please her; she looked into Grushenka's eyes in suspense; in them she saw the same ingenuous and trustful expression, the same blithe serenity—"Perhaps she's excessively naive!" Katerina Ivanovna thought hopefully. Meanwhile, Grushenka, seemingly enchanted by the "charming hand", was slowly raising it to her lips. But she suddenly stopped short for two or three seconds, just when it was quite close to them, as though considering something.

"D'you know what, my angelic young lady," she suddenly drawled in a most tender and dulcet tone. "I won't kiss your hand after all," and she burst into tinkling laughter.

"Just as you please— But what's the matter with you?" exclaimed Katerina Ivanovna with a sudden start.

"You can remain with the recollection that you kissed my hand, but I didn't kiss yours." There was a sudden gleam in her eyes, her gaze fixed with terrible intensity on Katerina Ivanovna.

"What insolence!" Katerina Ivanovna suddenly exclaimed, evidently realising something. She flushed crimson and jumped up from her seat. Grushenka, too, rose unhurriedly to her feet.

"So I shall describe to Mitya how you kissed my hand just now, but I didn't kiss yours at all. How it will make him laugh!"

"Get out, you hussy."

"For shame, young lady, for shame! Such words don't become you at all, dear young lady."

"Get out, trull that you are!" Katerina Ivanovna screamed, every feature quivering on her quite distorted face.

"A trull, am I? Wasn't it you, an unmarried girl, who used to visit a gentleman for money in the dark of evening, offering your beauty for sale? I'm in the know."

Katerina Ivanovna shrieked and was about to rush at Grushenka, but was forcibly held back by Alyosha.

"Not a step, not a word more! Say nothing and make no reply. She'll go away—go at once!"

It was at that instant that, alarmed by the shriek, the two aunts came running into the room, followed by the maid. They all hurried to her side.

"Go away I shall," said Grushenka picking up her cape from the sofa. "See me home, dear Alyosha, will you?"

"Go away, hurry away!" cried Alyosha imploringly, clasping his hands.

"Do come, dear Alyosha! I've something very special to tell you on the way! It was for you that I arranged that scene, my dear. Be a good boy and see me home. You'll understand things a little later, and approve."

Alyosha turned away, wringing his hands. Grushenka ran out of the house with a ringing laugh.

Overcome by an attack of hysteria, Katerina Ivanovna was sobbing convulsively, with all the others fussing about her.

"Didn't I warn you?" said the elder of the two aunts. "I tried to hold you back from taking such a step—you're too impulsive— How could you have risked taking it! You have no knowledge of such creatures, and she's said to be worse than all the others— No, you're too self-willed!"

"She's a tigress!" Katerina Ivanovna screamed. "Why did you hold me back, Alexei Fyodorovich, I'd have thrashed her—thrashed her thoroughly!"

She was unable to control herself in Alyosha's presence; perhaps she did not want to.

"She should be flogged in public on the scaffold, by the executioner—"

Alyosha backed towards the door.

"Good God!" Katerina Ivanovna suddenly exclaimed, throwing up her hands. "How could he! How could he have acted so caddishly, so cruelly! He actually told that slut what happened on that fateful and eternally accursed day! 'Offering your beauty for sale, dear young lady!' She knows of it! Your brother's a scoundrel, Alexei Fyodorovich!"

Alyosha wanted to speak, but couldn't bring out a single word. His heart contracted painfully.

"Go away, Alexei Fyodorovich. I feel so ashamed, so awful! Tomorrow—I beg you on bended knees, come tomorrow. Don't condemn me, and forgive me. I don't know what I shall do to myself!"

Alyosha was almost reeling as he went out into the street. He, too, was on the verge of tears. He was suddenly overtaken by the maid.

"The young lady forgot to give you this letter from Madame Khokhlakov. She's had it since dinner-time."

Alyosha took the little pink envelope quite mechanically and slipped it absently into his pocket.

11.

Another Reputation Ruined

It was a little over a verst from the town to the monastery and Alyosha walked at a fast gait along the road, which was almost deserted at that hour. Darkness was falling and objects only thirty paces ahead could hardly be made out. Half-way towards his destination there was a cross-roads, where a figure could be discerned under a solitary brittle-willow. Scarcely had Alyosha reached the cross-roads when the figure darted from his place and made for him, shouting in a fierce voice:

"Your money or your life!"

"Can it be you, Mitya?" cried the astonished Alyosha, who had been quite taken aback.

"Ha, ha, ha! You weren't expecting me, were you? I was wondering where I should wait for you. Near her house? But there are three roads leading from there, and I could have missed you. So I finally decided to wait for you here, because you would be certain to pass this way since there's no other road to the monastery. Well, let me have the truth. Squash me as you would a cockroach— But what's wrong with you?"

"Nothing much, brother Mitya—I got quite a fright. Oh, Dmitri! The sight of Father's blood—" and Alyosha burst into tears. He had been close to tears for a long time, but now something seemed to snap in his heart. "You almost killed him—you cursed him—and just now—playing a joke on me here—'Your money or your life!' "

"So what of that? Is it improper? Does not meet the situation?"

"'Oh, no, I was merely—"

"Stay! Look at the night! How dark it is; what clouds, and how strong the wind that has arisen! As I stood concealed here under the brittle-willow, and waiting for you, I suddenly thought of myself (as God is my witness!): 'Why live on in this misery? What is there to wait for? Here's a willow-tree; I have my shirt and a handkerchief which I can twist into a rope in a jiffy. Then there are my braces—why should I go on burdening the earth and dishonouring it with my vile presence?' And then I heard you—Good Lord, it was as though something had suddenly dawned on my mind: so there does exist a man I love: there he is—that man, that dear brother of mine, whom I love more than I do anyone in the world, the only one I do love. And I felt such a gush of love for you—I loved so dearly at that moment that I thought: I'll fall on his neck at once! But then a stupid thought occurred to me: 'I'll amuse him; I'll give him a scare', so like a fool I called out, 'Your money!' Forgive my playing the fool—it was only a piece of nonsense. As for what's in my heart—that's quite proper— Well, to hell with it all: tell me what went on over there? What did she say? Crush me, strike me down, don't spare my feelings! Did she go into a frenzy?"

"No, it wasn't like that— It was quite different, Mitya. I found the two of them together—there."

"The two of whom?"

"Both of them: Grushenka was at Katerina Ivanovna's."

Dmitri Fyodorovich was dumbfounded.

"It can't be!" he cried. "You're raving! Grushenka at her house?"

Alyosha described all the happenings from the moment he had entered Katerina Ivanovna's house. He spoke for about ten minutes; it cannot be said that it was a fluent or coherent account but he did seem to make things clear, conveying the most significant words that had been spoken, and the most significant actions, and at times vividly describing his own feelings through some single detail. His brother listened in silence, his gaze fixed on him in an intense glare, but it was clear to Alyosha that his brother had realised everything and taken in every fact. As the story proceeded, his expression grew, not so much gloomy as bodeful. He frowned and clenched his teeth, his glare became more fixed, intent and menacing— It was all the more surprising when the expression of fierce anger suddenly changed with inconceivable rapidity: the compressed lips parted and Dmitri Fyodorovich burst into the most uncontrolled and unaffected laughter. He literally shook with laughter, so that for a while he was unable to utter a word.

"So she didn't kiss her hand! So she ran off without kissing it!" he exclaimed in a kind of morbid delight—it might have been called brash had it not been so spontaneous. "And the other one screamed she was a tigress! Well, a tigress she is! And she should be flogged in public? Indeed, she should—I'm of the opinion she should have been, long ago! You see, dear boy, she should be flogged like that but first I must recover my senses. I can understand that queen of insolence—that's her all over, she-devil that she is; she expressed herself in full in that hand-kissing business! She's the queen of all the she-devils one can imagine in the world! She's magnificent in her own way! So she made off for home, did she? I'll—h'm—I'll run over to her place! Don't blame me, Alyosha; I agree that strangling's too good for her—"

"But what about Katerina Ivanovna?" Alyosha asked sadly.

"I can see right through the other one too, as I've never seen before! It's like the discovery of all the four continents of the world—all five, that is to say! What a step to take! And it was the same Katya, the finishing school girl, who wasn't afraid to come running to an absurd and unmannerly army officer out of the magnanimous idea of saving her father, and at the risk of being mortally insulted! But her pride, the urge to run that risk, that challenge to fate, that boundless defiance! You say her aunt had tried to dissuade her. That aunt of hers is an overbearing creature, and sister to the general's widow in Moscow. She was even more stuck-up until her husband was caught embezzling government money, lost everything, his estate and everything else, and the haughty lady now had to sing small and keep that way. So she tried to dissuade Katya, who wouldn't listen to her. 'I can overcome anything,' she thought, 'control everything, so I can bewitch Grushenka, should I wish to.' Who is to blame if that was what she thought in her overweening pride? Do you think it was on purpose that she kissed Grushenka's hand first, that it was done with some ulterior motive? Nothing of the kind: she was genuinely drawn to Grushenka, no, not to Grushenka but to her ideal, her illusion, for, you see, it is *'my* own ideal' and *'my* own illusion!' Dear Alyosha, how did you manage to escape from those women? Did you tuck up your cassock and run away? Ha, ha, ha!"

"But, Mitya, you don't seem to realise how much you wronged Katerina Ivanovna by telling Grushenka of what took place on that day. Grushenka at once flung it in her face, the fact that 'she used to visit a gentleman for money in the dark of evening, offering her beauty for sale!' Mitya, could you have wronged her more?" Alyosha was most of all tormented by the thought that his brother seemed glad of Katerina Ivanovna's having been humiliated, though that could not possibly have been true, of course.

"Bah!" Dmitri Fyodorovich exclaimed, suddenly striking his forehead with a palm and frowning fiercely. Only now did he really realise—though Alyosha had told him everything at once—how he had wronged Katerina Ivanovna and why she had called him a scoundrel. "Yes, I did perhaps tell Grushenka about that 'fateful day', as Katya calls it. Yes, I did tell her—I remember it now. It was then, at Mokroye when I was drunk and the Gipsy girls were singing— But I was sobbing, on my knees and in tears in my reverence for Katya, and Grushenka showed understanding. She understood everything and she was crying herself— Oh, hell! Could it be otherwise this time? She was in tears then but now—now she has thrust 'a dagger into the heart'. That's what women are like!"

He looked down and sank into thought.

"Yes, I'm a scoundrel, a base scoundrel," he suddenly said gloomily. "It makes no difference whether I wept or not; I'm a scoundrel all the same! Tell her I accept that name, if that's any consolation. Well, enough of that. Good-bye. What's the use of talking? There's no room for cheerfulness here. You go your way, and I'll go mine. And I don't want to see you any more except until the very last moment comes round. Farewell, Alexei!" He pressed Alyosha's hand, his eyes lowered, as was his head, then strode off towards the town. Alyosha gazed after him, unable to believe he had made off so abruptly.

"Stay, Alexei, I have another confession to make to you alone!" said Dmitri Fyodorovich, suddenly turning back. "Look at me, look closely: here, look here, a terrible disgrace is in preparation." (As he said "here" he smote himself in the chest with a fist, with a strange expression as though the disgrace was located and kept on his chest, in some place, perhaps in a pocket or sewn into a bag suspended from his neck.) "You already know what I am: a scoundrel, and recognised as such! But you should know that, whatever I have done before or may do in the future, nothing—nothing at all—can compare in vileness with the disgrace I now bear—at this very moment—within my breast—here, here—which is now under way and active, though I have the power to quell it—I can quell it or give it its head, mark you! Well, I'll give it the reins, and not curb it! I told you everything just now, but this is something I held back because I wasn't brazen enough to tell you! I can still call a halt; by doing so, I can regain half of my lost integrity tomorrow, but halt I will not, I'll carry out my vile scheme, and you can bear witness that I am saying that in advance and in full awareness! Darkness and destruction! There's nothing to explain, and you'll learn everything in due course. The evil-smelling back alley and the she-devil! Farewell. Don't pray for me, for I'm unworthy of that. Besides, it is quite unnecessary, quite unnecessary—I don't need it at all! I'm off!"

And he made off suddenly, this time in earnest, and Alyosha wended his way towards the monastery. "How can it be that I'll never see him again? What did he mean?" The idea seemed absurd. "I'll make a point of seeing him tomorrow; I'll find him. The things he says!"—

He made a detour of the monastery and, crossing the pine grove, went straight to the hermitage. He was admitted at once, although that was not the usual practice at so late an hour.

His heart was in a tremor as he entered Father Zossima's cell. Why, oh why, had he left this place? Why had the *starets* sent him forth into the "world"? Peace and holiness reigned here, while there all was gloom and confusion, in which one lost all bearings and went astray.

In the cell were the novice Porfiri and the hieromonach Father Paissi; the latter would call hourly to inquire after the health of Father Zossima, whose condition, as Alyosha learnt with dread, was becoming worse and worse. Even the evening talk he usually conducted with the brothers could not take place this time. As a rule, the monks would gather in his cell, after the evening service and before retiring for the night, to confess aloud the transgressions of the day, their sinful dreams, thoughts, temptations, and even quarrels among themselves, if there had been any. Some would confess on bended knees; the *starets* would settle differences, reconcile, instruct, impose penance, and give his blessing and absolution. It was against such fraternal "confessions" that the opponents of the *starets* institution had risen up, maintaining that it was a profanation of the sacrament of confession and bordered on sacrilege, although it was nothing of the kind. Representations were even made to the diocesan authorities that such confessions, far from achieving any good purpose, actually and deliberately led into sin and temptation. Many of the brothers, it was claimed, found it irksome to visit the *starets* in that way and did so against their will because of the others and for fear of being thought proud and rebellious in spirit. It had been said that, before going to attend the evening confession, some would come to previous understanding: "I will say I lost my temper with you this morning and you'll bear out my words", so as to have something to say and have done with. Alyosha was aware that such things did actually happen at times. He also knew of the resentment against the custom of having letters from home being brought to the *starets* to be opened and perused before being delivered to the addressee. It was assumed, of course, that all this was done freely and sincerely, in good faith, for the sake of voluntary submission and salutary guidance, but it did sometimes prove to be most insincere, artificial and false. Yet the older and more experienced of the monks stood their ground, arguing that "those who have entered these walls in all sincerity so as to win salvation will no doubt find all these acts of obedience and sacrifice salutary and highly beneficial; on the contrary, those who find them irksome and voice complaint are no true monks and ought not to have taken up the monastic life; their place is in the world outside. Safety from sin and the devil cannot be found even in the church, let alone the outside world, so sinfulness should not be encouraged".

"He's losing strength and is quite drowsy," Father Paissi whispered to Alyosha after giving him his blessing. "He's even hard to awaken, and we shouldn't do that. He woke up for about five minutes, and asked for his blessing to be sent to the brothers, whose nightly prayers for him he requested. He intends to take the Eucharist in the morning again. He remembered you, Alexei, and asked whether you had gone away, and was told you were in town. 'That was what I gave him my blessing for. His place is there, and not here for the time being'— those were the words he spoke of you. He remembered you with love and concern for you—do you realise what grace has fallen to your lot? But why has he decided you should spend some time in the world outside? It can only mean he has foreseen something in your fate! Only bear in mind, Alexei, that, if you return to the world outside, it must be to perform the duty your *starets* has placed on you, and not for the frivolous vanity and the pleasures of this world—"

Father Paissi left the cell. Alyosha had not the least doubt that the *starets* was at the point of death, though he might live on for a day or two. Alyosha firmly and positively decided that, despite his promise to see his father, the Khokhlakovs, his brother and Katerina Ivanovna, he would not leave the monastery on the morrow, but would stay at Father Zossima's side until he passed away. His heart was brimming over with love, and he reproached himself bitterly that, while he had been in town, he could have forgotten, even if only momentarily, him whom he had left on his death-bed at the monastery, a man he revered more than anyone in the world. He entered the *starets*'s cubicle, knelt down, and bowed low to the ground to the sleeper, who was slumbering peacefully, his breathing regular and almost imperceptible. His face was calm.

Returning to the other room, where the *starets* had received his visitors that morning, Alyosha prepared for his night's rest. He hardly undressed but removed his boots, after which he lay down on the hard and narrow leather-covered couch he had slept on nightly for a long time, bringing nothing but a pillow with him. He had long ago forgotten to use the mattress his father had shouted to him about shortly before. He merely took off his cassock to use as a blanket. Before lying down to sleep, he fell on his knees and prayed, for some time. In his fervent prayer, he did not ask God to shed light on his perplexity; he craved for nothing but the joyous and tender emotion that had always visited him after the praising and the glorifying of the Lord that usually comprised his bedtime prayer. That joy always brought him untroubled slumber. As he was praying, he happened to feel in his pocket the little pink envelope Katerina Ivanovna's maid had handed him after overtaking him in the street. He felt a little perturbed, but completed his prayer, and then, after some hesitation, opened the envelope. It contained a letter signed by Lise, Madame Khokhlakov's young daughter, the one who had poked fun at him that morning in the presence of the *starets*.

"Dear Alexei Fyodorovich," she wrote, "I am writing to you without anybody's knowledge, even Mother's, and I realise how wrong it is. But I cannot go on living unless I tell you what has been born in my heart, something that nobody except the two of us should know until the time is right. But how am I to tell you what I want so much to say? Paper, they say, cannot blush, but I assure you that is untrue, and that it is blushing just as I am now. Dear Alyosha, I love you, and have loved you since childhood, since our Moscow days, when you were not at all what you are now; I shall love you all my life long. I have chosen you in my heart, so as to unite with you, and end our lives together in old age. Of course, on condition that you leave the monastery. As for our age, we shall wait as laid down by law. By that time I shall get well without fail, and be able to walk and dance. There can be no doubt on that score.

"I have considered everything, as you can see, but there is one thing I cannot make up my mind about: what will you think of me on reading this? I am for ever laughing and being naughty. I made you angry this morning, but I assure you, before taking up pen to write this, I prayed to the icon of the Mother of God; I'm still praying and almost in tears.

"You hold my secret in your hands; I do not know how I shall look you in the face when you come tomorrow. Oh, Alexei Fyodorovich, what if I am again unable to restrain myself, like the silly girl I am, and burst into laughter just as I did this morning when I was looking at you? You may take me for a nasty scoffer and not believe my letter. That is why I implore you, dear, if you have any compassion for me, not to look too straight into my eyes when you come tomorrow because, when they meet yours, I may suddenly burst into laughter, especially as you will be wearing that long coat of yours— Even now, I feel cold all over when I think of it, so when you come in, don't look at me at all for a while, but look at Mother or out of the window.

"There, I've written you a love letter. Oh dear, what have I done? Don't despise me, Alyosha, and forgive me if I have done anything bad and upset you. And now the secret of my reputation, which has perhaps been ruined for ever, is in your hands.

"I'm sure I'll cry today. Good-bye till our meeting, till our *terrifying* meeting. Lise.

"P.S. Alyosha, be sure, be sure to come without fail.

Lise."

It was with amazement that Alyosha read and reread the letter; he thought for a while, and then suddenly burst into a soft and sweet laugh. Then he gave a start, for his laugh seemed sinful to him. But an instant later, he laughed again, just as softly and just as sweetly. He slowly replaced the note in the envelope, crossed himself and lay down. His vexation of spirit suddenly passed away. "O Lord, have mercy on all these people; preserve them, the unfortunate and the turbulent, and give them guidance. All ways are thine: save them according to Thy ways. Thou art love; Thou wilt send joy to all!" he murmured as he crossed himself, and then sank into peaceful slumber.

PART TWO

BOOK FOUR

Pangs of Anguish

1.

Father Ferapont

Alyosha was awakened early in the morning, before the break of day. The *starets* had woke up feeling very weak, but wished to get up and be seated in an arm-chair. His mind was perfectly clear; though his face looked extremely tired, it was serene and almost joyful, and the eyes cheerful, kindly and welcoming. "I may not live through this new day," he said to Alyosha, after which he expressed a desire to confess and receive the Eucharist at once. Father Paissi had always been his confessor. The two sacraments were followed by the ministering of extreme unction. The hieromonachs were assembling, and gradually the cell began to fill with hermitage inmates. Meanwhile, daylight had set in, and monks began to arrive from the monastery as well. When the service ended, the *starets* wished to take leave of everyone there and kissed them all. The cell being too small for so many people, the earlier arrivals went out to make room for the new-comers. Alyosha was standing by the side of the *starets*, who had returned to his arm-chair. He spoke and taught as much as he was able to. Though weak, his voice was still quite firm. "I have been instructing you for so many years and consequently have been speaking aloud for so long that I've got into the habit of speaking and instructing you as I speak, so much so that I've found it almost harder to be silent than to speak, dear Fathers and brethren, even now, despite my weakness," he said good humouredly, looking with fond joyfulness at the group surrounding him. Alyosha was able later to recall something of what he said at the time. Though his voice was fairly steady and his speech distinct, it was somewhat disconnected. He spoke of many things, seeming anxious to say everything, to give expression once again, before his dying hour, to everything he had not been able to say during his life-

time. He did not do so merely for the sake of giving istruc-
tion; it was as though he wished to pour forth his heart once more
in a thirst to share his joy and ecstasy with all, without exception.

"Love one another, Fathers," the *starets* said (as far as Alyosha could recollect later). "Love God's people. We are no holier
than the laity just because we have come here and shut ourselves in within these walls; on the contrary, by the very fact of
having come here each of us has learnt of himself that he is worse
than all laymen are, than all people on earth are— And the
longer the monk lives within his walls, the more acutely must
he be aware of that. Otherwise he should not have come here
at all. But when he realises that he's not only worse than the
laity are, but is responsible to all men, for all and everything,
for all human transgressions—both of the world at large and of
individuals—then and only then will the aim of our fellowship
be attained. For you must know, my dear ones, that every single
one of us is without any doubt responsible for all without
exception in this world, and not only for the sins of the world,
for he bears a personal responsibility for all men and for every
man on this earth. That awareness is the essence of the monastic
way of life, and indeed of every man's life. For the monk is not
a different kind of man but merely what all men on
earth should be like. Only then will our hearts be filled
to overflowing with a love that is boundless and
world-embracing, and knows no surfeit. Then each of you
will be able to win the world through love and, with
his tears, wash its sins away— Each should keep watch
over his heart and constantly confess his sins to himself.
Have no fear of your sins even when you become aware
of them, if only you repent of them, but present no conditions to God. Again I say to you: eschew all pride. Be
not proud—either with the humble or with the great. Have
no hate for those who reject you and heap shame, abuse
and slander on you. Have no hate for atheists, false teachers
and materialists, even those of them that are evil, let alone
those that are good, for there are among them many that
are good, especially in our times. Remember them in your
prayers thus: 'O Lord, save those who have no one to

pray for them, and also save those who do not wish to pray to you.' And add at once: 'It is not out of pride that I make this prayer, O Lord, for I am vile, more than anybody else'— Love God's people, and do not allow strangers to lead the flock astray, for, if you slumber in your sloth and contumely, or, worse still, greed, they will come from all sides to drive your flock astray. Ceaselessly expound the Gospels to the people— Exact no bribes— Do not love silver and gold, or hoard them— Have faith and hold the banner fast. Hold it high—"

Incidentally, the *starets* spoke more disconnectedly than set forth above or than Alyosha recorded his words afterwards. At times his speech broke off, as though he was mustering his strength; his breathing would become laboured, but he seemed in a kind of ecstasy. He was listened to with emotion, though many wondered at his words, which they found obscure— Later they all recollected his words. When Alyosha had occasion to leave the cell for a moment, he was struck by the general suspense and expectancy among the crowd of monks in the cell and near it. With some, the expectancy had something of alarm in it, and with others it was solemn. It was a general expectation that something immediate and great would come to pass when the *starets* breathed his last. From one point of view, this anticipation was somewhat lacking in dignity, as it were, but even the most austere of the older monks were not unaffected by it. The gravest of all was the face of the old hieromonach Paissi. The reason for Alyosha's leaving the cell was his being mysteriously summoned, through a monk, by Rakitin, who had arrived from the town with a strange letter from Madame Khokhlakov. The latter informed Alyosha of a curious and highly opportune piece of news, referring to the old woman from our town, an NCO's widow named Prokhorovna*, who had come the day before, among the other devout and simply women, to be blessed by the *starets*. It was she who had

---

*The use of the patronymic without the Christian name in addressing an elderly man or woman expresses affection and sometimes condescension on the part of the speaker. It is usually, but not always, a feature of peasant speech.—*Tr.*

asked him whether it was right to have prayers offered for the repose of her son Vassili's soul: he was stationed in Irkutsk in faraway Siberia and had not written for already a year. The *starets* had given her a severe reply, forbidding any such thing, calling it something akin to witchcraft. Then, forgiving her on account of her ignorance, he had added in consolation, "as though looking into the book of the future" (as Madame Khokhlakov put it in the letter), "that her son Vassya* was most certainly alive, and that he would soon return home or else would write, and that she should go home and wait there. And imagine," Madame Khokhlakov went on enthusiastically, "the prophecy has come true, even literally, and more than that". No sooner had the old woman returned home than she was handed a letter from Siberia, which had been awaiting her. But more was to come: in his letter, penned when passing through Yekaterinburg, Vassya informed his mother that he was returning to European Russia together with an official and "hoped to embrace his mother" some three weeks after receipt of the letter. Madame Khokhlakov urgently and beseechingly asked Alyosha to inform the Father Superior and the monastic fraternity of this new "miracle of prediction": "It should be made known to all, all!" she exclaimed in conclusion. The letter must have been penned in the greatest haste, for the writer's state of excitement was apparent in every line. But there was nothing for Alyosha to inform the monks of, for they already knew everything when Rakitin had sent a monk to Alyosha with a message, he had also asked him to "most respectfully inform the reverend Father Paissi that he, Rakitin, had something of such importance to tell him that it did not brook a moment's delay; he humbly begged forgiveness for being so presumptuous". Since the monk had passed Rakitin's message on to Father Paissi before seeing Alyosha, there was nothing left for the latter to do, on reading the letter, but to give it to Father Paissi to bear out the story. Even that austere and cautious man, though he frowned on reading of the "miracle", could not fully suppress some inner emotion. His

*Diminutive of Vassili.—*Tr.*

eyes glistened, and a grave and rapt smile suddenly came over his lips.

"We shall see even greater things!" were the words that suddenly escaped from him.

"We shall, indeed, we shall!" the monks repeated, but Father Paissi, frowning again, asked all of them not to speak of the event to anyone "until it is borne out more fully, since there is a great deal of frivolousness among the laity, and, besides, the entire matter may have come about in a natural way", he added cautiously, as if to salve his conscience, but hardly seemed to believe his own reservation, as his listeners could well see. Of course, the whole monastery at once learnt of the "miracle", as did many from outside who had come to attend divine service. But none seemed more impressed by the miracle than the visiting little monk "from the monastery of St. Sylvester", a small community at Obdorsk in the Far North. He had paid his respects to the *starets* on the previous day and, standing near Madame Khokhlakov, he pointed at that lady's "healed" daughter and feelingly asked the *starets*: "How can you make so bold as to perform such things?"

He was now somewhat at a loss, and scarcely knew what to believe. The evening before, he had visited Father Ferapont in the latter's cell, which stood apart from the others, beyond the apiary and had been overawed by the meeting, which had made an extraordinary and terrifying impression on him. This Father Ferapont was the aged monk, a great observer of fasting and silence, whom we have already mentioned as an opponent to Father Zossima and, more important, to the entire *starets* institution, which he regarded as a harmful and idle innovation. He was a highly dangerous opponent, though he scarcely spoke a word to anybody because of his practice of silence. He was dangerous mainly because his views were shared by many of the monks and, besides, many visitors from among the laity honoured him as a very saintly man and hermit, though they clearly saw that he was no doubt a fool for Christ's sake. It was this latter fact that attracted them. This Father Ferapont never called on the *starets* Zossima. Though he did live in the hermitage, he was not excessively bothered with its regulations, again for the reason that he behaved just like a saintly fool. He was about seventy-five if not more, and lived beyond the hermitage apiary, in a corner formed by two walls, in an old and ramshackle wooden cell put up long before, in the last century, for Father Iona, another great observer of fasting and silence, who had reached the age of a hundred and five and of whose saintly deeds many curious stories were told at the monastery and in the neighbourhood. Some seven years before, Father Ferapont had at last gained permission to move into this secluded cell, which was in fact just a peasant log hut, though it resembled a chapel, for in it were an extraordinary number of icons with little lamps constantly burning before each of them, all of them offerings from outside. He was supposed to attend to them and keep the lamps burning. He was said (quite truly) to live on no more than two pounds of bread for three days. This bread was brought to him every third day by the bee-keeper, who lived on the spot; even to this man, who waited on him, Father Ferapont seldom spoke even a word. The four pounds of bread, together with the Sunday wafer regularly sent to him by the Father Superior after late mass, comprised his weekly rations. The water in his pitcher was changed every day. He rarely attended mass. His visiting admirers would see him kneeling in prayer sometimes all day long, without looking about himself. If addressed, he was brief, abrupt, strange and always almost rude. There were occasions, true very rare, when he would enter into conversation with visitors, but he would usually limit himself to some strange utterance which always greatly puzzled the visitor, and would then relapse into silence, despite all pleadings. He was an ordinary monk, and had never been ordained. A very strange rumour existed, though only among the ignorant, that Father Ferapont held communication with heavenly spirits and conversed with them alone, which was why he was silent with people. Following directions from the bee-keeper, another taciturn monk, the Obdorsk visitor reached Father Ferapont's cell. "Since you're a stranger, he may speak to you, but perhaps you won't get a word from him," the bee-keeper had warned him. It was with the greatest fear, as he later said, that the little monk drew near. At that rather late evening hour, Father Ferapont was sitting on a low bench outside the door of his cell, under the rustling leaves of a huge old elm. The air was becoming a little chilly with the approach of dusk. The Obdorsk monk prostrated himself before the saintly man and asked for his blessing.

"Do you want me to do the same, monk?" said Father Ferapont. "Rise!"

The monk got up.

"One is blessed who blesses another, so sit down by my side. Where are you from?"

What struck the poor little monk most of all was Father Ferapont looking so vigorous, his rigorous fasting and advanced years notwithstanding. He was tall, erect and straight-backed, and, though his face was thin, its complexion was fresh and healthy. He was of powerful physique, and no doubt still possessed considerable strength. Despite his years, his once black and even now merely grizzled hair and beard were still quite thick. The eyes were grey, large, and luminous, but so bulging as to be awe-inspiring. His accent showed he came from the north of the country. He wore a long rust-coloured peasant-style coat of coarse homespun cloth and was girded about with a length of rope. His neck and chest were bare. From under the coat could be seen a canvas shirt that must have been worn for several months for it was almost black with dirt. Under his coat, it was said, he wore iron chains weighing some thirty pounds, this for the mortification of the flesh. His bare feet were thrust into a pair of dilapidated old shoes that were falling apart.

"I'm from St. Sylvester, a little monastery at Obdorsk," the visitor said meekly, while his inquisitive little eyes kept a sharp if somewhat frightened watch on the hermit.

"I've been there, at Sylvester's. Stayed there. Is Sylvester well?"

The monk blinked.

"What a muddle-headed lot you are! How do you observe the fasts?"

"Our fare follows the ancient monastic rules. No meals

are served on Mondays, Wednesdays and Fridays during Lent. On Tuesdays and Thursdays the monks get white bread, stewed fruit laced with honey, cloudberries or pickled cabbage and oatmeal. On Saturdays there's fresh cabbage soup, pea soup with noodles, and porridge—all these with hempseed oil. On week-days, besides the cabbage soup, we have dried fish and porridge. Between Monday and Saturday evening on Holy Week, that is, for six days, we live on nothing but bread and water, and that sparingly; and nothing is cooked. If possible, we do not eat every day but as is in order for the first week in Lent. Nothing is eaten on Good Friday, and likewise on Saturday, when the fast is broken at three o'clock with a little bread and water followed by a single cup of wine. On Holy Thursday we have some food cooked without oil, and the same wine; sometimes we have only uncooked food for, as laid down for Holy Thursday by the Council of Laodicea: 'For it is unseemly to permit the partaking of food on the Thursday of the last week in Lent, and thus dishonour the whole of Lent.' That's exactly the way we do things. But," the monk went on, growing a little bolder, "what is all that compared with you, great Father, who live on nothing but bread and water all the year round, even including Holy Easter, and the bread we eat in two days lasts you a whole week. Such strict abstinence is wondrous indeed."

"But what about mushrooms?" Father Ferapont asked suddenly.

"Mushrooms?" the little monk repeated in puzzlement.

"That's exactly what I meant. I can do without their bread, which I don't need at all. I can go into the forest and live on mushrooms or berries, but the people here can't do without their bread, so they're tied up with the devil. Nowadays the unbelievers say there's no need for so much fasting. That statement smacks of overweening pride and an absence of faith."

"Oh, how true," the monk sighed.

"And did you see the devils in their midst?" Father Ferapont asked.

"In whose midst?" the monk inquired timidly.

"When I went to the Father Superior's on Whit Sunday last year—I haven't been there since—I saw a devil on one man's chest, hiding under his cassock, with only his horns sticking out. Another monk had a devil peeping out of a pocket, his eyes like gimlets, but he was afraid of me. Yet another had a devil in his insides, in that unclean belly of his, while another had a devil clinging to his neck, and he was carrying him about quite unawares."

"And you, d'you—see them?" the monk inquired.

"I tell you I do, I see right through them. As I was leaving the Father Superior's I saw one of them hiding from me behind the door. He was a big fellow, an arshin and a half in height, perhaps a little taller, with a long, thick brown tail. Its tip happened to be in the door crack. Being no fool, I slammed the door to, pinching the tail tight. He squealed and struggled to get away, so I made the sign of the cross thrice over him and that was the end of him; he was as dead as a squashed spider. I suppose he's rotted away, in the corner, stinking horribly, yet they over there don't see or smell it. It's a year since I was there. I'm letting you know all this because you're a stranger."

"Awesome are your words! And, great and blessed Father," the monk said with growing boldness, "are they true, the great things spoken of you even in the distant parts—that you are in constant touch with the Holy Spirit?"

"He does descend at times."

"How does he descend? In what shape?"

"As a bird."

"The Holy Spirit in the shape of a dove?"

"Sometimes it's the Holy Spirit and sometimes the Holy Ghost. The Holy Ghost is different and can appear in the shape of another bird: now a swallow, now a goldfinch and sometimes a tomtit."

"But how do you know him from an ordinary tit?"

"He speaks."

"But how does he speak, in what language?"

"In human language."

"And what does he tell you?"

"Why, today he told me that a fool would turn up and ask me senseless questions. You want to know too much, monk."

"Awesome are your words, most blessed and holy Father,"

said the latter, shaking his head. Incidentally, an expression of distrust gleamed in his timid little eyes.

"You see that tree, don't you?" Father Ferapont asked after a short silence.

"I do, blessed Father."

"You take it for an elm, but I see it as a different picture!"

"What as?" asked the monk after a fruitless pause.

"It happens at night. D'you see those two boughs? At night it is Christ stretching out His arms and seeking me. I see it quite clearly, and quake. It's awesome, oh, so awesome!"

"How can it be awesome if it's Christ Himself?"

"Why, he can take me up and carry me up to Heaven."

"Alive?"

"In the spirit and power of Elias. Haven't you heard of that? He'll take me in his arms and carry me up."

Though the Obdorsk monk returned to the cell he now shared with one of the brothers in a state of great perplexity after this conversation, his heart was undoubtedly more inclined towards Father Ferapont than to Father Zossima. First and foremost, he stood for fasting, and he found nothing strange in so strict an adherent of fasting as Father Ferapont "seeing marvels". Of course, his words smacked of the absurd, but surely the Lord knew what lay hidden in them; besides all fools for Christ's sake were capable of far stranger words and actions. As for the devil's tail being pinched in the door crack, that was something he was ready and eager to believe, not only in the figurative but also in the literal sense. Besides, even prior to his visit to the monastery, he had been greatly prejudiced against the *starets* institution, of which he had known only from hearsay. Like many others, he regarded it as definitely a harmful innovation. After his first day at the monastery, he had noticed the subdued grumbling among some of the unthinking monks who were opposed to the institution. Besides, he was meddlesome and quick-witted by nature, insatiably inquisitive about all things. That was why the electrifying news of the fresh "miracle" worked by the *starets* Zossima reduced him to extraordinary bewilderment. Later Alyosha could recall how, among the monks gathered about the *starets* and outside his cell, the figure of the inquisitive visitor from Obdorsk could be constantly seen darting from group to group, listening to everything and questioning all and sundry. At the time, however, Alyosha had paid little attention to him and it was only afterwards that he called it to mind— Besides, he had other things to think of: the *starets* Zossima, again feeling tired, had gone back to bed and, as he was closing his eyes, had thought of him and had him sent for. Alyosha at once returned at the run. With the *starets* at the time were only Father Paissi, the hieromonach Father Iosif and the novice Porfiri. Opening his weary eyes and fixing them on Alyosha, the *starets* suddenly asked him:

"Are your folk expecting you, my son?"

Alyosha hesitated.

"Have they no need of you? Did you promise anyone yesterday that you would call today?"

"I did promise—my father—my brother—and others as well—"

"You see. You must go without fail. Don't feel sad. Know that I won't die without saying my last word on earth in your presence. It is to you that I shall say that word, my son, and bequeath it to you. To you, my dear son, for you love me. And now go to them you've promised to see."

Alyosha obeyed at once though it was hard for him to leave. Yet his soul filled to the brim with rapture at the promise that he, Alyosha, would be there to hear his last word on earth and, above all, that it would be bequeathed to him, as it were. He was about to make a hurried departure so as to get through with his affairs in town and return as soon as possible, when Father Paissi pronounced a few parting words, which produced a powerful and unexpected impression on him. The Father did so as they were leaving the cell together.

"Constantly bear in mind, my young friend," he began directly and without any preliminaries, "that secular science, which has amassed tremendous force, has subjected to scrutiny, especially during the past century, everything divinely bequeathed to us in Holy Writ. After their ruthless analysis, the

222

scientists of this world have preserved absolutely nothing of what was previously held sacred. But they have delved only into the particulars and, with a blindness that is amazing, have overlooked the whole. Yet that whole stands unshakable before their eyes just as before, and the gates of hell shall not prevail against it. Has it not lived for nineteen centuries, and does it not live on today in the impulses in individual souls and in movements of the masses? It lives on, just as unshakable as before, in the impulses of the souls of those very atheists who have demolished everything! For even those who have denied Christianity and rebel against it have, in essence, been cast in the image of Christ and remain so, for neither their wisdom nor the fervour of their hearts has been able to create a higher ideal of man and his dignity than that provided of old by Christ. All attempts made towards that end have produced nothing but monstrosities. Keep that especially in mind, my young friend, for your departing *starets* is sending you forth into the world. Perhaps, as you recall this great day, you will not forget these words of mine, which have been spoken as a heartfelt parting message, since you are young, and sore are the temptations of this world, and beyond your strength to endure. And now, orphaned youth, go."

With these words, Father Paissi gave Alyosha his blessing. As he was leaving the monastery and giving thought to those sudden words, Alyosha realised that, in this austere monk, who had previously been so severe towads him, he had now met a new and unexpected friend, a new and loving guide: it was as though the dying *starets* had bequeathed Alyosha to him. "Perhaps that's what actually passed between them," he suddenly thought. The unexpected homily he had just heard—that if nothing else—spoke of Father Paissi's warmth of heart: he had hastened to equip a young mind as soon as possible for the struggle against temptations and to safeguard his young charge with a rampart stronger than which he could imagine nothing.

2.

At His Father's

First of all, Alyosha set out for his father's. As he drew near to the house, he recalled that, on the previous day, his father had strongly insisted that he should find a way of entering without his brother Ivan's knowledge. "Why was that?" Alyosha now thought suddenly. "If Father wishes to say something to me alone on the quiet, why should I enter on the quiet? Perhaps he meant to say something else in his excitement, but couldn't make up his mind," he decided. Nevertheless, he felt greatly relieved when Marfa Ignatievna, who opened the wicket (Grigori being ill in bed at the lodge), told him, in reply to his question, that Ivan Fyodorovich had gone out a couple of hours before.

"And Father?"

"He's up and having his coffee," Marfa Ignatievna replied somewhat stiffly.

Alyosha went in, and found the old man sitting alone at the table, in slippers and an old overcoat, looking through some accounts in a somewhat abstract fashion, for want of something better to do. He was quite alone in the house, Smerdyakov having gone out to do some shopping for dinner. But it was not the accounts that engaged his thoughts. Though he had risen early and was trying to keep his spirits up, he looked tired and weak. He had tied a red handkerchief about his forehead, on which some big purple bruises had appeared during the night. His nose, which had also become badly swollen during the night, was covered with several minor bruises, which decidedly gave the whole face a peculiarly sinister and irritable look. The old man was himself aware of that, and gave Alyosha an unfriendly look as the latter entered.

"The coffee's cold," he exclaimed sharply. "I'm not offering you any. I'm having nothing but lenten fish soup today, and I'm not inviting anybody to share it. What has brought you here?"

"To find out how you're feeling," Alyosha said.

"Indeed. Besides, I myself told you yesterday to come. It's all a lot of rubbish. You needn't have gone to the trouble. Incidentally, I was sure you'd turn up straight away."

This was spoken with the utmost hostility. Meanwhile he rose to his feet and anxiously examined his nose in the looking-glass (perhaps for the fortieth time that morning). He then set about arranging the red handkerchief on his forehead to the best advantage.

"Red's better. A white one smacks of the hospital," he observed pompously. "Well, how are things over there? How's your *starets*?"

"He's in a bad way, and may die today," Alyosha replied, but his father was not even listening and had forgotten the question as soon as he had asked it.

"Ivan is out," he said suddenly. "He's doing all he can to get Mitya's fiancée for himself. That's why he's staying on here," he added maliciously, regarding Alyosha with a wry face.

"Did he tell you that himself?" Alyosha asked.

"Yes, he did, and quite a while ago. Imagine, he did so some three weeks ago. After all, he didn't come here either to murder me by stealth, did he? There must be something behind his coming here!"

"Oh, no, why are you saying such things?" said Alyosha, looking highly embarrassed.

"True, he doesn't ask for money, but he won't get a brass farthing from me nevertheless. I want you to know that I intend to go on living on this earth as long as I can, my dear Alexei Fyodorovich; that's why I shall have need of every copeck, and the longer I live, the more I shall need it," he continued, pacing the room from corner to corner, his hands in the pockets of his loose and soiled overcoat of yellow summer calamanco. "I'm still a man, only fifty-five in fact, and I want to go on being a man in the full sense for another twenty years. When I'm old, I'll become odious, and none of them will come to me of their own free will, and it's then that I'll be needing my money. So that's why I'm saving up more and more for myself alone, my dear son Alexei Fyodorovich. I want that to be known to you, because I intend to go on living to the end in my abomination. Make no mistake on that score. There is sweetness in vice: all condemn it but live in it, only they do so on the sly, while I'm frank about it. It's for my being so outspoken that all those vice-lovers fall upon me. As for your paradise, Alexei Fyodorovich, I want no part in it, I would have you know. It isn't a proper place for a gentleman, even if it does exist. In my opinion, a man falls asleep and never wakes up, and then comes nothingness, mark my words. Order prayers for the repose of my soul if you wish, and to hell with you if you don't. That's my philosophy. Ivan talked sense here yesterday, even if we were all drunk. Ivan's a braggart with no real learning or, for that matter, any particular education at all. He keeps mum, and grins at you in silence—that's the only way he makes an impression."

Alyosha listened to him in silence.

"Why doesn't he speak to me? And if he does, he's so puffed up; your Ivan's a scoundrel! I can marry that Grushenka straight-away if I feel like it. You see, money will get you anything, Alexei Fyodorovich. That's what Ivan's afraid of, so he keeps an eye on me all the time to keep me from marrying. It's why he is prodding Mitya to marry Grushenka: he hopes to prevent Grushenka from getting me (as though I'll leave him my money if I don't marry her!). On the other hand, if Mitya does marry Grushenka, Ivan will take over his rich fiancée—that's his scheme! Your Ivan's a scoundrel!"

"How worked up you are. It's after what happened yester-day. Why don't you go and lie down?" said Alyosha.

"There: you say such things, yet I don't get angry with you," the old man observed suddenly, as though the thought had oc-curred to him for the first time. "Had Ivan said that, I would have resented it. It's with you alone that I've had kindly mo-ments, for I'm an ill-natured man."

"You're not ill-natured but simply with a kind of twist in you," said Alyosha, smiling.

"Listen, I had a good mind to get that ruffian Dmitri behind bars today, and I still don't know what I'll decide on. Of course, in these fashionable times of ours, it is accepted that fathers and mothers should be regarded as a prejudice but I would think that even today the laws do not permit old fathers being pulled about by the hair or kicked in the mug on the floor at their own homes, or any bragging of coming to murder them—and all that with witnesses standing by. If I wanted to, I could make him knuckle under and have him locked now for what he did yesterday."

"So you don't want to lodge a complaint, do you?"

"Ivan't talked me out of it. I'd snap my fingers at Ivan if it weren't for something I must take into account."

And bending over Alyosha, he continued in a confidential undertone:

"If I get the scoundrel behind bars, she'll hear of it and dash off to see him. But if she hears today that he has beaten up a feeble old man like me within an inch of his life, she may well drop him and come over to see me—that's the way she's made: she simply must be contrary. I can see right through her. Now won't you have some brandy? Take some of the cold coffee and I'll add a quarter of a glass of brandy to it. It improves the taste tremendously."

"No, no, thank you, but I'll take that roll, if you don't mind," said Alyosha and, taking a three-copeck French roll from the table, he put it into a pocket of his cassock. "And I don't think you should have any more brandy," he suggested apprehensively, looking into the old man's face.

"You're quite right; it rasps on the nerves instead of soothing them. Well, just another little glass— I'll get it from the cupboard—"

He unlocked the cupboard, poured himself a glass, gulped it down, then locked the cupboard and put the key back in his pocket.

"That's enough. A single glass won't finish me off."

"You're kindlier now," said Alyosha with a smile.

"H'm. I don't need the brandy to make me love you, but I'm a scoundrel when I have to deal with scoundrels. Why doesn't Ivan go to Chermashnya? It's because he wants to spy on me to find out how much I'll give Grushenka if she comes here. They're scoundrels—all of them! Besides, I don't recognise Ivan at all. Where did he spring from? He has none of our soul in him. Indeed, why should I leave him anything? I don't intend

227

to draw up any will—you should all know that. As for Mitya, I'll squash him like a cockroach. I squash black-beetles under my slipper at night. They squelch when you tread on them. Your Mitya will squelch too. I say, *your* Mitya because you love him. Well, you love him, and I'm not afraid that you do. But if Ivan loved him, I would fear that love. But Ivan loves nobody. Ivan is not one of our kind, and people of his ilk are not our kind of people; they're like the chaff, which the wind driveth away— A silly thought occurred to me yesterday when I told you to come here today: I wondered if I could find out through you about Mitya—if I let him have a thousand or two, would he agree, pauper and scoundrel that he is, to get out of these parts altogether for five years or, better still, for thirty-five, only without Grushenka. Give her up completely, eh?"

"I'll—I'll ask him—" Alyosha muttered. "If you let him have all of the three thousand, perhaps he'd—"

"Rubbish! You needn't ask him now, there's no need at all! I've changed my mind. It was a stupid idea that came into my pate yesterday. I won't give him anything, not even a stiver. I need my money for myself," the old man cried, waving a hand. "As it is, I'll squash him like a black-beetle. Not a word to him, or he may have hopes. And there's nothing more for you to do here, so be off. That fiancée of his—that Katerina Ivanovna, whom he has so carefully kept out of my way—will she marry him or not? I think you called on her yesterday, didn't you?"

"Nothing could make her abandon him."

"That's the kind of men these delicate young ladies hanker after: rakes and scoundrels. All these pallid young ladies are a trashy lot, I tell you, and so different from—well, never mind— If I were his age and had my looks of those days (for I was far better looking at twenty-eight than he is), I would have made the same conquest as he has. He's a blackguard! But he'll never, never get Grushenka— I'll trample him into the mud!"

The last words were now spoken in fury.

"You'd better be off, too," he snapped. "There's nothing more for you to do here today."

Alyosha went up to him to say good-bye, and kissed him on the shoulder.

"Why are you doing that?" the old man asked, somewhat taken aback. "We'll be meeting again. Or won't we?"

"Of course, we shall. I did it just like that."

"And I said it so, just like that, too—" said the old man, gazing at him. "Listen, listen!" he shouted after him, "come here again soon. I'll have some fish-soup made for you, something special, not like today's. Be sure to come! Make it tomorrow, d'you hear, tomorrow!"

No sooner had the door closed after Alyosha than he went back to the cupboard and tossed off another half-glass.

"That's enough!" he muttered, and cleared his throat. He relocked the cupboard, pocketed the key, and then went into his bedroom, lay down in his bed quite spent, and instantly fell asleep.

3.

Becomes Involved with Some Schoolboys

"Thank goodness he didn't ask me about Grushenka," Alyosha thought, in his turn, on leaving his father's house in the direction of Madame Khokhlakov's, "or else I would have had to tell him about my meeting with Grushenka yesterday." Alyosha had a painful feeling that the opponents had mustered fresh strength during the night, and had hardened their hearts with the coming of day. "Father's exasperated and in an evil temper; he's thought up something and will carry it through. And what about Dmitri? He, too, has become ever more unyielding overnight; he's, probably, exasperated and rancorous too, and has something up his sleeve, I suppose— Oh, I simply must manage to get hold of him today—"

However, Alyosha's thoughts were soon distracted by an occurrence which, though trifling, made a strong impression on him. Soon after crossing the square and turning a corner to reach Mikhailovsky Street, which runs alongside Bolshoi Street but is separated from it by a ditch (ditches criss-cross all our town), he caught sight of a small group of young schoolboys between the ages of nine and twelve, no more, gathered below at a footbridge. They were on their way home from school, with school knapsacks on their backs or leather satchels slung over their shoulders, some in jackets, others in overcoats; some even wore high boots, the tops pushed down to crease about the ankles in the elegant style affected by boys pampered by well-to-do parents. The group were engaged in eager conversation, evidently discussing something; Alyosha could not pass by children without a sense of involvement. It had been the same in Moscow: though he was drawn to tots of three or thereabouts, he also enjoyed the company of schoolchildren of ten or eleven. So, anxious though he felt, a sudden desire to join them and strike up a conversation came over him. As he drew near them and looked into their rosy-cheeked and animated faces, he saw that every one of them had a stone in his hand, some even two. On the opposite side of the ditch, at some thirty paces from the group, another boy was standing at a fence. He was a schoolboy, too, with a satchel by his side, about ten years old or even less, judging by his size, pale of face and sickly, and with flashing dark eyes. He was keeping a sharp eye on the group of six boys, evidently his schoolmates, in whose company he had just come out of the school-house, and with whom he seemed to be on terms of some hostility. Alyosha went up to the group and, addressing one of them, a fair, curly-haired and pink-cheeked boy in a black jacket, remarked as he looked into his face:

"When I used to carry a satchel like yours, I always slung it over my left shoulder so as to keep my right hand free to reach into it. Yours is on your right-hand side, which makes it awkward to get into."

Alyosha began in this business-like vein without any premeditated guile, in the only way a grown-up can hope to win the trust of a child, the more so of a group of children. One should break the ground in a practical and serious manner so as to be on terms of full equality. This was a something Alyosha felt instinctively.

"But he's left-handed," another boy at once retorted, a well set-up and healthy-looking boy of eleven. The other five kept their eyes fixed on Alyosha in silence.

"He even throws stones with his left hand," a third boy remarked.

It was at that instant that a stone fell among the group, grazing the left-handed boy but hitting nobody else, though it had been carefully and strongly aimed by the boy on the other side of the ditch.

"Bang him with your stone! Let him have it, Smurov!" they all shouted, but Smurov, the left-hander, stood in no need of encouragement and hurled his missile, which failed to hit his target, falling to the ground. The boy on the other side of the ditch, whose pockets were visibly bulging with stones, threw another missile at the group, this time straight at Alyosha, striking him painfully on the shoulder.

"He was aiming at you. He hit you on purpose. You're a Karamazov, a Karamazov, aren't you?" the boys shouted, laughing. "Well, now boys, all together. Shoot!"

Of the six stones volleyed at the boy, one struck him on the head. He fell down, but immediately jumped to his feet and set about furiously returning the fire. The exchange of shots did not flag, the pockets of many of the group being well stocked with stones.

"How can you! For shame—six against one! Why, you might kill him!" Alyosha cried.

He leapt forward to intercept the hail of stones and shield the boy on the other side of the ditch. Three or four of the boys desisted for a while.

"He started it first," yelled a red-shirted boy in a childish treble. "He's a rotter who stuck a penknife into Krasotkin a short while ago, making him bleed. Only Krasotkin didn't want to tell on him, but he deserves a good hiding."

"But what for? You rag him, I suppose. Don't you?"

"He's aimed another stone at your back. He knows who you are," the children shouted. "It's you he's aiming at, not us. Come on, boys, let him have it again. Don't miss him this time, Smurov!"

A fresh exchange began, this time very viciously. The boy across the ditch suffered a hit in the chest. He screamed and began to cry, and then ran off uphill towards Mikhailovsky

Street. "See, he's run away in a funk! Tow-beard's son!" the boys yelled.

"You don't know yet, Karamazov, what a bounder he is," said the boy in the jacket, his eyes flashing. He was probably the eldest in the group. "Killing's too good for him."

"What's wrong with him?" Alyosha asked. "Is he a sneak?"

The boys exchanged somewhat derisive glances.

"You're going that way, to Mikhailovsky Street, aren't you?" the same boy went on. "Well, you can catch up with him. Look, he's stopped again; he's looking at you in waiting."

"He's looking at you—looking at you," the boys chanted.

"You'd better ask him what he thinks of a tow-beard—a tattered one. Just ask him that."

There was an outburst of laughter, with Alyosha and the boys eyeing each other.

"Don't go there; he'll hurt you," Smurov cautioned him in a loud voice.

"I won't ask him about that tow-beard, for I suppose that's how you rag him, but I want to find out why you hate him so—"

"You'll find out all right," the boys laughed.

Alyosha crossed the foot-bridge and went uphill along the fence, straight towards the shunned boy.

"You'd better look out," the boys called after him in warning. "He won't be afraid of you. He'll stick his knife in you when you're off your guard—just as he did to Krasotkin."

The boy stood motionless, waiting for him. When he came close to him, Alyosha saw a boy of no more than nine, undersized and sickly, with a pale, thin and elongated face and large dark eyes which regarded him resentfully. He wore a shabby old overcoat far too small for him, his bare wrists sticking out of the sleeves. There was a large patch on the right knee of his trousers, and a big hole heavily blackened with ink gaped at the toe of his right boot. Both pockets of his overcoat were full of stones. Alyosha came to a standstill two paces away from him, with a questioning look in his eyes. Sensing from their expression that Alyosha had no intention of attacking him, the boy grew less defiant and was even the first to speak.

"They're six to one against me," he said suddenly, his eyes flashing. "But I'll lick them all."

"That stone must have hurt you badly," Alyosha remarked.

"But I got Smurov on the head!" the boy cried.

"They said you know who I was, and aimed a stone at me for some reason. Is that true?"

The boy glowered back at him.

"I don't know who you are. Do you know who I am?" Alyosha insisted.

"Let me alone!" the boy suddenly exclaimed bitterly, without, however, budging from the spot, as though expecting something to happen. Again there was a malicious gleam in his eyes.

"All right, I'll go away," said Alyosha. "Only I don't know who you are and I'm not ragging you. They told me how you should be baited, but I've no intention of doing that. Good-bye!"

"You monk in fancy trousers!" cried the boy, watching Alyosha with the same resentful and defiant look and taking up a defensive posture, expecting Alyosha would certainly fall upon him now. But Alyosha turned back, looked at him and walked off. Before he had taken three steps, he was hit painfully in the back by a stone hurled by the boy, the biggest in his pocket.

"So you hit from behind? They were telling the truth when they said that you attack on the sly?" said Alyosha, again turning round. This time the stone the enraged boy threw was aimed straight at his face, and Alyosha was barely able to shield it with an arm, the stone striking him on the elbow.

"You should be ashamed of yourself! Have I done you any harm?" he cried.

The boy waited in silent defiance, expecting that Alyosha would certainly attack him now but, seeing that he had no intention of doing so, he grew quite vicious, just like a little wild animal. He flew at Alyosha and, before the latter could stir, the malicious boy lowered his head, seized Alyosha's left hand in both of his and painfully bit his middle finger. His teeth sank into the flesh, and he did not let go for some ten seconds. Alyosha cried out in pain, trying with all his might to release it. The boy finally let go and retreated to his former place. The finger had been bitten to the bone, close to the nail, and was bleeding badly. Alyosha took out his handkerchief and bound it tight about the injured hand. The bandaging took almost a full minute, during which the boy stood waiting. At last Alyosha raised his gentle eyes towards him.

"Well," he said, "you see how painfully you've bitten me. That's enough, isn't it? Now tell me how I've wronged you."

The boy looked at him in surprise.

"Though I've no idea who you are and this is the first time I've seen you," Alyosha continued in the same even tone of voice, "but I must have done you some wrong, for otherwise you wouldn't have hurt me so much. So tell me what I've done that puts me in the wrong."

Instead of replying, the boy burst into a loud and tearful wail and suddenly dashed off. Alyosha followed him slowly towards Mikhailovsky Street and, for a long time, could see the boy running in the distance, without slackening his pace or looking back, and probably still blubbering. He made up his mind to seek out the boy without fail as soon as he found the time, and clear up the puzzling occurrence, which had so mystified him. He had no time for it at the moment.

4.

At the Khokhlakovs'

He soon reached the Khokhlakov home, a handsome, two-storey brick house, one of the finest in our town. Though Madame Khokhlakov spent most of her time in another gubernia, where she had an estate, or else in Moscow, where she had another house of her own, she also owned a house in our town, which she had inherited from her family. Besides, her estate in our uyezd was the largest of her three estates, yet she had hitherto visited our gubernia on very rare occasions.

She ran out to meet Alyosha in the hall.

"Have you received the letter about the new miracle?" she asked in rapid and nervous tones.

"Yes, I have."

"Has it been brought to the public notice? He's actually

restored a son to his mother!"

"He'll die today," said Alyosha.

"I know, for I've heard of it. Oh, how eager I am to have a talk with you about it all, with you or somebody else. No, with you, with you! What a pity it's impossible for me to see him! The whole town's electrified: people are in a state of expectancy. But now—d'you know we have Katerina Ivanovna here now!"

"Oh, how very fortunate!" Alyosha exclaimed. "Then I'll be able to see her here. She told me yesterday to be sure to come and see her today."

"I know, I know everything about it, everything. I've heard all the details about yesterday's happenings at her place—and all the horror with that—creature. *C'est tragique*, and if I were in her shoes—I don't know what I'd have done had I been in her shoes! But your brother, too, Dmitri Fyodorovich—goodness gracious! I'm quite at a loss, Alexei Fyodorovich: just imagine, your brother's here with her—not that dreadful brother of yesterday, but the other one, Ivan Fyodorovich; they're engaged in a very important conversation— If you could only realise what's going on between them! It's something terrible! It's like a pang of anguish; it's some frightful and quite incredible happening. The two are simply destroying themselves without any cause at all. They're aware of it and even seem to relish it. I've been looking forward to seeing you, just longing for your coming! The main thing is that it's something I can't put up with—that's the worst of it. I'll tell you everything presently, but there's something else and most important I've got to say. Its importance just seems to have slipped my memory: tell me, why is Lise in hysterics? The moment she heard your footsteps, she became hysterical."

"*Maman*, it's you who are hysterical now, but not me," Lise's voice came suddenly twittering from the next room. The door was just slightly ajar, and there was a catch in the voice as though she was on the verge of bursting into laughter but was doing her utmost to stifle it. Alyosha had at once noticed that the door was ajar and surmised that Lise was trying to catch sight of him from her wheelchair, but he could not discern anything.

"There's nothing surprising about that, nothing at all, Lise.

Your whims are enough to drive me into hysterics too. Only she's so ill, Alexei Fyodorovich. She was feeling bad all night, feverish and moaning. I thought that morning and Herzenstube would never come. He says that he can't make anything of it and that we must wait. That's what he always says. She screamed and became hysterical as you were approaching the house, and insisted on being wheeled back into her former room here—"

"I didn't at all know he was coming, Mother, and it wasn't because of him, that I wanted to be wheeled into this room."

"That's not true, Lise. Julia ran to let you know Alexei Fyodorovich was coming. You told her to be on the lookout for him."

"Mother dear, that was not said very cleverly. But if you want to make up for it and say something very clever, then, Mother dear, tell our esteemed visitor Alexei Fyodorovich that he has shown a lack of cleverness by making so bold as to call on us today after what took place yesterday, and despite his being a laughing-stock."

"You are going too far, Lise, and I assure you I shall have to resort to severity with you. Who's made a laughing-stock of him? I'm so glad he's come; I need him terribly. Oh, Alexei Fyodorovich, I'm so unfortunate!"

"But what's wrong with you, Mother darling?"

"Oh, Lise, it's all because of your whims, your restlessness, your sickness, that awful night of fever, and that unbearable and everlasting Herzenstube—that everlasting, everlasting man! And, most important—everything, in fact everything—! And now, even this miracle! Oh, how it has amazed and shaken me, dear Alexei Fyodorovich! And now there's that tragedy in the drawing-room, which is simply more than I can bear—I tell you in advance that it's more than I can bear. It may be a comedy perhaps, not a tragedy. Tell me, will the *starets* Zossima live till tomorrow, will he? Dear God! What's going on in me? I keep closing my eyes and see it's all nonsense, a lot of nonsense!"

"I'd like to ask you to let me have some kind of bandage," Alyosha suddenly put in, "to bind my finger with. I've hurt it badly, and it's extremely painful."

236

He unbound the bitten finger, the handkerchief soaked in blood. Madame Khokhlakov gave a scream and shut her eyes.

"Good Heavens, what a wound! It's frightful!"

As soon as Lise, through the crack in the door, caught sight of the finger, she flung the door wide open.

"Come in, come in here at once," she exclaimed with imperative insistence. "And no nonsense now, please! Good Lord, why were you standing there all the time without saying anything about it? He may have lost a lot of blood, Mother! Where and how did it happen? First of all, get some water, some water! The wound must be washed thoroughly. Simply put the finger in cold water to ease the pain, and keep it there. Hurry up with the water, Mother, bring it in a basin. Do hurry!" she concluded in a nervous tone. She was quite frightened at the sight of the wound; it had completely unnerved her.

"Shouldn't we have Herzenstube sent for?" Madame Khokhlakov cried.

"You'll be the death of me, Mother. Your Herzenstube will come and say he can make nothing of it! Get the water! For goodness' sake, Mother, go and hurry Julia, who's for ever dawdling and can never be fast. Hurry up, Mother, or I'll die—"

"Oh, it's nothing much!" exclaimed Alyosha, taken aback by their alarm.

Julia came running with the water, and Alyosha put his finger in the basin.

"For goodness' sake, Mother, get some lint and that muddy-coloured caustic liquid for cuts—I forget what it's called! We've got some, got some!— You know where it's kept, Mother. The bottle's in your bedroom, in the righthand cupboard—a big bottle, as well as the lint—"

"I'll fetch everything at once, Lise, only don't get worked up and don't worry. See how staunchly Alexei Fyodorovich is putting up with his trouble. And where could you have got this nasty wound, Alexei Fyodorovich?"

Madame Khokhlakov hurried out of the room, which was what Lise had been waiting for.

"In the first place," she said rapidly to Alyosha, "answer my question: where did you get that wound? After that, I'll talk to you about something quite different. Well?"

Instinctively feeling that to her time was precious before her mother returned, Alexei told her rapidly and tersely, but in precise and clear terms, and omitting what was unessential, about his strange encounter with the schoolboys. Lise threw up her hands when she had heard the story.

"How could you have got yourself mixed up with a lot of little schoolboys, and you in that costume of yours!" she cried out angrily, as if she even had some right to him. "Why, after that, you're nothing but a boy, just a little boy, as little as can be! Yet you must find out somehow about that bad little boy and let me know, for there's something behind what happened. And now for the second matter, but first a question: can you talk sensibly about something trifling, despite the pain, Alexei Fyodorovich?"

"Of course, I can. Besides, there's no pain to speak of now."

"That's because your finger's in the water. It will have to be changed before it gets warm. Julia, run and fetch a piece of ice from the cellar, and another basin of water. Now that she's gone, I can speak: please, dear Alexei Fyodorovich, return the letter I sent you yesterday; return it at once, for Mother may be back at any moment, and I don't want—"

"I haven't got it with me."

"That's not true, you've got it with you! I knew you'd answer that way. It's there in that pocket. All night long I was regretting that stupid jest. Please return the letter at once!"

"It's over there."

"But you must not consider me a child, just a little, little girl, after that letter, with such a stupid jest. Forgive that stupid joke, but you simply must bring me the letter, if you really haven't got it with you now. Be sure to bring it today, without fail."

"I can't possibly do that today, because I'm going to the monastery, and shan't be able to come to see you for two, three or even four days, because the *starets* Zossima—"

"Four days? What nonsense! I suppose you must have laughed at me quite a lot."

"Not in the least."

"Why not?"

"Because I believed everything in the letter."

"That's an insult!"

"In no way. As soon as I read it, I decided it would be that way because I shall have to leave the monastery when the *starets* Zossima dies. I'll resume my studies and sit for my examinations. When the legal age is reached, we'll marry. I'll love you. Though I've not had the time to give thought to the matter, I don't believe I'll find a better wife, and the *starets* has told me to get married—"

"But I'm a cripple who's wheeled about in a chair," Lise laughed, flushing crimson.

"I'll wheel you about myself, but I'm sure you'll get well by that time."

"You must be mad," said Lise nervously, "to jump to such a ridiculous conclusion from a joke like that! Oh, here comes Mother, perhaps just at the right moment, too. Mother, why are you always late? How could you be so long? Here's Julia, too, with the ice!"

"Oh, Lise, don't talk at the top of your voice like that! Please, don't. Your screaming drives me— What could I do if you yourself put the lint somewhere else? It took me so long to find. I suspect you did it on purpose."

"But how was I to know he'd come with a finger bitten through? Otherwise, I might really have done it on purpose. Mother, my angel, you're beginning to say the most clever things."

"Never mind the clever things, but why all that emotion over Alexei Fyodorovich's finger and everything else? Oh, my dear Alexei Fyodorovich, what oppresses me is not anything in particular, and not some Herzenstube, but everything taken together, everything as a whole—it's something I can't put up with."

"Enough of Herzenstube, Mother, quite enough," cried Lise, laughing gaily. "Hurry with the lint and water. It's simply Goulard water, Alexei Fyodorovich. I've recollected the name—it's an excellent lotion. Just imagine, he had a fight with some boys in the street as he was coming here, and one of the boys bit his finger. Isn't he just like a little boy himself? Could he think of getting married after that, for, imagine, he wants to marry, Mama. Just think of him married! Isn't it funny? Isn't it awful?"

And she kept on laughing her nervous titter, gazing mischievously at Alyosha.

"But why should he get married, Lise; for what reason? It's quite out of place for you to speak of it—when that boy may have had rabies."

"Oh, Mother! Do boys ever have rabies?"

"Why not? You seem to imply that I've said something silly. Your boy may have been bitten by a mad dog, and he may have become rabid himself and bitten someone else nearby in his turn. How beautifully she's bandaged your finger, Alexei Fyodorovich! I couldn't have done it half as well. Does it still hurt?"

"Just a little."

"And aren't you afraid of water?" asked Lise.

"Come, enough of that, Lise. I may have been somewhat hasty in speaking of the boy having rabies, and you're already drawing conclusions. Katerina Ivanovna simply came rushing here as soon as she learnt you'd come, Alexei Fyodorovich. She's expecting you and eager to see you—just dying to see you, in fact."

"Oh, Mother, do go there alone. He's in no condition to go there now; he's in such pain."

"I feel no pain at all," said Alyosha, "and I can very well go there."

"What? Are you leaving? How can you?"

"But why not? I'll come back when I get through there and we'll be able to talk to your heart's content. I'd very much like to see Katerina Ivanovna straightaway, because I'm anxious to get back to the monastery as soon as I can today."

"Take him away, Mother, and at once. You needn't trouble to come back after seeing Katerina Ivanovna. Go straight back to your monastery—that's the place for you! And now I want to get some sleep. I didn't get a wink of sleep last night."

"Oh, Lise, all this is only joking on your part, but I do

wish you'd really get some sleep!" Madame Khokhlakov exclaimed.

"I don't understand in what way I've—" Alyosha muttered. "I'll stay on for another three minutes or so, even for five minutes."

"Even five! Take him away, Mother! He's monstrous!"

"Have you gone out of your mind, Lise? Let's go, Alexei Fyodorovich. She's too capricious today, so I don't want to irritate her. Nervous women are so difficult, Alexei Fyodorovich! But perhaps she'll really be able to get some sleep after all. How good it is that you've made her feel sleepy so soon. What a piece of luck!"

"Oh, Mother, you say the nicest things. I'd like to kiss you for it."

"Let me kiss you, too, Lise. Listen, Alexei Fyodorovich," Madame Khokhlakov said in a rapid and impressively mysterious undertone, as they were leaving. "I don't want to influence you or lift the veil; when you go in, you'll see for yourself just what is taking place there. It's appalling, a most unimaginable comedy: she loves your brother Ivan Fyodorovich, but is doing her utmost to persuade herself that she loves your other brother Dmitri Fyodorovich. It's dreadful! I'll go in with you and stay on to the end if I'm not turned out."

5.

Anguish in the Drawing-room

But the talk in the drawing-room was already coming to a close. Though she looked determined, Katerina Ivanovna was in a state of considerable excitement. Ivan Fyodorovich was making ready to leave when Alyosha and Madame Khokhlakov entered the room. He looked somewhat pale, which made Alyosha give him an uneasy glance: something that had been keeping Alyosha in doubt, a problem that had been causing him keen anxiety for quite a while, was now on the point of being resolved. During the past month, it had several times been suggested to him in various quarters that his brother Ivan was in love with Katerina Ivanovna, and moreover, intended to win her from Mitya. Until quite recently, the idea had seemed preposterous to Alyosha, though it had been causing him much concern. He loved both his brothers and was in dread of such rivalry between them. And now, on the previous day, Dmitri himself had suddenly told him in so many words that he was even glad of brother Ivan's rivalry, which would be much to his (Dmitri's) own advantage. But in what way? Help him to marry Grushenka? That was something Alyosha considered the most impossible step, an act of despair. Besides, until the evening before, Alyosha had been perfectly sure that Katerina Ivanovna was herself passionately and steadfastly in love with his brother Dmitri—but that had only been until the evening before. Moreover, he had for some reason imagined she could not love a man like Ivan, but did love Dmitri just for what he was, despite the utterly unbelievable nature of such a love. But, during the previous day's scene with Grushenka, a new idea had vaguely suggested itself to him. The word "anguish", which Madame Khokhlakov had just pronounced, almost made him start: on the night before, towards daybreak, as he had lain half awake, he had suddenly cried out, "Anguish, what anguish!" as though reacting to something he had dreamt. All night long, he had had a dream about the previous day's scene at Katerina Ivanovna's. He was now deeply impressed by Madame Khokhlakov's forthright and emphatic assertion that Katerina Ivanovna was in love with his brother Ivan, and, out of some caprice, some urge of anguish, was in fact deceiving and tormenting herself with an imaginary love of Dmitri prompted by some sense of gratitude. "Perhaps her words do express the full truth!" he thought. But in that case, where did Ivan stand? Alyosha somehow felt instinctively that Katerina Ivanovna was of a domineering nature, a trait she could display towards a man like Dmitri, but decidedly not a man like Ivan. For Dmitri alone could (of course, only in the long term) ultimately submit to her, and do so "for his own happiness" (which was what Alyosha would have even liked)—but not Ivan. No, Ivan could never submit to her; such submissiveness would bring him no happiness. That was the opinion Alyosha had, for some reason, un-wittingly formed of Ivan. And now all these doubts and reflec-tions flashed across his mind the moment he entered the draw-ing-room. There was also another irresistible and sudden thought: "But what if she loves nobody, neither one nor the other?" I shall note that Alyosha seemed abashed by such thoughts of his, and had reproached himself for them whenever they had occurred to him during the past month. "After all, what do I really know about love and women, and who am I to draw such conclusions?" he would think reproachfully after any such thought or conjecture. Yet he could not help thinking of the matter. He instinctively felt, for instance, that the rivalry be-tween his two brothers had become only too important a matter in their lives, something too much depended on. "One viper devouring the other," his brother Ivan had said on the previ-ous day when speaking with irritation of his father and his broth-er Dmitri. So, as he saw it, his brother Dmitri was a viper and had perhaps been one for a long time. Could it have been since the time Ivan had met Katerina Ivanovna? Of course, the words had escaped involuntarily from Ivan's lips, but that gave them an added significance. If that was so, what chance was there for peace? Were there not, on the contrary, fresh grounds for hatred and hostility in their family? Above all, who was Alyosha to feel sorry for? What should he wish each of them? He loved them both, but what should he wish each of them in the midst of such frightful contradictions? One could easily lose one's bearings in such a muddle, and uncertainty was some-thing Alyosha's heart could not tolerate, for his love was always of an active nature. He was incapable of loving pas-sively; when he loved someone, he at once set about helping that person. To do that, he had to have some definite purpose in view, and know for sure what was really necessary to each of them; when he became convinced that his purpose was a true one, it would be natural for him to help each of them. However, instead of some clear purpose, he saw nothing but uncertainty and confusion in everything. The world "anguish" had been spoken! But what was he to make even of that anguish? He could not make head or tail of all that disarray!

On catching sight of Alyosha, Katerina Ivanovna said in rapid and joyous tones to Ivan Fyodorovich, who had risen from his seat, preparing to leave:

"Just a moment! Please stay on for a while. I'd like to hear the opinion of this person, in whom I have implicit confidence. Don't leave either, Katerina Ossipovna," she went on, addressing Madame Khokhlakov. She seated Alyosha by her side, while Madame Khokhlakov sat down facing her, next to Ivan Fyodorovich.

"All of you here are my friends, all I have in the world, my dear friends," she began fervently, in a voice that quivered with sincere tears of suffering, making Alyosha' heart go out to her. "Alexei Fyodorovich, you witnessed yesterday's—dreadful scene, and saw my state. You did not see that, Ivan Fyodorovich, but he did. I don't know what he thought of me yesterday, but there's something I do know: if the same thing were to happen today, right now, I would voice the same sentiments as I did yesterday—the same sentiments, the same words, and the same actions. You remember my actions, Alexei Fyodorovich, don't you? You restrained me from one of them"—(She turned red as she said this, her eyes flashing.) "I tell you, Alexei Fyodorovich: I can't get reconciled to anything that has taken place. Listen, Alexei Fyodorovich, I don't even know whether I love *him* now. I find him *pitiful*, and that doesn't make for love. If I love him, if I'd go on loving him, then perhaps, I wouldn't feel pity for him now, but, on the contrary, would hate him—"

Her voice trembled and tears glistened on her eyelashes. Alyosha started inwardly. "The girl is truthful and sincere," he thought, "and—and she no longer loves Dmitri!"

"Indeed, indeed!" Madame Khokhlakov exclaimed.

"Just a moment, dear Katerina Ossipovna. I haven't said what is most important and conclusive, and what I decided last night. I'm aware that my decision may be a terrible one—for me, but I foresee that I will never change it all my life long, not for anything in the world. My decision has been approved and praised by Ivan Fyodorovich, my dear, kind and always magnanimous adviser, the only friend I have in the world, a man with a deep insight into the human heart—my decision is known to him."

"Yes, I approve of it," said Ivan Fyodorovich in a low but firm voice.

"But I'd like Alyosha (oh, forgive me, Alexei Fyodorovich, for calling you simply Alyosha)—I'd like Alexei Fyodorovich to tell me, in the presence of both my friends, whether I'm right or wrong. I have an instinctive feeling, Alyosha, my dear brother (because you *are* my dear brother)," she went on rapturously, taking his cold hand in her hot one, "I have a feeling that, despite all my suffering, your decision and your approval will set my mind at ease, because your words will enable me to calm down and grow reconciled to my fate—I feel that!"

"I don't know what you're going to ask me," said Alyosha, colouring. "What I do know is that I'm very fond of you and, at this very minute, wish you more happiness than do for myself! But you see, I know nothing at all about such things—" he suddenly hastened to add, for some reason.

"What is most important in these matters now, Alexei Fyodorovich, is integrity and a sense of duty, and I don't know what else, but something perhaps higher than a sense of duty. My heart prompts that irresistible feeling, which is so compelling. To put the matter in a nutshell, my mind is made up: even if he does marry that—creature," she went on emphatically, "whom I shall never, never be able to forgive, *I shall never abandon him!* From now on, I shall never abandon him, never!" she said with an outburst of pallid and agonised ecstasy. "I don't mean I'll pursue him, get in his way at every turn, or torment him—oh, no! I'll go away to some other town, anywhere you like, but I shall keep an unwinking eye on him all my life long. When he grows miserable with that woman, which is bound to happen very soon, let him come to me, and he'll find a friend, a sister, in me— Of course, nothing but a sister, and it will always be that way, but he'll at last realise that this sister is a sister indeed, who loves him and has sacrificed her whole life for him. I'll achieve that; I'll insist on his getting to know me for what I am and telling me everything, without feeling ashamed of anything!" she exclaimed in a kind of frenzy. "I'll be the god he'll pray to—that's the least he owes me for his treachery and for what I had to live through yesterday because of him. And let him see, throughout his life that, despite his faithlessness and treachery, I'll be true to him and keep my promise to him till the end of my days. I'll—I'll turn only into a means for his happiness or—how should I put it—into an instrument, an engine, for his happiness, and throughout my life, all of it, he shall see that, as long as he lives. That is my decision! And it has Ivan Fyodorovich's full approval."

She was gasping for breath. She may have been anxious to express the thought in a more dignified, skilful and natural manner, but what she said was too hurried and too forthright. There was much youthful impulsiveness in her words; much was merely a reflection of her resentment of the events of the previous day and an inner urge to hold her head high—she was well aware of that herself. She suddenly looked downcast and her eyes grew sullen. This was at once noticed by Alyosha, who felt a twinge of compassion in his heart. At this point, Ivan said something that made matters worse.

"I've merely voiced my opinion," he said. "Coming from anybody else, all this would have been morbid and laboured; with you, it's different. Anybody else would have been wrong, but you are right. I don't know how it's to be explained, but I see that you're sincere to the highest degree, which is why you're right—"

"But that's only at this very instant— But what does that instant spring from? From nothing but yesterday's insult—that's the significance of this instant!" cried Madame Khokhla-kov, in a sudden outburst; though reluctant to intervene, she had been unable to keep herself in check and had blurted out a very true thought.

"Indeed, indeed," Ivan broke in with sudden vehemence, obviously annoyed at having been interrupted. "That's so, but with any other woman that instant would have sprung from yesterday's impression and would be only fleeting, but with Katerina Ivanovna that instant will continue throughout her life. What for others is nothing more than a promise is for her a never ending and burdensome duty, sombre perhaps but unflagging. She will be sustained by this sense of a duty performed. Your life, Katerina Ivanovna, will henceforth proceed in a melancholy contemplation of your own feelings, your self-abnegation and your sorrow; however, that suffering will become alleviated later, and your life will turn into a serene contemplation of a firm and proud design fulfilled, one that is proud in its own way and, in any case, motivated by despair but triumphantly carried out; that consciousness will ultimately bring you the fullest satisfaction, and will reconcile you to everything else—"

This was said with some unmistakable malice and evidently on purpose, even perhaps without the least desire to conceal his intention, in other words, to show that he was speaking with intention and in derision.

"Goodness, how far you are from the mark!" Madame Khokhlakov again exclaimed.

"Why don't you speak up, Alexei Fyodorovich? It's terribly important for me to hear what you will say!" cried Katerina Ivanovna, bursting into sudden tears.

Alyosha rose from the sofa.

"It's all right, quite all right!" she continued, still weeping. "I'm simply upset and affected by last night, but the presence of two such friends as your brother and you gives me strength—because I know—that you two will never abandon me—"

"I'm sorry to say," said Ivan Fyodorovich suddenly, "that I'm leaving for Moscow, perhaps tomorrow, and will have to leave you for a long time— Unfortunately, there's nothing I can do about it—"

"Tomorrow—to Moscow!" Katerina Ivanovna exclaimed, her face suddenly contorted. "But—good heavens, how fortunate!" she cried in a completely different tone, her tears vanishing without a trace. The change in her was instantaneous, and simply amazed Alyosha. The poor and insulted girl who had just been weeping as if her heart would break had suddenly yielded place to a self-possessed woman extremely pleased with a turn of events that had even gladdened her.

"Oh, it's not my having to take leave of you that is fortunate—of course not!" she suddenly corrected herself, as it were, with the charming smile of a well-bred lady. "The idea simply couldn't occur to a friend like you. On the contrary, I feel unhappy at losing you" (she suddenly ran up to Ivan Fyodorovich, and, taking his two hands in her own, pressed them warmly); "what is fortunate is that you will be able to tell my aunt and my sister Agafya in person about the horror of my present situation: you can be quite frank with Agafya, but you must spare my dear aunt's feelings, and act as you are best able to. You can't imagine how miserable I felt yesterday and this morning, wondering how to write them that dreadful letter, because there are things that simply can't be conveyed in a letter— but now I'll find it easier to write because you'll be there to explain. Oh, I'm so glad. But that is the only reason for my gladness, believe me. You are, of course, indispensable to me— I'll rush off to write the letter," she suddenly concluded, and even made to leave the room.

"But what about Alyosha? What about his opinion, which you were so eager to learn?" cried Madame Khokhlakov, her words carrying a tart and testy undertone.

"I haven't forgotten," said Katerina Ivanovna, stopping suddenly. "And why are you so short with me at such a moment, Katerina Ossipovna?" she cried with bitter reproach. "I stand by what I said. I need his opinion, nay his decision! As he says, so shall it be: that's how I, on the contrary, am hanging on your lips, Alexei Fyodorovich— But what's wrong with you?"

"I could never have thought it possible!" the distressed Alyosha suddenly cried. "I could never have imagined it!"

"What do you mean?"

"He's leaving for Moscow and you exclaimed that you were glad—and you did that intentionally! Then you went on to explain that it wasn't his departure that gladdened you and that, on the contrary, you were sorry—to be losing a friend; but that, too, was a piece of play-acting—in a stage comedy!"

"A stage comedy? What do you mean!" cried the astonished Katerina Ivanovna, frowning and flushing crimson.

"Why, no matter how much you assure him that you're sorry to lose a friend in him, yet you insist on telling him point-blank that his departure is fortunate," Alyosha said with almost breathless emotion; he remained standing at the table.

"I don't understand what you're talking about—"

"I don't know either— It's as if something has suddenly dawned on me— I know it's unfair, but I'll say it anyway," Alyosha continued in the same trembling and faltering voice. "It has dawned upon me that perhaps you don't love my brother Dmitri at all—and have never loved him from the very outset— Besides, Dmitri doesn't love you at all—and hasn't loved you from the very outset; he only holds you in honour— I don't quite know how I've made so bold as to say all this, but somebody's got to speak up because—because nobody here is ready to speak the truth—"

"What truth?" cried Katerina Ivanovna with something hysterical in her voice.

"It's the following," Alyosha gabbled, seeming to throw all caution to the winds. "Have Dmitri come here— I'll find him—let him come and take you by the hand, then take brother Ivan by the hand, and then join your hands together. You're tormenting Ivan only because you love him—you're tormenting him because your love for Dmitri springs from emotional anguish—and not from a true feeling. You've simply persuaded yourself that you do—"

His voice tapered off into silence.

"Why, you're a religious crackpot, that's what you are!" Katerina Ivanovna snapped, her face white and her lips twisted in anger. Ivan Fyodorovich burst into laughter and rose to his feet, hat in hand.

"You are mistaken, my good Alyosha," he said, with an expression Alyosha had never before seen on his face, an expression of youthful sincerity and powerful and irresistibly candid emotion, "Katerina Ivanovna has never cared for me! She was always aware of my love for her, though I never said a word about it to her; she was aware of it but never cared for me. She has never stood in need of my friendship, not for a single day. She was too proud for that, yet she kept me by her side out of a constant thirst for vengeance. Through me and on me

249

she gave vent to her vengeance for all the insults continually heaped on her by Dmitri ever since their first meeting— For their first meeting has rankled in her heart as an insult. Such is her heart! I've actually done nothing but listen to her protestations of love for him. I'm going away, Katerina Ivanovna, but you should know that you really love nobody but him. And the more he insults you, the more you love him. That is the source of your anguish. You love him for what he is, even if he does insult you. Should he reform, you would give him up at once and stop loving him. But you need him so as to constantly contemplate your act of devotion and be able to upbraid him with his faithlessness. And it all comes of your pride. Oh, there's been a great deal of humiliation and self-abasement here, but it all comes of pride— I'm too young and have loved you too much. I know that I shouldn't have told you all this, and that it would have been more dignified on my part simply to go away; that would have caused you less offence. But then, I'll be going away far from here and will never return. It's for good— I don't want to witness any more of your anguish— Well, there's nothing more for me to add, for everything has been said— Farewell, Katerina Ivanovna, you have no reason to be angry with me because I've been punished a hundred times more than you have, if only because I'll never see you again. Farewell. I don't want your hand. You've tormented me too wilfully for me to forgive you at this moment. I'll forgive you later, but I don't want your hand now."

Den Dank, Dame, begehr ich nicht!

he added with a wry smile, proving, incidentally quite unexpectedly, that he could quote Schiller from memory, something that Alyosha would never have believed before. He left the room without even taking leave of Madame Khokhlakov, the hostess. Alyosha threw up his hands in dismay.

"Ivan," he cried after him, quite at a loss, "come back, Ivan. No, nothing can make him come back!" he exclaimed with sudden and sorrowful insight. "It's all my fault, all mine, because I began it! But Ivan's words were spiteful and unfair, yes, unfair and spiteful—" he said, speaking as one almost demented.

Katerina Ivanovna suddenly left the room.

"You've created no mischief at all; your behaviour was splendid, quite angelic," Madame Khokhlakov said in a rapid and ecstatic whisper to the sorrowful Alyosha. "I'll make every effort to dissuade Ivan Fyodorovich from leaving—"

To Alyosha's extreme distress, her face was radiant. It was at that moment when Katerina Ivanovna suddenly returned with two hundred rouble notes in her hands.

"I want to ask you to do me a great favour, Alexei Fyodorovich," she began, addressing Alyosha in an apparently calm and level voice, as though nothing out of the ordinary had just taken place. "A week ago—yes, it was a week ago, I believe—Dmitri Fyodorovich behaved in a hasty and unfair fashion—even outrageously. There's a disreputable place here—some kind of tavern, and it was there that—he met that discharged army officer, a junior captain, whom your father had employed on some business. For some reason, Dmitri Fyodorovich flew into a temper against this man and, grabbing him publicly by the beard, dragged him out into the street—in that humiliating way, pulling him along quite a distance. They say that man's son, quite a child, who attends school here, ran alongside them, crying aloud and begging for his father, appealing to people in the street to defend him, but meeting with nothing but laughter. You must forgive me, Alexei Fyodorovich, but I can't recall such shameful behaviour of *his* without indignation—behaviour only Dmitri Fyodorovich can be capable of in anger—and carried away by his passion! I can't even put it in words—I simply can't. Words fail me. I've made inquiries about the poor man and learnt that he's quite poverty-stricken. His name is Snegiryov. He was guilty of some misdemeanour in the army, for which he was discharged from the service. I don't know much about the matter, but he and his unfortunate family of sick children and his wife—she's quite insane, I believe—have been reduced to abject penury. He's been in this town for quite a long time, doing odd jobs and working for a while as a copy-clerk, but has been unable to collect any pay. As I happened to look at you—I mean, I thought—I don't know how to put it,

251

for I'm so mixed up—you see, I wanted to ask you, Alexei Fyodorovich, my kind-hearted Alexei Fyodorovich, to go to him on some pretext—I mean, to that captain—oh, dear, I can't get it all straight—and, with the delicacy and consideration you alone are capable of (at this, Alyosha suddenly coloured), hand him this monetary assistance—these two hundred roubles. He'll probably accept it—I mean, you'll persuade him— Or perhaps I'm mistaken—I don't know! You see, this is not by way of compensation to prevent him from lodging a complaint (as he means to, I believe), but just as an expression of sympathy, of my desire to help him. It comes from me, Dmitri Fyodorovich's fiancée, and not from him— In short, you'll find some way to do it— I'd go there myself, but you'll be able to do it far better than me. He lives in Ozerny Street, at the house of a Mrs. Kalmykov— Please don't refuse to do me this favour—but now—I'm feeling somewhat tired. Good-bye—"

She turned and disappeared behind the portière so suddenly that Alyosha had no time even to utter a word, though he had something to say. He wanted to ask her for forgiveness, to blame himself, or at least, say something, for his heart was full, and he was loth to leave without doing so. But, grasping his hand, Madame Khokhlakov led him out of the room. She halted in the hall and continued in the same whisper as before.

"It's all her pride; she's struggling against it, but she's kind-hearted, charming and magnanimous," she exclaimed in an undertone. "Oh, I do love her, especially at times, and how glad I feel at the way things are developing! Dear Alexei Fyodorovich, I can now tell you something you didn't know before: all of us—her two aunts, myself—well, all of us, even Lise, have for the past month been hoping and praying for only one thing—that she will give up your favourite brother Dmitri, who ignores her and doesn't love her at all, and marry Ivan Fyodorovich, an educated and superior young man, who loves her to distraction. We've been plotting to bring that about and that may be the only reason I'm staying on here—"

"But she's been in tears again, because of her injured feelings!" Alyosha exclaimed.

"Never believe a woman's tears, Alexei Fyodorovich. In

cases like this one, I'm always on the men's side, not the women's."

"You're pampering and spoiling him, Mama," came Lise's thin, thin voice from the other side of the door.

"No, I've been the cause of it all; I'm terribly at fault!" the disconsolate Alyosha kept repeating in acute remorse for his behaviour and even hiding his face in his hands in shame.

"Quite the reverse, you acted angelically, quite angelically, I'm prepared to repeat that a thousand times over."

"Mother, how did he behave angelically?" Lise's voice could be heard again.

"When I witnessed it all," Alyosha continued as though he had not heard Lise's words, "I somehow imagined that she loved Ivan, and that was why I said such a silly thing— What will happen now?"

"Who to? Who to?" Lise cried, "you probably want to be the death of me, Mother! I'm asking you something, but you simply don't answer my questions."

At that moment, the maid came running in.

"There's something wrong with Katerina Ivanovna. She's crying, in hysterics and convulsions."

"What the matter?" cried Lise with alarm in her voice, "Mother, I'll be the one who'll be having hysterics, not she!"

"Lise, don't scream like that, for heaven's sake stop tormenting me! You're still at an age when you shouldn't know everything grown-ups do. I'll be back directly and tell you everything you can be told. Goodness gracious! I'm coming, coming! Hysterics—that's a good sign, Alexei Fyodorovich, excellent indeed. It's just what she needs. In such cases, too, I'm always against women, against all these women's tears and hysterics. Run along, Julia, and tell her I'm coming at once. She has only herself to blame for Ivan Fyodorovich leaving like that. But he won't go away. Lise, stop your screaming, for goodness' sake! Oh, yes, it's not you who are screaming, but me. Do forgive your mother, but I'm utterly delighted, delighted! Did you notice, Alexei Fyodorovich, how youthful Ivan Fyodorovich looked as he was leaving—when he said all that, and left? I found him such an educated person, so scholarly, and he

253

suddenly spoke out with such ardour, frankness and youthfulness, with such youthful inexperience, and it was so absolutely wonderful, wonderful just like you—and the way he recited that German verse, so much like you too! Well, I'm off. Do hurry to deliver her message, Alexei Fyodorovich, and hurry back here. Do you want anything, Lise? For heaven's sake, don't delay Alexei Fyodorovich, not even for a second. He'll be back with you presently—"

She dashed off at last. Alyosha was about to open the door to see Lise before leaving.

"Not for anything in the world!" Lise cried out. "It's out of the question now! Speak through the door. How have you become an angel? That's all I want to learn."

"Through an awful piece of stupidity, Lise! Good-bye."

"Don't dare go away like that!" Lise cried.

"I feel so unfortunate, Lise! I'll be back directly, but I'm in deep, deep sorrow!"

And he ran out of the room.

6.

Anguish in a Cottage

Alyosha was grieved to the heart in a way he had never before felt. He had rushed in and made a mess of things, and in what? In matters of the heart! "What do I know of such things? What can I make out in them?" he kept asking himself for the hundredth time, and colouring as he did so. "I can put up with a sense of shame, for that is the punishment I deserve, but the trouble is that I will no doubt be the cause of fresh misfortunes—and imagine: the *starets* sent me to reconcile and bring together. Is this the way to bring together?" At this point, he suddenly recalled what he had said about "joining their hands together", and again a sense of shame came over him. "Though I acted in all sincerity," he suddenly concluded, "I've got to be more sensible in future," and the conclusion he drew did not even make him smile.

The errand entrusted to him by Katerina Ivanovna would

take him to Ozerny Street, close to where his brother Dmitri was staying at a house located in a by-lane, so Alyosha decided to call on him before going on to his destination, though he had a feeling that he would not find him at home. He suspected that Dmitri would perhaps try to keep out of his way, but he positively had to be found. Time was running out and the thought of the *starets*, who was breathing his last, had been with him ever since he had set out from the monastery.

There was something in the charge entrusted to him by Katerina Ivanovna that aroused his keen interest: when she made mention of the little schoolboy, the junior captain's son, who had run, crying aloud, alongside his father, it had suddenly occurred to Alyosha that this must have been the schoolboy who had bitten his finger when he, Alyosha, had asked him in what way he had wronged him. Alyosha now felt almost certain of it, without knowing the reason why. This line of thought was a relief to him, distracting him as it did from dwelling on the "blunder" he had committed, and he decided to torment himself no longer with remorse but carry on with his purpose, come what may. The thought fully restored his equanimity. As he turned into the by-lane towards Dmitri's, he felt he was hungry, so he took out of his pocket the French roll he had brought from his father's and ate it as he walked along, thus fortifying himself.

Dmitri was not in. The people of the house—an old carpenter, his old wife and their son—regarded Alyosha with suspicion even. "He hasn't spent the last three nights here, and may have gone away somewhere," the old man said in reply to Alyosha's insistent inquiries. Alyosha realised that he was obviously speaking on instructions he had been given. Asked whether he was at Grushenka's or again in hiding at Foma's (Alyosha was purposely outspoken in the matter), the three looked at him with positive alarm. "They're probably fond of him," Alyosha thought, "and are on his side. That's good."

At last, in Ozerny Street, he found the Kalmykov house the captain lived at. It was a dilapidated little affair, one side sunk lower than the other, with its three little windows facing the street, and a neglected yard, in the middle of which stood a solitary cow. The entrance into the house was from the yard through a door leading into a passageway, on the left side of which lived the old landlady and her elderly daughter, both apparently deaf. In reply to his question about the captain, which he had to repeat several times, one of the two finally realised that he was asking about their tenants and pointed across the passageway to a door leading into the tenants' quarters, which proved to be an ordinary living room. Alyosha was about to take hold of the latch to open the door when he was taken aback by the utter quiet beyond it, though he had been told by Katerina Ivanovna that the retired captain was a family man. "They're either all asleep," he thought, "or they may have heard me come and are waiting for me to open the door, so I'd better knock again," and he did so. There was a reply, though not immediately, but perhaps some ten seconds later.

"Who's there?" someone shouted in a harsh and excessively angry voice.

At this, Alyosha opened the door and stepped across the threshold, finding himself in a fairly spacious room which was cluttered up both with inmates and household belongings of every description. On the left was a massive whitewashed brick stove, from which a clothes-line hung with a variety of tattered washing ran across the entire room to the window. On either side of the room, right and left, was a bedstead covered with a knitted counterpane. On one of them, on the left, was a pyramid of four cotton-encased pillows, each smaller than the one beneath, but there was only a single pillow—a very small one—on the opposite bed. The nearer corner was partitioned off from the rest of the room by a curtain or bed sheet slung over a rope. On the other side of the screen could be seen some more bedding made up on a broad bench with a chair placed at one end. A plain deal table with a square top had been moved from the nearer corner to the middle window. The three windows, each with its four greenish and grimy glass panes, admitted very little light and were tightly shut, so that it was rather stuffy and darkish in the room. On the table was a frying-pan with the remnants of some fried eggs, a half-eaten slice of bread, as well as a half-quart vodka bottle with the dregs of the stuff that cheers on the bottom. Sitting on a chair beside the left-hand bed was a woman of some ladylike appearance, wearing a print dress. She was thin of face and sallow of complexion, her sunken cheeks at once betraying her sickness. What struck Alyosha most of all was the expression in the poor lady's eyes—a blend of intent inquiry and the utmost arrogance. Until she began to speak and while Alyosha was explaining the purpose of his call to the captain, the gaze of her big brown eyes kept travelling from one speaker to the other with the same questioning and arrogant expression. Standing at the lady's side and next to the left-hand window was a rather plain-looking girl with thin reddish hair, poorly though neatly dressed, who eyed Alyosha with disdain as he came in. To the right, also at a bed, sat another female creature, a pitiful little thing of perhaps twenty, but a hunchback and a cripple with withered legs, as Alyosha was subsequently told. Her crutches stood nearby, in a corner between the bed and the wall. The poor girl's gentle and remarkably beautiful eyes rested on Alyosha with mild serenity. At the table, finishing the fried eggs, sat a man of about forty-five, short of stature, thin and weakly built, with reddish hair and a scanty reddish beard very much like so much tow (the resemblance and especially the word tow at once came to Alyosha's mind, for some reason, as he later recalled). It was obviously the gentleman who had shouted "Who's there?" from the other side of the door, since there was no other man in the room. As Alyosha entered, the man seemed to jump up from the bench he was sitting on at the table and, wiping his mouth with a tattered napkin, dashed up to the caller.

"It's a monk collecting for his monastery. He's come to just the right place!" the girl standing at the left-hand corner said in a loud voice. But the gentleman who had dashed up to Alyosha immediately turned on his heels to face her, and replied in an excited and somehow faltering voice.

"No, Varvara Nikolayevna, it's not that. You've guessed wrong! Permit me, in my turn, to ask you," he went on, suddenly turning back towards Alyosha, "what has induced you to visit—these lower depths?"

Alyosha looked closely at the man, whom he now saw for

257

the first time. There was something awkward, fussy and irritable about him. Though he seemed to have been drinking, he was not at all high. His face was expressive of a certain extreme effrontery and, strange as it might have seemed, at the same time, undisguised cowardice. He was like a man long used to humiliating bowing and scraping but now determined to assert himself. Or, better still, like one terribly eager to hit you but terribly afraid that you'll get in first. In his words and the intonation of his rather shrill voice was a kind of clownish humour, now spiteful, now timid, but unmaintainable for any length of time, and constantly faltering. He seemed to quiver all over, his eyes goggling, as he spoke of the "lower depths", and dashed up so close to Alyosha that the latter involuntarily retreated a step. The man wore a dark and very shabby nankeen overcoat, stained and patched. His checkered and light-coloured trousers of some very thin material, long out of fashion, were so rumpled at the bottom, and therefore so short, that the impression was that he had worn them in his boyhood and grown out of them.

"I'm—Alexei Karamazov—" Alyosha began.

"I'm more than capable of realising that," the man snapped out, intimating that he was well aware of Alyosha's identity. "In my turn, I'm Junior Captain Snegiryov, sir, by your leave, and it's desirable that I should learn exactly what has induced you—"

"Oh, I've called just like that. I'd like to have a word with you—if you'll only permit me—"

"In that case, here's a chair, and kindly be seated. That's what they used to say in the old-style comedies, 'Kindly be seated!' and, with a rapid movement, the captain took hold of a vacant chair (a plain wooden chair, with no upholstery) which he placed almost in the very middle of the room; then, snatching another and similar chair for himself, he sat down facing Alyosha, and again so close to him that their knees were almost touching.

"Nikolai Ilyich Snegiryov, sir, former junior captain in the Russian infantry, sir, and, though disgraced for his vices, a captain still. Yet, sir, I should style myself Captain Cap-in-hand, for it has been only during the second half of my life that I've had to be humble to others, sir, a habit one acquires when one has come down in the world."

"Very true," Alyosha said with a smile, "but is it acquired involuntarily or by choice?"

"As God is my witness, it's done involuntarily. There was a time when I never knew the meaning of humbleness, but then came a sudden fall, from which I rose a humbled man. It's the work of some higher power. I see you take an interest in present-day problems. But in what way could I have aroused such interest, since I live in circumstances that do not permit hospitality?"

"I've come because of—that affair."

"Over *that* very affair?" the captain put in impatiently.

"Yes, that encounter of yours with my brother Dmitri Fyodorovich," Alyosha blurted out awkwardly.

"What encounter, sir? Oh, you mean *that* encounter, sir. So, it's about that business of the tattered tow-beard?" the man asked, moving up so close that their knees actually knocked against each other. His lips were compressed in a thin line.

"What do you mean by tow-beard?" Alyosha muttered.

"He's come to complain about me!" cried a voice that was familiar to Alyosha. It came from behind the curtain and belonged to the schoolboy he had recently had to deal with. "It was me who bit his finger!"

The curtain was pulled aside and Alyosha saw his recent enemy lying in the corner under the icons, on a bed made up on the bench and a chair. The boy was lying under his overcoat and an old quilt. He was evidently ill, his glittering eyes showing that he was feverish. He eyed Alyosha without fear, not as he had done earlier, as if to say, "Here, at home, I'm beyond your reach."

"What d'you mean: bit his finger?" cried the captain, half rising from his chair. "Did he actually bite your finger?"

"He did. He was engaged in stone-throwing against some boys in the street. There were six of them against him alone, so I went up to him, but he hurled a stone at me, and then another one at my head. When I asked him what I had done to him, he made a dash at me and bit my finger very painfully, I don't know for what reason."

"I'll give him a thrashing, sir, I'll thrash him right away," cried the captain, now really jumping up from his chair.

"But I haven't come to complain; I'm just telling you how it came about— I don't want him to be punished. Besides, he seems quite ill—"

"Did you actually think I'd thrash him, sir—that I'd take my dear little Ilya and thrash him in your presence just to satisfy you? Would you like it done at once, sir?" asked the captain, turning abruptly towards Alyosha as though he would hurl himself at him. "I'm sorry, sir, about your finger, but wouldn't you like me, before I thrash Ilya, to chop off four fingers of mine with this very knife and in your presence, for your just satisfaction. I think four fingers should be enough to satisfy your thirst for vengeance. A fifth one wouldn't be necessary, would it, sir?" He suddenly stopped short, and seemed to be choking. Every muscle of his face was twitching and working, and he looked most defiant and quite beside himself.

"Now I understand everything, I think," Alyosha replied in a low and sad voice, without rising from his chair. "So your son's a good boy, who loves his father and attacked me because the man who offended you is my brother— I understand now," he repeated thoughtfully. "But my brother Dmitri Fyodorovich repents of his behaviour—I know that, and if it's possible for him to call on you, or better still, to see you again at the same place, he'll apologise to you publicly—if you so wish."

"You mean he pulls out my beard and then asks for forgiveness—thus, so to speak, squaring all accounts. Is that the case?"

"Oh, no! On the contrary, he'll do anything you wish and in any way you wish!"

"So if I were to ask his grace to go down on his knees before me at that selfsame inn—it's called *The Metropolis*—or in the town square, would he do it?"

"Yes, he'd even go down on his knees."

"You've moved me to the bottom of my heart, sir. Touched me to tears and pierced me to the heart. I'm excessively sensitive. And now allow me to introduce my family: my two daughters and my son—my litter, so to   say. Who will love them should I die, sir, and, as long as I'm alive, who but they will love me, miserable wretch that I am? That is the wonderful thing the Lord has arranged for every man of my ilk, sir, for it's essential for a man like me to be loved by somebody at least, sir—"

"Oh, how truly spoken!" Alyosha exclaimed.

"Do stop that clowning. Some fool comes along, and you put us to shame," the girl at the window unexpectedly cried, addressing her father wih an air of disdain and contempt.

"A little patience, Varvara Nikolayevna, permit me to follow my course," her father cried to her emphatically but with full approval as he regarded her. "That's the kind of person she is," he went on, turning again to Alyosha.

> And there was nothing in all of Nature
> That he could find himself willing to bless.

"I really ought to have used the feminine: 'That she could find herself willing to bless.' And now let me introduce you to my wife, Arina Petrovna, a legless lady aged forty-three; oh, her legs can move, but just a little. She's of lowly origin. Smooth your features, Arina Petrovna: this is Alexei Fyodorovich Karamazov. Rise to your feet, Alexei Fyodorovich," he said, taking him by the arm and suddenly pulling him up with a force that could not have been even expected of him. "You're being introduced to a lady, so you must rise to your feet. He isn't *that* Karamazov, Mother, who—h'm—and all that, but his brother, resplendent in modest virtues. But first, Arina Petrovna, permit me, my dear, permit me to kiss your hand."

And he kissed his wife's hand respectfully, and even tenderly. The girl at the window turned her back indignantly on the scene, while the arrogantly questioning expression of the wife's face yielded to one of extraordinary sweetness.

"How do you do? Won't you sit down, Mr. Chernomazov*?" she asked.

---

*The surname *Karamazov* literally means *swarthy, dark-skinned*, from the Turkic prefix *kara*—black. The lady has mistakenly used the Russian equivalent *cherny*.—Tr.

"Karamazov, Mother, Karamazov. We're of lowly origin," he again whispered.

"Well, Karamazov, or whatever, but I'll keep on saying Chernomazov— Do sit down. Why did he make you rise from your seat? A legless lady, he says. Well, I've got legs all right, but they're swollen like barrels, while the rest of me is all shrivelled. I used to be stout once, but I'm as thin as a pin now—"

"We're of lowly origin, sir, lowly origin," the captain again prompted.

"Father, oh Father," the hunchbacked girl, who had hitherto been silent, burst out, and suddenly covered her eyes with her kerchief.

"You buffoon," the girl at the window rapped out.

"That's the kind of news we have," said the mother, spreading out her hands and pointing at her daughters. "It's just the way clouds appear: they will pass on and then we'll have our music again. In the past, when we were army people, we used to have a lot of such visitors of course. I'm not drawing any comparison, sir. If you like somebody, go ahead and like him. The deacon's wife would come and say, 'Alexander Alexandrovich is an excellent soul, but Nastasia Petrovna is of the spawn of hell.' 'Well,' I would make reply, 'it's all a matter of somebody liking somebody else, but you're a little heap that smells bad.' 'You're the kind of person that must be kept in her place,' she said, to which I replied, 'Who have you come to teach, you common slattern?' 'My breath is sweet, while yours reeks,' she said. 'Well,' I replied, 'you'd better ask the officer gentlemen whether my breath is sweet or otherwise.' Ever since then, I simply couldn't get it out of my mind, so much so that, when the general who was here for Holy Week called when I was sitting here at this very place, I asked him, 'Your Excellency, shouldn't a gentlewoman breathe fresh air?' 'Yes,' he said, 'but you should open the window or the door because the air here isn't very fresh.' That's what they all say. But what's my air got to do with them? The dead smell even worse, don't they? 'I'm not making your air worse,' I say. 'I'll order a pair of shoes and go away'. Don't have any hard words for your mother, my darlings. My dear Nikolai Ilyich, haven't I tried ever so hard to please you? My only joy is little Ilya, who comes back from school and loves me. He brought me an apple yesterday. Do forgive your mother, my dears; forgive a lonely woman, but why is it my breath has become so nasty to you?"

The poor woman burst into sobs, the tears streaming down her face, at which the captain ran up to her.

"Mother, dear, Mother dear, dry your tears. You're not a lonely woman! We all love you! Everybody adores you!" and again he began to kiss both her hands and stroke her face with his palms. Snatching up the dinner napkin, he suddenly began to wipe her tears away. Alyosha even fancied that tears were glistening in his eyes. "Well, you've seen and heard, haven't you?" he exclaimed turning in sudden fury to Alyosha and pointing at the poor feeble-minded woman.

"I've seen and heard," Alyosha muttered.

"Father, Father, are you—how can you—with him? Let him alone!" the boy suddenly cried, rising up on his bed, his flashing eyes fixed on his father.

"Enough of your clowning and showing off your silly antics, which don't get you anywhere!" Varvara Nikolayevna cried from her corner, in a high temper and even stamping her foot.

"This time you're quite right in showing your anger, Varvara Nikolayevna, and I hasten to satisfy you. Don your hat, Alexei Fyodorovich, and I'll take my cap. Let's go, sir. I have something of importance to tell you, only outside these walls. The girl sitting over there is my daughter Nina Nikolayevna. I forgot to introduce her to you. She's an angel from heaven— who had flown down to us, mortals—if you can only understand that—"

"There he goes, trembling all over, as if he's having convulsions," the indignant Varvara Nikolayevna continued.

"And the one who's just stamped her foot and dubbed me a clown is another angel in the flesh, sent down from heaven, and quite right in calling me that, sir. Come along, Alexei Fyodorovich, we've got to get through with the matter—"

And, seizing Alyosha by an arm, he led him out of the house, straight into the street.

7.

And Out of Doors

"The air's fresh here, while it's quite stale in my apartments, in every sense even. Let's walk at a leisurely pace. I'd very much like to engage your interest, sir."

"I, too, have an important matter to discuss with you," Alyosha remarked, "only I don't know how to set about it."

"I'm quite aware you must have had some business to discuss with me, for otherwise you'd never have called. Or perhaps you have come to complain about my boy. That's quite unbelievable! Yes, about my boy! I couldn't explain things in there, but I can now describe the scene to you. You see, the tow was much thicker only a week ago—I'm referring to my beard— that's what they called my beard, I mean, the schoolboys. Well, there was your brother Dmitri Fyodorovich pulling me by the beard. He actually dragged me out of the tavern into the town square just at the moment the boys were coming out of school, Ilya among them. The moment he caught sight of me in such a situation, he ran up to me, crying, 'Daddy, Daddy,' he got hold of me and flung his arms about me, trying to release me, and shouting to my assailant, 'Let him go! Let him go! It's my Dad! Forgive him, sir!' He clung to him with his little hands, and actually kissed that very hand, yes, sir, he kissed it. I remember his face at that moment— I haven't forgotten it and never shall!"

"I swear my brother will express his most sincere and full repentance," Alyosha exclaimed, "even if he has to go down on his knees in that very square—I'll make him do that, or he's no brother of mine!"

"Oh, so it's all still in preparation. It doesn't come straight from him, but springs from the prompting of your generous heart, sir. You should have said so! In that case, let me tell you of your brother's highly chivalrous and soldierly magnanimity, as expressed by him at the time. When he left off dragging me by my tow-beard and released me, he said to me, 'You're an officer and so am I. If you can find a decent man to act as your second, send him along: I'll give you satisfaction, even if you are a rogue.' That's what he said. A truly chivalrous soul! We made off, Ilya and I, but the picture of what took place with his progenitor has become imprinted for ever in his soul's memory. No, I can lay no claim to any privileges of the nobility. Judge for yourself: you've been to our mansion, and what did you see there? Three ladies, one of them a feeble-minded legless cripple, another a legless hunchback, and the third with the use of her legs, but too clever by half, a student eager to return to St. Petersburg to work on the banks of the Neva for the emancipation of Russian women. I'm not speaking of Ilya; he's only nine and quite alone in the world, should I die, so what will become of all of them—that's what I'm asking you, sir! If that is so, then, should I challenge him to a duel, and if he kills me there and then, what's going to happen? What's to become of all of them? It'll be far worse if he doesn't kill me, but only maims me: I won't be able to make a living, but that mouth of mine will remain to be fed, and who is to do the feeding, for them as well as for me? Perhaps Ilya should be taken away from school and sent out to beg for alms every day? That's what it means to me to challenge him to a duel. Duelling's all stuff and nonsense, and nothing else."

"He will ask you to forgive him, he'll stand on his knees in the middle of the square," Alyosha again exclaimed, his eyes flashing.

"I wanted to take him to court," the captain continued, "but consult our legal code, and you'll see I won't get much in the way of damages for the injury offered me. And then I was suddenly summoned by Agrafena Alexandrovna, 'Don't dare even to think of doing that!' she shouted. 'If you bring a charge against him, I'll have it brought to the public notice that he beat you up for your knavery, and that will land you in court.' The Lord alone knows how that knavery came into being, and on whose instructions some small fry like me became involved—didn't they come from her and Fyodor Pavlovich? 'And what's more,' she added, 'I'll send you packing, so that you'll never earn another copeck from me. I'll also tell my merchant friend (that's what she calls the old gentleman: my merchant friend), and he'll have no more dealings with you either.' So I thought to myself: if the merchant lays me off, where else can I get any earnings. Those two are the only sources left, for your father Fyodor Pavlovich has not only stopped trusting me for some other reason, but wants to drag me into court after gaining possession of some receipts carrying my signature. That's why I'm lying low, and you've seen our lower depths, haven't you? And permit me to ask you: did he bite your finger very painfully—I mean Ilya? I didn't want to go into details at my abode, in his presence."

"I am afraid he did, very much so. He was in a state of fury. It's quite clear to me that he was wreaking vengeance on me as a Karamazov, for your sake. But if only you could have seen how he engaged in stone-throwing against his fellow-schoolboys! It's very dangerous: they could have killed him. They're children, and silly. A flying stone can easily break a skull."

"He was hit by a stone today, only not on the head but on the chest, just above the heart, where it left a big bruise. He came home crying and moaning, and now he's been taken ill."

"And, you know, he's always the first to attack them all. He's embittered on your account. I'm told he stuck a pen-knife into a boy's side—his name's Krasotkin—a short while ago—"

"I've heard of that too. It's a dangerous business. Krasotkin is a local official, and it can all end up in trouble—"

"I'd like to advise you," Alyosha went on warmly, "to keep him away from school for a while till he cools off—and his anger passes."

"Yes, his anger, sir," the captain repeated. "That's just what it is. He's a little fellow, but his anger is great. You don't know all of it, sir. Allow me to describe the story in some detail. You see, all the schoolboys began to badger him over the 'tow-beard' business. Schoolchildren are a ruthless lot: taken singly they're God's angels, but in a group they're often ruthless, especially at school. They set about teasing him, thus stirring up his noble spirit. An ordinary boy, a spiritless son, would have knuckled under and felt ashamed of his father, but this one rose up against them all for his father's sake—one against the whole lot. For his father, and for truth and justice, sir. What he had to put up with when he kissed your brother's hand and cried out to him, 'It's my Dad! Forgive him, sir!' is something the Lord alone knows, and I too. And that is how our children—I mean not yours but ours, the children of the despised but honourable poor—learn, even at the age of nine, what justice on earth means. The rich never get an opportunity, and, throughout their lives, will never delve into such depths, while my Ilya, at the moment he kissed his hand in the townsquare—at that very moment, realised the meaning of justice. The truth of it entered his very soul and crushed it for ever, sir," the captain went on heatedly and in a kind of frenzy, striking his left palm with his right fist, as though wishing to express how "the truth of it" had crushed his Ilya. "He fell ill with fever that very day, and was delirious all night. He said little to me all that day, and was even quite silent, but I only noticed he kept looking at me from his corner. For most of the time, however, he turned towards the window, pretending to be doing his homework, though I could see his mind was not set on it. I got a little drunk the next day, sinner that I am, to drown my troubles, so I don't remember much. Mother, too, began to cry—I am very fond of Mother, sir—so I spent my last money on drink to drown my sorrows. You shouldn't despise me for that, sir. The drinkers are the most kind-hearted people in Russia, and the most kind-hearted among us are the heaviest drinkers. So there I was, lying down all day, so I don't remember much of what Ilya was going through, but it was on that very day that the boys were making mock of him at school, from the very morning, sir. 'Wisp of tow,' they shouted, 'your father was dragged out of the tavern by his tow-beard, and you were running alongside, begging for him to be forgiven.' On the third day, he came home from school, looking wretched and pale. 'What's wrong?' I asked him but got no reply. Well, there can be no conversation at my mansion without Mother and the girls joining in. Besides, the girls had got to know all about it, even on the very first day. Varvara Nikolayevna set about nagging me. 'Can anything making sense come of clowns and buffoons?' 'You're quite right,' I said, 'nothing sensible can come of such people, Varvara Nikolayevna.' For the time being we ended on that note. So in the evening, I took the boy out for a walk. You should know, sir, that we've been in the habit of going out for walks every evening, along the road we are following now—from our gate to that big boulder over there, which stands solitary at the wattle fence, where the town's common grazing grounds start—a lonely but pleasant spot. So there we were, walking along. Ilya and I, his hand in mine, as is our wont. His is a very small hand, the fingers thin and cold; he suffers with a weak chest, you know. 'Daddy,' he said, 'Daddy!' 'Yes?' I said; I could see that his eyes were flashing. 'The way he treated you, Daddy!' 'That couldn't be helped, Ilya,' I said. 'Don't make it up with him, Daddy, don't make it up. The boys say he paid you ten roubles for that.' 'No, Ilya,' I said, 'I won't ever take any money from him.' At this, he began to tremble all over, took my hand in his, and kissed it again. 'Daddy,' he said, 'challenge him to a duel. The boys say you're a coward and won't challenge him, but will take his ten roubles.' 'I can't challenge him to a duel,' I replied, and told him in short what I've just explained to you. He heard me out, and then went on: 'Daddy!' he said, 'Daddy, don't make it up with him all the same. When I grow up, I'll challenge him myself, and kill him!' His burning eyes were flashing. After all, I'm his father, so I had to tell him some words of truth. 'To kill is a sin,' I said, 'even in a duel.' 'Daddy,' he said, 'Daddy, then I'll knock him down when I grow up. I'll knock his sword out of his hand with my sword, fall upon him, knock him to the ground, raise my sword over him and say, "I could easily kill you but I'll spare you—so there!"' So you can see, sir, what's been going on in that little head of his these two days. He must have been dwelling day and night, to the point of obsession, on wreaking vengeance with his sword. But then he began to return home from school badly beaten—I learnt of that the day before yesterday, and you're quite right, sir: I won't send him to that school any more. I grew frightened for him when I got to know that he was standing up alone to the whole class and defying them all, that he had grown bitterly resentful, and that his heart was ablaze. So we went for a walk again. 'Daddy,' he asked, 'Daddy, the rich are more powerful than all the rest in the world, aren't they?' 'Yes,' I said, 'there's nobody in the world more powerful than a rich man.' 'Daddy,' he said, 'I'll get rich, become an army officer and defeat them all. The tsar will reward me, I'll come back here, and nobody will dare—' He was silent for a while, and then went on, his lips still quivering, 'Daddy,' he said, 'what an evil town this is.' 'Yes,' I replied, 'it isn't what you'd call a nice town!' 'Daddy, let's move to another town, a nice town, where nobody knows of us.' 'We shall,' I said. 'We shall, Ilya, as soon as I've saved up some money.' I was glad to have an opportunity to distract him from his gloomy thoughts, and we began to imagine how we would move to another town, and buy a horse and cart for the purpose. We'd put Mother and the sisters inside it, cover them up, and we'd walk alongside. 'I'll give you a lift from time to time, but I'll walk at your side, because the horse has to be spared: it can't pull all of us. And that's how we'll set out.' The prospect delighted him, especially that we would have a horse of our own and that he would drive it himself. It's common knowledge that Russain boys have horses in their blood. We talked for quite a while. Thank goodness, I thought to myself, I've distracted him from his gloomy thoughts and consoled him. That was the day before yesterday, in the evening, but things again took a change last night. He had set out for school in the morning as usual, but came home very, very depressed. In the evening, I took him by the hand and we went out for a walk. He was silent, and would not talk. A wind had arisen, the sun was hidden behind the clouds, and autumn was in the air; it was getting dark. We were walking along, both in low spirits. 'Well, son, how will we get ready for our travels?' I asked him with the intention of resuming our conversation of the day before. He said nothing but I could feel his fingers tremble in my hand. 'Ah,' I thought, 'there's been some fresh trouble.' We had reached this very boulder, and I sat down on it. Lots and lots of kites were flapping and whirling in the sky—

there must have been about thirty of them. You see, the kite season's in. 'Well, Ilya,' I said, 'isn't it time for us to get our last year's kite flying? I'll get it mended—where have you put it?' Again my boy said nothing; he was looking away, standing sideways to me. Then came a gust of wind that sent the sand swirling—he suddenly ran up to me, threw his arms about my neck and pressed himself against me.

"You should know children that are silent and proud and hold back their tears for a long time will suddenly break down when trouble strikes, so that the tears flow in torrents rather than in drops, sir. His warm tears wetted all my face. He sobbed, shaken with emotion and clinging to me, while I sat there on the boulder. 'Daddy,' he cried, 'dear Daddy, how he humiliated you!' I, too, burst into tears, sir, and there we sat, trembling in each other's arms. 'Daddy, dear Daddy!' he said. 'Ilya, Ilya, my dear boy!' I replied. Nobody saw us then, except for God above. Perhaps he'll record it to my credit. You have your brother to thank for it all, Alexei Fyodorovich. No, sir, I won't thrash my boy for your satisfaction!"

He had resumed his former note of resentful buffoonery, but Alyosha felt that the man trusted him and that, had there been anyone else in his, Alyosha's place, the captain would not have let himself go like that and been so outspoken. This encouraged Alyosha, who was on the verge of tears himself.

"Oh, how much I'd like to make it up with your boy!" he exclaimed. "If you could bring it about—"

"Why, yes, sir," the captain replied in a low voice.

"And now I have something quite different to say to you," Alyosha went on excitedly. "Please listen to a message I have for you. Dmitri, that brother of mine, has also insulted his fiancée, a most noble-minded girl you've probably heard of. I have the right to tell you of the way he's insulted her; in fact, I'm even in duty bound to do so, for when she learnt of the way he had offended you and of your unfortunate circumstances, she commissioned me to bring you—at once, this very day— her offer of help—but only from her, not from Dmitri, who has thrown her over. No, not from me, his brother, or from anyone else, but from her alone! She implores you to accept this help

270

from her—you've both been insulted by one and the same man—in fact, she thought of you when she had suffered a similar insult from him—similar in its cruelty. This means a sister coming to the aid of a brother— She's asked me to persuade you to accept these two hundred roubles as from a sister. No one will ever learn of it, so that it cannot give rise to any malicious gossip—here's the two hundred roubles. I swear you must accept it, for otherwise—otherwise all men can only be enemies to one another! But brothers do exist in the world— Yours is a noble heart—you will understand—you simply must!"

And Alyosha held out two crisp rainbow-coloured, hundred-rouble bank-notes to him. The two were standing at the fence, close to the big boulder, and there was no one in the vicinity. The notes seemed to produce a powerful impression on the captain: he gave a start, but at first apparently out of nothing but astonishment—he had never even dreamt of anything of the kind, and such an outcome was the last thing he had ever expected. Even in his wildest dreams he could not have imagined help from anyone, and, moreover, so munificent. He took the notes and for a whole minute was almost incapable of answering. Something quite new flashed across his face.

"Is that for me—for me? Such a lot of money—two hundred roubles! Goodness, I haven't set eyes on such money for the last four years! And she calls herself a sister—is that really true?"

"I swear that everything I've told you is the truth!" cried Alyosha. The captain turned red.

"Listen, my friend, listen to me: if I accept it, that won't mean I'm a scoundrel, will it? You won't look upon me as a scoundrel, will you, Alexei Fyodorovich? No, Alexei Fyodorovich, just listen to me, listen," he went on rapidly, touching Alyosha with both hands, "you're trying to persuade me by telling me it's being sent by a 'sister', but inwardly, in your heart, won't you feel contempt for me if I accept, eh?"

"No, no, of course not. I swear by my salvation that I won't! It will never be known to anyone: only to you, her, myself, and another lady, a great friend of hers—"

"Never mind the lady! Listen, Alexei Fyodorovich, hear me out: the moment has come for you to hear me out, for you

271

can't even understand what these two hundred roubles now mean to me," the poor man continued, whipping himself into a kind of turbulent and almost uncontrollable excitement. He seemed bewildered, his words tumbling out as though he was afraid he would not be allowed to have his say. "Apart from its having been honestly acquired from so esteemed and holy a 'sister', do you know that I'll now be able to provide medical treatment for Mother and my daughter Nina, my hunchbacked angel? Dr. Herzenstube once visited me out of the kindness of his heart, and examined them both for a whole hour. 'I can't make anything of it,' he said, 'but the mineral water can be got at the local chemists (he made out a prescription for it) it is certain to do her good.' Besides, he advised medicinal foot-baths, with medicine he also prescribed. The mineral water costs thirty copecks and she'll have to take perhaps forty jugs of it. So I took the prescription and put it on the shelf under the icon, where it's still lying. For Nina he prescribed baths with some kind of solution in them, hot baths, daily, in the morning and in the evening, but how on earth are we to arrange such treatment in our mansion, with no servants, no help, no bath-tubs and no water? And Nina is all rheumatic—I haven't told you of that yet—and her entire right side aches at night. She suffers great pain, but, can you believe it, that angel from heaven bears it with fortitude so as not to disturb us; she doesn't utter a groan for fear of waking us up. We eat whatever we can get, yet she'll take only what's left over, and fit only for dogs. 'I'm taking it out of your mouths; I'm a burden to you'— that's the expression in her angelic eyes. We try to serve her, but that oppresses her. 'I'm unworthy of it, quite unworthy; I'm an undeserving and useless cripple.' Undeserving? Why, her angelic sweetness will win us salvation on high; it would be hell in our house without her, without her gentle speech! Even Varvara has grown milder under her influence. And don't judge Varvara Nikolayevna too harshly either. She, too, is an angel, and has also undergone humiliation. She came to us in the summer, bringing with her sixteen roubles she had earned by giving private lessons. She put it by to pay for her return fare to St. Petersburg in September, that is, now. But we took her money and spent it, and she now has nothing to go back on—that's how it is. Besides, she can't go back anyway, because she works her fingers to the bone for us, much like a work-horse: she gives us her care, does the mending and the washing-up, sweeps the floor, and puts Mother to bed—and Mother's petulant, Mother's tearful and Mother's quite mad!— With these two hundred roubles I'll be able to hire a servant, d'you realise that, Alexei Fyodorovich? I'll be able to afford medical treatment for my dear creatures, send Varvara back to her studies in St. Petersburg, buy some beef and give them all some decent food. Good Lord, it's what I've been dreaming of!"

Alyosha felt terribly glad to have created such happiness and to have gained the poor man's consent to make himself happy.

"Stay, Alexei Fyodorovich, stay!" exclaimed the captain, as he burst into frenzied speech, quite carried away by a new flight of fancy. "Do you realise that we—Ilya and I—will now really be able to achieve our ambition: we'll buy a horse and covered cart—a black horse, for he's set his heart on a black horse—and we'll start out the way we spoke of the day before yesterday. There's a lawyer I know in K... Gubernia, an old friend of my childhood, who has let me know through a relia-ble acquaintance, that if I come to his parts, he'll take me on as a clerk in his office—who knows: perhaps he will— So I'd just put Mother and Nina in the cart, give Ilya the reins, and I'd walk and walk alongside until I got them all there— Goodness if I could only collect a bad debt into the bargain, there'd be enough for that, too!"

"There will, there will!" Alyosha exclaimed. "Katerina Iva-novna will let you have some more, as much as you like. Besides, you know, I, too, have got some money, take as much as you need, as you would from a brother or a friend, you'll pay me back later—(You'll get rich—I'm sure you will). Then, you couldn't have hit on a better idea, than moving to another gubernia! It will be the salvation of you, especially for your lit-tle boy Ilya—and you must do so before the winter, before the cold sets in. You must write to me from there, and we would remain brothers— No, that's no empty dream!"

So pleased did Alyosha feel that he felt like embracing the

man. But he stopped short as he glanced at the captain, who now stood with neck outstretched, his lips protruding, and his face pale and frenzied. His lips were moving as though trying to pronounce something, but no sounds came from them. It was somehow weird.

"What's wrong with you?" said the startled Alyosha.

"Alexei Fyodorovich—I—you—" the captain muttered, his voice faltering, and gazing at him with a strange glare, like one who has made up his mind to hurl himself down a precipice, but at the same time with a grin on his lips. "I—you— Wouldn't you like me to show you a conjuring trick, sir," he suddenly said in a rapid and firm whisper, his speech faltering no longer.

"What kind of trick?"

"A conjuring trick, a piece of hocus-pocus," the captain went on in the same whisper, his mouth twisted on the left side, his left eye screwed up, and his gaze still fixed unflinchingly on Alyosha.

"But what's the matter with you?" cried the latter, really alarmed. "What kind of trick do you mean?"

"This one," the captain suddenly squealed. "Look!"

And displaying the two bank-notes, which during the entire conversation he had been holding by one corner between the forefinger and thumb of right hand, he suddenly crumpled them savagely, and squeezed them tight in his right fist.

"D'you see that! Do you?" he shrieked, pale and frenzied. Suddenly raising his fist, he flung the two crumpled notes on the sand. "D'you see that?" he again shrieked, pointing a finger at them. "There you are!"

Suddenly raising his right foot, he began trampling the notes under his heel, gasping for breath and exclaiming with every spurning movement.

"There, so much for your money! So much for your money! So much for your money!" He suddenly jumped backwards and drew himself up before Alyosha, his figure expressive of boundless pride.

"Inform those that sent you that the tow-beard does not sell his honour!" he cried, an arm raised skyward. He then turned on his heel and dashed off. Hardly had he run five paces when he turned round and waved to Alyosha. He ran on another five paces and turned round for the last time, but now his face was no longer contorted in laughter but, on the contrary, quivering with tears. In a choking voice throbbing with sobs, he gabbled:

"What could I say to my boy if I accepted money for our shame?" With these words, he made off, this time without looking back. Alyosha's glance followed him with inexpressible sorrow. Ah, how well he understood that, until the very last instant, the poor man had not known that he would crumple the bank-notes and fling them to the ground. The running man did not look back and Alyosha knew he would not do so. He had no desire to run after him and call him, and he knew why. When he was already out of sight, Alyosha picked up the two bank-notes. They were much crumpled and crushed into the sand, but were intact and even rustled like new when Alyosha smoothed them out. He folded them, put them in his pocket, and set out for Katerina Ivanovna's to report on the outcome of his mission.

BOOK FIVE

Pro Et Contra

1.

The Betrothal

Again, Madame Khokhlakov was the first to meet Alyosha. She looked flustered, for something important had taken place: Katerina Ivanovna's hysterics had ended in a fainting fit, followed by an "awful and terrible weakness; she lay down, her eyes turned up till the whites showed, and became delirious. She's still feverish, so I've had Herzenstube and her aunts sent for. The aunts have already come, but Herzenstube hasn't turned up yet. They're waiting in her room. Something's sure to happen, and she's still unconscious. What if it proves to be brain fever?"

Madame Khokhlakov looked profoundly alarmed as she said all this. "It's very serious this time," she kept reiterating after practically every word, as though everything that had taken place with her previously had been no serious matter. Alyosha listened to her with despondency: he made an attempt to describe the recent happenings, but she interrupted him after the very first words. She had no time to listen, and asked him to stay with Lise and wait for her to come.

"Lise, my dear Alexei Fyodorovich," she whispered almost in his ear, "Lise has just sprung a strange surprise on me, but so touchingly that I find it in my heart to forgive her everything. Imagine, the moment you left, she suddenly began to sincerely regret having poked fun at you today and yesterday. In fact, she wasn't making mock of you in any way, but was merely joking. Her regret was so sincere that she was almost in tears, so that I couldn't help feeling surprised. She never used to repent when she poked fun at me, but always made a joke of it. And, you know, she's constantly making fun of me. But this time she's quite earnest, quite earnest. She holds your opinion in high esteem, Alexei Fyodorovich, so don't take offence or harbour any grudge against her. I try all the time to spare her

276

feelings because she's really a clever girl; don't you think so! She's just been telling me you were her childhood friend—'the closest friend of my childhood', as she put it—just imagine: the closest friend—and where do I come in? She has most serious sentiments on that score, and even memories, but the thing is the turns of speech and the words she uses, the most unusual words, the kind you'd never expect, yet they come tumbling out. For instance, the recent instance of a pine. A pine-tree stood in our garden in her very early years. It may still be standing there for all I know, so there's no point in speaking of it in the past tense. Pines are not like people—they don't change for a long time, Alexei Fyodorovich. 'Mama!' she said, 'I remember that pine as in a dream—it's a pine I just pine to see again!' You see: a pine I just pine to see—that's the way she put it, but I may have got it all mixed up. *Pine* is a stupid word, but she said something so original on the matter that it's something I can't express. Besides, I've forgotten it all. Well, goodbye, I'm terribly shocked and am probably going out of my mind. Oh, Alexei Fyodorovich, I've gone out of my mind twice in the past and undergone medical treatment. Do go to Lise and cheer her up in the way you always do so well. Lise!" she called out, going up to her door, "I've brought Alexei Fyodorovich here, whom you've hurt so unfeelingly. He's not angry with you at all, I can assure you. On the contrary, he's surprised you could have thought so!"

"*Merci, maman*. Do come in, Alexei Fyodorovich."

Alyosha entered her room. Lise, who looked somehow embarassed, suddenly flushed crimson. She seemed to be ashamed of something and, as always happens in such cases, she burst into rapid speech about extraneous matters, as if they were the only things of interest to her at the moment.

"Mother has just told me all about the two hundred roubles, Alexei Fyodorovich, and about your mission—to that poor officer—as well as the awful story of his ill-treatment; Mother, you know, told it in such an unintelligible way, skipping over so many things, yet I couldn't help crying when I heard. Well, did you hand him the money, and how is the unfortunate man at present—?"

"The trouble is that I didn't give it to him, and it's quite a story," Alyosha replied as though his failure to hand over the money was causing him the greatest concern, yet Lise could clearly see that there was something else on his mind and that, he, too, was looking away and trying to keep off the subject. Alyosha seated himself at the table and began his account; at the very first words, he shed all his embarrassment and was able to fully win Lise's interest. He spoke under the influence of a deep feeling and the powerful impression he had recently gained. His story was well told and circumstantial. Even in the past, during Lise's childhood in Moscow, he had liked coming to see her and tell her of happenings in his life, what he had read, or recollections of his boyhood. At times, they would indulge in flight of fancy and think up all kinds of stories, most of them merry and amusing. They now felt carried back to the old times in Moscow two years before. Lise was deeply moved by his story, for Alyosha was able to portray little Ilya with genuine sympathy. When he gave a detailed description of the scene of the unfortunate man stamping the money, Lise clasped her hands, crying out with uncontrollable emotion:

"So you didn't give him the money, and let him run off without it? Goodness, you should have dashed after him and caught up with him—!"

"No, Lise, it's better that I didn't run after him," said Alyosha, rising from his chair and anxiously pacing the room.

"How can it be better? Why better? They've got nothing to eat, and will starve!"

"No, they won't, because the two hundred roubles will be theirs without fail. He's sure to take the money tomorrow. He's quite sure to," said Alyosha, pacing the room thoughtfully. "You see, Lise", he continued, halting suddenly in front of her, "I made a mistake myself but even that mistake has worked out for the best."

"What mistake, and how has it worked out for the best?"

"It's like this: he's cowardly and weak-willed. He's been through hard times, but has kept a kind heart. I keep on wondering why he should have taken offence and trampled the money under foot, because, I can assure you, he did not know until the very last instant that he was going to trample on the bank-notes. There were several things to give him offence, it seems to me—and it couldn't have been otherwise in his situation— First of all, he felt angry with himself for having shown too much joy in my presence over the money and not having concealed it from me. Had he been just pleased but not overjoyed; had he not shown it but pretended to have scruples as others do when accepting money; had he equivocated, then he could have put up with things and taken the money. What he actually did was to show his joy too frankly, and that was too mortifying. Oh, Lise, he is a truthful and kind-hearted man, and that's the trouble in such cases! His voice was so faint and feeble while he was speaking to me, and he spoke at such a rate, sniggering in such a strange way or perhaps weeping—yes, he was in tears of delight—and he spoke of his daughters—and a situation he had been promised in another town— But hardly had he poured out his heart just a little when he was suddenly overcome with shame at having opened himself up to me like that. That's why he's developed such a hatred for me. He's one of the hyper-sensitive poor. What rankled most in him was his excessively rapid acceptance of me as a friend, and his having yielded to me so soon. At first, he almost flew at me so as to intimidate me, but then, when he saw the money, he began embracing me. Yes, he practically embraced me, touching me with his hands. It must have been at that very moment that he felt his humiliation, and it was then that I made that blunder, a very serious one, by suddenly saying that the money might not be enough to enable him to move to another town and that he could count on some more, indeed, I myself would give him as much of my own money as he needed. This simply flabbergasted him, for why should I come rushing forward with my help? You know, Lise, it's terribly hard for a humiliated man to have others considering themselves his benefactors—I've heard of that before and been told of it by the *starets*. I can't find the words to express it, but I've often witnessed it. Besides, it's exactly what I myself feel. The main thing is that, though he did not know until the last moment that he would trample on the bank-notes, he did have a presentiment that he would do

279

so—that's certain. It was because of that presentiment that he was so worked up— Though it has turned out so badly, it's all for the best. I even think that nothing better could have happened—"

"But why, why could nothing better have happened?" Lise exclaimed, looking at him in great surprise.

"Because, Lise, had he taken the money and not trampled on it, he would have shed tears of humiliation an hour or so after returning home. Yes, that would certainly have happened. He would have wept and perhaps called on me the first thing in the morning to fling the notes in my face or trample on them as he did today. As it was, he went off terribly proud and triumphant though he knows he has 'ruined himself'. That's why nothing can now be easier than to make him accept the same two hundred roubles not later than tomorrow, because he has vindicated his honour by tossing the money back and trampling on it— When he did that, he couldn't have possibly known that I'll bring it back tomorrow. And he stands in desperate need of the money. Though he now feels proud of himself, he'll be thinking even today of the aid he has forfeited. He'll be thinking of it even more during the night and will dream of the money in his sleep; by the morning he'll probably be prepared to come running to me to beg forgiveness. I will appear at that very moment. 'You've proved that you're a proud man, so please take the money and forgive us,' I'll say, and this time he'll take it!"

Alyosha felt quite carried away as he uttered the words "and this time he'll take it". Lise even clapped her hands.

"Oh, how true that is—it's something I've realised so terribly suddenly! Oh, Alyosha, how have you come to know all that? You're so young, yet you can read people's hearts— I'd never be able to think of anything so convincing—"

"The main thing now is to persuade him that he's on an equal footing with us though he is accepting money from us," Alyosha continued just as fervently, "and not only on an equal footing but even on a higher one—"

"On a higher footing—how excellently put, Alexei Fyodorovich, but go on, go on!"

"I'm afraid I haven't put it very well by speaking—on a higher footing—but never mind, because—"

"Oh, it doesn't matter, it doesn't matter in the least! Forgive me, dear Alyosha— You should know that I hardly respected you till now—or rather, I did respect you on an equal footing, but now I shall look up to you on a higher footing— Don't be angry with me, dear, for my seeming to be playing with words," she went on feelingly. "I'm a ridiculous little girl, while you—you are— Listen, Alexei Fyodorovich, don't you think that all our reasoning—I mean, your reasoning—no, rather our reasoning—smacks of contempt for him, for that unfortunate man? I mean our dissecting his soul as though from a position of superiority, and our being so certain he'll accept the money?"

"No, Lise, there's no contempt in that," Alyosha replied unhesitatingly, as though he had expected the question. "I turned the matter over in my mind on the way here. Indeed, what contempt can there be when we are of the same stuff as he is, when everybody's like that. For we are just the same as he is, and no better. Even if we were better, we would still be the same as he is were we to find ourselves in his position— I can't speak for you, Lise, but I consider that in many respects mine is a petty soul. But his is no petty soul but, on the contrary it's full of noble feeling— No, Lise, there's no contempt for him in this! You should know, Lise, that my *starets* has said that people should be cared for as though they were children; indeed, some need care as though they were patients at a hospital—"

"Oh, Alexei Fyodorovich, dear friend, let's care for people as we would for the sick!"

"Let us, indeed, Lise. I'm ready for that, only not quite. I'm very impatient at times, and at others I don't see things in their proper light. With you it's quite different."

"Oh, I don't believe that! How happy I feel, Alexei Fyodorovich!"

"It's good of you to say so, Lise."

"You're an amazingly good man, Alexei Fyodorovich, but you seem a bit priggish at times— Yet you aren't. Please go to the door, open it gently, and make sure Mother isn't listening,"

Lise suddenly said in a rapid and nervous whisper.

Alyosha did so and reported that nobody was listening there.

"Come here, Alexei Fyodorovich," Lise continued, flushing more and more, "give me your hand—like that. Listen, I have a great confession to make to you: yesterday's letter was written in earnest, and not in jest—"

She covered her eyes with a hand; obviously feeling greatly ashamed to have made such a confession. Suddenly she seized his hand, and kissed it rapidly three times.

"Oh, Lise, that's wonderful," Alyosha exclaimed joyfully. "I was absolutely certain you had written in earnest."

"Fancy that: he was certain!" she cried, pushing his hand away without letting go of it, colouring terribly, and laughing a happy little laugh. "I kiss his hand and he says, 'That's wonderful.'" The reproach, however, was undeserved: Alyosha, too, was all of a flutter.

"I'd like nothing better than to please you always, Lise, but I don't know how to do it," he murmured, blushing too.

"Alyosha, dear, your manners are cold and audacious. You see: he has deigned to choose me as his wife, and lets things stand at that! He's already quite certain I wrote in earnest—what d'you say to that? It's audacity—that's what it is!

"Was it bad of me to feel certain?" asked Alyosha, bursting into laughter.

"Why no, Alyosha, quite the contrary, it was awfully good," said Lise, regarding him with tender and happy eyes. Alyosha, who was standing at her side, his hand still in hers, suddenly bent down and kissed her on the lips.

"Really, what's come over you?" cried Lise, casting Alyosha into utter confusion.

"Forgive me if I shouldn't have— It may have been terribly stupid of me— You said my manners were cold, so I kissed you. I now see it was silly of me—"

Lise laughed, hiding her face in her hands.

"And you in that garment of yours!" she exclaimed between her peals of laughter, but suddenly stopped laughing, becoming very serious and even severe.

"We'll have to wait with our kissing, Alyosha, because

neither of us is good at it, and there's still a long time to wait," she concluded abruptly. "Better tell my why you've chosen me, such a fool, a sickly little fool, you, who are so clever, think so well, and are so observant? Oh, Alyosha, I'm terribly happy, because I'm quite unworthy of you!"

"But you are quite worthy, Lise. In a few days I'll be leaving the monastery for good. I shall have to marry when I go out into the world—that I know very well. That's what *he* has commanded me to do. Who could be better for me than you are—and who except you will take me? I've been giving the whole matter thought. In the first place, you've known me since your childhood; secondly, you possess many qualities that are absent in me. You are more cheerful in soul than I am; what's most important, you're more innocent than I am, for I've been in contact with many, many things— Oh, you may not know it, but I'm a Karamazov, too. What's wrong in your laughing and joking, and poking fun at me as well; go ahead, it only makes me glad— But your laughter is that of a little girl; of yourself you think like a martyr—"

"A martyr? What do you mean?"

"Yes, Lise. Your question whether we felt contempt for that unfortunate man in dissecting his soul could have come only from a martyr— You see, I don't know how to express it properly, but I think that such questions could have arisen only in one who is himself capable of experiencing suffering. As you sit in your invalid chair, you must have turned over many things in your mind—"

"Give me your hand, Alyosha; why are you taking it away?" said Lise in a failing voice, weak with happiness. "Listen, Alyosha, what will you wear, what kind of suit, when you leave the monastery? Don't laugh my question away and don't be angry; it's very, very important to me."

"I haven't thought of that yet, Lise, but I'll wear any clothes you like."

"I want you to wear a dark-blue velvet jacket, a white piqué waistcoat, and a grey trilby hat— Tell me, did you believe me yesterday that I didn't love you when I said I didn't mean what was written in my letter?"

"No, I didn't".

"Oh, what an unbearable and incorrigible man you are!"

"You see, I knew that you—loved me perhaps, but I pretended to believe that you didn't, so as to make it—less embarrassing for you—"

"That's even worse! Both worse and better than anything else. I'm terribly in love with you, Alyosha. Before you came here last time, I put my good luck to a test: I decided to ask you to return the letter. Had you just taken it calmly out of your pocket to give it back (as might always have been expected of you) that would have meant that you didn't care for me, felt nothing for me, and that you were a stupid and worthless boy, which would have spelt my ruin. But you left the letter behind in your monastery cell and that gave me comfort. Isn't it true that you left it there on purpose because you had a feeling I'd ask for it? You did, didn't you?"

"Oh, no Lise. You see, I've still got the letter with me, and I had it with me then, too, in this pocket. Here it is."

And, with a laugh, Alyosha produced the letter, which he showed her at a distance.

"Only I won't give it back to you. Look at it from where you are."

"Why? So you were lying to me, you—a monk!"

"I suppose I was," said Alyosha, laughing too. "I did that so as to keep the letter. It's very precious to me," he suddenly added with deep emotion, and blushed again. "It always will be, and I won't let anybody else have it!"

Lise looked at him with admiration.

"Alyosha," she murmured again. "Go to the door and have a look to see if Mother's listening."

"All right, Lise, I'll have a look, but wouldn't it be better not to? Why should your mother be suspected of such meanness?"

"Meanness? What kind of meanness? If you mean eavesdropping on her daughter, then she has every right to. There's nothing mean in that," cried Lise, flushing. "You may rest assured, Alexei Fyodorovich, that when I'm a mother myself and have a daughter like me, I shall most certainly eavesdrop on her."

"Would you really, Lise? That wouldn't be right."

"Goodness, what kind of meanness could that be? If it were a matter of ordinary small talk and I went in for eavesdropping, then that would be meanness. But here it's a matter of her own daughter being closeted with a young man— Listen, Alyosha, you should know that I, too, will be keeping an eye on you as soon as we get married, and, besides, that I shall open all your letters and read them— So you've been informed in advance—"

"Of course, if that's how—" Alyosha murmured, "only it's not right—"

"Oh, how contemptuous! Alyosha, dear, don't let's quarrel from the very outset—but I might as well tell you the whole truth: of course, eavesdropping's not at all right, and, of course, I'm all wrong and you're right, but I'll eavesdrop all the same."

"Do so, then, but you'll never catch me at anything blameworthy," said Alyosha with a laugh.

"And then, Alyosha, will you obey me? That, too, has to be decided in advance."

"Very willingly, Lise, and without fail, but not in major questions. Even if you're not in agreement with me in the most important things, I shall act as my sense of duty bids me to."

"So you should. Know, then, that I'm ready to yield to you, not only in the most important things but in all things, and I'm giving you my solemn promise to do so—in all things and throughout my lifetime," Lise exclaimed with ardour. "And I gladly promise that, gladly! Moreover, I give you my word that I'll never eavesdrop on you, nor read a single letter of yours, because you're right, and I'm wrong. No matter how tempted I may feel to eavesdrop on you, I won't, because you consider it ignoble. It is as though you are my providence now— Tell me, Alexei Fyodorovich, why have you been so sad all these days—both yesterday and today; I know you've been having a lot of worry and trouble, but I can also see that you have some special worry, a secret one perhaps, haven't you?"

"Indeed, I have, Lise," said Alyosha despondently. "I see you do love me, since you've realised that."

"What is it? What's the cause? Can you tell me?" said Lise in timid entreaty.

"I'll tell you, Lise, later," said the embarrassed Alyosha. "You wouldn't understand if I told you now. Besides, I don't think I'll be able to explain it at present."

"I also know that your brothers and your father are causing you a lot of worry. Aren't they?"

"Yes, my brothers as well," said Alyosha, as though deep in thought.

"Alyosha, I don't like your brother Ivan Fyodorovich," Lise suddenly observed.

With some surprise, Alyosha took note of the remark, which he did not take up.

"My brothers are bent on self-destruction," he went on, "and so is my father. Together with themselves, they are destroying others. It comes from the 'earthy Karamazov force', as Father Paissi put it the other day—earthy, unbridled and crude— I don't even know whether the spirit of the Lord hovers above that force. I only know that I, too, am a Karamazov. But am I a monk, a monk? Am I really a monk, Lise? You said a moment ago that I was a monk, didn't you?"

"I did."

"Perhaps I even have no faith in God."

"You have no faith? What's the matter with you?" said Lise in a low and guarded voice. However, Alyosha made no reply. Perhaps in these excessively sudden words of his there was something very mysterious and very subjective, perhaps even obscure to himself but undoubtedly causing him much torment.

"And now, apart from everything else, the finest man on earth, my friend is departing this life. If you only knew, if you only knew, Lise, how I'm bound, how closely knit in soul I am to that man! And now I shall be alone— I shall come to you, Lise— In the future we shall be together—"

"Yes, together, together! From now on we shall be together always and for the rest of our lives. And now, kiss me. I permit it."

Alyosha did so.

"And now, go. Christ be with you!" (She made the sign of the cross over him.) "Go quickly *to him* whilst he is still alive. I see it was cruel of me to hold you back. I shall pray for you and for him today. We shall be happy, Alyosha, we shall, shan't we?"

"I think we shall, Lise."

As he left Lise, Alyosha decided not to see Madame Khokhlakov, and was about to leave the house without saying goodbye to her. But no sooner had he opened the door to go downstairs than he found himself facing Madame Khokhlakov. From her very first words Alyosha realised that she had been on the wait for him.

"This is terrible, Alexei Fyodorovich. It's all a lot of childish nonsense, quite ridiculous. I hope you realise you shouldn't think—it's all dreams. It's utter foolishness, nothing but foolishness!" she exclaimed, somewhat aggressively.

"Only don't say that to her," said Alyosha, "for it will upset her, which is bad for her."

"Those are sensible words coming from a sensible young man. Am I to infer that you agreed with her only because you wished to avoid irritating her by contradicting her, and all that out of compassion for her ailing condition?"

"Oh, no, in no way. I spoke to her in all earnest," Alyosha declared firmly.

"Being in earnest is unthinkable here. In the first place, I'll never be at home to you any more; secondly, I'll leave this town and take her away. You may rest assured on that score."

"Why do that?" said Alyosha. "It's all still far off. We may have to wait another year and a half perhaps."

"Oh, that's perfectly true, of course, Alexei Fyodorovich, and during those eighteen months you'll quarrel and part a thousand times. Oh, I'm so unfortunate, so unfortunate! It may be a trifling matter, but it's been a blow to me. I'm just like Famusov in the last scene; you're Chatsky, and she's Sofia, and, imagine, I've come running here on purpose to intercept you on the staircase; in the play, too, the crucial event takes place on the staircase.* I overheard everything, and I could have dropped to the floor. So that accounts for her dreadful night and her hysterical condition! It spells love to the daughter and death

---

*The reference is to the concluding scene in the celebrated comedy *Wit Works Woe* (1824) by Alexander Griboyedov.

to the mother. I might as well be in my grave. And a second and most important matter: what kind of letter has she written to you? Let me see it at once, at once!"

"I can't do that! And now tell me: how is Katerina Ivanovna? I've got to know."

"She's still delirious and hasn't regained consciousness yet. Her aunts are here, but all they do is to sigh and turn up their noses at me. Herzenstube called and grew so alarmed that I was quite at a loss how to calm him down, and actually wanted to send for a doctor. I had him taken home in my carriage. And now, on top of everything, there's you and this letter! True, we still have another eighteen months ahead of us. I implore you, Alexei Fyodorovich, for the sake of all that's sacred, for the sake of your dying *starets*, show the letter to me, her mother! You can hold it in your hand at a distance if you like, and I'll read it that way."

"No, I won't show it to you, Katerina Ossipovna. I won't do that, even were she to give her permission. I'll come again tomorrow and we can talk over a great many things, but now I must be off. Good-bye!"

And Alyosha ran downstairs into the street.

2.

Smerdyakov with Guitar

Indeed, he was pressed for time. Even while he was saying good-bye to Lise, the idea had flashed across his mind that he should, through some wile, get hold of his brother Dmitri, who was, obviously, keeping out of his way. It was already quite late, the time being three o'clock in the afternoon. Alyosha longed with all his heart to get back to the monastery to be with his "great" departing friend, but the need to see his brother Dmitri outweighed everything else: with every hour, a sense of some impending and terrible disaster grew ever stronger in Alyosha's mind. He could not, perhaps, say definitely what that disaster might consist in, and what he should tell his brother at the moment—"Even if my benefactor dies whilst I'm away, I shall at least have no cause to reproach myself till the end of my days with having been in a position to forestall something and failing to do so through passing by and hurrying to my own home. In acting thus, I shall be fulfilling his behest—"

His idea consisted in his coming upon his brother Dmitri unawares by climbing over the wattle fence just as he had on the previous day, entering the garden, and lying in wait in the pergola. "If he isn't there," Alyosha thought, "I'll wait there in hiding till the evening if need be, without tipping off Foma or the women of the house. If he's waiting for Grushenka to put in an appearance, he may very well come into the pergola." Incidentally, Alyosha did not give much thought to the details of his scheme, but decided to carry on with it even if it meant that he would not get to the monastery that day.

Everything went off smoothly: he climbed over the fence almost at the same place as on the previous day, and stole unobserved into the pergola. He did not want to be seen: both the landlady and Foma (if he were there) would side with his brother and obey his orders, that is to say, would not let him into the garden, or else would warn Dmitri in good time that he was asked for and awaited. The pergola was empty. Alyosha sat down on the same seat as he had on the day before, and began to wait. He looked about himself and found that the pergola looked far more dilapidated than had seemed to him on the previous day: it now looked positively ramshackle. The weather was just as clear as it had been yesterday. On the green-painted table in the pergola there was a circular stain probably made by the brandy spilt over from his brother's wine-glass the day before. Idle and irrelevant thoughts kept floating across his mind in the way they do at a time of tedious waiting; for instance, he asked himself what had made him sit down on the same seat as on the day before, and not on another. He finally felt quite saddened by the suspense and the uncertainty. He had not been sitting there for more than fifteen minutes when several chords were suddenly struck on a guitar very close by. Some person or persons were sitting, or had just sat down, in the thick of the bushes twenty paces, no more, from him. Alyosha suddenly recollected that, after leaving his brother in the pergola the previous day, he had seen, or merely glimpsed, a low and old green-painted garden bench on the left, amidst the shrubbery at the fence. Some new arrivals must have just occupied it. But who could they be? Suddenly a man began to sing in a saccharine falsetto, accompanying himself on a guitar:

> *With love so strong*
> *For my dear I long.*
> *The Lord have mer-r-cy*
> *On her and me!*
> *On her and me!*
> *On her and me!*

There was a pause in the singing, which was in a lackey-style tenor, the song itself smacking of the servants' quarters. Then another voice, a woman's, asked in a melting if timid tone, albeit mincingly:

"Why haven't you been to see us for such a long time, Pavel Fyodorovich? Why do you always look down on us?"

"Not at all," a man's voice replied politely, but with firm and no-nonsense dignity. The man was obviously in command of the situation, and the woman was trying to ingratiate herself with him. "The man must be Smerdyakov," Alyosha thought. "At least, the voice is his, and I expect the lady is the landlady's daughter from Moscow, the one who has a train to her dress, and comes to Marfa Ignatievna for the soup—"

"I simply dote on poetry if it has a lilt to it," the woman's voice continued. "Why don't you go on?"

The voice broke into song again.

> *What care I for wealth*
> *If my dear keeps her health?*
> *The Lord have me-r-r-cy*
> *On her and me!*
> *On her and me!*
> *On her and me!*

"It sounded nicer last time," the woman's voice remarked. "After *wealth*, you sang *If my sweetheart keeps her health*. It sounded far tenderer. You must have forgotten it today."

"Poetry's tomfoolery," said Smerdyakov curtly.

"But I do enjoy a nice bit of verse."

"If it's verse, it must be arrant tomfoolery. Just consider: whoever in the whole world ever speaks in rhyme? Were we to start speaking in rhyme, even if ordered to by the authorities, would we be able to say much? No, verse gets one nowhere, Maria Kondratievna."

"What a clever man you are! How have you come to be so knowing?" said the woman's voice ever more ingratiatingly.

"I could have made much more headway and got to know far more if I'd been born under a luckier star. I could have shot dead in a duel anyone who said I'm disreputable because I'm the fatherless offspring of Smelly Lizaveta. In Moscow, they used to throw it in my face, because the story reached them from Grigori Vassilievich. He rebukes me for rebelling against my birth. 'You opened her womb,' he says. I don't mind about the womb, but I'd have preferred being killed in it to coming into the world. It was on all tongues in the market-place, and your mother, too, tried to tell me out of her tactlessness, that she used to go about with her hair all matted, her height being only two arshins and *a wee little bit*. Why put it that way when she might have just said a little over two arshins, like all people say. Wanted to make it sound tearful, but that's the kind of tears to be expected from a muzhik, the feelings of an oaf. Can the Russian muzhik experience the feeling of a man of refinement? His ignorance makes him incapable of any feeling. Since my childhood, the words 'a wee little bit' have always put my back up. I hate all of Russia, Maria Kondratievna."

"You wouldn't say such things if you were an army cadet or a young hussar; you'd have drawn your sabre in defence of all Russia."

"I not only have no desire to be a hussar, Maria Kondratievna but, on the contrary, want all soldiering to be abolished."

"But who will there be to defend us should an enemy come?"

"There's no need for that. In 1812 there was a vast invasion of Russia by the French Emperor Napoleon I, father of the present one,* and it would have been a good thing had the French conquered us: a clever nation would have subdued a very stupid one and taken it over. Our way of life would have become quite different."

"Is their way of life over there so much better than ours? Any of our elegant young men is worth any three young Englishmen," she said tenderly, her words probably being accompanied with the most languorous of glances.

"It's all a matter of taste, I think."

"And you're just like a foreigner yourself, just like a high-born foreigner. I say that despite my sense of modesty."

"If you really care to know, the people over there and over here are very much alike in their vices. They're all rogues tarred with the same brush, the only difference being that over there they sport patent-leather boots, while our scoundrel stinks in his squalor, and sees nothing bad in that. The Russian people need to be flogged, as Fyodor Pavlovich quite rightly said yesterday, though he's quite mad, as are all his children."

"But you yourself have said you have such respect for Ivan Fyodorovich."

"Well, he's called me a stinking lackey. He thinks I may rebel, but he's mistaken. If I had a well-lined pocket, I'd have gone off long ago. Dmitri Fyodorovich is worse than any lackey, both in behaviour, mind and in his beggary; he's a good-for-nothing, yet he's looked up to. I realise I'm only a broth-cook, but with good luck I could start a cafe and restaurant in Petrovka Street in Moscow. That's because I'm a first-class chef, better than any one of them in Moscow, except the chefs from abroad. Dmitri Fyodorovich hasn't got a copeck to his name, yet if he challenged the son of the premier count in Russia to a duel, the challenge would be accepted, and yet is he a better man than I am? He's far stupider than me. Think of the money he's simply poured uselessly down the drain!"

"I think a duel's simply wonderful," Maria Kondratievna

*An obvious error. Napoleon III (1808-1873) was a nephew of Napoleon I.—*Tr.*

suddenly remarked.

"In what way?"

"It's dreadful but brave, especially when young officers empty their pistols at each other over some young lady. It's just lovely. Oh, if we girls were allowed to look on, I'd be most eager to see a duel."

"It's all very well if you're pulling the trigger, but it's a silly feeling if the other pistol is aimed straight at your mug. You'd run away, Maria Kondratievna."

"And what about you? Would you really run away?"

But Smerdyakov deigned no reply. After a minute or so of silence, he struck up another chord, and his falsetto continued with the concluding lines:

> *Whatever you say*
> *I'll go away*
> *And be merry and gay*
> *In a town far away.*
> *No grief for me*
> *As you will see.*
> *I'll cast off all care,*
> *And life will be fair.*

It was at that moment that the unexpected happened: Alyosha gave a sudden sneeze, at which the couple on the bench immediately fell silent. Alyosha rose to his feet and walked towards them. It was indeed Smerdyakov, all dressed up, his hair pomaded and almost curled, and in patent-leather boots. His guitar was lying on the bench. The lady was Maria Kondratievna, the landlady's daughter, clad in a light-blue dress with a train two arshins long. She was quite young and would have been quite good-looking if her face had not been so round and terribly freckled.

"Will my brother Dmitri be back soon?" Alyosha asked as calmly as he could.

Smerdyakov rose slowly to his feet, the lady following suit.

"Why should I be informed of his whereabouts?" Smerdyakov replied in a low voice, distinct and scornful. "It isn't as if he was in my charge, is it?"

"I was simply asking if you did know," Alyosha explained.

"His whereabouts are unknown to me and I haven't the least desire to know."

"But my brother made a point of telling me you would let him know of happenings in the house, and that he had your promise to inform him when Agrafena Alexandrovna came."

Smerdyakov slowly raised his eyes in an unperturbed gaze.

"How did you get in here this time, seeing as how the gate was locked and barred an hour ago," he said with a keen glance at Alyosha.

"I got in from the back-street over the fence and went straight into the pergola. You'll forgive me, I hope," he went on, addressing Maria Kondratievna. "I was in a hurry to get hold of my brother."

"Oh, how could I take it amiss," she drawled, flattered at being apologised to. "You see, Dmitri Fyodorovich himself often gets into the pergola in the same way. It often happens that we don't even know he's here, and lo! he's in the pergola."

"I'm anxious to find him. I must see him or find out from you where he is now. Believe me, it's on a very important matter."

"He never tells us," Maria Kondratievna gabbled.

"Even when I'm here on a friendly call," Smerdyakov again began, "he keeps pestering me something cruel with his endless questions about the master: how things are with him, all the comings and goings, and whether I have anything else to report. On two occasions he even threatened to murder me."

"Murder you?" Alyosha exclaimed in surprise.

"D'you think that would present much difficulty, what with his temper, as you yourself witnessed yesterday? 'If,' he says to me, 'you let Agrafena Alexandrovna in to spend the night here, your goose is cooked.' I'm in terror of him, and if I wasn't in mortal terror even more, I'd report him to the authorities. The Lord alone knows what he's capable of."

" 'I'll grind you to powder in a mortar,' he told him only the other day," Maria Kondratievna added.

"As for the mortar, that may be mere talk," Alyosha remarked. "If I could see him now, I could say something to him on that score, too—"

"There's only one thing I can tell you," said Smerdyakov, seeming to make up his mind. "I come here to see my friends and neighbours, why shouldn't I? On the other hand, Ivan Fyodorovich sent me, the first thing in the morning, to his lodgings in Ozerny Street without any note but with a message that Dmitri Fyodorovich should be sure to dine with him at the local inn, the one in the town square. I went there but did not find him at home, though it was eight o'clock already. 'He was in,' I was told, 'but now he's gone.' I suppose there's some secret arrangement there. It may be that at this very minute he's over there at the inn with Ivan Fyodorovich, as Ivan Fyodorovich hasn't been home for dinner, and Fyodor Pavlovich dined alone an hour ago, and is having a nap. But I'd like to ask you most earnestly not to mention me or what I've told you, or else he'll do me in without any cause."

"So brother Ivan invited Dmitri to have dinner with him at the inn?" Alyosha asked rapidly.

"Yes, sir."

"At the Metropolis Inn in the town square?"

"That's right, sir."

"It's quite possible!" Alyosha exclaimed, much excited. "Thank you, Smerdyakov. That's an important piece of news. I'll go there directly."

"Only don't give me away, sir," Smerdyakov called after him.

"Oh, no. I'll just happen to drop in by chance. Don't worry."

"Why go that way, I'll unlock the gate for you," Maria Kondratievna exclaimed.

"No, I'll again take the short cut over the fence."

The news had taken Alyosha aback, and he hurried to the inn. It was not at all befitting to enter the place in a cassock, but he could make inquiries on the staircase and have them called out. Scarcely had he reached his destination when one of the upstairs windows was flung open and his brother Ivan shouted to him:

"Alyosha, can you come up here to me? I'd appreciate it greatly."

"Of course I can, but what about this garment of mine?"

"I'm in a private room. Walk up to the porch and I'll run down to meet you."

A moment later, Alyosha was sitting next to his brother. Ivan was dining alone.

3.

The Brothers Get to Know Each Other

Ivan, however, was not in a private room but in a partitioned-off section of the public room, at a window, where the diners could not be seen by the rest of the public. It was the first room from the entrance, with a bar-counter running along the side-wall. Waiters were constantly dashing to and fro. The only other customer in the room was an elderly retired army officer, who was having his tea in a corner. In the other rooms, however, there was the bustle typical of such place: voices were calling out loud for the waiters, beer-bottle corks were popping; billiard balls were clicking, and an organ was droning. Alyosha knew that Ivan never patronised that particular inn, and was in general no frequenter of such places, so he must have come there, he thought, to keep an appointment with his brother Dmitri. The latter, however, had not turned up.

"I'll order some fish-soup or something else for you; after all, you don't live on tea alone, do you?" cried Ivan, evidently delighted to have got hold of Alyosha. He had finished his dinner and was having his tea.

"Let me have some fish-soup and then the tea. I'm quite famished," said Alyosha in a merry voice.

"Won't you have some cherry jam? They have it here. Don't you remember how fond you were of cherry jam when you were a kid and living at Polenov's?"

"You still remember that? So come along with the jam. I'm still fond of it."

Ivan Fyodorovich rang for the waiter and ordered fish-soup, tea and jam.

"I remember everything, Alyosha. I remember you until

you were eleven and I was in my fifteenth year. There's such a difference between fifteen and eleven that brothers are never on close terms at such ages. I don't even know whether I was fond of you then. During the first years after I left for Moscow, I never recollected you at all. Then, when you came to Moscow, we met somewhere on a single occasion. And now I've been living here for over three months, but we haven't exchanged a word. I'm leaving tomorrow, and, as I sat here, I thought to myself: how can I see him to bid him good-bye and at that very moment you happened to pass by?"

"Were you very anxious to see me?"

"Very much so, and I want us to get to know each other better once and for all. And then to part on that note. In my opinion, the best time to get to know people is just before parting with them. I've seen you watching me all these three months, and seen the look of constant expectation in your eyes. That's something I can't put up with, which is why I've kept away from you. But I've ultimately come to respect you: this young fellow, I decided, has a firm grip on life. Note that, though I'm joking, I'm speaking in earnest. You have got a firm grip on life, haven't you? I admire such firm people whatever their stand may be, even when they are such little fellows like you. Towards the end, I felt no dislike for your expectant look; on the contrary, I finally took a liking to it— You seem to have grown fond of me for some reason, Alyosha, haven't you?"

"I have, Ivan. Brother Dmitri has said of you, 'Ivan can keep a secret,' but I say of you, 'Ivan is a riddle.' You are still a riddle to me, though I'm beginning to see through you, and only since this morning."

"What do you mean?" Ivan laughed.

"And you won't get angry?" Alyosha asked, laughing in his turn.

"Well?"

"I mean you're just the same kind of young man as all other young men of twenty-three are, just as young, youthful, nice and fresh—a callow youth, in fact. Well, have I offended you?"

"On the contrary, I'm amazed at the coincidence!" Ivan exclaimed with warm good humour. "Would you believe it:

ever since our recent meeting at her place, I've kept thinking of it: the callowness of twenty-three, and now you've suddenly seen through the whole thing, and begun with it. D'you know what I was saying to myself as I sat here? It was this: even if I shed my belief in life; even if I lose faith in a woman I hold dear; even if I lose faith in the order of things; even if I become convinced that, on the contrary, everything is disorderly, accursed and satanic chaos; even if I succumbed to all the horrors of human disillusionment—even then I shall want to live a full life and, having raised the cup to my lips, I won't tear them away from it until I've drunk it to the last drop! Incidentally, I shall probably cast the cup aside by the time I'm thirty, even if I haven't quite drained it, and depart—I know not where. But I'm perfectly sure that until I'm thirty my youth will triumph over everything—every disillusionment and all distaste for life. I've asked myself many times whether there is in the world any despair that can subdue that frenzied and, perhaps, unseemly thirst for life, and have decided that nothing of the kind seems to exist, that is to say, until I turn thirty, and then I'll lose all desire, I think. Some of the consumptive and snotty-nosed moralists—especially the poets—call that thirst for life low. True, it is partly a Karamazovian trait— that thirst for life, regardless of everything— It's very much a part of your make-up, too, but why is it low? There's an awful lot of centripetal force on our planet, Alyosha. I have a longing to live on, and I'm doing so, even in the teeth of logic. I may not believe in the order of things, yet the sticky young leaves that unfold in the spring are dear to me, as is the blue sky; I hold some people dear, whom—can you believe it?—one loves without knowing why; also dear to me are some men's supreme achievements that I may have lost faith in long ago but still revere in my heart out of habit. Well, here comes your fish-soup. Try it; it's excellent. They know how to make it. I want to travel in Europe, Alyosha; I'll go there from here. I know I shall be only going to a graveyard, but it's a very, very precious graveyard indeed, so there! The dead that lie there are precious; every stone that lies over them speaks so eloquently of such ardent life that is no more, such burning faith in their high mission, their truth, their struggle and their learning that I know I shall fall to the ground, kiss those stones and weep over them—while feeling convinced that it's long been a graveyard, and nothing more. It will not be out of despair that I shall weep, but simply because the tears I shed will make me feel happy. I will revel in my own emotions. What I love is the sticky young leaves of spring and the skies of blue—so there! It is not with the mind, not through logic, that one loves, but with one's insides, one's bowels; it is a love of one's first youthful power— Can you make anything of my twaddle, Alyosha, or can't you?" said Ivan, bursting into laughter.

"I understand it only too well, Ivan: one wants to love with all one's insides and bowels—you've expressed it so well, and I'm terribly glad that you've got such a thirst for life," Alyosha exclaimed. "I think that people should first and foremost hold life dear."

"You mean love life more than its meaning?"

"Most certainly, love it dearer than logic, as you have said, yes, indeed, dearer than logic, and only then will I understand its meaning. It's something I've been vaguely aware of for a long time. You've done and achieved half of your work: you love life. You now have to achieve the other half, and you are saved."

"Are you really out to save me, though I have, perhaps, not perished! And what does it consist in—that second half of yours?"

"In the need to resurrect your dead, who have perhaps never died at all. And now for tea. I'm glad we're having this talk, Ivan."

"I see you're in a kind of inspired mood. I simply love such *professions de foi* from such—religious novices. Yours is a firm nature, Alexei. Is it true you're thinking of leaving the monastery?"

"It is. My *starets* is sending me out into the world."

"Consequently, we shall see each other in the world; we shall meet before I turn thirty and begin to turn away from the cup. Father doesn't want to turn away from his cup till he's seventy, or even eighty, as is his ambition; he himself has said so. It's a serious matter with him, though he's a buffoon. He's taken a rock-firm stand on sensualism—though I suppose there's nothing else to stand on after thirty— But it's low to hold on until seventy—that's better done till one is thirty—one can retain 'a shadow of nobleness' by self-deception. Have you seen Dmitri today?"

"No, I haven't, but I have seen Smerdyakov." And Alyosha told his brother rapidly but in detail of his meeting with Smerdyakov. Ivan suddenly began listening with concern, even asking him to expand on some details.

"Only he asked me not to tell brother Dmitri what he had said of him," Alyosha added.

Ivan frowned and grew thoughtful.

"Is it because of Smerdyakov that you're frowning?" asked Alyosha.

"Yes, because of him. Well, to hell with him. I really did want to see Dmitri, but it's become unnecessary now—" said Ivan with reluctance.

"Are you leaving so soon, brother?"

"I am."

"But what of Dmitri and Father? How will it all end between them?" Alyosha asked anxiously.

"You're on the same subject again! What's that got to do with me? Am I my brother Dmitri's keeper?" Ivan began in sharp irritation, but suddenly gave a bitter smile. "That was how Cain replied to God about his murdered brother, eh? Perhaps, that's what you're thinking at this moment, isn't it? But damn it all, I really can't stay on here as their keeper, can I? I've wound up my affairs and am leaving. Do you actually think I'm jealous of Dmitri, and that for the last three months I've been trying to win his beautiful Katerina Ivanovna away from him. Damn it, I've had my own affairs to attend to. I've completed them and am leaving. You witnessed the way I completed them."

"You mean with Katerina Ivanovna?"

"Yes, with her, when I put paid to everything once and for all. What's all this about? What's Dmitri to do with me? He's not in the picture at all. I had my own affairs to attend to with

Katerina Ivanovna. You know that, on the contrary, Dmitri behaved as though he'd reached an understanding with me. I never asked him to, but he's solemnly passed her on to me with his blessing. It's all so ridiculous. No, Alyosha, if you only knew what a sense of relief I feel! So here I was, seated at dinner and—would you believe it?—felt like ordering some champagne to celebrate my first hour of freedom. Ugh, close on six months—and all suddenly cast off, at one go. Why, even yesterday I had no inkling that, if I wanted to, I would find nothing easier than to have done with it!"

"Are you speaking of your love, Ivan?"

"I am, if you like. Yes, I fell in love with that young lady, that boarding-school miss. I had a bad time with her, and she made things very hard for me. I devoted so much time to her—and now it's all suddenly over. I spoke with inspiration there a short while ago, but no sooner had I left than I burst into laughter. Would you believe it? Yes, I mean exactly what I say."

"Even now you speak of it with such gaiety," Alyosha remarked, looking him intently in the face, which had indeed grown suddenly cheerful.

"How on earth was I to know I didn't love her in the least! Well, well. It appears that I don't. But how drawn I felt to her! I felt attracted even while I was making my speech. I like her awfully even now, yet nothing can be easier than parting with her. Do you think I'm putting on side?"

"No, I don't, only it may not have been love."

"My dear Alyosha," Ivan laughed, "don't get involved in disquisitions on love! It's unseemly for you to do so. The way you came sailing into the discussion this morning was simply amazing. I've forgotten to embrace you for it— And how she tormented me! I was indeed a witness to so much anguish. Oh, she was well aware I loved her! And it was me she loved, and not Dmitri," Ivan insisted blithely. "Dmitri was simply a source of anguish. Everything I said to her was nothing but the truth. The trouble, the gist of the matter, is that it will take her perhaps fifteen or twenty years to realise that she does not love Dmitri at all, and that it's me she loves, a man she has tormented. She probably won't ever realise that, despite the lesson she was taught today. Well, it's better this way: I got up and left for good. How is she now, by the way? What happened after I left?"

Alyosha told him of her hysterics and that she was still apparently unconscious and delirious.

"Is Madame Khokhlakov telling the truth?"

"I think she is."

"I'll have to ask after her. Incidentally, no one has ever died of hysterics. So what if she's been hysterical: it was out of His love that God sent woman hysterics. No, I won't go there. Why should I intrude again?"

"Yet you told her she never loved you, didn't you?"

"I did so on purpose. What will you say, Alyosha, to some champagne to celebrate my freedom? Oh, if you only knew how glad I feel!"

"No, Ivan, I don't think we should have any champagne," Alyosha said suddenly. "Besides, I feel dispirited."

"You've been feeling low for quite a while. I've seen that for a long time."

"So are you leaving definitely tomorrow morning?"

"Morning? I didn't say it would be on the morning— Yet it may very well be in the morning. Believe me, I've been having dinner here today exclusively to avoid dining with the old man—he's become so loathsome to me. I would have left long ago if it were a question of him alone. But why are you so put out by my going away from here? We have all the time in the world before I do so—an eternity, time without end!"

"What kind of eternity can it be if you're leaving tomorrow?"

"How can that affect the two of us?" said Ivan with a laugh. "We'll have time enough to have our say and talk out what has brought us here. Why do you look so surprised? Tell me: what have we come here for? To talk of my love for Katerina Ivanovna? Of the old man and Dmitri? Of my going abroad? Of Russia's parlous state? Or about the Emperor Napoleon? Tell me: are we here for that?"

"No, not for that."

"Then you know very well why we're here. Other people are

taken up with one kind of problem, while we fledgelings are concerned with something else; in the first place, we are here to settle some long-standing questions—that is our prime concern. The entire youth of Russia are talking of nothing but long-standing questions. Especially now, when their elders have suddenly become preoccupied with practical matters. What has brought that look of expectation into your eyes during these past three months? Has it been there so as to ask me, 'What do you believe in? Or have you no belief at all?' That has been the actual meaning of your glances these three months, Alexei Fyodorovich, hasn't it?"

"I suppose it has," said Alyosha with a smile. "You aren't making fun of me now, are you?"

"Me make fun of you? I wouldn't want to upset my little brother, who has been looking at me so expectantly during the last three months. Look me in the face, Alyosha: I'm just as much of an urchin as you are, except that I'm not in the novitiate. And what have these Russian boys been engaged in to date? I mean, certain of them. Take this foul tavern, where they get together in some corner. They haven't ever known each other till now, and when they leave this place they won't meet for another forty years. Yet what are they going to discuss during that fleeting minute in the tavern? Nothing but world-scale questions, such as: does God exist? Is there immortality? Those who do not believe in God will speak of Socialism or anarchism, the refashioning of mankind after some new pattern. So you see, it all boils down to the selfsame questions, only taken from the opposite end. And so many Russian boys, who do original thinking—a multitude of them—do nothing nowadays but talk about eternal questions. Isn't that so?"

"Indeed it is," said Alyosha, regarding his brother with the same gentle and inquiring smile, "to genuine Russians such questions as whether God and immortality exist, or, as you put it, questions taken from the 'opposite end', stand first and foremost, which is how they should."

"So you see, Alyosha, it's sometimes not at all a clever thing to be a Russian, yet one cannot imagine anything more stupid than what Russian boys engage in nowadays. But there's a

Russian boy named Alyosha that I'm terribly fond of."

"How neatly you've brought that in!" Alyosha suddenly laughed.

"Well, tell me what to begin with—give the command: shall it be with God? Does God exist?—that's the question."

"Begin with anything you wish, even with the 'opposite end'. Didn't you declare yesterday at Father's that there is no God?" said Alyosha regarding his brother searchingly.

"I said that yesterday at dinner at Father's place just to tease you, and saw how it made your eyes sparkle. But now I'm not averse from having a talk with you, and say so in all earnest. I want to draw closer to you, Alyosha, because I have no friends. I want to have a try. Well, just imagine that I, too, perhaps accept the existence of God," said Ivan with a laugh. "That comes as a surprise to you, doesn't it?"

"Of course, it does, if only you're not speaking in jest."

"'In jest?' I was said to be speaking in jest yesterday when we were with the *starets*. You see, my dear fellow, there lived, in the eighteenth century, an old sinner who said that if there was no God, He would have to be invented: *s'il n'existait pas Dieu il faudrait l'inventer*. And, indeed, man has invented God. What is so strange and would be so marvellous is not God's actual existence, but that such an idea—the idea of the necessity of God—should have occurred to so vicious and evil an animal as man—an idea so sacred, so moving and wise that it stands to man's credit. As for me, I decided long ago not to speculate whether it was man who created God, or God who created man. Of course, I have no intention of taking up all the present-day axioms on the matter, which so exercise the minds of our Russian boys and have all been deduced from European hypotheses: what is a hypothesis over there immediately turns into an axiom with the Russian boy, and not only with boys but probably with their professors as well, for our Russian professors are quite often nothing but the selfsame Russian boys. I therefore avoid all hypotheses. For what is the task now facing us? It consists in my being able to explain my essence to you as quickly as possible, that is to say, to let you know what kind of man I am, what I believe in and hope for? Isn't that so?

I therefore declare that my acceptance of God is simple and straightforward. However, here's something that should be taken note of: if God exists and if He really did create the earth, then, as we know perfectly well, He created it in accordance with Euclidean geometry and, in creating man's mind, endowed it with the notion of only three spatial dimensions. Yet there have been, and even still are, geometricians and philosophers—and even outstanding ones—who doubt whether the entire Universe or, in a broader sense, the whole of existence, was created only according to Euclidean geometry, and even make so bold as to fancy that two parallel lines, which, Euclid says, cannot ever meet on earth could perhaps meet somewhere in infinity. I have arrived at the conclusion, my dear Alyosha, that if I can't grasp even that, how can I understand the question of God. In all humility I confess that I haven't the abilities needed to deal with such questions. My mind is Euclidean and earthbound, so how am I to deal with what is not of this earth. And I would advise you, too, friend Alyosha, never to give thought to that, and especially to whether God does or does not exist. All such questions are quite alien to a mind created with the idea of only three dimensions. And so I accept God, and do so, not only willingly but with full acceptance of His wisdom and His purpose, which are inscrutable to us; I believe in the order and meaning of life; I believe in the eternal harmony in which we are supposed to merge one day; I believe in the Word, towards which the Universe is straining and which itself was 'with God' and itself is God—well, and so on and so forth, and thus to eternity. Many words have been enunciated on that score. So I seem to be on the right road, eh? Well, just fancy: in the final analysis, I do not accept this world of God's and, though I know it exists, I do not acknowledge it at all. It is not God that I do not accept—you must understand that—but the world created by Him, and I cannot agree to accept it. I shall qualify my words by adding that I have a childlike confidence that the sufferings will be healed and smoothed away; that the humiliating absurdity of human contradictions will vanish like a miserable mirage, like a vile fabrication of the human Euclidean mind,

20-721

which is so puny and is as minute as an atom, and finally that, at the world's finale, at the moment of eternal harmony, there will come to pass and appear something so precious that it will suffice for all hearts, allay all resentment and atone for all the crimes of mankind and all the blood it has spilt, and suffice to make it possible, not only to forgive but even to justify everything that has come about with mankind—let all that come to pass and appear, but it's something I do not accept, and do not wish to! Even let the parallel lines meet for me to see it with my own eyes—I shall see it and say they have met, but still I won't accept the fact. Therein is my essence, Alyosha; that is my thesis. I have said that to you in all earnest. I deliberately began our discussion in the most inane manner possible but led it up to my confession because that's all you need. It was not something about God you wanted to hear, but only what your beloved brother lives by. And I've told you that."

Ivan suddenly concluded his lengthy and vehement speech with a kind of marked and unexpected feeling.

"But why did you begin 'in the most inane manner possible'?" asked Alyosha, looking thoughtfully at him.

"At least, to follow the Russian pattern, in the first place: Russians talk on such matters in the most inane manner. Secondly, the greater the inanity, the closer to the point. The greater the inanity, the clearer things become. Inanity is short-lived and ingenuous, whilst intelligence twists and turns, and hides in holes and corners. Intelligence is vile, while inanity is straightforward and honest. I have brought the matter to my condition of despair and the more inanely I have presented that condition of mine, the more it has been to my advantage."

"Will you explain to me why you refuse to 'accept the world'?" said Alyosha.

"Of course, I will: it's no secret, and it's what I've been trying to lead up to. My dear little brother, it's not you I want to corrupt or shift from your rock; perhaps, I want to get healed through you," said Ivan, with a sudden smile like that of a gentle child. Never before had Alyosha seen him smile like that.

4.

Rebellion

"I have a confession to make to you," Ivan began. "I've never been able to understand how one can love one's neighbours. To my mind, it is one's neighbours that cannot be loved, with the possible exception of distant ones. I remember reading about a certain 'John the Compassionate' (a saintly man) who, when a hungry and freezing traveller asked him to let him warm himself, lay down with him in his bed, embraced him and began to breathe into his mouth, which was festering and fetid from some horrible disease. I'm convinced he did so out of some false obsession, a sense of duty-inspired love, and as a self-imposed penance. If you would love a man, he must keep in hiding, for love will vanish the moment he shows even a little of his face."

"The *starets* Zossima has often mentioned that," Alyosha observed. "He has also said that a man's face often prevents people with little experience of loving others from loving him. But then, mankind harbours a great store of love that is almost Christlike, as I know for myself, Ivan—"

"Well, that's something I know little of as yet and can't understand: neither can a countless multitude of people. The question is: does it come of man's evil qualities, or does it lie in their very nature. As I see it, a Christlike love of others is a kind of miracle that is impossible on earth. Of course, Christ was God. But we are not godlike. Let us assume that I, for instance, am capable of deep suffering but nobody else can ever learn the depth of my suffering because he is someone else, and not me; besides, it is rare for a man to recognise another as a sufferer (as though that were some distinction). Why do you think he won't recognise the fact? It may be because I smell bad or have a stupid face, or perhaps because I once trod on his toes. Besides, suffering can be of different kinds; there is the humiliating brand, which degrades me—going hungry, for instance. That is something any benefactor of mine will not object to, but he will rarely put up with a somewhat higher brand of suffering—for some idea, for instance, because he may happen to cast a glance at me and suddenly see that I haven't got the kind of face which, his fancy tells him, a man suffering for an idea ought to have. That makes him immediately deprive me of his benefactions, and not out of any hardness of heart. Beggars, especially those of the genteel brand, should never show themselves in public but should ask for alms through the newspapers. In the abstract, one may still love one's neighbour, sometimes even at a distance, but almost never at close quarters. If the world were like a stage, a ballet performance, for instance, where, if beggars appear, they do so in rags of silk and tattered lace, prancing gracefully as they beg for alms, then they might, perhaps, evoke admiration—admiration, but not love. But enough on that score. I simply wanted you to see my point of view. I wanted to speak of the sufferings of mankind in general, but, perhaps, we should rather confine ourselves to the sufferings of the children alone. That will reduce the volume of my argument by nine-tenths, but I think it is better to keep to the children, though that will be all the more to my disadvantage, of course. But, in the first place, children can be loved even at close range, even if they're dirty and ugly (though it seems to me that children's faces can never be ugly). In the second place, I won't speak about grown-ups also for the reason that, besides being revolting and undeserving of love, they await retribution: they have eaten of the apple and become 'as gods', knowing good and evil. They still continue to eat of it. But the children have not eaten of it and are as yet guiltless. Do you love little children, Alyosha? I know that you do, so you will understand why it is that I now want to talk of them alone. If they, too, suffer terribly on earth, it is, of course, because of their fathers; they are punished for their fathers, who have eaten of the apple—but such reasoning comes from another world, and is beyond the comprehension of the human heart down here on earth. No innocent creature should suffer for another, especially when it is so innocent! Regard me with surprise, Alyosha, for I'm also terribly fond of little children. And please note: cruel people, passionate and rapacious—the Karamazovites—are sometimes extremely fond of children. While they are still small—

up to the age of seven, for instance, children stand far removed from grown-ups: they seem to be quite different creatures, quite different in nature. I once knew a robber, who was behind bars. During his career of crime he had murdered entire families in houses he had broken into at night for the purpose of robbery; he would also murder several children for good measure. But he had a strange affection for children when he was in prison. He would never tire of watching them, from the window of his cell, at their play in the prison courtyard. He even taught a little boy to come and stand at his window, and they became great friends— Oh, why am I telling you all this, Alyosha? My head is aching somehow and I feel sad."

"You are speaking in such a strange way," Alyosha remarked with concern, "as if you were somehow unsettled in your mind."

"Incidentally," Ivan Fyodorovich went on, seeming not to hear his brother's words, "a Bulgar I recently met in Moscow told me of the mass atrocities committed throughout Bulgaria by the Turks and the Circassians for fear of a general uprising of the Slavs. With fire and sword they lay waste to the land, rape women and children, nail prisoners to fences by the ears, leave them that way till the next morning, when they hang them—that's the way they behave and it beggars discription. People sometimes speak of man's 'brutal' cruelty, but that is unfair and insulting to dumb brutes: beasts can never be as cruel as man is, so ingenious and refined in cruelty. The tiger will gnaw and tear at its prey—it's all it can do. It would never occur to it to nail people to fences by the ears for the night, even were it able to do so. Those Turks, incidentally, derived exquisite pleasure from torturing children—from cutting unborn babies out of their mothers' wombs with daggers, to tossing babies in the air and impaling them on their bayonets before their mothers' eyes. Doing so for the mothers to see gave them particular delight. But here's a scene that greatly interested me: imagine a baby in its mother's trembling arms, surrounded by Turks who have entered the house. They want their bit of fun, so they fondle the baby, laughing aloud to amuse it. When they succeed, a Turk levels a pistol some four inches from its face. The child chuckles in joy and stretches out its little hands to take hold of the pistol. The Turk pulls the trigger and blows out its brains— Artistic, eh? Incidentally, the Turks are said to be very fond of sweetmeats."

"Why are you telling me all this, brother?" Alyosha asked.

"I think that if the Devil doesn't exist and has therefore been created by man, then the latter has created him in his own image and likeness."

"In that case, just as he created God."

"How good you are at 'cracking the wind of the poor phrase', as Polonius has it in *Hamlet*," said Ivan with a laugh. "You've turned my own words against me, and I'm glad of it. Yours must be a fine God if man created Him in his own image and likeness. You just now asked me why I was telling you all this: well, you see, I'm given to collecting certain facts and, would you believe it, I copy out and collect from newspapers and stories, from practically anywhere, anecdotes of a certain kind, and I've already got a good collection of them. Of course, the Turks are in the collection, but they are foreigners after all. I've also got some choice selections from Russian life—even better than the Turkish ones. You know, we go in more for flogging—the birch and the cat—that's a national institution with us. Nailing by the ear is unthinkable here, for we're Europeans after all, but the birch and the cat are part and parcel of our life and can't be taken away from us. Flogging seems to have gone out of fashion abroad. Perhaps their mores have become purer, or they may have passed the appropriate laws banning one man from flogging another, so they have made up for it in another way just as purely national as ours; indeed, it is so national that it would seem impossible in our country, though, I believe, it is striking root here too, particularly since the time the religious movement appeared among our upper classes. I have in my possession a most charming little pamphlet, translated from the French, which describes the execution in Geneva, quite recently, only some five years ago, of a scoundrel and murderer, Richard by name, a young man of twenty-three, I think he was, who repented of his crimes and was converted to the Christian faith shortly before being beheaded. This Richard was born out of wedlock; when he was six, his parents had made a *gift* of him to some Swiss mountain shepherds, who brought him up to work for them. He grew up there in the manner of some wild little animal. He was not taught anything; on the contrary, at the age of seven he was sent to tend the flock in the cold and the wet, scarcely fed or clothed. Of course, in doing so, the shepherds gave no thought to him and felt no remorse; on the contrary, they considered themselves entitled to treat him in that way, for he had been given to them as chattel, so that they did not even think it necessary to feed him. Richard himself testified that during those years he, like the Prodigal Son in the Gospels, had yearned for the mash the pigs were fed to fatten them up for the market. He was never given even that and was thrashed whenever he stole from the pigs. And that was how he spent his childhood and his youth until he grew up and was strong enough to make off and live by stealing. This savage began to earn money as a day-labourer in Geneva, spending his earnings on drink. He lived like a brute and ended up by murdering and robbing an old man. He was caught, tried and condemned to die. They have no place for sentimentality over there, you see. In prison, he was immediately surrounded by pastors, members of various Christian fraternities, lady philanthropists and the like. He was taught how to read and write, had the Gospel expounded to him, was exhorted, worked on, coaxed and constantly drummed at. Finally, he solemnly confessed to his crime. He was converted and himself wrote to the court that he was a monster who had at last seen the light of God and been vouchsafed grace. He became the focus of exalted attention from the whole of philanthropic and religious Geneva. Members of the upper classes and well-bred circles hastened to see him in prison; he was embraced and kissed: 'You are our brother on whom grace has descended.' Richard himself could only weep with emotion: 'Indeed, grace has descended upon me! In my childhood and youth I was glad to get pig feed, but now grace has descended on me too, and I shall die in the Lord!' 'Yes, yes, Richard, die in the Lord: you've shed blood and must die in the Lord. Even if you're not to blame that you did not know the Lord when you envied the pigs, their feed and were beaten for stealing it (which was very wrong of you, for it is forbidden to steal), you've shed blood and must die.' And so the last day came round. The enfeebled Richard was in tears and could do nothing but keep on repeating, 'This is my finest day: I'm going to the Lord!' 'Yes,' exclaimed the pastors, the judges and the lady philanthropists, 'this is your happiest day, for you are going to the Lord!' In carriage or on foot they all followed the tumbril that was taking Richard to the place of execution. At last they arrived there. 'Die, our brother,' they shouted to Richard, 'die in the Lord, for you've been granted grace!' And so, covered with brotherly kisses, brother Richard was dragged on to the platform, placed on the guillotine and had his head lopped off in brotherly fashion, for he also had found grace. Yes, it was all characteristic. The pamphlet has been translated into Russian by some Lutheranising philanthropists from the Russian upper classes and distributed free of charge as supplements to newspapers and other publications, with the aim of edifying the Russian people. Richard's case is interesting in its national flavour. Although with us it would be absurd to chop off a brother's head simply because he's become our brother and been granted grace; we, I repeat, have our own brand, which is hardly any worse. The infliction of pain by flogging is our historical, immediate and specific form of enjoyment. The poet Nekrassov has some lines about a muzhik belabouring his nag about the eyes, 'its meek eyes'. Who has not witnessed similar scenes, which are so typical of our land? He describes a feeble nag, badly overloaded, which can't drag the heavy cart out of a rut. The muzhik whips it savagely, and goes on doing so without realising, in the intoxication of inflicting punishment, what he is actually doing. Over and over again, he lashes at the horse mercilessly. 'Pull, no matter how weak you are! Even if you die, go on pulling.' The nag heaves away to no avail, so he begins to whip the poor and defenceless animal about its weeping 'meek eyes'. Frantic from the blows, it gives a tremendous pull, drags the cart out of the rut, and goes off, breathless and trembling, moving sideways with a skipping motion, unnatural and shameful— Nekrassov's description is heartrending. But it's nothing more than a horse here, and God himself has given us horses to be flogged. That's what the Tartars taught us, leaving us the knout for remembrance. But human beings, too, can be flogged. So we have a well-bred and educated gentleman and his good lady, who birch their own seven-year-old daughter—I have a detailed account of it. Daddy is pleased that the twigs have plenty of knots—'it will sting more', he says, as he sets about drubbing his own daughter. I know for certain that there are floggers who derive a sensual pleasure from every blow, literally sensual pleasure, which grows and grows with each fresh blow. The birching goes on for a minute, for five minutes, then ten, with ever mounting frequency and force. The child screams until its voice is gone, and it gasps for air. 'Daddy, daddy, dear daddy!' The matter is brought into court through some devilish and indecent play of chance, and counsel is engaged. 'A conscience for hire'—that's what Russians have long called the advocate. Counsel protests in loud terms against his client being taken to court. 'It's such a simple matter—an ordinary family matter: a father has thrashed his child and, to the shame of our times, it's been brought to court!' he contends. Convinced by his argument, the jury retire and return with a verdict of acquittal. The public roar with delight at the tormentor having been acquitted. Oh, it's such a pity I wasn't there: I'd have barked out a proposal that a scholarship should be founded and named after the tormentor!—What charming scenes these are! But I have even choicer things about children: I've collected very, very many facts about Russian children, Alyosha. Two parents, 'most respected people of good education and social standing', developed a hatred for their little daughter of five. You see, I aver most emphatically that a great many members of the human race possess a peculiar trait—a love of tormenting children, and children alone. Towards all other members of the human species these self-same tormentors even display goodwill and kindness, like the well-bred and human Europeans they are, but they are ever so fond of displaying cruelty to children, and, in this sense, have a love of children. It's the defencelessness of the little creatures that attracts the tormentors, the angelic trustfulness of the child, who has no other refuge or protection—that's what sets the tormentor's vile blood coursing. Of course, a wild beast lies concealed in every man, a fiend born of fury, of vicious and intoxicating delight from the screams of the tormented victim, an uncontrollable animal let off the chain, a wild beast begotten of disease, gout, liver trouble and other such things contracted through vice. The poor five-year-old girl was subjected to indescribable maltreatment by these educated parents, who beat, whipped and kicked her without themselves knowing why, until her whole body was covered with bruises. They finally achieved the height of refined cruelty: on cold and frosty nights, they would lock her till the morning in a privy if she had soiled her bedding at night (as though a child of five, deep in angelic slumber, could be trained at her age), and smeared her face with excrement, which they made her swallow—and it was her own mother who did that! And that mother could actually sleep when the groans of the poor child could be heard from that vile place! Can you understand that—a little creature, still incapable of realising what is happening to her, beats her aching breast with a tiny fist, in the dark and cold of that vile place, and sheds meek and burning tears addressed to 'dear, kind God' and begs His protection—can you understand the entire utter absurdity, my brother and friend, my pious and meek novice—can you understand why this grotesque business should be necessary and brought to pass? Without it, they say, man could not exist on earth, since he would not have known good and evil. But why on earth should he know such diabolical good and evil if the price is so high? Why, in that case, the entire world of knowledge is not worth that child's tears of prayer to 'dear, kind God'. I'm not speaking of the sufferings of grown-ups, for they've eaten of the apple and so to hell with them—let them all rot in Hell—but the little ones, the little ones! I'm tormenting you, Alyosha, and you look terribly upset. I'll stop, if you like."

"No, don't. I, too, want to undergo that torment," Alyosha said in a low voice.

"One more, only one more scene, and that, too, because it's so curious and so characteristic, but mostly because I've just come across it in a collection of historical facts—the *Archives* or *Olden Days* or something like that. I've forgotten the exact source, but I can look it up. This happened during the darkest days of the serf-owning system, in the early days of the century—and long live the liberator of the people.* There lived, in the early years of the century, a certain general, an extremely wealthy landowner with the highest connections, one of those (true rather the exception, even then) who, on retiring from army service, were almost certain that they had earned the right of life and death over their serfs. There were such people in those times. Well, this general settled down on his estate, with its two thousand serfs, considering himself high and mighty, and lording it over his poorer neighbours as though they were his hangers-on and existed only for his amusement. He kept hundreds of hounds in his kennels and almost a hundred whips, all mounted and in uniform. One day a little house-serf, a boy of only eight, happened to throw a stone in play, hurting a paw of the general's favourite hound. 'Why is my favourite hound limping?' the general asked, and was told that the boy had thrown a stone and hurt its paw. 'So it was you, eh?' the general said, looking the boy up and down. 'Have him locked up!' He was taken away from his mother and kept in the lock-up all night. Just after dawn, the general prepared for the hunt, all dressed up for the occasion and on horseback, surrounded by his hangers-on, his hounds, the whips and the huntsmen. To drive the lesson home, the house-serfs were mustered, with the culprit's mother in front of them all. The boy was brought from the lock-up. It was a chilly, gloomy and misty autumn day, just right for the hunt. The general had the child stripped naked. He was shivering and numb with fright, not daring to utter a sound— 'Make him run off!' the general ordered. The cry was taken up by the whips: 'Run, run!' they cried, and the boy dashed off. 'Yoicks, yoicks!' the general bawled, and set the entire pack of hounds on him. They hounded the child down before the

---

*The reference is to Tsar Alexander II, during whose reign (1855-1881) serf-ownership was abolished.—*Tr.*

315

mother's eyes, and tore him to pieces! The general was later declared *non compos mentis*, I believe. Well—what did he deserve? Should he be shot? Shot to satisfy our sense of morality? Tell me, Alyosha!"

"He should," said Alyosha in a low voice, looking up at his brother, his lips distorted by a pale smile.

"Bravo!" cried Ivan, with a kind of delight. "If you say so, then— Well, so much for the coenobite! That's the kind of imp that lurks in your heart, Alyosha Karamazov!"

"I've said something absurd, but—"

"But that is the crux of the matter—" cried Ivan. "Let me tell you, you postulant, that absurdities are absolutely essential on earth. The world rests on absurdities; perhaps nothing could come to pass without them. We know that we know!"

"What is it that you know?"

"I don't understand anything," Ivan went on, all wrought up, "and from now on I don't want to. I want to rest with the fact. I've long been determined not to understand anything. If I should want to understand something, I'd instantly be false to the fact, and I've decided to rest firm with the fact—"

"Why are you testing me?" Alyosha exclaimed in sad distress. "Won't you tell me at last?"

"Of course, I shall. That's what I've been leading up to. You're dear to me. I don't want to lose you and I won't give you up to your Zossima."

Ivan fell silent for a while, his face suddenly becoming very sad.

"Listen: I took only the children to make things more obvious. I shan't say a single word about the other human tears the earth is soaked in from crust to centre; I've narrowed down my theme on purpose. I'm nothing more than a bug and acknowledge in all humility that I can't make head or tail of why everything has been arranged as it is. So it's men themselves who are to blame: they were given Paradise, but wished for freedom and stole the fire from Heaven, knowing full well that they would become unfortunate, so there's nothing to pity them for.

Oh, with my miserable earthly Euclidean mind I only know that suffering exists with nobody to blame, that one thing emerges simply and directly from another, and that everything is in a state of flux and evens out—but all that is Euclidean balderdash; I know that, but I cannot agree to live by it! What is it to me that no one is to blame and that I know it? What I want is retribution, for otherwise I'll destroy myself. That retribution should come, not somewhere else and at some time in infinity, but here on earth and for me to see for myself. I have had faith and I want to see it for myself; if I'm dead by then, let me be resurrected, for if it all comes about without me, that would be a great pity. Surely I haven't gone through suffering so that some future harmony should be manured, for somebody else, with me, my evil deeds and my sufferings. I want to see with my own eyes the doe lie down by the lion's side and the victim of murder arise and embrace his murderer. I want to be here when all men will suddenly learn the purpose of it all. All the religions in the world are grounded in that desire, and I'm a believer. But then there are the children, and what am I to do with them in that case? That's a question I can't answer. I repeat for the hundredth time—there are a multitude of questions, but I've taken the children alone, for in this case what I have to say is incontestably clear. Listen: if all must suffer to pay for eternal harmony, what has that to do with the children, I ask you? It passes all understanding why they, too, should suffer, and why they should have to pay for that harmony with their sufferings? Why should they, too, have to become so much material to manure the soil for somebody's future harmony? Solidarity in iniquity among men is something I can understand, as well as solidarity in retribution, but it is not with the children that there can be solidarity in sin. And if the truth lies in their sharing responsibility with their fathers for all the crimes the latter have committed, then that truth is not of this world, and I fail to understand it. Some jester might say that the child would have grown up anyway, and fallen into sin, but the fact is that he did not grow up, but was torn to pieces by hounds at the age of eight. Oh, I'm not blaspheming, Alyosha! Of course, I realise what an upheaval of the Universe will

317

take place when everything in heaven and earth will blend in a single voice of praise, and all living things, past and present, will cry out, 'Righteous art thou, O Lord, for thy ways are revealed!' Of course, the height of knowledge will be achieved and everything will find explanation when the mother embraces the tormentor who has had her child torn to pieces by hounds, and the three cry aloud in tears, 'Righteous art thou, O Lord!' But the snag is that I cannot accept that harmony! And as long as I am on earth, I hasten to make use of a yardstick of my own. You see, Alyosha, it may indeed come about that, if I live to see that day or rise from the dead to see it, then I, too, may exclaim, together with all the rest, at the sight of the mother embracing her son's tormentor: 'Righteous art thou, O Lord', but I do not want to do that. Whilst there is still time, I hasten to shield myself, and therefore renounce the higher harmony completely. That harmony is not worth a single tear of the tormented child that beat its breast with its little fist and, with unexpiated tears, prayed in stinking privy to her 'dear, kind God'! It isn't worth those tears because they have not been atoned for. But they must be atoned for, since otherwise there can be no harmony. But how are they to be atoned? Is that possible? Not, surely, by their being avenged? But do I need that vengeance or Hell for the tormentors? What can Hell change once those have been done to death? And, if Hell exists, what kind of harmony can there be? I want to embrace and forgive; I want no more suffering. And if the children's sufferings go to swell the sum of the sufferings needed in payment for truth, then I assert in advance that the whole truth is not worth the price. Finally, I don't want the mother to embrace the tormentor who had her son torn to pieces by his hounds! She dare not forgive him! Let her forgive him for herself if she so wishes; let her forgive the tormentor for her boundless anguish as a mother; but she has no right to forgive the sufferings of her tortured child even were the child to forgive its tormentor. She dare not do so! And, if that is so, and the two do not dare to forgive him, where is harmony to be found? Is there, in the whole world, a creature that could give forgiveness, and had the right to? I want no harmony; out of my love for mankind I do not want it.

I prefer to remain with the unavenged sufferings. It's better for me to remain with my sufferings unavenged and my indignation unassuaged *even if I'm in the wrong.* Indeed, the price set on harmony is too high, and we can't afford the entrance fee. That is why I hasten to return my entrance ticket. If I'm a man of integrity, it's my duty to return it at the earliest opportunity. That's exactly what I'm doing. It's not that I don't accept God, Alyosha; I'm merely most respectfully returning the ticket to Him."

"But that's rebellion," said Alyosha softly, lowering his eyes.

"Rebellion? I wouldn't have liked to hear that word from you," said Ivan earnestly. "Can one live in a state of rebellion—and I want to go on living. Tell me frankly—I conjure you—answer me: imagine that you are yourself engaged in creating the fabric of human fate, with the aim of ultimately bringing men happiness and giving them peace and contentment at last, but for that, to come about, it is essential and inescapable that a tiny being should be tortured to death—that very child that beat its breast with its little fist—and that the edifice should be founded on its unavenged tears: would you agree to be the architect on those terms? Answer, and tell me the truth!"

"No, I would not," said Alyosha in a low voice.

"And can you allow the idea that those you are building for would agree to accept happiness at the cost of the unatoned blood of a little victim and, having accepted it, remain happy for all time?"

"No, I can't allow the idea," Alyosha exclaimed, his eyes flashing. "Ivan, you've just asked whether there exists in the world a being that could forgive, and had the right to? But that being does exist, and he can forgive anything and anybody—*and for everything*, because he himself gave his innocent blood for all and everything. You've forgotten him, but it is on him that the edifice rests, and it is to him that people will cry out, 'Righteous art thou, O Lord, for thy ways are revealed!' "

"Oh, 'the one without sin' and his blood! No, I haven't forgotten him. On the contrary, I was wondering all the time why you didn't bring him in for so long, since in their arguments, your kind usually bring him forward. I hope, Alyosha,

I won't make you laugh if I tell you that I once wrote a poem, about a year ago. If you don't mind wasting another ten minutes on me, I'll tell it to you."

"You've actually written a poem?"

"Oh, no, I haven't actually written one," Ivan laughed. "I haven't ever penned even a couple of verses in my life. But I've thought up this poem in prose and memorised it. I thought it up at a moment of uplift. You'll be my first reader, or listener rather. Indeed, why should an author forego even a single listener?" said Ivan with a grin. "Shall I tell it or not?"

"I'm all ears," said Alyosha.

"My poem is entitled *The Grand Inquisitor*; it's quite absurd, but I'd like you to hear it."

5.

The Grand Inquisitor

"Even here," said Ivan with a laugh, "we can't do without a preface, that is to say, without a literary preface, and I'm not much good as an author. You see, the action takes place in the sixteenth century, a time when, as you probably remember from your school-days, it was customary for poetical works to call celestial forces down to earth. I will make no mention of Dante in this connection. In France, the law clerks as well as the monks at monasteries would stage entire performances in which the Madonna, angels, saints, Christ and God Himself appeared on the stage. In those days, it was all done so ingenuously. In *Notre Dame de Paris*, Victor Hugo describes an edifying performance provided in the Hôtel de Ville free of charge for the Paris public during the reign of Louis XI, in honour of the birth of the Dauphin. It was entitled *Le bon jugement de la très sainte et gracieuse Vièrge Marie,* and in it she appeared in person to pronounce her *bon jugement*. Similar performances were sometimes given in Moscow before the times of Peter the Great: the same kind of almost dramatic plays based on scenes in the Old Testament especially. Also common, apart from dramatic performances, were numerous tales and poems, in which saints, angels and all the host of Heaven would take part when required. Our monasteries also engaged in the translation, the copying and even the writing of such poems—even under the rule of the Tartars. For instance, there exists one such poem (from the Greek, of course), *The Ordeal of Our Lady*, with descriptions of a boldness in no wise inferior to Dante's. She visits Hell, her ordeal being under the guidance of the Archangel Michael. There she sees the sinners and the torment they undergo. Incidentally, there are, among them, a most diverting class of sinners, kept in a burning lake: those of them that become immersed so that they cannot get out have been 'forgotten by God'—an expression of extraordinary depth and forcefulness. Shocked and in tears, Our Lady kneels before the throne of God, begging forgiveness for all the sinners she has seen in Hell, without any distinction. Her talk with God is of vast interest. She beseeches Him and refuses to leave; when God points to her son's hands and feet nailed to the cross and asks her: 'How can I forgive his tormentors?' she bids all the saints, martyrs, angels and archangels to kneel together with her and beg for mercy for all, without distinction. She ultimately wins from God deferment from torment between Good Friday and Trinity Sunday every year, at which the sinners in Hell offer thanks to the Lord, crying out to him: 'Righteous art thou, O Lord, in thy judgement.' Well, then, my little poem would have been in the same vein had it appeared at the time. In my poem, he appears on the stage; true, he says nothing in the poem, but merely appears and goes his way. Fifteen centuries had elapsed since he has promised to come into his kingdom, fifteen centuries since the prophet had written, 'Behold, I come quickly.' 'But of that day and that hour, knoweth no man, no, not the angels which are in heaven, neither the Son, but the Father,' as He himself said whilst still on earth. But mankind was awaiting his coming with the selfsame faith and the selfsame longing. Oh, even with greater faith, for fifteen centuries had passed since man had been vouchsafed signs from heaven:

> *Believe that which the heart doth say,*
> *No signs from heaven descend today.*

"Nothing beside remained but faith in the promptings of the heart! True, many miracles were worked at the time. There were saintly men who brought about wondrous cures, and the *Lives* of certain righteous men tell us that they were visited by the Queen of Heaven herself. But the Devil does not slumber, and doubt began to appear in mankind as regards the truth of such miracles. It was at that time that a frightful new heresy arose in the north of Germany. A great star 'burning as it were a lamp' (that is to say, a church) 'fell upon the rivers and upon the fountains of waters, and they were made bitter'. Such heresies began blasphemously to deny miracles. But ever more ardent grew the faith of those that remained devout. Just as before, there ascended to him the tears of a mankind that awaited his coming, loved him, placed their hopes in him, and longed to suffer and die for him, as they had done in the past— For so many centuries had mankind prayed with fervent faith: 'O Lord, appear unto us', for so long had mankind called out to him that, in his boundless mercy, he at last deigned to descend to those who prayed. True, even before that, he had visited certain righteous men, martyrs and holy hermits, as is recorded in their *Lives*. In our country, the poet Tyutchev, who implicitly believed in the truth of what he said, proclaimed:

> *You it was, my land, that Mary's*
> *Saintly son, disguised as bondsman,*
> *Tireless walked, His lone cross bearing—*
> *You it was that blessed He loudly.* *

"And it was really so, I can assure you. And lo! he wished to appear, if only briefly, to the people—to those in torment and suffering, sunk in rank iniquity, but loving him like innocent babes. The scene of my story is Spain, the city of Seville,

---

*From Fyodor Tyutchev's *Hamlets poor*—translated by Irina Zheleznova.—*Tr.*

during the most frightful times of the Inquisition, when throughout the land, fires were lit daily at the stakes to the glory of
God, and

> *Evil heretics were burnt*
> *In impressive autos-da-fé.*

"Of course, this was not the second coming, when, as he promised, he would appear in all his heavenly glory at the end of
time, and which would be as sudden as 'the lightning that
cometh out of the east and shineth even unto the west.' No, he
merely wished to visit his children if only briefly, and to where
the faggots were crackling about the stakes of the heretics. In
his boundless mercy, he once again walked among men in the
same human semblance as fifteen centuries before, in the course
of three years. He walked along the sultry streets of that
southern city where, only on the day before, almost a hundred
heretics had been simultaneously burnt at the stake by the Cardinal, the Grand Inquisitor, in an 'impressive auto-da-fé', *ad
majorem gloriam Dei*, in the presence of the king, the court,
knights, cardinals, the fairest ladies of the court and the po-
pulace of Seville. He appeared modestly and inconspicuously,
yet—and that was so strange—he was universally recognised.
That might have been one of the best passages in my poem—I
mean, why he was recognised.

"Drawn to him by some irresistible force, the people sur-
round him and throng about him, and follow in his footsteps.
Without a word, he walks among them with a gentle smile of
infinite mercy. In his heart burns the sun of love, and from his
eyes stream rays of Light, Enlightenment and Power, which,
shed upon the people, move their hearts to a responsive love.
He stretches forth his hands to them, blesses them, and from
the least contact with him, even with his garments, there ema-
nates a healing virtue. From the midst of the crowd, an old
man, blind since childhood, cried out, 'Lord, heal me that I
may see thee!' The scales seem to fall from his eyes, and the
blind man actually sees him. The weeping people kiss the
ground he treads. Children scatter flowers before him, singing

and crying out 'Hosanna!' 'It is he, he himself!' they all repeat, 'it must be he, no one but he!' He halts on the steps of Seville Cathedral at the moment weeping mourners are carrying an uncovered white coffin into the temple: in it lies a little girl of seven, the only child of a prominent citizen. The coffin is bedecked with flowers. 'He will raise up your child!' come shouts to the weeping mother from the crowd. The canon, who has come out to meet the coffin, frowns in perplexity, but the dead child's mother falls at his feet with a wail. 'If thou art he' she cried, holding her hands out to him, 'then raise my child from the dead!' The cortege comes to a standstill and the coffin is lowered on to the steps at his feet. He looks on with compassion and his lips once again softly pronounce the words *Tabitha cumi*, 'and the maiden arose'. The little girl sits up in the coffin and looks about her, smiling, her wondering eyes wide open. In her hands is the bunch of white roses that lay in the coffin. There is commotion, cries and sobbing in the crowd, and it is at that very moment that the Cardinal himself, the Grand Inquisitor, passes by the cathedral as he crosses the square. He is an old man of almost ninety, tall and erect of carriage, his face gaunt and his eyes sunken, though they gleam with a light like fiery coals. Oh, no, this time he is not in his magnificent cardinal's vestments of the previous day, in which he appeared in public when the foes of the Roman faith were being burnt; no, he is now wearing only his old, coarse monk's cassock. He is followed at some distance by his sombre assistants and servants, as well as by his 'holy' guards. He halts before the crowd and watches the scene from afar. He has seen everything. He has seen the coffin placed at his feet, the young girl raised from the dead, and his face darkens. He knits his beetling grey brows and his eyes blaze ominously. He stretches forth a finger and orders the guard to seize the man. Such is his power and so completely have the people been cowed into submissiveness and trembling obedience that the crowd part before the guards who, amidst the deathlike hush that has suddenly fallen, lay hands on him and take him away. The crowd immediately, like one man, bow down to the ground before the old inquisitor, who gives them a silent blessing and passes on. The guards lead their captive into a gloomy and narrow-vaulted cell in the old building of the Holy Inquisition, where he is incarcerated. The day passes and night falls, the dark, hot and stifling night of Seville. The air is redolent of laurel and lemon blossoms. In the gloom of night, the iron door of the cell suddenly opens and the old Grand Inquisitor himself slowly enters, a lantern in his hand. He is alone, and the door at once clangs to behind him. He stands at the door and for a minute or two, gives his face a long scrutiny. Finally, he goes up slowly to him, places the lantern on the table, and says, 'Is it you? You?' Receiving no reply, he at once adds, 'Do not reply; be silent. Indeed, what is there for you to say? I know full well what you will say. Besides, you have no right to add anything to what you already said in the past. Why have you come to get in our way? For you've come to hinder us, and you know that yourself. But do you know what will happen tomorrow? I know not who you are, and do not wish to: whether it is really you or only a semblance, tomorrow I shall condemn you and burn you at the stake as the most reprobate of heretics, and those very people who kissed your feet today will, at a wave of my hand, rush to heap up the coals at your stake tomorrow. Do you know that? Yes, perhaps you do know that,' he added reflectively, never for a moment removing his gaze from the captive."

"I don't quite understand what you mean, Ivan," said Alyosha with a smile. He had been listening in silence all the time. "Is this some riotous imagining, or some mistake on the part of the old man, some unbelievable *quid pro quo*?"

"Accept it as the latter," Ivan said with a laugh. "If you have been so spoilt by present-day realism that you can't put up with any play of the imagination, then let it be so. True, the old man is ninety years old and his obsession may have driven him out of his mind. He may have been struck by his captive's appearance. Finally, it may simply have been an illusion born of delirium, a vision seen, before his death, by a man of ninety who has been overwrought by the burning of a hundred heretics at the auto-da-fé of yesterday. What difference does it make to the two of us whether this is a *quid pro quo* or some riotous imagining? What matters is that the old man has to speak his mind, that he speaks out finally for all the ninety years of his life, and says aloud what he has been silent about all those ninety years."

"And is the captive silent as well? He just looks at him without saying a word?"

"Yes, that's how it has to be, even in any case," Ivan laughed again. "The old man himself remarks that he has no right to add anything to what has already been said in the past. That, if you will, is, in my opinion at least, the most fundamental feature of Roman Catholicism: 'You have entrusted everything to the Pope, so that everything is now in the Pope's hands; there's no need now for you to come, and, at least for a while, do not hinder us.' They do not only speak in that vein, but also write—at least the Jesuits do. I've read of that in the writings of their theologians. 'Have you the right to reveal to us even a single mystery of the world you've come from?' the old man asks him, and goes on to reply to his own question, 'No, you have not, so that nothing can be added to what has already been said in the past, and men shall not be deprived of the freedom you stood up for so firmly when you were on earth. Anything you reveal anew will encroach on men's freedom of faith, for it will come as a miracle, and their freedom of faith was more precious to you than anything else, even then, a thousand and a half years ago. Did you not say so often, "I will make you free"? And now, you have seen these "free" people,' the old man suddenly adds with thoughtful irony— 'Yes, the work has cost us dear,' he goes on, looking severely at him, 'but we have at last completed it in your name. For fifteen centuries we have had no end of trouble with that freedom, but now it's all done with, and for good. You don't believe it's done with and for good, do you? You look mildly at me and do not even vouchsafe me your indignation? Let me tell you that now, even now, these people are more convinced than ever before that they are completely free, yet they themselves have brought their freedom to us and laid it submissively at our feet. But it is we that have brought that about. Was it that which you wished, the kind of freedom you wanted?' "

"Again I don't understand," Alyosha broke in, "is he being ironical, or joking?"

"Not in the least. It stands to his credit and that of his followers, he thinks, that they have at last subdued freedom, and done so to make people happy. 'For it is only now,' he says (referring, of course, to the Inquisition) 'that it has become possible, for the first time, to think of men's happiness. Man was created a rebel, but can rebels enjoy happiness? You were given warnings,' he goes on; 'there was no lack of warnings and signs, but you paid no heed to the warnings, and rejected the only road that could lead to people's happiness; fortunately you passed that matter on to us when you departed. You gave your promise and confirmed it by your own word, you have authorised us to bind and loose, and you cannot, of course, even think of depriving us of that right now. Why, then, have you come to hinder us?' "

"But what is meant by 'no lack of warnings and signs'?" Alyosha asked.

"That is the very core of what the old man has to voice.

" 'The dread and wise spirit, the spirit of self-destruction and non-being,' the old man went on, 'that great spirit spoke to you in the wilderness, and the books tell us that he apparently "tempted" you. Wasn't it so? And can anything truer be said than what he revealed to you in his three questions, which you rejected, and what the books call the "temptations"? And yet, if an absolutely real and stupendous miracle was ever worked on earth, it was on that day, the day of those three temptations. The miracle lay in the asking of the three questions. Were it imaginable, just as an instance and for the sake of argument, that the dread spirit's three questions vanished without a trace in the books, that they had to be restored, thought up anew and invented so as to bring them afresh into the books, and that, to do so, we had to assemble all the world's sages—rulers, high priests, scholars, philosophers, and poets—and set them the task of thinking up and devising three questions, such that would not only be in keeping with the magnitude of the event but, in addition, would express in three words, in three terse human sentences, the entire future history of the world and mankind,

then do you think that all the wisdom on earth, brought together, could produce anything similar in force and profundity
to the three questions that were actually put to you then in
the wilderness by that mighty and wise spirit? From those
questions alone, from the miracle of their appearance, one can
understand that you are dealing, not with the transient human
mind but with one that is eternal and absolute. For those questions blend in one whole and foretell the entire further history
of mankind, and three images are produced in which all the irresolvable contradictions of human nature throughout the world
come together. That could not be clearly seen at the time, for
the future was still unknown, but now, when fifteen centuries
have elapsed, we see that everything in those three questions
was so perfectly anticipated and foretold and has been so fully
accomplished that nothing can be added to them or deducted.

" 'Decide, then, for yourself who was right: you or he who
asked you those questions. Just call the first question to mind:
though not in the literal sense, its meaning was the following,
"You would go into the world, yet you are going so empty-
handed, with some promise of freedom, which, in their simplicity and inborn unruliness, they cannot even grasp, are afraid
of and dread—since man and human society have never found
anything more intolerable than freedom! Do you see these
stones in this bare and parched desert? Turn them into loaves,
and mankind will run after you like a flock, grateful and obedient, though for ever quaking lest you withdraw your hand,
thus depriving them of your loaves." But you did not wish to
deprive man of his freedom and rejected the offer, for, you
thought, what kind of freedom is one in which obedience
is bought with loaves? You objected that man does not live by
bread alone, but you should know that, for the sake of that
very bread, the spirit of the earth will rise up against you,
grapple with you and overcome you, and all will follow him,
exclaiming, "Who is like unto the beast, who has given us fire
from heaven!" Are you aware that centuries will pass, and
mankind will proclaim, by the lips of its sages and men of science, that crime does not exist and, consequently, neither does
sin; there exist only the hungry. "First feed them, and then

demand virtue of them!"—that is what they will write on the banner they will raise against you and which will destroy your church. On the site of your church there will be erected a new edifice, the dread Tower of Babel will go up again and, while, like the previous one, it will not be completed, you could have yet forestalled that new tower and reduced human suffering by a thousand years, inasmuch as it is to us that they will come after a thousand years of heartbreak with their tower! They will then seek us again below the ground, hiding in the catacombs (for we shall again be persecuted and tormented): they will find us and cry out to us, "Feed us, for those who have promised fire from heaven have not given it to us on earth." And then we shall complete their tower, for that can be done by those who feed them, and only we can do that in your name, but we shall be lying in saying that it is in your name. Oh, never, never will they feed themselves without us! No science will ever give them bread as long as they remain free, but it will all end in their laying their freedom at our feet and saying, "Better enslave us but give us food." They will at last come to understand that freedom and ample earthly bread for all are inconceivable together, for it will never, never be possible for them to divide the bread equally. They will also realise that they can never be free either, because they are puny, vicious, paltry, and rebellious. You promised them bread from heaven, but, I again repeat, can it stand comparison with earthly bread in the eyes of the weak, for the ever vicious and for the ever ingrate tribe of man? And even if, for the sake of bread from heaven, you are followed by thousands and tens of thousands, what will become of the millions and scores of thousands of millions of creatures unable to forego the earthly bread for the sake of the heavenly? Or is it only the tens of thousands of the great and strong that are dear to you, while the other millions, countless as the sand of the sea, who are weak but love you, are to serve only as material for the great and strong? No, the weak are also dear to us. They are vicious and unruly, but towards the end will become obedient. They will marvel at us and regard us as gods because we, having taken them in our charge, have consented to tolerate freedom and rule them—so dreadful will they find it towards the end to be free! But we shall tell them that we obey you and that we rule them in your name. We shall again deceive them, for we shall keep you away from us. That deception will cause us suffering, for we shall have to lie. That was the meaning of the first question in the wilderness, and that is what you rejected for the sake of that freedom, which you exalted over everything else. And yet the great secret of this world lay hidden in that question. By accepting the "loaves" you would have assuaged man's universal and age-long craving, both in the individual and in the human race taken together, a craving expressed in the question, "Who is to be worshipped?" Having achieved freedom, man knows nothing more endless and nagging than the pressing urge to find someone to worship. But man seeks to worship what is already indisputable, so much so that all people will agree to its universal worship. For these miserable creatures are concerned not so much with finding what I or somebody else can worship but with finding something all can believe in and worship, and do so *all together*. It is this need of *community* of worship that has been the main source of anguish to every man as an individual and to mankind as a whole since the beginning of time. For the sake of that community of worship, they have put each other to the sword. They have set up gods and called out to each other, "Give up your gods and come and bow down to ours, or else death to you and your gods!" And it will thus be until the end of the world, even when the gods, too, vanish from the earth: they will fall down before idols just the same. You knew, you could not but know, this underlying mystery of human nature, but you rejected the only infallible banner held out to you to make all men worship you absolutely: the banner of earthly bread, and rejected it in the name of freedom and bread from heaven. Now behold what you did further—and again all in the name of freedom! I say to you that man has no worry more harassing than that of finding somebody to whom he can hand over, with the greatest celerity, the gift of freedom the unfortunate creature has been born with. But only he can win possession of men's freedom who will allay their consciences. An infallible banner was given to you together with the bread: if you provide him with bread, man will worship you, for there is nothing more unequivocal than bread is, but if, at the same time, anyone besides you gains possession of his conscience, oh, he will then cast your bread away and follow him who has seduced his conscience. In that you were right. For the secret of man's existence lies, not merely in living but in an awareness of the purpose of life. Without a clear idea of what to live for, man will not agree to live, and will rather destroy himself than remain on earth, even if there is an abundance of loaves about him. That is true, but what was the outcome? Instead of gaining control over men's freedom, you enhanced it even more! Or perhaps you forgot that man's peace of mind, and even death, are dearer to him than freedom of choice in the knowledge of good and evil? There is nothing more seductive to man than his freedom of conscience, but nothing can cause greater torment. Instead of firm foundations for setting men's consciences at rest once and for all, you chose everything that was unconventional, conjectural and indeterminate, everything that was beyond men's strength: you acted as though you had no love at all for them. And who was it that acted thus? It was he who had come to give up his life for them! Instead of gaining control over men's freedom, you multiplied it and burdened man's spiritual realm with its torment for ever and ever. You wanted man's freely given love so that he should follow you freely, lured and captivated by you. Instead of the firm ancient law, man was to decide for himself and with a free heart, what is good and what is evil, having only your image before him as guidance. But why did it not enter your mind that he would finally reject even your very image and your truth were he to be weighed down with so fearful a burden as freedom of choice? They will at last cry out that the truth does not lie in you, since it was impossible for them to be left in perplexity and torment more than you did by leaving them with so many cares and irresolvable tasks. Thus, it was you yourself who laid the foundation for the destruction of your kingdom, so do not blame anyone else for that any more. Yet was it that which was offered to you? There exist three forces, the only ones on earth capable of overcoming and holding captive for all time the consciences of these weakly rebels and do so for their own happiness. Those forces are: the miraculous, the mysterious, and authority. You rejected all three, and set an example to others to do the same. When the wise and awesome spirit set you on a pinnacle of the temple and said unto you: "If thou be the Son of God, cast thyself down from hence: for it is written, He shall give his angels charge over thee, to keep thee; and in their hands they shall bear thee up, lest at any time thou dash thy foot against a stone; thou shalt then learn whether you are the Son of God and shalt show them how great is thy faith in thy Father." But, when you had heard his words, you turned down his proposal, and did not yield to him and did not cast yourself down. Oh, you acted proudly and magnificently of course, just like God, but the weak and rebellious tribe of men—are they gods? Oh, you were perfectly aware at the time that, by making a single step and making a single movement to cast yourself down, you would at once be tempting God and would lose all your faith in him; you would crash down on the earth you had come to save, and the wise spirit that tempted you would rejoice. But, I repeat, are there many like you? Could you have actually imagined, even fleetingly, that people, too, could withstand such temptation? Has human nature been created in such a way as to reject the miraculous, and remain true to the free decision of the heart even at such fearful moments of life, moments of the most fearful, fundamental and agonising problems of the spirit? Oh, you knew that your feat would be recorded in books and handed down through the ages to reach the furthermost corners of the earth; you hoped that, by following you, man would remain with God, without standing in need of miracles. You did not know, however, that as soon as man rejected miracles, he would immediately reject God as well, since it is not so much God that man seeks, as miracles. And as man is incapable of doing without miracles, he will think up miracles, new ones of his making, and now bow down to miracles worked by the medicine-man, and the witchcraft of hags, even if he has been rebellious, heretical and godless a hundred times over. You did not come down from the cross when you were being shouted at, mocked and reviled: 'Let him now come down from the cross, and we will believe him.' You did not come down because, again, you were averse to enslaving man through a miracle, and yearned for faith freely given, not for a miracle. You longed for freely given love, not the servile raptures of the slave in the face of a power that has terrified him for all time. But here, again, your judgement of men was too high, for they are of course slaves, though created rebels. Look about you and judge for yourself. Fifteen centuries have gone by: look at them. Whom have you elevated to your own level? Man, I swear, has been created weaker and viler than you thought! Can he, can he do what you did? By holding him in such high esteem, you acted as though you had lost all compassion for him, because you demanded too much of him—you, who loved him more than yourself! Had you shown him less esteem, you would have asked less of him, and that would have stood closer to love, since his burden would have been lighter. He is weak and vile. He is now everywhere rebelling against our rule, and takes pride in his rebellion—but what of that? It is the pride of a child, a schoolboy. They are like little children who have run riot and chased the schoolmaster out of the classroom. Yet their escapade will come to an end, and will cost them dear. They will tear down their temples and will drench the earth with blood. But the foolish children will ultimately realise that, though they are rebellious, they are spineless rebels, who cannot live up to their own rebelliousness. Dissolved in foolish tears, they will at last realise that he who created them rebels must no doubt have done so in order to hold them up to ridicule. That is what they will say in their despair, and their words will be blasphemous. That will make them feel even more unfortunate, for human nature cannot endure blasphemy and will, in the end, always wreak vengeance for it. And so, unquiet, perturbation and misery—such is men's present lot after all you suffered to bring them freedom! Your great prophet says figuratively and in a vision that he has seen all those who took part in the first resurrection, and that they were sealed twelve thousand from each of the tribes. But if there were that number, they must have been like gods, not men. They had endured your cross and scores of years in the bare and barren wilderness, living on locusts and roots—and you can, of course, point with pride at these children of freedom, their freely offered love, and free and magnificent sacrifice in your name. But remember: they numbered only several thousands, and, moreover, they were gods. But what of the others? Can the rest, the weak ones, be held to blame for being unable to endure what the men of might could? Why should the weak soul be blamed for lacking the capacity for such awesome gifts? Can you really have come only to the chosen, and for the chosen alone? If that was so, that is a mystery, and beyond our understanding. And if it is a mystery, we, too, have the right to preach a mystery, and teach them that what is important is not the freely made decision of their hearts, and not love, but a mystery they must obey blindly, even despite their consciences. That is what we have done. We have rectified your work and grounded it in *the miraculous, the mysterious, and authority*, and men have rejoiced that they are again being led like a flock and that their hearts have at last been unburdened of the awesome gift that brought them so much anguish. Tell me: were we right in teaching and acting thus? Was it not for love of mankind when, humbly recognising its weakness and lovingly lightening its burden, we allowed its weak nature even to sin, but only with our permission? Why have you now come to hamper us in our work? And why are you looking at me so searchingly and in silence, with your gentle eyes? Grow angry with me, for I do not want your love, because I do not love you. And what have I to conceal from you? Do you think I do not know who I am talking to? Everything I have to tell you is already known to you—I can read it in your eyes. And is it for me to conceal our secret from you? Perhaps it is just that which you want to hear from my lips? Listen, then: we are with *him*, and not with you—that is our secret! We have long been with *him*, not with you—a matter of eight centuries. It was exactly eight hundred years ago that we took from him what you rejected so scornfully—the final gift he offered you after showing you all the kingdoms of the earth: from him we took Rome and the sword of Caesar, and proclaimed ourselves the only earthly rulers, sole rulers, though we have not yet succeeded in bringing our work to full completion. But whose is the fault? Oh, the world is only at its beginning, but it has begun. It has long to await its consummation, and the earth has still much to suffer, but we shall accomplish the task and become Caesars, and then the time will come for us to give thought to the universal happiness of people. But even then, you could have taken up the sword of Caesar. Why did you reject that last gift? By accepting the mighty spirit's third counsel, you could have fulfilled all that man seeks on earth, that is, someone to worship and entrust his conscience to, and how to finally unite all people in an incontestable, harmonious and common ant-hill, since the need for world-wide union is the third and last anguish of men. In all its entirety, mankind has always striven to organise without fail on a worldwide scale. There have been many great peoples with great histories but the higher such peoples stood, the greater was their misfortune, for they were more acutely aware than others of the need for a world-wide union of all people. The great conquerors—the Tamerlanes and the Genghis Khans—swept across the earth like whirlwinds, in their attempts to conquer the world, but even they, albeit unconsciously, expressed mankind's selfsame vast need to achieve worldwide and overall union. By accepting the world and the imperial purple, you could have founded a world realm and brought about universal peace. For who else is to rule men but those who control their consciences and their bread? We have taken the sword of Caesar, and, having done so, have rejected you and followed *him*. Oh, there will elapse many a century of turmoil created by the free mind, their science and anthropophagy, because, having begun to build their Tower of Babel without us, they will end up with anthropophagy. It will be then that the beast will come crawling to us to lick our feet, which it will bespatter with tears of blood from its eyes. And we shall bestride the beast and raise the cup with the inscription: 'Mystery'! Then and only then will the reign of peace and happiness for men set in. You take pride in your elect, but you have only your chosen few, while we shall soothe all men. And besides, many of the chosen ones, those men of might who could have been among the elect, have finally wearied of awaiting you and have carried—and will continue to carry—elsewhere the powers of their spirit and the ardour of their hearts and will end up by raising their banner of *freedom* against you. But that banner was raised aloft by you yourself. With us, however, all will be happy, and will no longer engage in rebellion or mutual destruction, as is the case everywhere under your freedom. Oh, we shall persuade them that they will only become free when they renounce their freedom, place it in our hands, and submit to us. Well, shall we be right, or shall we be lying? They will see for themselves that we are right, for they will recall what enormities of enslavement and turmoil your freedom has brought them. Freedom, untrammelled thinking and science will lead them into such quandaries and confront them with such portents and irresolvable mysteries that some of them—the stiff-necked and the defiant—will destroy themselves; others—defiant but puny—will destroy one another, while yet others—the rest: the weak and unfortunate, will come crawling to our feet and cry out, "Yes, you were right; you alone possess his mystery, and we are returning to you to beseech you to save us from ourselves." As they get loaves from us, they will of course see quite clearly that we are taking from them loaves they have made with their own hands, and are distributing the loaves among them, without any miracle-working; they will see that we have not turned stones into loaves, but they will verily rejoice more at getting the bread from our hands than at the bread itself! For only too well will they remember that, in the past when they were without us, the loaves they had earned turned to stones in their hands, but as soon as they returned to us, the very stones turned into loaves in their hands. Only too, too keenly will they realise what it means to submit for all time! They will know no happiness until they understand that. But who was it, tell me, that contributed most to such lack of understanding? Who split up the flock and scattered them along uncharted paths? But the flock will be gathered anew and submit to us, and this time for ever. And then we shall give them unclouded and modest happiness, the happiness of the weak creatures they have been created as. Oh, we shall at last persuade them to eschew pride, for you exalted them and thereby

336

taught them pride; we shall prove to them that they are weak, merely pitiful children, and that the happiness of a child is sweeter than any other kind. They will grow timid, look towards us and cling to us in their fear, like chickens to the mother-hen. They will marvel at us and be terrified by us, yet be proud that we are so powerful and wise that we have been able to subdue such a turbulent flock of so many millions. In their debility, they will quake at our wrath; their minds will grow timid, and they will be as tearful as children and women, but, at the least sign from us, they will just as readily go over to merriment and laughter, innocent joy and the happy songs of childhood. Yes, we shall make them work, but their life during their leisure hours will be like that of children at play, with children's songs in chorus and innocent dancing. Oh, we shall also permit them sin, for they are helpless and weak, but they will love us like children for allowing them to sin. We shall tell them that any sin will be forgiven if it has been committed with our permission; we permit them to sin because we love them; as for punishment for those sins—well, that is something we shall assume for them. We shall take them upon ourselves, and they will adore us as their benefactors who have taken on their sins in the sight of the Lord. And they will have no secrets from us. We shall allow or forbid them to live with their wives and mistresses, and to have or not to have children—all in the measure of their obedience, and they will submit to us with merriment and joy. The will come to us with everything—the most afflictive secrets weighing on their consciences, and we shall hand down our decisions, which they will gladly accept, for they will relieve their minds of the terrible anxiety and present agony of personal and free decision. And they will all be happy, all those millions of creatures, with the exception of the hundred thousand that govern them. We alone—the guardians of the mystery—we alone will be unhappy. There will be thousands of millions of happy children, and the hundred thousand sufferers who have accepted the curse of the knowledge of good and evil. They will die in peace, fade away peacefully in your name, but they will find nothing but death beyond the grave. However, we shall keep the secret, and, for their own happiness, we shall allure them with the prospect of heavenly and eternal reward. But even were there anything at all in the world to come, it would not, of course, be for the like of them. They say and they prophesy that you will come and again conquer, come with your chosen ones, your proud and mighty ones, but we shall say that they have saved only themselves, while we have saved all. It has been said that the harlot that sits upon the beast and holds the *mystery* in her hands shall be put to shame, and that the weak will again rebel, rend her purple robe asunder and strip her "vile" body naked. But then I shall stand up and show you the thousands of millions of happy creatures that have known no sin. We, who have, for their happiness, shouldered their sins—we shall stand up before you and say, "Pass judgement on us if you can, and dare." Know that I fear you not. Know that I, too, have lived in the wilderness, that I, too, fed upon locusts and roots, that I, too, blessed the freedom you blessed men with, and that I, too, was preparing to join the number of your chosen ones, the strong and the mighty, thirsting to make myself of their number. But I came to my senses and refused to serve madness. I returned and joined the host of those who have *rectified your work*. I left the ranks of the proud and returned to the meek, for the happiness of those meek. What I say to you will come about, and our kingdom will be set up. I repeat: tomorrow you will see the obedient flock, who, at a sign from me, will hasten to heap up the hot coals about the stake I shall burn you at, for you have come to hinder our work. If anyone has deserved to go to the stake, it is you. I shall have you burnt tomorrow. *Dixi!*' "

Ivan stopped. He had been carried away by his discourse and had spoken with ardour. A sudden smile appeared on his face when he ended.

Alyosha, who had been listening to him in silence, had made several attempts to interrupt him towards the end but had restrained his agitation with an effort, now burst into a spate of speech.

"But—but that's absurd!" he exclaimed, flushing. "Your poem is in praise of Jesus, and not to his detraction—as was your purpose. And who will believe what you have said about freedom? Is that, is that, how it should be understood? Is that the understanding of the Orthodox church— That pertains to Rome—and not to all of Rome—that is not true; it pertains to the worst elements in Catholicism, the Inquisitors and the Jesuits! Besides, so fantastic a person as your Inquisitor could never have existed. What are the sins of men that have been shouldered? Who are the guardians of the mystery, who have taken on some kind of curse for men's happiness? When have they been seen? We know of the Jesuits—they are ill spoken of, but are they like those you've described? They are not like that at all, not in the least— They are simply the Romish army for the world-wide kingdom on earth, under an emperor—the Roman high priest—that's their ideal, but it contains no mysteries or elevated sadness— It's the most ordinary lust for power, for filthy earthly gains, the enslavement of others—a kind of future system of serf-ownership, with them as the masters—that's all they're after. They may not even believe in God. Your suffering Inquisitor is nothing but a figment of the imagination—"

"Just a moment," Ivan laughed, "don't get yourself worked up so! You say he's a figment of the imagination? Let it be so! Well, he is, of course. But let me ask you: do you really think that the entire Catholic movement of the last few centuries has consisted in nothing but a lust for power, for filthy gains? Is that what Father Paissi has been teaching you?"

"Oh, no, on the contrary, he once told me something rather the same as you have—only not quite, of course, not quite the same," Alyosha quickly qualified his statement.

"Quite a valuable admission, nevertheless, despite your 'not quite the same'. What I'm asking you is this: why is it that your Jesuits and Inquisitors have united only for filthy material gains? Why shouldn't there happen to be among them a single sufferer tormented by some great sorrow and with a love of mankind? Let's assume that, among those who are after filthy material gains, one man is to be found—only one man like my old Inquisitor, who himself fed on roots in the wilderness and frenziedly sought to subdue the flesh so as to make himself free and perfect, yet loved mankind all his life long; suddenly his eyes are opened and he realises that there is no supreme moral satisfaction in achieving perfection of the will, while seeing millions of God's other creatures remain mere travesties of what they should be, that they will never be able to cope with their freedom; that the pitiful rebels will not bring forward any giants to complete the tower, and that it was not for the sake of such simpletons that the great idealist dreamt of harmony. When he realised that, he turned back and joined—the clever ones. Can't that possibly have happened?"

"Whom did he join? Who are the clever ones?" Alyosha exclaimed almost heatedly. "They possess no such cleverness, and have no particular mysteries or secrets— Nothing but godlessness—there's all their secret. Your Inquisitor doesn't believe in God—that's all there is to his secret!"

"That may be true! You've put your finger on it at last! That's really the case, and therein alone lies the whole secret. But isn't that actual anguish, at least for a man like that, who has dedicated his whole life in the wilderness to what he has considered his mission but cannot be cured of his love for mankind? In his declining years, he has arrived at the firm conclusion that nothing but the counsels of the great and terrible spirit can in some measure create a tolerable existence for the puny rebels, those 'uncompleted experimental creatures made in travesty'. When that conclusion sinks in, he sees that the instructions have to be followed which have been handed down by the wise spirit, the terrible spirit of death and destruction; to that end, he must accept lies and deception, and consciously lead men towards death and destruction, deceiving them along the whole road, for them not to notice where they are being led, so that, along the road at least, the miserable and blind creatures may consider themselves happy. And, mark you, the deception is committed in the name of him whose ideal the old man has believed in so fervently all his life long! Is not that a misfortune? And even should only one such man find himself heading the entire army of those 'craving for power, for filthy gains alone', would not even one such man suffice for tragedy to emerge? Moreover, one such leader would suffice to finally create a genuinely guiding idea for the entire Roman Catholic cause, with all its armies and Jesuits—the supreme idea of that church, I tell you in all earnest that I firmly believe that such a man has never been lacking among those who have headed the movement. There may have been such individuals among the Roman high priests: who can tell? This accursed old man, who loves mankind so stubbornly and in his own way, may possibly exist even now in the shape of a host of such individual old men, and not fortuitously but by common consent, as a kind of secret society set up to guard the mystery, guard it from the weak and unfortunate, so as to make them happy: who can tell? That must be the case, and that's how it should be. I have a feeling that something like that mystery underlies even the Freemasons' creed, which is why they are so hated by the Catholics, who see them as rivals engaged in demolishing the singleness of the idea, whereas there should be one fold and one shepherd— However, in defending my concept, I must look like an author who bridles at your criticism. So enough of the matter."

"Perhaps you're a Freemason yourself!" Alyosha burst out. "You do not believe in God," he added, this time more in deep sorrow. Besides, it seemed to him that his brother was regarding him somewhat derisively. "But how does your poem end?" he suddenly asked, his glance cast downwards. "Or was that the end?"

"I meant to make it end as follows: When the Inquisitor fell silent, he awaited his captive's reply for some time. His silence weighed heavily on the old man. He had seen the captive listening to him with quiet intentness all the time, looking straight into his eyes and evidently unwilling to raise any objection. The old man would have liked him to say something, however bitter and terrible. But suddenly, without a word, he drew near the old man and kissed him gently on his bloodless lips. That was the entire reply. The old man started. The corners of his mouth quivering slightly, he went to the door, opened it and said, 'Go, and return no more—never, never!', and let him out into the dark of the city. The captive departed."

"And the old man?"

"Though the kiss burns in his heart, he holds on to his idea."

"And so do you, don't you?" Alyosha asked sorrowfully.

Ivan laughed.

"It's all been a lot of rubbish, Alyosha, a meaningless poem by a dunderhead student, who has never penned even a couple of verses. Why have you taken it in all earnest? Do you really think I'll be going straight there, to the Jesuits, to join the host of those who are rectifying his work? Gracious, what is all that to me? I've told you that all I want is to reach the age of thirty, and then—dash the cup to the floor!"

"But what about the sticky young leaves, the dear graves, the blue skies and the woman you love? How will you go on living? How will you be able to love them?" Alyosha exclaimed sorrowfully. "Is that possible, with such a hell in your breast and your mind? No, you are leaving to join their ranks—and if you don't, you'll kill yourself; you won't be able to endure it!"

"There is a force that can withstand anything," said Ivan, this time in cold derision.

"What kind of force?"

"The Karamazovian—the force of the Karamazovian baseness."

"Does that mean sinking into debauchery and stifling the soul with corruption? Does it?"

"Perhaps even that—but only till thirty. But I may manage to avoid that until that time, and then—"

"But how will you avoid it? In what way? With ideas such as yours, that's impossible."

"Again, in the Karamazovian manner."

"You mean: 'Everything is permitted'? Is that what you mean?"

Ivan frowned and suddenly turned strangely pale.

"Ah, you've taken up the phrase I used yesterday, which so offended Miusov—and which brother Dmitri so naively and eagerly took up and paraphrased, haven't you?" he asked with a wry smile. "Indeed, 'everything is permitted' since the statement has been made. I'm not withdrawing it. And Mitya's wording is not at all bad either."

Alyosha regarded him in silence.

"When I made up my mind to leave these parts, I thought I

had at least you in the world, brother," Ivan suddenly said with unexpected feeling, "but I now see, my dear recluse, that there's no place for me in your heart either. I'll never renounce the 'everything is permitted' formula, so will you renounce me for that, eh?"

Alyosha rose to his feet, went up to him without a word and gently kissed him on the lips.

"That's a piece of literary appropriation!" Ivan cried in sudden delight. "You've stolen that from my poem! Thank you all the same. Get up, Alyosha. Let's be going. It's time for the two of us."

They left the place, but halted at the exit.

"Here's what I want to say, Alyosha," Ivan said in a steady voice. "If I really find room in myself for the sticky young leaves, I shall only love them in recollection of you. It will suffice for me to be aware that you're here somewhere, and I won't lose my wish to live on. Is that enough for you? Accept that as an expression of my love for you, if you wish. And now take the road to the right, and I'll turn leftwards—and enough of it all, d'you hear, enough of it. I mean that, even if I weren't leaving tomorrow (and I think I will, for certain) and we happened to meet again somewhere, do not say another word to me on these matters. I emphatically request that of you. The same refers to brother Dmitri: never even attempt to speak to me again about him," he added with sudden irritation. "Everything's been said and thrashed out, hasn't it? For my part, I make this promise to you: when, on reaching thirty, I shall want to 'dash the cup to the floor', then, wherever you may be, I'll come for another talk with you—even from America. You may be sure of that. I'll come expressly for the purpose. It will also be most interesting to have a good look at you then, to see what kind of person you've become by that time. That's a solemn promise, as you can see. In fact, we may be parting for seven or even ten years. And now go to your *Pater Seraphicus*. He's at death's door, after all. If he dies while you're away, you may be angry with me for having kept you. Good-bye, kiss me again, like that, and go—"

Ivan turned away suddenly and went his way without

343

looking back, much in the way Dmitri had left Alyosha on the previous day, though that parting had been quite different. The strange resemblance flashed like an arrow through Alyosha's distressed mind, so sorrowful and dejected at the moment. He waited a little, gazing after his departing brother. For some reason, he noticed that his brother was swaying as he walked and that, if seen from behind, his right shoulder seemed lower than his left one, something he had never noticed before. But now he, too, turned away and almost ran to the monastery. Darkness was falling and he felt something like fear; some new feeling was mounting within him, which he was unable to account for. The wind had risen just as on the evening before, and the ancient pines were rustling gloomily about him as he entered the monastery grove. "*Pater Seraphicus*—he must have got the name from somewhere—but where from?"—flashed through Alyosha's mind. "Ivan, poor Ivan, when shall I see you— Ah, here's the hermitage, thank goodness! Yes, indeed, it is he, *Pater Seraphicus* who will save me—from him, and for ever!"

Several times, later in life, he wondered with sudden perplexity how, after parting with Ivan, he could have quite forgotten his brother Dmitri, whom, only several hours earlier that morning, he had resolved to locate without fail, and not to leave without doing so, even if it meant not going to the monastery at all that night.

6.

Very Vague As Yet

On parting with Alyosha, Ivan Fyodorovich set out for home, towards his father's house. Strange to say, however, a sudden sense of dejection overcame him; moreover, his dejection grew the closer he approached his destination. What was strange was not so much his gloom as his total inability to account for its cause. He had often had occasion to feel depressed previously, so there was nothing surprising in his feeling like that, for on the morrow he was preparing to make a clean break with everything that had brought him here, and he was preparing to make an entirely new start in life and enter upon a new and entirely unknown future; he would again be quite alone, harbouring many hopes without any clear awareness of what he could look forward to, expecting so much from life and unable to determine anything either in his expectations or even desires. Though an apprehension of the new and the unknown did oppress him, that was not all that was worrying him. "Can it be a loathing for my father's house?" he thought. "It looks like it, for I'm sick and tired of it; though I realise that I'll be crossing the hateful threshold for the last time, I can't help detesting it—"Yet that was not the cause. Could it be his parting with Alyosha and the talk that had taken place between them? "I'd been silent with the world for so many years and never deigned to speak up, and here suddenly came out with a spate of balderdash." In fact, it might have all stemmed from a young man's vexation at his callowness and youthful vanity, his inability to fully express himself, especially with a creature like Alyosha, whom he had counted on a great deal in his heart of hearts. That, too, doubtlessly had played a part, i. e. his vexation at himself. It could not have been otherwise, but that was not all. "I'm sick unto death of this dejection but I can't say just what I'm after. Perhaps I'd better simply stop thinking—"

Ivan Fyodorovich had tried to "stop thinking" but that had been of no avail. What was so vexing about his feeling of dejection was its being somehow fortuitous and coming from without; he felt that. It was as though some impediment—some creature or object—was obtruding itself somewhere, in the way something may dangle before your eyes without being noticed by you because you are busy or engaged in some engrossing talk; yet that impediment may well get on your nerves and even upset you until you finally realise the cause and remove the offending object, which may be something trifling and ridiculous: some article left lying about in the wrong place; a handkerchief that has fallen on the floor; a book that has been mislaid and not returned to its rightful place in the bookcase, and the like. In a vile and irritated frame of mind, Ivan Fyodorovich finally reached the parental house, and, at a distance of some fifteen paces from the wicket-gate, cast a glance in its direction and at once realised what had been distressing him so much.

On the bench by the wicket-gate sat the servant Smerdyakov, enjoying the cool of the evening and, at the first glance at him, Ivan Fyodorovich realised that it was the servant Smerdyakov who had so oppressively been at the back of his mind, and that it was this very man he could not tolerate. Everything now fell into place and became quite clear. From Alyosha's recent account of his meeting with Smerdyakov something gloomy and abhorrent had suddenly penetrated his heart, evoking in it a feeling of anger in response. During their talk, Smerdyakov had been forgotten for a while, though lurking in his mind, but as soon as Ivan Fyodorovich parted with Alyosha, and was making his way alone to the house, the forgotten sensation returned rapidly into the foreground of his consciousness. "Why should this contemptible blackguard disturb me so much!" he thought with exasperation.

In fact, Ivan Fyodorovich had indeed taken an intense dislike to the man of late and especially during the past few days. He had begun to notice within himself a mounting feeling bordering on hatred for the creature. This sentiment may have been heightened because something quite different had come about at the outset when Ivan Fyodorovich had just come to our parts. He had then suddenly taken a marked interest in Smerdyakov, and had even found him highly original. He had himself encouraged Smerdyakov to talk to him, always, however, wondering at a certain incoherence or rather restlessness of his mind, and unable to make out what it was that so constantly and relentlessly disturbed "that contemplator". They discussed questions of philosophy as well, and even why there had been light on the first day, whereas the sun, the moon and the stars were created only on the fourth day, and how that was to be understood. However, Ivan Fyodorovich soon realised that it was not the sun, the moon and the stars that interested Smerdyakov, and that though those heavenly bodies were objects of curiosity to Smerdyakov, they were practically of little interest to him; he was after something quite different. In one way or another, Smerdyakov began to display and express an overweening vanity, and an injured vanity at that. That was something Ivan Fyodorovich disliked intensely. It marked the beginning of his aversion for the man. Then had come rowdy scenes in the house, Grushenka had put in an appearance, the trouble with Dmitri had begun, and the house was in disarray—that, too, had been discussed by the two, but though Smerdyakov always grew highly agitated whenever the subject came up, his true feelings were quite impossible to ascertain. Indeed, there was cause for considerable surprise in the unreasonableness and oddity of some of his desires, which escaped him in all their usual obscurity. He was constantly trying to nose out things and asking oblique but obviously farfetched questions, never, as a rule, giving reasons, suddenly falling silent at the crucial moment of his inquiries or turning to some other subject. But what ultimately irritated Ivan Fyodorovich most and filled him with such repugnance was the peculiar and ever more offensive familiarity that Smerdyakov began to evince towards him. Not that he ever forgot himself to the point of rudeness; on the contrary, he always addressed him most respectfully, but things worked out in such a way that, for some reason, Smerdyakov now seemed to consider himself bound to him by some understanding. His tone of voice was always suggestive of some kind of secret compact between them, something pronounced by the two, known to them alone and even beyond the comprehension of other mortals busy with their own affairs. Even here, however, Ivan Fyodorovich was long unable to understand the real cause of his growing repugnance, and it was only recently that he had realised what was at the root of it all. With a sense of squeamish irritation, he now tried to enter the wicket without a word or a glance at Smerdyakov, who, however, rose from the bench in a way that at once intimated to Ivan Fyodorovich that he wanted to speak to him on an important matter. Ivan Fyodorovich gave him a glance and halted, and the very fact that he had come to a sudden standstill and not walked past as he had intended a moment before exasperated him unbearably. He looked with angry disgust at Smerdyakov, his haggard face of a eunuch, the hair swept forward on his temples and the little tuft fluffed up above the forehead. His left eye was screwed up in winking irony, as if to imply,

"Why are you passing me by? You can't do that. Can't you see that the two of us, clever people that we are, have something to talk over?" Ivan Fyodorovich was all atremble.

"Go away, you scoundrel! I'm no company for a fool like you!" he was on the point of exclaiming, but, to his utter astonishment, he said something quite different.

"Is Father still asleep or up?" he asked in a low and humble voice, much to his own surprise, and suddenly, just as unexpectedly, sat down on the bench. For a moment, a sense of fear came over him, as he later recollected. Smerdyakov stood facing him, his hands clasped behind his back, his glance expressing self-assurance and almost severity.

"He's still asleep, sir," he said unhurriedly. ("You were the first to speak, not I!" he seemed to say.) "I'm surprised at you, sir," he added, after some silence, lowering his eyes with affected coyness, advancing his right foot and playing with the toe of his patent-leather boot.

"Why are you surprised at me?" Ivan Fyodorovich asked with severe abruptness, doing all he could to maintain his self-control, and suddenly realising with revulsion that he was feeling a keen curiosity which he had without fail to satisfy before leaving.

"Why don't you go to Chermashnya, sir?" asked Smerdyakov, suddenly raising his eyes with a smirk of familiarity. "If you're a clever man, you should understand why I'm smiling," his screwed-up left eye seemed to be saying.

"Why should I go to Chermashnya?" asked Ivan Fyodorovich in surprise.

Smerdyakov fell silent again.

"Fyodor Pavlovich himself has begged you to, sir, hasn't he?" he unhurriedly said at last, as if he himself attached little importance to the reply: "I'm putting you off with an explanation of little account, simply to say something," he seemed to imply.

"The devil take it, can't you speak more clearly? What is it you're after?" Ivan Fyodorovich cried out angrily at last, meekness yielding place to rudeness.

Bringing his right foot up to his left one and drawing himself up, Smerdyakov kept his glance fixed on Ivan Fyodorovich with the same calmness and the same smirk.

"There's nothing of substance to say—it was just by way of conversation—"

Another pause ensued. It lasted almost a full minute. Ivan Fyodorovich knew that he should rise to his feet at once and show his anger. There stood Smerdyakov before him, as though in expectation. "I'll wait and see whether you will blow up in anger or not." At least, that was Ivan Fyodorovich's impression. Finally, he made a movement to rise. Smerdyakov at once seized the opportunity.

"I'm in a terribly awkward situation, sir, and don't even know how to help myself," he suddenly said firmly and distinctly, sighing as he concluded. Ivan Fyodorovich sat down again at once.

"The two are quite out of their minds, sir, behaving just like little children," Smerdyakov continued. "I mean your father and your brother Dmitri Fyodorovich. He, I mean Fyodor Pavlovich, will be getting up directly, and start pestering me every minute with the question, 'Why hasn't she come? Why hasn't she?' and carry on like that till midnight and even later. And if Agrafena Alexandrovna doesn't turn up (for I don't think she has the slightest intention of doing so), he'll be at it again, tomorrow morning: 'Why hasn't she come? Why hasn't she turned up? When will she come?' as if I were to blame for it all. On the other hand, sir, your brother turns up somewhere close by, with a gun in his hand as soon as it grows dark or even earlier. 'Look out,' he says to me, 'you rogue of a broth-cook: if you fail to see her and let me know she's come, I'll kill you on the spot.' When the night has gone and morning has come, he starts tormenting me something cruel, just like Fyodor Pavlovich: 'Why hasn't she come? When will she show up?' and again I'm to blame that his lady-friend hasn't put in an appearance. The two of them grow angrier and angrier with every day and hour, sir, so that I sometimes think that it would be better to do away with myself than live in such fear. I can't trust either of them, sir."

"Then why did you get involved?" Ivan Fyodorovich asked

irritably. "Why did you have to begin acting as informer for Dmitri Fyodorovich?"

"But how could I help doing so, sir? In fact, I did nothing to get involved in it, if you want to know the truth, sir. I kept quiet from the very outset, and didn't dare to object to anything. It was him who made me his agent, his watchman, so to speak. Since then, he has only one thing to say to me: 'I'll kill you, rogue that you are, if you miss her!' I'm certain, sir, I'm going to have a long epileptic fit tomorrow."

"What do you mean?"

"I mean a long epileptic fit, sir, a very long one, lasting several hours or even a day or two perhaps. I once had an attack lasting three days; it was when I fell from the loft. The convulsions went on and off for three whole days, and during all that time I couldn't come to my senses. Fyodor Pavlovich, your father, had Herzenstube, the local doctor, sent for, who put ice on the top of my head, as well as some other remedy—it could have been the death of me, it could, sir."

"But it's impossible to tell when an attack is coming on, they say, or name the exact hour. So how can you say you'll have a fit tomorrow?" Ivan Fyodorovich inquired with keen and exasperated curiosity.

"True enough, sir. You can't tell beforehand."

"Besides, you fell from the loft then."

"I go up to the loft every day, sir, and I may very well fall from there tomorrow. And if it isn't that, I may fall into the cellar, for I have to go down there every day too, sir."

Ivan Fyodorovich gave him a long look.

"You're talking nonsense, I see, and I don't quite get your meaning," he said in a low but menacing voice. "Do you intend to stage a fit tomorrow to last for three days, eh?"

With eyes fixed on the ground and again playing with the toe of his right foot, Smerdyakov set it down, advanced his left foot instead, raised his head and said with a grin:

"Even if I could work that trick, sir, I mean, pretend to throw a fit, which isn't at all hard for an experienced man to do, I have every right to do so to save myself from death, for even if Agrafena Alexandrovna were to come to see his father whilst I'm sick in bed, he couldn't very well hold a sick man responsible and ask, 'Why didn't you report it to me?' He'd be ashamed to."

"Damn it all!" Ivan exclaimed, his face contorted in sudden anger. "Why are you always trembling for your life? All my brother's threats are nothing but words spoken in anger. He won't do you in; if he kills somebody, it won't be you!"

"He'll kill somebody like a fly—me in the first place, sir. But there's something else I'm even more afraid of: being taken for an accomplice of his when he does something daft to his father."

"But why should you be taken for an accomplice?"

"They'll consider me an accomplice, sir, because I let him know of those signals very much on the quiet."

"What signals do you mean? Let whom know? Express yourself more clearly, damn you!"

"I must admit quite frankly," said Smerdyakov with affected slowness of speech, "that there's a secret understanding between me and Fyodor Pavlovich. As you know (if you do know of it), he has, during the past few days, been locking himself in as soon as night or even evening falls. You've been going to your room upstairs early of late, and you didn't go out anywhere at all yesterday, so you may not know, sir, how carefully he locks himself in for the night. Even if Grigori Vassilievich himself happens to come, he won't unlock the door till he recognises him by his voice. But Grigori Vassilievich hasn't ever come of late, because I've been the only one to wait on him in his rooms since that business with Agrafena Alexandrovna began— And on his orders, sir, now I, too, sleep in the lodge, only I don't go to bed till midnight, but keep watch in the yard in case she turns up, for he's been expecting her during the last few days like one who's gone out of his mind. This is the way he argues, sir: 'She's scared of him—of Dmitri Fyodorovich (he calls him Mitya), so she'll come in stealthily by the back entrance late in the night. So you be on the look-out, he says, till midnight or even later. If she turns up, you run up to my door and knock on it or on the garden window twice at first, very gently, and then another three times, more rapidly. That

351

will tell me that she's come, and I'll open the door for you very quietly. Besides, he gave me another signal in case something is urgent: two rapid knocks at first, and then, after an interval, a single knock, only much louder. That will mean that something sudden happened and that I've got to see him at once, so he'll unlock the door and let me in for me to report to him. That's all in case Agrafena Alexandrovna can't come in person but sends somebody with a message. Besides, Dmitri Fyodorovich may turn up, too, so I'm to let the master know that he is nearby. He's terribly afraid of Dmitri Fyodorovich, so that even if Agrafena Alexandrovna were to have come already and be locked in with him, and Dmitri Fyodorovich is close by in the meantime, I will have to let him know about it at once by knocking three times: so the first signal of five knocks will mean that Agrafena Alexandrovna has come; the second signal of three knocks will mean I have something urgent to tell him. He has instructed me several times how the signals are to be given, and explained their meaning to me. And seeing as he and I are the only people in the whole world who know of these signals, he'll unlock the door without any hesitation or calling out (for he's terrified of calling out aloud). Well, all the signals are now known to your brother Dmitri Fyodorovich."

"Why are they known to him? Did you tell him? How did you dare to let him know?"

"Out of the selfsame fear of him. How could I keep it back from him, sir? Dmitri Fyodorovich kept bullying me all the time: 'You're deceiving me; you're concealing something from me! I'll break both your legs for you, I will!' Then I let him know of the secret signals for him to fully see my slavish devotion to him and be satisfied that I'm not deceiving him but telling him everything I know."

"If you think he'll use the signals to gain entry, don't let him in."

"But how can I keep him out if I'm laid up with a fit, even if I could dare try to prevent him, knowing the kind of headstrong man he is, sir."

"The devil take it all! Why are you so sure you're going to

have a fit, damn you? Are you making mock of me?"

"Would I dare to do so, sir, and is it a laughing matter, when I'm so scared? I feel I'm in for a fit; I have a feeling that fear alone will bring it on, sir."

"Oh, hell! Grigori will have to keep watch if you're laid up. Warn Grigori in advance not to let him in. He'll never do it."

"Without orders from the master, I'll never dare let Grigori Vassilievich know of the signals, sir. As for Grigori Vassilievich hearing him come and not letting him in, I must tell you, sir, that he's been ill ever since yesterday and Marfa Ignatievna intends to start giving him her treatment tomorrow. That's the arrangement. The treatment she gives is an uncommon one: she knows the recipe for a powerful infusion of herbs, which she always keeps ready. It's a secret of hers, and she gives Grigori Vassilievich this secret medicine of hers three times a year, sir, when his lumbago gets so bad that he simply can't move, as though he was paralysed, yes, three times a year, sir. She takes a towel, steeps it in the stuff and rubs his back with it for half and hour, till it's all dry, and his back is red and swollen. Then she makes him drink the rest over a certain prayer—no, not all of it, for she keeps some for herself, because it's a rare occasion, and drinks it, too. The two of them, I tell you, never take strong drink, so they drop off at once and sleep it off for a long time. Grigori Vassilievich almost always recovers afterwards, sir, but Marfa Ignatievna always has a headache when she awakes. So if she carries out her intention tomorrow, sir, he won't hear anything and won't be able to keep Dmitri Fyodorovich out. They'll be fast asleep, sir."

"What a tall story! And all this will coincide, as if on purpose; you'll be having your bout of the falling sickness, and the two will be dead asleep!" Ivan Fyodorovich cried out. "Are you by any chance scheming to have it happen like that, all at once?" he burst out with a menacing scowl.

"How could I arrange that, sir—and with what purpose, when it all depends on Dmitri Fyodorovich alone, what he's set his mind on— If he's determined to do something, he'll do it, sir. If he isn't, can it be for me, sir, to bring him here on purpose so as to push him into your father's room?"

"But what for should he go into Father's rooms, and on the quiet, too, if, as you yourself say, Agrafena Alexandrovna won't be coming at all," Ivan Fyodorovich went on, turning white with anger. "That's what you've been saying all the time, and ever since I came to live here I've been sure that the old man has been imagining things, and that the slut will never come to him. Why should Dmitri break into the old man's quarters if she doesn't come? Speak up! I want to know what's in your mind!"

"You know very well why he'll go there, so what difference does it make what's in my mind? He'll go there out of sheer malice or because my illness may make him suspicious. He'll grow doubtful and search the rooms in his impatience, the way he did yesterday, to make sure she hasn't slipped past him. He knows for certain that Fyodor Pavlovich has a big envelope ready, with three thousand roubles enclosed, under three seals and tied round with a pink ribbon, and an inscription in his own hand: 'To my angel Grushenka, should she wish to come', to which he added three days later, 'and my little chick'. It's that which makes things so suspicious, sir."

"Rubbish!" cried Ivan Fyodorovich, almost beside himself. "Dmitri will never come to rob for money and murder his father into the bargain. He could have killed him yesterday on account of Grushenka like the savage and crazy fool he is, but he'll never commit robbery!"

"He's badly in need of money, sir, very hard up, indeed, Ivan Fyodorovich. You've no idea how badly he needs it," Smerdyakov explained with the utmost composure and explicitness. "Besides, he considers the three thousand his own, as he himself told me: 'Father still owes me exactly three thousand', were his words. And apart from all that, Ivan Fyodorovich, there's another piece of pure truth you should consider: it's almost certain that Agrafena Alexandrovna will make him marry her, if she has a mind to, I mean the master, Fyodor Pavlovich, of course, if she has a mind to. And she may wish to. I've been saying she won't come, but she may be after bigger things—I mean, becoming the mistress of this house. I know for certain that her merchant Samsonov told her quite frankly it wouldn't be a bad idea at all, and he laughed as he said that. And she has her wits about her, sir, has she. Why on earth should she marry a pauper like Dmitri Fyodorovich? That's why, Ivan Fyodorovich, now that you know everything you should consider: if that happens, then neither Dmitri Fyodorovich nor you and your brother Alexei Fyodorovich will get anything, not a single rouble, after your father's death, because she'll marry him only to get all his fortune settled on her. Were your father to die now, sir, before anything of the kind has come about, then each of you would get a cool forty thousand right away, even Dmitri Fyodorovich, whom he hates like poison. That's because he's made no will— And Dmitri Fyodorovich is very much aware of it."

A kind of spasm seemed to distort Ivan Fyodorovich's features, and he suddenly turned red.

"After everything you've said," he suddenly interrupted Smerdyakov, "why are you advising me to go to Chermashnya? What's behind your words? Supposing I leave and all that takes place here?" He had difficulty in drawing his breath.

"Very true, sir," said Smerdyakov in a low and sober tone, while keeping a close eye on Ivan Fyodorovich.

"What d'you mean 'very true'?" asked the latter, controlling himself with an effort, a menacing flash in his eyes.

"I said that because I'm thinking of you, sir. If I were you, I'd have done with everything here—rather than stay on in this set-up—" Smerdyakov replied, looking most candidly into Ivan Fyodorovich's flashing eyes. They both fell silent.

"You seem to be an utter idiot, and, what's more—a thorough scoundrel!" cried Ivan Fyodorovich, rising suddenly from the bench. He was on the verge of passing through the wicket-gate when he suddenly stopped and turned towards Smerdyakov. Then there happened something strange. Ivan Fyodorovich suddenly bit his lip spasmodically as it were, clenched his fists, and seemed on the verge of falling upon Smerdyakov, who at once noticed it at any rate, started, and shrank back. However, the instant passed off safely for Smerdyakov, and Ivan

Fyodorovich turned back into the wicket-gate without a word, seeming somehow perplexed.

"If you care to know, I'm leaving for Moscow early tomorrow morning—and that's all!" he suddenly said in a loud and distinct voice full of anger, later feeling surprised with himself that he had had to say just that to Smerdyakov.

"That's the best thing for you to do, sir," the latter at once replied, as though it was something he had anticipated, "except, of course, that you can easily be reached there by telegram, sir, should there be some cause."

Ivan Fyodorovich halted again and turned quickly towards Smerdyakov. But something seemed to have come over the latter too. He suddenly shed all his familiarity and casual tone; his face expressed the keenest attention and eagerness, albeit timid and cringing: "Haven't you got anything more to say? Won't you add anything?" were the questions to be read in the gaze he fixed on Ivan Fyodorovich.

"But couldn't I be reached in Chermashnya just as well—should anything happen?" Ivan Fyodorovich said suddenly bawling for some reason.

"Yes, you could be sent for—from there, too—" Smerdyakov mumbled almost in a whisper, looking disconcerted but keeping his gaze fixed intently on Ivan Fyodorovich's eyes.

"Only Moscow's farther away, while Chermashnya is closer, so are you worried about my travelling expenses when you insist that I should go to Chermashnya? Or do you feel sorry for my having to make such a big detour?"

"Very true, sir," Smerdyakov mumbled, his voice faltering, an odious smile on his face, and making ready to jump back convulsively should the need arise. But, to his surprise, Ivan Fyodorovich broke into a laugh and rapidly entered through the wicket, still laughing. Anyone looking into his face would have seen that his laughter did not spring from any lightness of heart. He himself could not have possibly accounted for his state at the moment. His movements and gait looked quite convulsive.

7.

"Talking to a Clever Man Is Always Worth While"

So did his speech. On meeting with Fyodor Pavlovich as he entered the drawing-room, he suddenly called out to him, waving his hands, "I'm going upstairs to my room. See you later", and walked past, even trying to keep his eyes away from his father. The old man was very possibly too hateful to him at the moment, but so undisguised a display of hostility had been unexpected even by Fyodor Pavlovich. The old man evidently had something urgent to tell him, which was why he had wanted to intercept him in the drawing-room. On hearing so courteous a greeting, he stopped short without a word, his eyes following his son's progress up the stairs and along the mezzanine with a quizzical look, till he passed out of sight.

"What's the matter with him?" he promptly asked Smerdyakov, who had followed hard on Ivan Fyodorovich's steps.

"He's angry over something," Smerdyakov muttered evasively. "Who can tell why!"

"Oh, to hell with him! Who cares for his anger, anyhow? Fetch the samovar in and then off with you. Is there any news?"

There followed a series of questions of the kind Smerdyakov had complained of to Ivan Fyodorovich, to wit, the expected lady visitor. We shall skip them all. Half an hour later, the house was locked up, and the crazed old man kept pacing his rooms in tremulous expectation of hearing, at any moment, the prearranged five-knock signal, peering at times through the windows into the darkness of the night, but discerning nothing.

Though the hour was already very late, Ivan Fyodorovich was still awake and wrapped in thought. He went to bed late, at about two o'clock. However, we shall not go into the course of his thoughts; this is not the right time to delve into his soul, whose turn will come. Were we to try to describe any of those thoughts, we would find it hard to do so, because they were not really what could be called thoughts but something very vague and, above all, flurried. He felt completely at a loss, and overcome by strange and almost unexpected desires, for instance he felt an overwhelming urge, after midnight, to go downstairs, open the front door, go into the lodge and give Smerdyakov a good hiding. Were he to be asked why, he would have been quite unable to give any explicit reason except perhaps that the servant had become hateful to him as one who had humiliated him more outrageously than anyone in the world could have done. On the other hand, there came over him several times during that night a kind of inexplicable and humiliating timidity which—he felt—seemed even to drain him of all his physical strength. His aching head was swimming, and a feeling of hatred rankled in his heart as though he had to wreak vengeance upon somebody. He hated even Alyosha as he recalled their talk, and at moments he hated himself too. He had almost forgotten to give thought to Katerina Ivanovna, which greatly surprised him afterwards, the more so for his clearly remembering how, that very morning with Katerina Ivanovna, he had boasted so extravagantly that he would leave for Moscow the next morning, while in his heart of hearts a still small voice had whispered, "What nonsense: you won't go anywhere, for it won't be so easy for you to tear yourself away as you are now bragging." Long, long afterwards, as he recollected that night, Ivan Fyodorovich would recall with particular revulsion how he would suddenly get up from the sofa, open the door softly, as though fearful of being seen, go out on the staircase and listen to his father's movements in the rooms downstairs—listen with beating heart and bated breath for a long while, driven by some strange curiosity. Why he had done all that, or why he had listened so—he could not of course tell. All his life long he was to call his behaviour "vile" and, in the deepest recesses of his heart, thought of it as the basest action of all his life. At the moment, he had not even felt any hatred for his father, but for some reason had felt merely intensely curious: how the latter was pacing his rooms and what he might possibly be doing; he imagined and pictured to himself how he must be peering through the dark windows, halting suddenly in the middle of the room and listening, listening intently for the knocks to come. Ivan Fyodorovich twice went out on the staircase to listen in that way. At about two o'clock, when everything was quiet and his father had retired, Ivan Fyodorovich, too, went to bed with the firm desire to fall asleep at once, for he felt quite worn out. Indeed, he suddenly sank into sound and dreamless slumber, but woke up early, at seven o'clock, when day had broken. On opening his eyes, he was surprised to feel a surge of extraordinary energy within himself; he jumped out of bed and rapidly got dressed, pulled out his portmanteau and immediately set about packing it. Fortunately, he had received his linen back from the laundress the morning before. He even smiled at the thought that things had worked themselves out perfectly and that there was nothing to delay his sudden departure. And his departure would indeed be quite sudden. Though, on the previous day, Ivan Fyodorovich had said (to Katerina Ivanovna, Alyosha, and then Smerdyakov) that he would be leaving on the morrow, he had not thought of departing when he went to bed—he remembered that very well; at least, he had never thought that the first thing he would do on getting up in the morning would be to pack his portmanteau. At last, the portmanteau and travelling bag were ready: it was at about nine o'clock when Marfa Ignatievna came in with the usual daily question: "Where will you be having breakfast, sir, here or downstairs?" Ivan Fyodorovich went downstairs looking almost blithe, though there was something distrait and hurried in his words and gestures. After an affable greeting to his father and even a special inquiry after his health, he did not bother to wait for the end of his father's reply, but at once announced that he was leaving for Moscow for good in an hour's time, and asked for the carriage to be sent for. The old man showed not the least surprise at the news, most indecently forgetting to express his regret at his son's departure. Instead, he suddenly grew very flustered as he recalled some highly important business of his own.

"That's the kind of fellow you are! You could have told yesterday—well, never mind, things can be arranged all the same. Please do me a great favour, my dear boy, and stop over at Chermashnya on the way. It's only a left-hand turn from Volovya station, a matter of some twelve versts, and there you are at Chermashnya!"

"Sorry but I can't. It's eighty versts from here to the railway station, and the train for Moscow starts at seven in the evening. I shall just make it."

"You can catch your train tomorrow or the day after, but please turn off to Chermashnya today. It won't cost you too much effort to ease your father's mind, will it? If I hadn't some business to attend to here, I'd have run over there myself long ago, because the deal there is urgent and important, but I can't get away at the moment— You see, I have two stands of timber there, at Begichevo and Dyachkino on some wasteland. The Maslovs, an old merchant and his son, are offering me a mere eight thousand for the timber, while only a year ago a buyer showed up, who offered me twelve thousand, but he wasn't a local man—that was the main point. Nothing can be sold locally because the Maslovs—father and son—who are worth hundreds of thousands, have things very much their own way here. You have to take it or leave it, because no one around here dares bid against them. Last Thursday, the Ilyinskoye priest suddenly wrote to me that Gorstkin, a merchant I happen to know, had turned up. His only value is that he isn't a local man, but comes from Pogrebovo, so he isn't afraid of the Maslovs. He says he'll pay eleven thousand for the timber, mark that! He'll be staying there only for another week, the priest writes. Couldn't you go over there and clinch the deal?"

"Well, write to the priest, and he'll attend to it."

"He can't do that. He has no eye for business. An excellent man: I could trust him with twenty thousand for safekeep without taking a receipt for the money, but he has no business sense. Just like a child in such matters. Why, a crow could gull him. And imagine, he's a man of learning. Now this Gorstkin looks like a bumpkin and affects peasant dress, but he's a knave through and through—which is very common with us here. He's a liar—another feature in him. Why, he can tell you such lies that you start wondering why he should do so. The year before last, he told me a whopper about his wife having died and his having married another woman, and it was all untrue, just imagine: his wife never died, she's alive to this day and gives him a thrashing twice a week. So, you see, we've got

360

to find out whether he's lying or telling the truth when he says he wants to buy the timber for eleven thousand."

"But I can't be of much use in such matters: I've no eye for business either."

"Hold on! You'll manage because I'll instruct you how to deal with Gorstkin, for I've conducted business with him for quite a while. You see, you've got to keep an eye on his beard— a nasty, thin, reddish beard. If it quivers and he speaks in an angry tone, then it's all right—he's speaking the truth and means business, but if he strokes his beard with his left hand, and grins, that means he's out to cheat you. Never look into his eyes, because they won't tell you anything. He's too deep for that, the rogue, but watch his beard! I'll give you a note for him. Though his name's Gorstkin, it should be Lurcher. Only don't say that to him or it will give him offence. If you come to terms with him and see it's all right, write to me at once. All you have to write is, 'He's not lying'. Hold out for eleven thousand; you can knock off a thousand, but no more. Just think: eight and eleven—a difference of three thousand. It's as good as finding the three thousand. It's not so easy to find a buyer, and I'm in desperate need of money. Let me know that he's in earnest, and I'll run over myself and clinch the deal. I'll find the time somehow. Why should I rush off there now if the priest may have thought the whole affair up? Well, will you go there or not?"

"I haven't got the time. You must excuse me."

"Oh, do your father a favour! I won't forget it. You're heartless people, the whole lot of you! What is a day or two to you? Where are you off to now—to Venice? Your Venice can wait for another couple of days. I could have sent Alyosha, but he's quite at sea in such things. I'm asking you solely because you're a clever fellow—don't I see that? You don't trade in timber, but you've got a pair of eyes. All you've got to see is whether the man means business or not. Look at his beard, I say: if it quivers, he's in earnest."

"So you're impelling me to go to that damned Chermashnya, eh?" cried Ivan with a malicious grin.

Fyodor Pavlovich did not notice the malice, or chose not to, but he did seize on the grin.

"So you're going, after all, aren't you? I'll just go and dash off a note for you."

"I don't know whether I shall go. I really don't know. I'll make up my mind on the way."

"Why do that on the way? Make up your mind right away! Come on, my dear fellow! If you settle the matter, write me a couple of lines, give the note to the priest, and he'll send it on to me without delay. I won't keep you any longer—go on to your Venice. The priest will take you to Volovya station in his carriage—"

Delighted with the turn things had taken, he dashed off the note, ordered the carriage to be ready, and had some refreshment and brandy served. When the old man felt pleased, he always grew effusive, but this time he seemed more reserved. For instance, he made no mention at all of Dmitri Fyodorovich. Having to say good-bye to Ivan did not affect him in the least, and he even seemed at a loss as to what to say, which Ivan Fyodorovich at once noticed. "He must be thoroughly tired of me," he thought. It was only when he was seeing his son off from the porch that the old man appeared flustered, and even tried to kiss him, but Ivan Fyodorovich held out his hand for a handshake, with the obvious purpose of avoiding the embrace. This was understood by the old man, who drew back at once.

"Well, good luck to you, good luck!" he kept repeating from the steps. "Will you ever be coming back in your lifetime, I wonder. I'll always be glad if you do. Christ be with you!"

Ivan Fyodorovich got into the carriage.

"Good-bye, Ivan! Don't think too badly of me!" his father exclaimed in parting.

The entire household had gathered to give him a sendoff: Smerdyakov, Marfa and Grigori, whom Ivan Fyodorovich tipped ten roubles each. When he had seated himself in the carriage, Smerdyakov dashed up to adjust the rug.

"You see—I'm going to Chermashnya—" Ivan suddenly said, the words seeming to escape from his lips just as on the day before, but this time with a kind of nervous laugh. He recalled it long afterward.

"So people are right when they say that talking to a clever man is always worth while," Smerdyakov replied in a firm voice, and with a significant look.

The carriage drove off and picked up speed. The passenger felt ill at ease in his mind, but looked around eagerly at the fields, the hills, the trees, and the gaggle of geese flying high overhead in a cloudless sky. A sudden sense of well-being came over him. He tried to fall into conversation with the driver, and at first felt greatly interested in what the man had to say, but very soon realised that he had missed most of what the latter had said and, in fact, had not even caught the reply. He fell silent, for things were good as they were: the air was pure, cool and fresh, and the sky clear. Images of Alyosha and Katerina Ivanovna floated across his mind, but he smiled gently and waved the dear phantoms away. "Their time will come," he thought. They soon reached the post station, changed horses and galloped on to Volovya. "What did he mean by saying that talking to a clever man is always worth while?" he asked himself, and then suddenly gasped. "Why did I have to tell him I was going to Chermashnya?" On reaching Volovya station, Ivan Fyodorovich got out of the carriage, and several private coachmen approached him, haggling over the fare for the twelve versts to Chermashnya. He hired one of them and told him to harness the horses. He entered the station house, looked around, glanced at the station master's wife, and suddenly went outside again.

"I won't be going to Chermashnya. Will I make the seven o'clock train?"

"We can make it nicely. Shall we harness the horses?"

"Yes, right away. Will any of your fellows be in town tomorrow?"

"Why indeed, sir. Mitri here will."

"I want you to do me a service, Mitri. Call on my father, Fyodor Pavlovich Karamazov, and tell him I haven't gone to Chermashnya. Can you do it?"

"Of course, I can, sir. We've known Fyodor Pavlovich for a long time."

"And here's something for you, for I don't think he'll give you a tip," said Ivan Fyodorovich with a gay laugh.

"Of course, he won't!" Mitri replied, laughing too. "Thank you, sir. I'll do it without fail."

It was seven o'clock in the evening when Ivan Fyodorovich boarded the train for Moscow. "Away with the past; I've done for ever with my former world, and I don't want ever to hear of it or from it again. Onward towards a new life and new places, and no looking back!" But instead of any uplift, his soul was plunged into gloom, and his heart filled with a sadness he had never before experienced. He lay immersed in thought all night, and it was only at dawn, as the train steamed into Moscow, that he suddenly came to himself.

"I'm a scoundrel!" he whispered to himself.

As for Fyodor Pavlovich, he felt very pleased with himself after seeing his son off. For two whole hours he felt almost happy and sipped at his brandy; but there suddenly happened a most vexing and unpleasant event which utterly dismayed him at once: Smerdyakov, who had gone down into the cellar for something, fell from the top step. It was fortunate that this took place while Marfa Ignatievna was in the courtyard and heard him in time. She did not see him fall, but did hear the scream, the peculiar and eerie scream long familiar to her—that of an epileptic falling in a fit. Whether the attack had come on at the moment he was going down the steps and he must have lost consciousness as he fell, or whether, on the contrary, the attack had been brought on by the fall and the ensuing shock to one known to be prone to epileptic fits—that could not be made out, but he was found on the cellar floor writhing in convulsions and foaming at the mouth. It was thought at first that he must have suffered some injury—a broken arm or a leg—but, as Marfa Ignatievna put it, God had preserved him: nothing of the kind had happened, only there was some difficulty in getting him out of the cellar. But the neighbours were called in to help and the thing was done somehow. Fyodor Pavlovich was there all the time and lent a helping hand, evidently alarmed and somehow at a loss. Smerdyakov did not regain consciousness, however. The attacks ceased for a while, only to return later, so the general conclusion was that the same thing would occur as in the year before, when he had accidentally fallen from the loft. It was recalled that he had had an ice pack placed on his head at the time. Since there was still some ice in the cellar, Marfa Ignatievna sent for it; towards evening, Fyodor Pavlovich had Dr. Herzenstube sent for, who came at once. After a thorough examination of the sick man, Dr. Herzenstube (an elderly and most estimable man, and the most conscientious and considerate physician in all the gubernia) concluded that the fit was a most severe one and might be dangerous; for the time being, however, he could not quite understand it in its entirety, so that if the remedies prescribed would not help, he would try other ones the next morning. The sick man was put to bed in the hut, in a room next to Grigori and Marfa Ignatievna's. As for Fyodor Pavlovich, he had to put up with one inconvenience after another the rest of the day; dinner was cooked by Marfa Ignatievna, and, compared to Smerdyakov's, the soup was "like swill" and the chicken so tough as to be quite unchewable. To her master's bitter if justified reproaches, Marfa Ignatievna replied that the bird had been a very old one to begin with, and, as for herself, she had never been given a cook's training anyway. There was more trouble to come in the evening: Fyodor Pavlovich was informed that Grigori, who had been indisposed for two days, was now laid up with lumbago. Fyodor Pavlovich had tea as early as he could, and locked himself in the house. He was in a state of restless and anxious expectancy, for he was looking forward to Grushenka's coming that evening almost for certain. At least, Smerdyakov had practically assured him early that morning, "she had definitely promised to come". The old man's restless heart went pit-a-pat as he paced his empty rooms, listening. He had to keep his ears pricked, for Dmitri Fyodorovich might be on the look-out for her somewhere, and as soon as she tapped on the window (a couple of days previously, Smerdyakov had assured him he had told her where and how to knock) he had to unlock the door as quickly as he could and not keep her waiting in the hall even for a moment, lest—which heaven forfend—she might become apprehensive and make off. It was a trying time for Fyodor Pavlovich, yet never before had his heart been dilated with sweeter hope: this time it could be said almost with certainty that she would come!

BOOK SIX

The Russian Monk

1.

The *Starets* Zossima and His Visitors

Alyosha stopped short almost in amazement as he entered Father Zossima's cell, for he had come with anxiety and pain in his heart: instead of the dying man, perhaps already in a coma, he had feared to find, he saw the *starets* seated in his armchair, his face bright and cheerful if pale and tired, surrounded by visitors and talking to them in a calm and pleasant voice. He had, in fact, risen from his bed only a quarter of an hour before Alyosha's arrival. The visitors had assembled in his cell earlier and had been waiting for him to wake, having been firmly assured by Father Paissi that "the teacher will certainly get up to once again converse with those dear to his heart, as he himself promised this morning". Father Paissi had implicit trust in this promise, as indeed he had in every world spoken by the departing *starets*, so much so that, should he have seen him unconscious and even lifeless, but, having his promise that he would rise again to take leave of them, he would not have believed even perhaps in death, but would have waited for the dying man to open his eyes and keep his promise. In the morning, before he had fallen asleep, the *starets* Zossima had uttered: "I shall not die without the delight of more discourse with you, who are so dear to my heart, without looking once more into your dear faces, and pouring out my soul again." Those who had gathered for that discourse, probably their last with the *starets*, were his most devoted friends of many years. They were four in number: the hieromonachs Father Iosif and Father Paissi, the hieromonach Father Mikhail, the prior of the hermitage, who was not at all elderly or very learned; he was of humble origin but firm of spirit, and steadfast and simple in faith, austere in appearance but with a tender heart, a trait he kept concealed as though he even felt ashamed of it. The fourth visitor was a Father Anfim, an elderly and humble little monk of the poorest peasant class, almost unlettered, quiet and untalkative, scarcely speaking to anybody, the meekest of the meek, and looking as though he had been overawed by something great and terrible, and beyond his understanding. The *starets* was very fond of this timid man and had always regarded him with the deepest respect; there was hardly anybody with whom he had spoken fewer words, though the two had spent many years wandering all over holy Russia. That had been long before, some forty years back, when the *starets* had entered the monastic state in a poor and little known monastery in Kostroma Gubernia, and when, shortly afterwards, he had become Father Anfim's companion in his wanderings to collect donations for their obscure monastery. The entire company—host and visitors—were in the *starets*'s second room, where his bed stood, a room which, as already mentioned, was so small that there was scarcely room for the four (apart from the novice Porfiri, who remained standing) to sit round Father Zossima on chairs brought from the other room. It was already getting dark, and the room was lit up by the lamps and wax candles burning before the icons. On seeing Alyosha, who stood embarrassed in the doorway, the *starets* gave him a joyful smile and held out his hand.

"Welcome, my quiet one, welcome, my dear boy. Here you are at last. I knew you'd come."

Alyosha went up to him, bowed low to the ground and burst into tears. Something welled up in his heart, his soul was throbbing, and he wanted to sob.

"Come, come, it is too soon to mourn for me," said the *starets*, smiling and putting his right hand on Alyosha's head. "I'm sitting here and talking, as you see. I may live on for another twenty years, as was wished me by that dear and kindly woman from Vyshegorye, the one with the little girl Lizaveta in her arms. O Lord, remember both the mother and the little girl Lizaveta!" (He crossed himself.) "Did you take her offering to where I told you, Porfiri?"

He was referring to the sixty copecks donated by the cheerful woman for somebody "poorer than me". Such donations are made by way of voluntary penance and always in the form of money earned by one's labour. On the evening before, the *starets* had sent Porfiri to a poor widow with two children, whose house had been burnt down and who was now reduced to begging for alms. Porfiri hastened to let the *starets* know that he had fulfilled the errand and, as instructed, had passed on the money from an "unknown benefactress".

"Rise, my dear boy," the *starets* continued to Alyosha. "Let me have a good look at you. Have you been home and seen your brother?"

It seemed strange to Alyosha that he was asking so firmly and definitely only about one of his brothers—but which one? So it was perhaps for that brother that the *starets* had sent him away from himself the day before and that morning.

"I've seen one of my brothers," Alyosha replied.

"I'm referring to that one, the elder, to whom I bowed down to the ground yesterday."

"I saw him only yesterday, but was quite unable to find him today," said Alyosha.

"Hasten to find him, go again tomorrow and make haste; leave everything else and make haste. You may be in time to prevent something terrible from happening. When I bowed down to the ground before him yesterday, it was because of the great suffering that awaits him."

He fell suddenly silent and seemed wrapped in thought. His words were strange. Father Iosif, who had witnessed the low bow made by the *starets* on the previous day, exchanged glances with Father Paissi. Alyosha could hold himself back no longer.

"Father and teacher," he asked with deep emotion, "your words are hard to fathom— What kind of suffering awaits him?"

"Do not ask. I sensed something terrible yesterday—as though his eyes were expressive of his whole future fate. There was a look in them—I felt horrified momentarily in my heart by what the man is preparing for himself. I have seen the same expression on a man's face once or twice before—an expression that seemed to reflect that man's entire fate, which, alas, actually came about. I sent you to him, Alexei, because I thought that your brotherly face might help him. But everything, all our destinies, come from the Lord. 'Except a corn of wheat fall into the ground and die, it abideth alone: but if it die, it bringeth forth much fruit.' Remember that. Many times in my life I have blessed you in my thoughts for your face, Alexei; you should know that," the *starets* said with a gentle smile. "Now here is what I think of you: you will go forth from within these walls, but even in the outside world you will live like a monk. You will have many foes, but even your foes will love you. Many are the trials life will bring you, but it will be in them that you will find happiness and bless life, and make others bless it—which matters most. That is the kind of creature you are. Fathers and teachers," he went on, addressing his visitors with a gentle smile, "until this day I have never told even this youth why his face is so dear to me. I will tell you now: his face has been a remembrance and a prophecy. At the dawn of my days, when I was a little child, I had an elder brother, who died in his youth, before my eyes, when he was only seventeen. Later, as I travelled the road of life, I gradually became convinced that my brother had, as it were, shown me guidance and a sign from on high, since, had he never appeared in my life and never existed, I would never, so I believe, have donned the monastic habit and not entered upon that precious path. He first appeared to me in my childhood, and now, at the end of my journey, he seems to have come to me again. Fathers and teachers, I marvel at the fact that, while he bears but a remote resemblance to him in countenance, Alexei has seemed so much like him in spirit that I have many a time taken him for that youth, my brother who, at the ebb of my life, has returned to me mysteriously as a kind of reminder and inspiration, so that I've been even surprised at myself and my strange fancy. Listen, Porfiri," he said, turning to the novice who waited on him. "I've often seen an expression of distress on your face because you think I love Alexei more than I do you. Now you know the reason, but I love you too, and I've been grieved many a time by your distress. And now, my dear visitors, I'd like to tell you about that youth, my brother, for there has never been anything in my life more precious, more prophetic and moving. I feel deeply moved in my heart as I look back at my entire life as though living it anew—"

I must observe at this point that this last conversation held by the *starets* with those who visited him on the last day of his life has been preserved in part in writing, recorded from memory by Alexei Fyodorovich Karamazov some time after the *starets* breathed his last. I cannot say for certain whether the record contains everything he said that particular evening, or whether Alexei later augmented it with earlier notes of talks with his teacher. Besides, it is a continuous account, as though, in addressing his friends, the *starets* told them the unbroken story of his life, while later accounts would show without any doubt that things proceeded in a somewhat different manner, for the conversation that evening was of a general nature and, though the visitors rarely interrupted their host, they did at times speak for themselves and make a contribution to the talk. Besides, there could hardly have been any continuous narration by the *starets*, who at times gasped for breath, his voice failing him, and he even had to lie down on his bed to rest a while, though he did not doze off, and his visitors did not leave their seats. Once or twice, the conversation was interrupted by readings from the Gospels by Father Paissi. It is noteworthy, too, that none of them thought that he would die that very night, the more so because, on that last evening of his life, he seemed, after sleeping soundly in the daytime, to have found fresh strength which sustained him during his long conversation with his friends. It was, as it were, the last outpouring of his love which gave him a brief outburst of energy, for his life was suddenly cut short— But of that anon. At this point, I would like to state that I have decided not to give a detailed account of the conversation but to confine myself to the *starets*'s story according to Alexei Fyodorovich Karamazov's manuscript. It will be briefer and less tiring though, of course—and I repeat—Alyosha has drawn extensively of former conversations as well, which he has appended.

2.

From the Life of the Demised Hieromonach, the *Starets* Zossima, Recorded From His Own Words by Alexei Fyodorovich Karamazov

Biographical Notes

(a) *About the Youth, Father Zossima's Brother*

Beloved fathers and teachers, I was born in the town of V. in a remote gubernia in the north of the country. My father was of gentle birth, but of little consequence or rank. I have no recollection of him at all, for he died when I was only two years old. He left my mother a small wooden house and a small fortune sufficient for her and her children to live on without experiencing any need. There were two of us children: my elder brother Markel and myself, Zinovy. He was my senior by eight years, short of temper and irritable but kind-hearted and never sharp of tongue; he was most sparing of words, especially at home: with me, our mother and the servants. He did well at the Gymnasium but did not get on with his school-fellows, though he never quarrelled with them, as Mother later recalled. Some six months before his death, when he was over seventeen, he began to call on a man who led a very solitary life in our town, a political exile banished from Moscow for his free-thinking. He was a scholarly man and a distinguished university philosopher. For some reason, he took a liking to Markel, and always welcomed him at home. The youth would spend whole evenings with him throughout that winter, until, at his own request, the exile was summoned to St. Petersburg to take up a post in the government service, for he had influential patrons. When Lent came round, Markel refused to observe the fast, making mock of the season of penitence: "It's all nonsense," he would say, "there is no God," thereby horrifying Mother, the servants, and me, too, for though I was only nine, I was aghast at hearing such words. Our four servants were all serfs, bought on behalf of a landowner of our acquaintance. I can still remember Mother selling one of the four, our cook Afimya, a lame and elderly woman, for sixty roubles, and engaging a free servant in her stead. In the sixth week of Lent, my brother suddenly fell ill. He had always been ailing, with a weak chest, slight of build, and consumptive. He was quite tall, but thin and delicate, and his face was a handsome one. I suppose he caught a chill; anyway the doctor came and soon told Mother in a whisper that he had galloping consumption and would not live through the spring. Reduced to tears, Mother began to entreat my brother, albeit in guarded terms (mainly so as not to alarm him), to fast, attend divine service and take the sacrament, for he was not yet laid up. This made him angry and scoff at the church, yet he grew thoughtful: he realised at once that he was dangerously ill, which was why Mother was sending him to church to confess and take the sacrament while he was still strong enough to do so. Incidentally, he was aware that he had been in declining health for a long time, and a year before he had calmly observed to Mother and me at table, "I won't be with you for long; I may not live another year"; he seemed to have predicted the outcome. Holy Week came round three days later; beginning with Tuesday morning, my brother began to fast and attend divine service. "I'm doing it simply for your sake, Mother," he said, "to gladden you and set your mind at rest." Mother shed tears of joy mixed with grief. "It must be because his end is near, if there's been such a sudden change in him." He was unable to attend divine service for long: he took to his bed, and had to confess and take the sacrament at home. Easter was later that year, with clear, bright and fragrant days. He would lie coughing all night, I remember, and his sleep was poor, but in the morning he would always get dressed and try to sit up in an arm-chair. That's how I remember him: seated in the arm-chair, calm and gentle, a smile on his face, looking cheerful and joyous despite his illness. He was completely transformed in spirit—such a marvellous change had suddenly come over him! Our old nurse would enter the room and say: "May I light the lamp before the icon, my dear boy?" In the past, he did not permit it, and would even blow the flame out. "Light it, my dear, light it," he would now say, "I used to behave wretchedly when I prevented you from lighting it. You pray to God while you are lighting the lamp, and I will do the same while I rejoice, looking at you. So we shall be praying to one and the same God." Such words seemed strange to us, and Mother would go to her room and weep, but when she returned she would wipe her eyes and try to look cheerful. "Don't cry, Mother dear," he used to say, "I've still a long time to live and to rejoice with you; for life is full of gladness and joy!" "How can you feel joyful, my dear boy, when you burn with fever at night and cough as though your chest will burst?" "Don't cry, Mother," he would reply, "life is a paradise, and we are all in paradise, though we don't want to admit it; if we did, the whole world would be a paradise tomorrow." We all marvelled at his words, which he spoke so strangely and so positively; we were moved to tears. When friends came to see us, he would address them in the following words: "What have I done to deserve your love, my dear ones? Why do you love me for what I am, and how is it that I used to be unaware of it, and did not appreciate it?" When the servants entered his room, he kept on saying to them: "Why should you wait on me, my dear ones? I am unworthy of it. Should God spare me, and let me live on, I will serve you, for we should all serve one another." This would make Mother shake her head. "My dear boy," she would say, "it's your illness that makes you speak like that." "Mother darling," he would reply, "some have to be masters and others must be servants, but I want to be the servant of my servants: to be to them what they are to me. Besides, Mother, every one of us is at fault to all men for everything, and I most of all." This made Mother smile through her tears: "In what way are you at fault to others more than all the rest? There are murderers and robbers in the world, so what sins have you committed to accuse yourself more than anybody else?" "Mother, dear heart (he had taken to using such tender and unexpected words), Mother, my dearest one, know that, verily, each man is at fault to all others, for all the others, and for everything. I don't know how to explain it to you, but that is what I feel to the point of anguish. How could we have lived in anger and without the least awareness?" That was how he awoke every morning, with ever mounting joy and tenderness, vibrant with love. Whenever the doctor called—an elderly German Eisenschmidt by name—my brother would joke with him. "Well, doctor," he would say, "do you give me another day of life?" "Why only one day more?" the doctor would reply. "You're good for many a day yet, and for many months and years, too." "Why count the years and months?" my brother would exclaim. "Why count even the days, when a single day will suffice for a man to learn what happiness really means? My dear ones, why do we quarrel, boast to one another and bear grudges? Why not go into the garden, stroll about and enjoy ourselves there, love, embrace and appreciate one another, and bless our lives?" "Your son hasn't much longer to live," the doctor said to Mother as she was seeing him out. "I'm afraid his illness is affecting his mind." His windows gave onto the garden, which was full of shade, with old trees. The spring buds were burgeoning, and the early birds were chirping and singing at his windows. As he looked admiringly at them, he would suddenly beg their forgiveness. "Birds of God, messengers of joy, forgive me too, for I've sinned against you as well." That was something none of us could understand at the time, but he shed tears of joy. "Yes, all about me was the glory of heaven, with the birds, the trees, the meadows and the sky; I alone lived shamefully; I alone besmirched it all, and had no eyes for the glory and the beauty." "You take too many sins on yourself," Mother would say in tears. "Mother, dearest, my tears spring from joy, not grief. You see, I myself want to feel at fault with them, only it's something I can't put into words, for I don't even know how to love them. Even if I've sinned against all other people, yet they will forgive me, and that is happiness from paradise. Am I not in paradise now?"

There was a great deal more that I cannot recall or describe. However, I do remember going into his room when there was no one else there. It was a clear evening and the sun was setting, its slanting rays lighting up the whole room. On seeing me, he beckoned to me, and when I came up to him he put his hands on my shoulders, and looked me in the face with tender love; he said nothing but just looked at me like that for a minute or so: "And now," he said, "return to your play, and go on living for me!" I did so, and, in the course of my further life, I recalled many a time and with tears how he told me to go on living for him. He said many other wonderful and beautiful things, which we did not understand at the time. He died in the third week after Easter, in full possession of his mental faculties, though he could no longer speak. There was no change in him up to his very last hour: his expression was joyful, with eyes full of gladness; his look followed and sought us, and his smile never left his lips. There was a lot of talk about his death even in the town. It all left a deep but not excessive impression on me at the time, though I shed many tears at his funeral. I was very young then, a mere child but it did leave an indelible imprint on my heart, a deep-lying feeling. It was to spring to life and respond when the time came. That was exactly what came to pass.

(b) *On the Part Played by Holy Writ in the Life of Father Zossima*

There were now only two of us, Mother and myself. Very soon some good friends advised her to send her son to St. Petersburg: she had only one son now, and, as she was in more or less comfortable circumstances, she should follow the example of other people, since keeping me by her side might well mean depriving me of a brilliant career. So they persuaded Mother to take me to St. Petersburg and have me enrolled in the Cadet Corps,* after which I could enter the Imperial Guards. For a long time, Mother could not make up her mind, for she was loth to part with her only remaining son, but she finally decided to do so, though not without many tears, hoping it would be for my good. She took me to St. Petersburg and got me into the Corps, after which I never saw her again for she died three years later, grieving for the two of us. I inherited nothing but treasured memories from my parental

*A system of privileged military secondary schools in pre-revolutionary Russia, where boys of the nobility were trained for future army service as officers.—*Tr.*

home, for no memories can be more precious than those of one's earliest childhood at that home; that is almost always so if there is the least love and harmony in the family. In fact, precious memories may live on even of a bad home, if only one's soul is capable of seeking after the precious. Among my memories of home I number those of Biblical history, which I was eager to learn at home though I was only a child. I had an excellently illustrated book of stories from the Bible entitled *A Hundred and Four Sacred Stories From the Old and the New Testaments,* from which I learnt to read. It is still standing there on my bookshelf as a precious relic of the past. I remember how, even before I learned to read, I was visited by a kind of spiritual emotion when I was only eight years of age. I remember Mother taking me to church (I don't remember where my brother was at the time) to attend morning mass on the Monday before Easter. The weather was fine and I well remember, just as though I was witnessing it now, the incense rising from the censer and slowly floating upwards, while the rays of God's sun came streaming through a little window on the dome above, seeming to dissolve the incense as it rose in waves towards them. As I looked upwards, I felt deeply stirred by the sight, and for the first time in my life the first seeds of the word of God were consciously accepted in my soul. Then a youth stepped forth into the middle of the church, carrying a book so big that I thought at the time that he had difficulty even in lifting it; he placed it on the lectern, opened it and began to read, and it was then that, for the first time in my life I understood something, to wit, what is read in the temple of God. There was a man in the land of Uz, and that man was perfect and upright, and he had so much substance, so many camels, and so many sheep and she-asses; and his sons feasted in their houses. He loved them greatly, and prayed for them, for they may have sinned as they feasted. Now there came a day when Satan came to present himself before the Lord among the sons of God, saying he had been going to and fro in the earth and walking up and down in it. "And hast thou considered my servant Job?" the Lord asked Satan, and went on to boast of his great and holy servant. Now Satan laughed at God's words:

"Put him in my hands, and you will see that your servant will murmur against you and curse thee to thy face." And God put the righteous man he loved so well in the hands of Satan, who smote his children and his cattle, and scattered his wealth all at once, as with a thunderbolt from heaven. Then Job arose and rent his mantle, fell down upon the ground, and cried out: "Naked came I out of my mother's womb and naked shall I return thither: the Lord gave, and the Lord hath taken away; blessed be the name of the Lord now and for ever!" Forgive me my tears, fathers and teachers, for all my childhood seems to rise up again before me, and my breath comes just as it did then into the chest of a child of eight, and, just as then, I feel wonder, trepidation and joy, and my imagination was caught by the camels, by Satan who spoke like that with the Lord, and by the Lord, who gave up his servant like that to ruination, and by his servant, who cried out, "blessed be thy name, though thou chastiseth me", and then by the soft and sweet singing in the church, "Let my prayer rise up to thee", and then again by the incense from the priest's censer, and the prayers offered on bended knee! Ever since then—and I took it only yesterday—I've never been able to read that holy story without tears. It contains so much that is majestic, mysterious and passing the imagination! Later I would hear the words of the scoffers and the revilers—words of pride: how could the Lord give the most beloved of his righteous in the hands of Satan as a plaything, take away his children, smite him with sore boils, so that he had to take a potsherd to scrape away the corruption from his sores, and for what? Merely to be able to boast to Satan, "See what my saint can put up with for my sake!" But the greatness of it lies in its being a mystery—because in it are brought together the passing show of the earthly, and eternal truth. Here eternal truth takes effect in the presence of earthly truth. Here, just as in the first days of the Creation, the Creator, as he completes each day with the words of praise, "What I have created is good", considers Job and again takes pride in his creation. And, in praising the Lord, Job is serving, not only Him but everything He has created, for generation after generation, and for ever and ever, for he was predestined to do so. Good Lord, what a book and what lessons it teaches! What a book Holy Writ is, and how great are the miracle and the strength it endows man with! It is a mould of the world, of man and human characteristics; in it everything is shown and named for all time. And how many are the mysteries it reveals and resolves: God raises Job up again and returns his substance to him; many years pass, and he has other children and he loves them all, good Lord. But could he love those new children when the other ones were no more, lost to him? But, it may be asked, as he recollected them, could he be fully happy with the new children as he had been with the previous ones, no matter how dear the new children were to him? But he could, indeed he could: through the great mystery of human life, the old sorrow is gradually translated into quiet and gentle joy; the turbulent blood of youth yields place to the mellow serenity of old age. Every day I bless the sunrise and my heart sings to it as before, but I have greater love for the sunset, its long and slanting rays, and with it my quiet, gentle and tender memories, the dear images of a long and blessed lifetime—and over it all reigns the truth of God, tender, reconciling and full of forgiveness! My end is drawing near—I feel and know it, but, with every day that is left to me, I feel that my earthly life is in touch with a new life, infinite, unknown but at hand, in anticipation of which my soul trembles in rapture, my mind glows, and my heart weeps for joy— Friends and teachers, I have often heard, and of late ever more frequently, that our priests, and especially in our rural areas, have been complaining bitterly and on all sides of their miserable stipends and their humiliating status, declaring forthright, even in print—something I've seen with my own eyes—that they are unable to expound the Scriptures to the people because of the paucity of their stipends, and that if the Lutherans and heretics come to lead their flock astray, let them do so, because the stipends, they claim, are so small. Heavens, I think to myself, may the Lord grant that the stipends that are so precious to them be increased (because their complaint is also justified) but verily I say that if anyone is to blame for the matter, then half the fault is ours!

For even if he is short of time, even if he is right in saying that he is swamped under with work and church services, that is not the case all the time; surely he has at least an hour a week to remember God in. And then, he does not work all the year round. Let him gather about himself if only the children at first, one evening a week, and the fathers will learn of it and begin coming too. Such work does not call for mansions to be built for it; he should simply receive them at his home, without fearing that they will dirty it, for it will be only for an hour. Let him open the Book and begin reading from it without high-flown words and conceit, and without any sense of superiority, but with meekness and kindliness, rejoicing at the reading and at being listened to and understood; yourself loving the words, pause at times to explain some word ordinary folk do not understand. Have no worry, for they will understand everything: the hearts of the Orthodox will understand it all! Read to them about Abraham and Sarah, Isaac and Rebecca, about Jacob going to Laban and wrestling with God in a dream and then saying, "How dreadful is this place", and you will strike a chord in the peasant's devout mind. Read to them, especially to the children, how the brothers sold into bondage their own brother Joseph, a sweet youth, visionary and great prophet, and told their father he had been devoured by a wild beast, and showed him the youth's bloodstained clothes. Read to them of the brothers going down to Egypt afterwards for corn, and of Joseph, already in high favour at court and unrecognised by them, tormenting and accusing them, keeping back his brother Benjamin, while loving them all the time: "I love you, and, in loving you, I torment you." For he kept recollecting his past life, his being sold to the merchants at a well in the burning wilderness, and his weeping and beseeching his brothers, wringing his hands, not to sell him into bondage in a strange land; now, on seeing them again after so many years, he loved them again with a boundless love, but harassed and tormented them while loving them. And then he turned himself about from them, unable to bear the suffering of his heart, flung himself on his bed, and wept. Then he wiped his tears, went out to them, joyful and radiant and made himself known to them:

"I am Joseph your brother!" Let the priest go on to read how the aged Jacob rejoiced at learning that his dear boy was still alive and went down to Egypt, leaving his homeland and dying in a foreign land, uttering in his last words a great prophecy which during all his lifetime had lain mysteriously dormant in that meek and timid heart: from his offspring, from Judah, would come the hope of the world, the peace-maker and saviour! Fathers and teachers, forgive me and be not wroth with me for my engaging in childish talk about things you have long known and can teach me a hundred times better and more skilfully. It is my ardour that makes me speak in this way, so forgive me my tears, for I love that Book! Let him shed tears too, the priest of God, and he will see that the hearts of his listeners will expand in response. Only a small seed is needed, a tiny seed: plant it in the heart of the common man and it will not die, but live on there throughout his life, concealed within its recesses, in the midst of the gloom and the foulness of his sins, like a ray of light, a great token of remembrance. There's no need at all for much teaching and expounding, for he will simply take it all in. Do you think the common folk will not understand? Try also reading to them the moving and enthralling story of the fair Esther and the haughty Vashti; or the wonderful account of the prophet Jonah in the whale's belly. Neither should you forget the parables of Our Lord, mostly according to the Gospel of St. Luke (which is what I did), and then from the Acts of the Apostles, the conversion of Saul (that without fail, without fail!) and, finally, from the Lives of the Saints, say, the Life of Alexei, Man of God, and then Mary of Egypt, the greatest of the great, the joyful sufferer, seer of God and bearer of Christ in her heart—and these simple tales will touch them to the heart. And only one hour a week is needed even though his stipend is small, a single hour. He will see for himself that our people are kindly and grateful, and will repay him a hundredfold; mindful of their priest's zeal and his moving words, they will of their own accord help him in his field and in his house, and will pay him more respect than ever before: thus will his stipend increase. It is so simple a matter that we are sometimes afraid even to mention it for fear of being laughed at, and yet how true it all is! He who has no belief in God will never believe in God's people. But he who has faith in God's people will also behold his holiness even if he has never before believed in it. Only the people and their future power of the spirit will convert our atheists, who have lost touch with their native soil. And what is the use of Christ's word unless we set the example? Without the word of God, the people are doomed, for they yearn in soul for the Word and for all that is seen as good and beautiful. Long ago, in the days of my youth, almost forty years ago, Father Anfim and I walked the length and breadth of Russia, collecting alms for our monastery, and we spent one night on the bank of a big river in the company of some fishermen. We were joined by a handsome young peasant of about eighteen, who was in a hurry to get to his job next day working as a barge-tracker for some merchant. I noticed his clear and tender gaze as he looked before himself. It was a warm, light and calm night in July; a mist was rising from the broad and cool expanse of the river, and at times we could hear the soft splashing of fish. The birds were silent; it was the hush of beautiful night with everything praying to God. Only the two of us, the peasant lad and I, were not asleep, and we fell to speaking of the beauty of God's world and the great mystery of it all. Every blade of grass, every little insect, ant and golden bee—each of them has a marvellous knowledge of its path, and, though without intellect, testified to the mystery of God as a constant part of it. I could see that the dear lad's heart was glowing. He told me that he loved the woods and their wild birds: he was a bird-catcher, who understood every bird call, and could decoy any bird. "I know of nothing better than being in a forest," he said, "and all things are good." "Indeed," I replied, "all things are good and fair, because truth is all-pervading. Consider," I said to him, "the horse, that great animal which stands so close to man, or the lowly and pensive ox, which feeds him and works for him; consider their faces: what meekness, what attachment to man, who often beats them without mercy, what gentleness and trustfulness, what beauty they express. It is even moving to know that there is no sin in them, for everything but man is perfect and without sin, and

381

Christ was with them even before he came to us." "But," asked the youth, "can Christ really be with them?" "How could it be otherwise," I said to him, "since the Word is for all; all creation, all creatures, and every leaf pants after the Lord, sings God's glory, weeps to Christ, and, unbeknown to itself, does so through the mystery of their sinless life. Out there in the forest," I said to him, "wanders the terrible bear, dreadful and fierce but yet not to blame for being so." And I told him how a bear once came upon a great saint, who had found asylum in a little cell in a forest. The saintly man felt loving kindness for the animal, went up fearlessly to it, and gave it a piece of bread: "Go on your way," he said to the bear, "Christ be with you", and the fierce animal went obediently and meekly away, without doing him any harm. The lad was delighted by the bear going away without doing any harm, and that Christ was with him, too. "Oh, how good that is," he said, "how good and beautiful are all of God's works!" He fell into a quiet and sweet reverie. I saw that he had understood. He slept beside me, and his slumber was peaceful and sinless. May God bless the young! And I prayed for him before falling asleep myself. O Lord, send peace and light to thy people!

(c) *Reminiscences of the Starets Zossima's Adolescence and Youth While Still in the World. The Duel*

I spent a long time, almost eight years, in the Cadet Corps in St. Petersburg, my new surroundings obliterating many of my childhood impressions, though I forgot nothing of them. Instead, I acquired so many new habits and even opinions that I turned into a cruel, absurd and almost savage creature. I did acquire a superficial gloss of politeness and society manners together with a knowledge of French, but all of us, including myself, treated the soldiers in our service as so many cattle. I was perhaps worse than the rest, for I was more impressionable than my comrades. On receiving our commissions, we felt ready to spill our blood for the honour of our regiment, but hardly any of us realised the meaning of true honour; even had we learnt it, we would have been the first to ridicule it. We took almost pride in drink, rowdiness and dare-devilry. I don't say we were evil; all those young men were really good fellows, but their behaviour was reprehensible, mine being the worst. The main reason was that I had come into some money, so that, with all the abandon of youth, I gave myself up to a life of pleasure, into which I flung myself headlong and without restraint. Strange to say, I did a lot of reading then, even deriving great pleasure from books; however, the Bible was practically the only book I hardly ever opened at that time, though I never parted with it, always carrying it with me. Indeed, I treasured the Book, without being aware of it, "for an hour, and a day, and a month, and a year". After four years of this kind of army life, I found myself at last in the town of K., where my regiment was stationed at the time. The social life there was varied, bustling and gay, and marked by hospitality and wealth; I was well received everywhere, for I was lively by nature and, besides, I was reputed to be in comfortable circumstances, which means not a little in society. Then something took place that was the prelude to everything. I grew attached to a beautiful young girl, intelligent and virtuous, sunny and high-minded, and the daughter of esteemed parents. They were people of note, wealth and influence, who received me with warmth and cordiality. I imagined that the girl regarded me with favour. the mere thought of which set my heart aflame. Later I saw and realised that I was perhaps not so much passionately in love with her as full of admiration of her intelligence and elevated mind, for one could not feel otherwise. My vanity, however, prevented me from proposing to her at the time: it seemed hard on me, and galling, to have to give up the pleasures of my un-trammelled and licentious bachelor life while I was still so young and, moreover, with ample funds. Yet I did hint several times as to my intentions, though I put off taking the decisive step. Then I was unexpectedly seconded to another uyezd for two months. When I returned, I learnt that the girl had, in the meantime, married a wealthy local landowner, who, though my senior in years, was still comparatively young, and with excellent connections in the capital and in society, which I had not, a most well-bred man, and, besides, well educated, education being something I lacked completely. I was so overwhelmed by this sudden turn of events that I went quite out of my senses. The main thing was that, as I learnt at the time, the young landowner had been betrothed to her for quite some time and that I had often met him at her home, but, in my blind vanity, had failed to notice anything. It was this that mortified me most: how could I have overlooked something that was common knowledge? I was overcome with some sudden and irrepressible anger. With burning cheeks I began recalling how I had, on so many occasions, been on the verge of declaring my love to her and, as she had never even attempted to stop or dissuade me, I concluded that she must have been making fun of me. Of course, I realised on second thought that she had never done that; on the contrary, whenever I had begun to voice my feelings, she had invariably cut me short with some banter, or changed the subject. However, I was incapable of calm reflection at the time, and thirsted for vengeance. I recall with astonishment that my wrath and vengeful feeling were extremely distressing and alien to me because my easy-going nature precluded my harbouring rancour for long, which was why I had to keep my malevolence going, and I ended up by becoming repulsive and absurd. I bided my time till one day I was able to insult my "rival" in the presence of a large company, ostensibly over some irrelevant pretext, ridiculing an opinion he had voiced on important public event of the time (this was in 1826). I held him up to ridicule, so people said, in a witty and clever way, and then went on to demand an explanation from him, doing so in such ill-mannered terms that he accepted my challenge, despite the enormous difference between us, for I was so much his junior in years, of little consequence and inferior rank. I was later to learn for a fact that it was out of a feeling of jealousy that he had accepted my challenge; he had been somewhat jealous of me previously on account of his wife, who was his fiancée at the time. He now thought that if she learnt that he had swallowed my insult and not challenged me to a duel, she could not but come to despise him and waver in her love for him. I soon found a second—a fellow-officer, a lieutenant in our regiment. Although duelling was banned and severely punished in those days, it was even in vogue among the military—so strong and deep-rooted can brutal prejudices sometimes become. It was towards the end of June, and the encounter was due to be held somewhere in the outskirts of the town at seven o'clock the next morning, but there took place something that was to affect on my entire future. When I returned home that evening, in an ugly and savage temper, I flew into a rage with my batman Afanasy, and struck him in the face twice with all my strength, so that the blood streamed down his face. He had not been in my service long and I had sometimes struck him before, but never with such savage brutality. And believe me, dear, though forty years have passed since then, I still think of it with shame and pain. I went to bed, slept for three hours and woke up at daybreak. I got up at once since I did not want to sleep any more, went to the window, opened it—it faced the garden—and saw the sun rising. It was warm and beautiful, and the birds were breaking into song. "Why is it," I thought to myself, "that I have a feeling of shame and disgrace in my heart? Is it because I am about to shed blood?" No, I thought, that's not why. Am I afraid of death, afraid of being killed? Not at all, not at all— And I suddenly realised what it was: the beating I had given Afanasy the evening before! The scene arose before my eyes as though it was being re-acted: there he was in front of me while I struck him in the face as hard as I could, while he stood stiffly to attention, his head erect, his eyes fixed blankly on me as though on the parade ground, reeling from every blow but not daring to raise a hand to protect himself—and that was what a man had been reduced to —and here was a man beating a fellow-creature! What a crime! I felt as though a sharp dagger was piercing my heart. I stood as one bereft of reason, while the sun shone on, the leaves were rejoicing and gleaming in its rays, and the birds—the birds were praising the Lord— I covered my face with my hands, flung myself on my bed and burst into tears. And then I recalled my brother Markel and his parting words to our servants: "Why should you wait on me, my

385

dear ones? What have I done to deserve your love? Am I worthy of that?" "Indeed, am I worthy of that?" was the question that flashed suddenly through my mind. After all, what had I done to deserve that another man, one, like me, created in God's image, should serve me? For the first time in my life the question burned my brain. "Mother, my dearest one, each one of us is at fault to all men for everything, only people don't realise that. If they did—life would be a paradise at once!" "Dear Lord," I thought as I wept, "could that, too, be false? In truth, I was perhaps more at fault to all others than anyone, and certainly worse than anyone else in the world!" And I suddenly saw the whole truth in its full light: what was I about to do? I was out to kill a man, a good, intelligent and honourable man, who had done me no wrong. By killing him I would deprive his wife of happiness for the rest of her life, and thus torment and kill her, too. I lay there on the bed, my face buried in the pillow, and heedless of the passage of time. Suddenly my second, the lieutenant, called for me with the pistols. "Oh," he said, "I see you're up already. That's fine! It's time to set out. Let's be off!" I felt quite at a loss as to what I should do, but we went out to get into the carriage. "Just a moment," I said to him. "I'll be back directly. I've forgotten my purse." I ran back alone to my rooms and went straight to Afanasy's cubicle. "Afanasy," I said, "I struck you twice in the face yesterday; please forgive me." He gave a violent start, as though in fear, and stared back at me. I saw that my words were not enough, not at all enough, so I suddenly fell at his feet, in full uniform as I was, my forehead touching the ground. "Forgive me!" I said. At that he looked utterly confounded. "Your honour," he stammered, "sir, you shouldn't—I—I'm not worth it—" and burst into tears himself, as I had done, and, covering his face with his hands, turned to the window, shaken with sobs. I ran back to my fellow-officer and jumped into the carriage. "On we go!" I cried. "Ever seen a victor? Well, here is one before you!" I was in such an ecstasy that I went on laughing and talking, talking all the way, I don't remember what about. He looked at me: "Well, old man," he said, "you've certainly got spunk. I can see you'll stand up for the honour of the uniform!" So we reached our destination, where we were already awaited. We took up our positions at twelve paces apart. The toss had given him the first shot. I stood facing him blithely, without batting an eyelid, with love for him in my heart, for I knew what I would do. He fired, the bullet grazing my cheek and ear. "Thank God," I cried, "you haven't killed a man!" I clutched my pistol, turned back and flung it high into the trees. "There's where you belong!" I cried. Turning to my opponent, I said: "Sir, forgive me, stupid young fellow that I am, for the unprovoked insult and having forced you to fire at me. I'm ten times worse than you are, perhaps, even more. Tell that to the lady you esteem more than anyone else in the world." As soon as I said this, the three began shouting at me: "Really," said my opponent, who was quite annoyed, "if you didn't want a duel, why did you trouble me to come here?" "Yesterday," I replied blithely, "I was still stupid; today I know better." "As for yesterday," he said, "I can believe you, but as for today, I find it hard to agree with your opinion." "Bravo," I cried, clapping my hands, "I agree with you there, too. I've deserved it!" "Are you going to fire, sir, or not?" "I'm not," I replied, "but if you wish, you may fire at me again, though it would be better for you not to." The seconds were shouting, too, mine especially. "How can you disgrace your regiment like that, sir, by facing your opponent and then begging for his forgiveness? If I'd only known!" So I faced them all, no longer laughing. "Gentlemen," I said, "is it really so extraordinary in these times to find a man who will repent of his own folly and publicly confess to the wrong he has done?" "But not at a duel," my second exclaimed again. "Ah," I said, "that's exactly what's so surprising, for I should have done so as soon as we got here, before he fired his shot, and then I might not have led him into a great and mortal sin, but we ourselves have brought things to such an awful pass in society that it was almost impossible for me to do that; only after I faced his shot at twelve paces could my words have had any significance to him. Had I spoken as soon as we arrived here and before he had fired, he would have simply said that I was a coward, who had been frightened by the pistols and should not be listened to. Gentlemen," I cried suddenly, speaking straight from the heart, "look about you at God's gifts: the clear sky, the pure air, the tender grass, the birds. Nature is beautiful and blameless, while we, we alone, are godless and foolish, and don't realise that life is a paradise. We have only to want to understand that and it will at once be fulfilled in all its beauty, and we shall embrace one another in tears." I would have said more, but could not, my breath failing me, everything within me felt so fresh and sweet, and my heart was full of a happiness I had never felt before in my life. "It's all very proper and reasonable," my opponent said, "and you are certainly a most original person." "Laugh away," I said to him, laughing too, "but later you'll have words of praise for me." "Why," he said, "I'm quite ready to praise you now. Let's shake hands, for I believe you are really sincere." "No," I said, "not now, but perhaps later when I've become a better man and earned your esteem; then you'll shake hands with me, and do well." We went home, my second upbraiding me all the time, while I kept embracing him. When it came to the knowledge of my fellow-officers, they met to pass judgement on me the same day: "He's besmirched the uniform," they said, "so he must resign his commission." There were some who stood up for me: "He did face the shot," they said. "Yes, he did, but he was afraid to go on, and apologised during a duel." "But," my defenders object, "if he'd been afraid of going on, he'd have first fired and then asked for forgiveness, but he threw his loaded pistol into the trees. No, there's something else in this, something most unusual." I listened, feeling happy as I looked at them. "My dear friends and comrades," I said, "don't worry about my resigning my commission, because I sent in my papers this morning. As soon as I get my discharge from the service I shall enter a monastery. That's why I've resigned my commission." They all burst into loud laughter on hearing this. "Why didn't you say so before? Well, that explains everything. We can't pass judgement on a monk." They kept on laughing, not in scorn but in gay fashion. They all grew suddenly fond of me, even my most severest accusers, and could not make too much of me during the following month before my discharge came. "Oh, you monk!" they would say. They all had kind words for me and tried to dissuade me from entering a monastery, even pitying me: "What are you doing to yourself?" "No," some said, "he's a brave fellow, he faced the pistol shot, and he could have fired himself, but on the previous night he had a dream about becoming a monk, and that's why he's doing it." Almost the same change came over the town's society. I had never been an object of particular attention in the past, though I had been received cordially enough, but now I was suddenly known to all and was now invited to their homes: they did make fun of me, but could not help loving me. I shall observe here that although the duel was on all tongues, the army authorities hushed it up, because my opponent was a close kinsman of our general's and since no blood had been shed, and the entire matter resembled a jest, and, besides, I had resigned my commission, it was all actually taken as a jest. And then I began to speak out fearlessly, despite the ridicule, for, after all, it was kindly and without malice. Such talk took place mostly at evening parties, in the society of ladies, for it was they who were the best listeners and made their menfolk listen too. "But how can one be at fault for all?" they would ask, laughing in my face. "Can I, for instance, be at fault for you?" "But," I would reply, "how can you possibly understand it when the whole world has long embarked on a different road and we accept a downright lie as truth and, indeed, demand the same lie from others? Here I have, for once in my life, acted sincerely, and what does that lead you up to? Why, you look upon me as a freak. You may be fond of me," I said, "yet you make fun of me." "But how can we help being fond of such a man?" my hostess said, laughing aloud. The room was full of people. All of a sudden, I saw the young lady whose husband I had challenged and whom I had been planning to make my bride rise to her feet from among the other ladies. I had not noticed her arrival. She came up to me with hand outstretched. "May I tell you," she said, "that I am the first not to laugh at you, but, on the contrary, I want to thank you with tears of gratitude and express my esteem for the way you acted then." Her husband, too, came up, and then they all surrounded me and almost kissed me. I felt overjoyed, but my attention was especially attracted by an elderly gentleman who also approached me. Though I knew him by name, I had never made his acquaintance or exchanged a single word with him until that evening.

(d) *The Mysterious Visitor*

He had long been a government official in our town, where he held a very important position. He commanded general respect, was wealthy and known for his charitable works, having donated considerable sums to the alms-house and the orphanage, and spent a great deal on charity in secret, without any publicity, a fact that became known only after his death. He was about fifty, almost severe of mien and not given to conversation. He had been married for about ten years, and his wife, who was still young, had born him three children. I was sitting alone in my rooms on the following evening when the door suddenly opened and this gentleman walked in.

I should mention that I was no longer living in my old quarters, but had moved after sending in my resignation from the regiment. My landlady was an old woman, the widow of a civil servant, who had let me some rooms in her house, with service. I had moved from my old quarters simply because, on my return from the duel, I had sent Afanasy back to his company, for I was ashamed to look him in the face after the way I had behaved towards him—so prone is the ordinary man of the world to feel ashamed even of some of his finest acts.

"I've listened to you with great interest in different houses for the last few days," said my visitor, "and I'd like to make your acquaintance, as I am anxious to speak to you in some detail. Can you render me that great service, sir?" "Why, with the greatest pleasure, sir. Indeed, I shall consider it an honour," I said, feeling almost dismayed, so deep was the impression he produced from the first moment of his appearance in my room. For although people listened to me and were interested in what I had to say, no one had ever approached me before with so earnest and severe an air. And such a man had called on me of his own accord. He sat down. "I can see," he said, "that you're a man of great strength of character, for you were not afraid to serve the truth in a matter in which you risked incurring universal contempt for championing the truth." "Perhaps your praise is excessive, sir," I said. "No," he replied, "I'm not exaggerating. Believe me, it is far harder to perform an act like that than you think. That's what has impressed me so much and why I've come to see you. Can you, please, describe to me, if, that is, you don't think I'm being unduly inquisitive, what you felt at the moment you decided to apologise at the duel, if you can still remember it? Don't think me frivolous. On the contrary, in asking you this question, I have a secret motive of my own, which I will perhaps explain to you later if it please God to make us more closely acquainted."

I was looking him straight in the face as he spoke and suddenly felt I could trust him implicitly. Besides, my own curiosity was strongly aroused too, for I sensed there was some strange secret in his soul.

"You ask me to describe exactly what I felt at the moment when I asked my opponent to forgive me," I answered, "but first, I'd better tell you something I haven't yet told anyone else." And I told him what had passed between Afanasy and me, and how I had bowed down to the ground before him. "From that you can see for yourself," I concluded, "that it was easier for me at the duel, for a beginning had been made at home, and once I had started out on that road, the rest was not only easy, but also brought me joy and happiness."

After hearing me out, he gave me a very friendly look. "All this," he said, "is most interesting and I'll come to see you again and again." And after that, he began calling on me almost every evening. We would have become very close friends if he had ever spoken of himself. But he scarcely ever did so, but kept questioning me about myself. Yet I grew very fond of him and spoke to him about my feelings with perfect frankness for, I thought to myself: what do I care about his secret when I can see that he's a righteous man? He was, besides, such a serious-minded man and so much my senior, yet he would come to see a youngster like me and treat him as an equal. I learnt many useful things from him, for he was a man of high intelligence. "I've long thought that life is a paradise," he said to me suddenly. "It's always in my thoughts," he added unexpectedly. He looked at me with a smile. "I'm even more convinced of it than you are," he said. "You'll learn why later." As I listened to him, I thought to myself: "I suppose he wants to reveal some secret of his to me." "Paradise," he said, "lies concealed within every one of us; it now lies hidden within me, too; if I so wish, it will arrive for me on the morrow, and will remain with me for the rest of my life." I saw that he was speaking with deep feeling and was looking mysteriously at me, as though questioning me. "You were quite right in saying that every man is at fault for all other men and for everything, apart from his own sins; it's remarkable how you could have suddenly taken in that idea in all its fullness. It is indeed true that, when people have taken in that idea, the Kingdom of Heaven will become a reality to them and not just a dream." "But," I exclaimed sadly, "when will that come about? And will it ever come to pass? Isn't it nothing but a dream?" "Oh," he said, "I see you don't believe it. You preach it but you don't believe it yourself. You should know that this dream, as you call it, will undoubtedly come to pass—you can be certain of that, but not now, since every action obeys its own law. It's a process in the mind, something psychological. To recreate the world anew, men should themselves undergo a change of heart. Until you have actually become a brother to every other man, the brotherhood of men will not come about. No scientific advance and no common interest will ever make people able to share out their property and their rights equitably. They will never get enough to satisfy them and they will always murmur, envy and destroy one another. When will that come about, you ask me. Come it will, but first the period of human *isolation* will have to end." "What sort of isolation do you mean?" I asked. "Why," he replied, "the kind that is now prevalent and especially in our time, but has not yet reached its ultimate development, and its end is not yet in sight. For today everyone still strives to maintain his own personality as much as possible; everyone still wishes to experience within himself alone the fullness of life and yet, instead of achieving that fullness, all his efforts merely lead to complete self-destruction; instead of complete self-realisation they fall into complete isolation. All men have split up into separate units; everyone withdraws into his own hole, shuns his neighbour, goes into hiding and conceals everything he possesses, ending up in alienating himself from others and repelling them. He amasses wealth on his own, and imagines he is strong and secure, without realising, in his madness, that the more he amasses, the deeper he sinks into self-destroying impotence. For he is used to relying on himself alone and has developed into a separate unit cut off from the whole. He has accustomed his mind to have no faith in help from others, in men and mankind, and is only fearful of losing his money and the privileges he has acquired. Today the human mind is sceptically beginning to lose the awareness that the individual's true security lies, not in his isolated efforts but in universal human solidarity. But the time will certainly come for this dreadful isolation to end, and it will be generally realised, all at once, how unnaturally men have cut themselves off from one another. Such will be the trend of the times, and people will marvel at having been steeped in murky darkness for so long, and failing to see the light. And then shall appear the sign of the Son of man in heaven— But till then we must still hold the banner high and, even if he has to do it on his own, man has to set at least a single example and bring his soul out of its solitude so as to work for some great act of brotherly love, even if that means being regarded as a saintly fool. He must do so that the great idea shall not die—"

It was in such fervent and high-minded discourse that we spent evening after evening. I even gave up my social calls and visited the homes of my friends and acquaintances ever less frequently; besides, I was no longer in fashion to the same extent as before. I'm not saying this in condemnation of my friends, for they continued to like me and treat me good-naturedly, but simply to point out that vogue, in fact, wields no small sway in society, something which has to be acknowledged. I came to regard my mysterious visitor with admiration, for besides enjoying his high intelligence, I could not help feeling that he was nurturing some secret intention in his heart and was perhaps preparing himself for something extraordinary. Perhaps the thing he liked about me, too, was that I displayed no curiosity about his secret and did not question him about it, either directly or indirectly. But at last I noticed that he himself seemed to be anxious to reveal something to me. At any rate, this became fairly obvious about a month after he first began visiting me. "Do you know," he once asked me, "that people in town are becoming very curious about us both and are wondering why I see you so often? But let them wonder, for *everything will soon come to light*." He would sometimes grow agitated, and whenever that happened he would almost always get up and leave. He would sometimes fix a long and piercing look on me and I could not help thinking: "Now he is on the verge of saying something," but he would suddenly begin talking about something ordinary and familiar. He also began complaining frequently of headaches. And then one evening, after he had been talking with great fervour for a long time, he suddenly and to my great surprise turned pale, his face grew contorted and he looked me straight in the eye.

"What's wrong?" I asked. "Are you ill?"

He had, in fact, just been complaining of a headache.

"I—you know—I—I'm a murderer!"

He said this with a smile, but his face had turned as white as a sheet. "Why is he smiling?" was the thought that suddenly crossed my mind before I was able to realise anything properly. I turned pale myself.

"What are you saying?" I shouted.

"You see," he said with the same pale smile, "what it has cost me to utter the first word. Now I've done that and, I think, I'm on the right path. I'll follow it."

For a long time I could not believe him, and I did not when he first told me the story. That came only after he had been to see me three days in succession and told me everything in detail. My first thought was that he must be mad, but I ended up by finally becoming convinced, to my great grief and astonishment, that what he had told me was true. Fourteen years earlier, he had committed a heinous crime: he had murdered the widow of a rich landowner, a young and beautiful woman, who owned a house in our town. He had fallen passionately in love with her, declared his love, and tried to persuade her to marry him. But she had already given her heart to another, an army officer of high rank and good social standing, who was away on active service at the time, though she was expecting him to return soon. She rejected his proposal and asked him not to call on her again. His calls ended, but since he knew his way about her house, he gained entry into it at night through the garden and by the roof with great daring, for he ran the risk of discovery. But, as so often happens, crimes committed with extraordinary audacity are successful more often than not. Entering the attic through a skylight, he made his way to the living quarters by the attic stairs, knowing that the door at the bottom of the ladder was, through the carelessness of the servants, not always locked. He had correctly counted on this oversight. Making his way in the dark to the living quarters, he entered her bedroom, where a lamp was burning before the icon. It so happened that her two young maids had gone off without permission to attend a birthday party in the same street; the other servants slept in the servant's quarters or in the kitchen, in the basement. The sight of her asleep inflamed his passion and a vindictive and jealous rage gained possession of his heart; beside himself he ran up to her bed like a drunken man and plunged a knife into her heart before she could utter a cry. Then with fiendish and criminal intent, he contrived to make suspicion fall on the servants: he did not scruple to take her purse, open the chest of drawers with the keys from under her pillow and abstract some articles from it, just as some ignorant servant might have done, leaving the valuable securities behind and taking only the money. He also took some of the larger gold articles and left behind the smaller articles ten times as valuable. Besides, he also took some other articles, as keepsakes for himself, but of that later. Having done that dreadful thing, he returned the way he had entered. Neither on the next day, when the alarm was raised, nor at any time in his life did it occur to anyone to suspect the actual criminal! Besides, no one knew that he was in love with her, for he had always been of a reserved and unsociable disposition, and had no friend to open up his heart to. He was simply regarded as an acquaintance of the murdered woman, and not even a close acquaintance at that, for he had not visited her during the previous fortnight. Suspicion at once fell on her serf-servant Pyotr and as it happened, all the circumstantial evidence pointed to him, for he knew—and his mistress had made no secret of it—that, since she was to send off one of her peasants for army service, she had chosen him, as he had no relatives, and was of bad behaviour, besides. While he was drunk in a tavern, he had been heard to angrily threaten to kill her. Two days before her death, he had run off and lived in town at some unknown address. On the day after the murder, he was found lying dead drunk on the highway outside the town, with a knife in his pocket; for some unknown cause, his right hand was bloodstained. He claimed that his nose had been bleeding, but no one believed him. The two servant girls, on the other hand, confessed that they had gone to a party and that the front door had been left open against their return. There were many other similar clues which pointed to the innocent servant, and led to his arrest. He was put on trial for murder, but a week later he fell ill with a fever, and died in hospital without regaining consciousness. That was the end of the matter, and all were convinced—the authorities, the judges and society at large—that the crime had been committed by no one but the servant, who had died during his trial. Then the punishment began.

The mysterious visitor, now my friend, told me that, at the beginning, he was not in the least disturbed by qualms of conscience. He felt unhappy for a long time, but not for that reason, but because he was remorseful at having murdered the woman he loved and would never see again, and that, having murdered her, he had also killed his love, though the fires of passion still burned within him. He never gave thought at the time to having shed innocent blood, and to the murder of a human being. He could never have become reconciled to the idea that his victim could have become another man's wife, which was why he for a long time remained convinced at heart that he could not have acted otherwise. At first, he had been worried by the arrest of the servant, but the prisoner's sudden illness and subsequent death set his mind at ease, for the man quite obviously died (he argued at the time) not because of his arrest or his fright but because of a chill he had contracted while on the run, when he had been lying dead drunk on the ground all night. The theft of the articles and the money troubled him little, for (he argued again) the theft had been committed, not for gain but to avert suspicion. The sum stolen was small and he even donated it all, and even more, to the alms-house which had just then been founded in our town. He did this on purpose to set his mind at rest about the theft, and the strangest thing about it was that for a time, for a long time, in fact, he really was at peace with himself—he told me so himself. It was then that he began his very active career in the civil service. He volunteered for a very troublesome and difficult assignment, which occupied him for two years, and, as a man of strong character, at times he almost forgot about the crime he had committed; when he did recall it, he tried to dismiss it from his thoughts. He also did a great deal of philanthropic work, founding and endowing charities of every kind in our town; his name became known in Moscow and St. Petersburg, too, and he was elected to philanthropic societies there. Nevertheless, he began brooding painfully over the past, the strain becoming too great to bear. It was just then that he was attracted by a beautiful and intelligent girl, whom he soon married in the vain hope that marriage would dispel his dejection and that, by entering upon a new life and by zealously performing his duty towards his wife and children, he would find full escape from his old memories. But the reverse occurred. Already during the first month of his marriage he began to be worried continually by the thought: "My wife loves me, but what if she knew?" When she told him that she was going to have a baby, their first, he looked troubled: "I've created a life, but have taken another life away." More children were born: "How dare I love them, teach them, and bring them up? How can I speak to them of virtue, I who have shed blood?" They were beautiful children and he longed to caress them.

"But I can't look at their bright innocent faces: I'm unworthy." At last, he began to be bitterly and ominously haunted by the blood of his murdered victim, by the young life he had destroyed, by the blood crying out for vengeance. He began to have dreadful dreams. But, a man of stout heart, he put up with his suffering for a long time: "I shall atone for everything through this secret torment," he thought. However, the hope, too, was in vain: the longer it continued, the more intense did his suffering grow. His philanthropic work was winning him respect in society, though people were daunted by his stern and gloomy character, but the more he was respected, the more unbearable it was for him. He told me he had been thinking of suicide. But instead, he became obsessed by another dream, which he considered insane and impossible at first, but which finally became so obsessive that he could not rid himself of it: it was about rising up to confront the public to confess that he had committed a murder. For three years he carried the thought in his heart and he imagined all kinds of ways of carrying it out. At last, he came to believe with all his heart that, by publicly confessing to his crime, he would most certainly regain his peace of mind and set it at rest once and for all. Though he had come to this conclusion, his heart was filled with terror, for how was he to carry out his decision? And then the incident of my duel had taken place. "Looking at you, I made up my mind," he said to me. I looked back at him.

"Do you really mean," I cried, throwing up my hands, "that such a minor incident could have evoked such resolve in you?"

"My resolve had been mounting for three years," he replied. "That incident of yours merely gave the necessary impetus. When I looked at you, I reproached myself and envied you," he said to me almost in a severe tone.

"But you won't be believed," I observed. "Fourteen years have gone by."

"I have proof, irrefutable proof. I'll present it."

I wept then as I embraced him.

"Advise me on one thing, only one thing!" he said to me (as if everything now depended on me). "What about my wife and children? My wife will probably die of grief, and though my children will not lose their rank as noblemen, or their estate, they'll be the children of a convict, serving a life sentence. And what a memory, what a memory I shall leave behind in their hearts!"

I was silent.

"And to part with them, leaving them for ever? It is for ever, you know, for ever!"

I sat there praying in silence. At last, I rose to my feet. I felt fear in my heart.

"Well?" he asked, looking at me.

"Go," I said, "and confess in public. Everything passes; only the truth will remain. When they grow up, your children will understand how much magnanimity there was in your great resolve."

He left me as though his mind was really made up. Yet he kept calling on me every evening for over a fortnight, still preparing himself but unable to take the decisive step. He was tormenting my heart. One day he would come fully determined and say with deep feeling:

"I know I will gain paradise as soon as I confess. I've been in hell for fourteen years. I want to suffer. I shall accept my suffering, and begin a new life. You can go through life in false-hood, but there's no turning back. I dare not love my neigh-bour now, let alone my children. Dear God, surely my children will understand what I've gone through, and will not censure me! God lies, not in strength but in truth."

"Your great act of expiation will be understood by all," I said, "if not now, then later. For you have served the truth, the higher truth, which is not of this earth—"

And he would go away seemingly comforted, but he would come again the next day, pale and angry, and say scathingly:

"Every time I come to see you, you look at me with such curiosity, as if to ask, 'Haven't you confessed yet?' Give me some respite. Don't despise me too much. It's not as easy as you think. Perhaps I won't do it at all. You wouldn't denounce me then, would you?"

But, as a matter of fact, far from looking at him with foolish curiosity, I was afraid even to glance at him at all. I was quite ill from anxiety, and my heart was full of tears. I even could not sleep at night.

"I've just seen my wife," he went on. "Do you realise what a wife is? My children called out to me as I was leaving: 'Goodbye, Daddy. Hurry home to read *Children's Stories* to us.' No, you can't understand that! Another man's woes cannot make anyone wiser."

His eyes flashed and his lips quivered. Suddenly he struck the table with his fist so that the things on it jumped. It was the first time that so reserved a man had done such a thing.

"But is it at all necessary?" he cried. "Should I do it? No one was condemned by the court, no one was sentenced to penal servitude because of me and the servant died of natural causes. I've been punished by my suffering for the blood I shed. Besides, I won't be believed and no proof will ever convince them. Must I confess? Must I? I'm ready to suffer all my life long for the blood I've shed if only my wife and children are spared the shock. Would it be fair for them to face ruination through me? Are you sure we're not in error? Where does the truth lie? And will people recognise the truth? Will they appreciate it, respect it?"

"Good Heavens," I thought to myself, "at such a moment he thinks of other people's respect!" So sorry did I feel for him then that I believed I would share his fate if only it would bring him some relief. I could see he was beside himself. I was appalled, realising with all my soul, not only with my reason, what such resolve called for.

"Decide my fate!" he exclaimed again.

"Go and confess," I whispered to him. Though my voice was failing me, I whispered it firmly. Then I took up the New Testament from the table, the Russian translation, and showed him the Gospel of St. John, Chapter 12, Verse 24:

"Verily, verily, I say unto you, except a corn of wheat fall into the ground and die, it abideth alone; but if it die, it bringeth forth much fruit." I had read that verse before he came in.

He read it too.

"That's true," he said, but he smiled bitterly. "Yes," he said after a brief pause, "it's awful, the things you find in these books. It's easy to thrust them under another's nose. And who wrote them? Not men, surely?"

"The Holy Ghost wrote them," I said.

"It's easy for you to prattle like that," he said, smiling again, but this time almost with hatred.

I reopened the book at another place, and showed him the Epistle to the Hebrews, Chapter 10, Verse 31. He read out: "It is a fearful thing to fall into the hands of the living God."

He read it and flung down the book. He was even trembling all over.

"A fearful verse," he said. "You've chosen well, I must say." He rose from his chair. "Well," he said, "farewell. I may not come any more—we shall meet in heaven. So it's fourteen years since I 'fell into the hands of the living God'. That's how these fourteen years should be called, shouldn't they? Tomorrow I shall beseech those hands to release me—"

I wanted to embrace and kiss him, but I dared not—so distorted was his face and so sombre his look. He left. "Dear God," I thought, "what awaits that man!" I fell on my knees at the icon and wept for him before the Holy Virgin, our speedy mediator and helper. I had been kneeling like that for half an hour, praying in tears. It was already late, about midnight. Suddenly I saw the door open and he came in again. I felt surprised.

"Where have you been?" I asked.

"I think, I—I've forgotten something—my handkerchief, I think—" he said. "Well, even if I haven't forgotten anything, you won't mind my sitting down, will you?—"

He sat down on a chair. I stood over him. "Won't you sit down, too?" he said. I did so. We sat like that for a couple of minutes. He looked at me intently and suddenly smiled, I remember that well, then rose, embraced me warmly and kissed me.

"Remember," he said, "how I came to see you for a second

time. Do you hear? Remember that!"

It was the first time he had addressed me with the familiar *tu*. Then he left. "It will be tomorrow," I thought.

And so it was. I had no idea that evening that the next day was his birthday. I had not been out of doors for several days, so I could not have learnt it from anyone. He always gave big birthday parties, which were attended by the entire town. It was the same this time. And so after dinner, he walked into the middle of the room, a paper in his hand—a formal statement to the head of his department. And as that gentleman was present, he read it out there and then to the whole gathering. It contained a full account of the crime, in every detail. "I have cast myself out of the pale of society as a monster," he said in conclusion. "God has visited me—I want to suffer!" Then he produced and laid out on the table all the articles he thought would prove his crime, which he had kept for fourteen years: the gold articles belonging to the murdered woman, which he had taken to avert suspicion from himself; her locket and cross he had taken from her neck—with a portrait of her fiancé in the locket; her diary and, finally, two letters: her fiancé's letter to her about his speedy arrival and her reply, which she had begun but left unfinished on the table, intending to post it the next day. He had carried off the two letters—but why? Why had he kept them for fourteen years instead of destroying them as evidence against himself? And now here is what happened: they were all amazed and horrified, but no one would believe it, though they all listened with intense curiosity but they all thought that he was ill. A few days later it was definitely decided and agreed in every house that the unhappy man had gone mad. His superiors and the court authorities could not but institute criminal proceedings against him, but they soon dropped them: though the articles and letters he had produced gave them food for thought, but it was decided that even if they proved authentic, it was impossible to lay a charge of murder on the basis of that evidence alone. Besides, he could have obtained all those things from her as a friend of hers and a person who enjoyed her confidence. I heard afterwards, however, that the authenticity of the articles was proved by many of the murdered woman's friends and acquaintances, and that there was no doubt about them. But, again, the whole thing came to naught in the end. Five days later it was learnt that the sufferer had fallen ill and that his life was in danger. I cannot say what the illness was. It was rumoured that he had had a heart attack, but it also became known that, at his wife's insistence, the doctors had examined his mental condition and had come to the conclusion that he showed signs of insanity. I disclosed nothing though they rushed to question me, but for a long time they would not let me visit him, especially his wife. "It is you," she said to me, "who have unsettled him. He was always a gloomy man but during the last year he was seen to be unusually excited and do strange things, and then you came and ruined him. It was your endless discussions that brought it about, for he never left your room during a whole month." And it was not only his wife. Everyone in town pounced upon me and blamed me. "It's all your fault," they said. I kept silent but rejoiced at heart, for I could plainly see God's mercy to a man who had risen up and punished himself. But I could not believe in his insanity. At last, I was allowed to see him, for he insisted on taking leave of me. I went in and saw at once that not only his days but even his hours were numbered. He was weak, his face sallow, and his hands trembling. He was gasping for breath, but there was joy and elation in his eyes.

"I did it!" he said to me. "I've long been yearning to see you; why didn't you come sooner?"

I did not tell him I had not been allowed to see him.

"God has had pity on me and is calling me to him. I know I'm dying, but I feel happy and at peace for the first time after so many years. As soon as I'd done what had to be done I felt paradise in my heart. Now I dare to love my children and kiss them. I am not believed, and no one has believed me. Neither my wife nor the judges. Nor will my children ever believe in it. I see in that a sign of God's mercy to my children. I shall die and my name will be unslurred for them. Now I feel that God is near, and my heart rejoices as in paradise—I have done my duty."

He could not speak, he was gasping for breath, but pressed my hand warmly, looking fervently at me. But we did not talk for long, for his wife kept looking into the room while I was there. But he managed to whisper to me:

"Do you remember how I came back to you for a second time at midnight? I told you to remember it. Do you know what I came back for? It was to kill you!"

I gave a violent start.

"I went out from you that time into the darkness, and walked about the streets, struggling with myself. And suddenly, I felt such hatred for you that it was unbearable. 'No,' I thought, 'he's the only one who has tied my hands and is my judge, and I can't refuse to face my punishment tomorrow because he knows everything.' It wasn't that I was afraid you'd denounce me (the thought never even occurred to me), but I kept thinking: 'How could I face him again if I didn't make a clean breast of it?' And even if you'd been at the other extreme of the earth, as long as you were alive, I couldn't have endured the thought that you were alive, knew everything and were condemning me. I hated you as though you were the cause of it all, and were to blame for everything. I came back that time for I remembered that you had a dagger lying on the table. I sat down, asked you to sit down too and turned the matter over in my mind for a whole minute. If I had murdered you, it would be over with me even if I hadn't made my first crime known. But I was not thinking of that at all, and I didn't want to think of it at the moment. I just hated you and longed to avenge myself on you for everything. But the Lord vanquished the devil in my heart. I want you to know, however, that you were never closer to death."

He died a week later. The whole town followed his coffin to the graveside. The priest made a moving speech, the public lamenting the terrible illness that cut his days short. But the whole town turned against me, after the funeral, and even stopped receiving me. It is true that some, a few at first, but many more later on, began to believe his confession, and started calling on me frequently and questioning me with great interest and eargerness: for people love to see the downfall and disgrace of a righteous man. But I kept silent and soon left the town for good; five months later, by the grace of God, I entered upon the straight and glorious path, blessing the unseen finger which had shown it to me. To this day I have remembered Mikhail, the much-suffering servant of God, in my daily prayers.

3.

From the Discourses and Homilies of the *Starets* Zossima

(e) *Something About the Russian Monk and His Possible Significance*

Fathers and teachers, what is a monk? In the enlightened world, the word is nowadays uttered with derision by some, others using it even as a term of derogation. Things are becoming worse with the passage of time. It is true, alas it is true, that there are many idlers, gluttons, voluptuaries and insolent tramps among monks. Educated men of the world speak of this, saying: "You are idle and useless members of society. You live on the labour of others, you are shameless beggars." And yet think of the many meek and humble monks there are who yearn for solitude and fervent prayer in peace and quiet. These attract far less attention and are even passed over in silence, and how surprised many people would be were I to tell them that the salvation of the Russian land may well come again from these meek monks, who long for solitary prayer! For, in peace and quiet they are verily prepared "for an hour, and a day, and a month, and a year". In their solitude, they have kept the image of Christ pure and undistorted, kept it in the purity of God's truth, which they have received from the Fathers of old, the apostles and martyrs; when the time comes, they will reveal it to the sagging truth of the world. A great thought that. It is from the East that that star will shine forth.

That is how I see that monk; is that view false or arrogant? See whether, with the worldly and with everything in God's world that has elevated itself above the people, the image of God and His truth have been distorted? They possess science, but in science there is nothing but what is subordinate to the senses. The world of the spirit, however, the superior half of man's essence, is utterly rejected, dismissed with a kind of triumph, even with hatred. The world has proclaimed freedom, especially in recent times, but what do we see in that freedom of theirs: nothing but slavery and self-destruction! For the world says: "You have needs, so therefore satisfy them, for you have the same rights as the most wealthy and the most powerful. Do not be afraid to satisfy those needs, but even miltiply them." Such is the present-day doctrine of the world, and it is in it that freedom is seen. And what does that right to multiply needs lead up to? To the *isolation* and spiritual suicide of the rich, and to envy and murder among the poor, for the rights have been granted while the means of satisfying needs have not been indicated. It is averred that the world is getting more and more united and growing into a brotherly community through the contraction of distances and the transmission of ideas through the air. Alas, no faith can be placed in that kind of unity. By understanding freedom as the multiplication and the rapid satisfaction of needs, people distort their own nature, since such an interpretation merely engenders many senseless and foolish desires, habits and most absurd conceits. They live only to envy others, to engage in carnality and ostentation. They regard dinners, horses, carriages, rank and slaves to serve them as necessities, to satisfy which they sacrifice life, honour and love of mankind; they even kill themselves if they cannot satisfy them. We see the same thing among those who are not wealthy, while the poor drown their unsatisfied needs and envy in drink. But they will soon drown them in blood instead of drink—that's where they are being led. Is such a man free, I ask you? I knew a "fighter for an idea", who himself told me that when he had been deprived of tobacco in prison he had been made so wretched by this privation that he almost was ready to betray his "idea" just to get a little tobacco. And it is such a man who says, "I'm setting out to fight for mankind!" But whither can such a man set out, and what is he capable of? He may act on the spur of the moment, but he possesses no fortitude. It is no wonder that, instead of gaining freedom, people have fallen into slavery, and instead of serving the cause of brotherly love and the union of humanity, they have, on the contrary, sunk into *separateness* and isolation, as my mysterious visitor and teacher said to me in my youth. And that is why the idea of service to humanity, of brotherhood and of the oneness of mankind is becoming extinct in the world. Indeed, the idea is even met with derision, for how can a man eschew his habits, whither can such a slave set out if he is so accustomed to satisfying the countless needs he has created for himself? Living in isolation, what does he care for the whole of mankind. And a stage has been reached in which more and more things have been amassed but there is ever less joy in life.

The monastic way is another matter. People even make mock of obedience, fasting and prayer, yet it is only through them that the way lies towards genuine and true freedom: I eliminate all superfluous and unnecessary needs, subdue my proud and selfish will and chastise it through obedience, and, with God's help, thereby attain freedom of spirit, and with it spiritual joy! Which of the two is more capable of conceiving a great idea and serving it: the rich man in his isolation, or the man *liberated* from the tyranny of things and habits? The monk is reproved for his solitude: "You have sought solitude to find salvation within the monastery walls, and lost sight of brotherly service to humanity." But we shall see which will be more zealous in brotherly love. They fail to see that it is they, not we, who live in isolation. Since olden times it is we that have brought forth national leaders from our midst, so why should that not happen again now? The selfsame meek and humble fasters and observers of silence will rise up again and go forth to work for a great cause. The salvation of Russia lies in the people. And the Russian monasteries have, since time immemorial, been with the people. If the people live in isolation, then so do we. The people believe in our way, and the unbelieving leader will never achieve anything here in Russia, even if he is sincere at heart and an intellectual genius. Remember that. The people will meet the atheist and overcome him, while Russia will be united and Orthodox. Therefore, care for the people and protect their hearts. Educate them gently. That is your great duty as monks, for ours is a godly people.

(f) *Something About Masters and Servants and Whether It Is Possible for Them to Become Brother in the Spirit*

Dear God, it cannot be denied that common folk can also be sinful. And the fire of corruption is to be seen spreading hourly, coming from above. Isolation is also appearing among ordinary folk: kulaks and village usurers are emerging; the merchant, too, is already becoming ever more eager for honours and strives to seem educated, though he has no education whatever; to show that he is educated, he despicably spurns the ancient customs and is ashamed even of the faith of his fathers. He calls on princes, though he is merely a corrupted peasant. The common people are festering in drunkenness, and cannot give it up. And what cruelty to their families, their wives and even their children! It all stems from drunkenness. I've even seen ten-year-old children at factories: weak, sickly, rickety and already depraved. The stuffy workshop, the clanging of machinery, toil all day long, foul language, and drink and again drink— is that all a little child's soul needs? What he needs is sunshine, play, good examples on all sides, and just a little love. Monks! That must be put an end to: no more tormenting of children; you must rise up and preach that at once, right away! But God will save Russia, for though the ignorant peasant is corrupt and cannot give up his vile sins, he knows that they are cursed by God, and that he does wrong in sinning. Yet our people still believe in righteousness, have faith in God, and shed tears of devotion. It is different with the upper classes: they have taken up science, and desire to achieve justice on the foundation of reason alone, but without Christ as in the past; they have already proclaimed that crime and sin no longer exist. And they are right in their own eyes: if you have no God, what crime can there be? In Europe, the common people are already rebelling violently against the rich, and the people's leaders everywhere guide them towards bloodshed and teach them that their anger is justified. But "cursed be their anger, for it was fierce." Yet God will save Russia as he has saved her many a time. Salvation will come from the people, from their faith and their humility. Fathers and teachers, work to preserve the people's faith, for that is no dream: all my life long I have been struck by the genuine and magnificent sense of dignity in our great people. I have seen it myself and I can testify to it, I have seen it and marvelled, have seen it despite the vile sins and the poverty-stricken appearance of our people. They are not servile even after two centuries of slavery. They are free in appearance and bearing, but without the least insolence. They are neither vengeful nor envious. 'You are well-born, wealthy, intelligent and talented— that's all very well, and may God bless you. I honour you, but I know that I, too, am a man. By honouring you without envy, I show you my dignity as a man.' And, truly, if they do not say so (for they are still unable to do it) that is the way they *behave*. I have seen and experienced it myself, and (would you believe it) the poorer and lower our Russian peasant is, the more that splendid truth stands out in him, for the rich among them—the kulaks and the usurers—are already corrupted in great measure, for much of which our own negligence and oversight are responsible! But God will save his people, for Russia is great in her humility. I dream of looking into our future, and I already seem to see it clearly, for it will come to pass that even the most corrupt man among our wealthy will ultimately become ashamed of his wealth, in the face of the poor, who, seeing his humility, will understand and gladly give way to him responding with kindness to his noble shame. That is how it will end up, believe me: everything is indicative of it. Equality is to be found only in man's spiritual dignity, and that will be understood only in our land. When men become brothers, there will be brotherhood as well, but there can never be any fair division of wealth before we have brotherhood. It is we who have preserved the image of Christ, which will shine forth like a precious diamond to the whole world— It shall surely come to pass!

Fathers and teachers, a most moving incident once befell me. During my wanderings, I came across my former batman Afanasy one day, in the gubernia town of K. This was eight years after I had seen him last. He chanced on me in the marketplace, recognised me, ran up to me and was so delighted to see me that he almost fell on my neck. "Good gracious, sir, is it you? Can it really be you that I see?" He took me to his home. He had been discharged from the army, was married, with two little children. He and his wife earned a living as stall-holders in the market. His room was a humble one, but spick and span, and joyful. He made me sit down, got the samovar ready, sent for his wife, as though my visit called for a special celebration. He led his children up to me: "Give them your blessing, Father." "Who am I, an ordinary humble monk, to bless them?" I replied. "I'll say a prayer for them, and as for you, Afanasy Pavlovich, I've been praying for you daily since that very day," I went on, "for it was you who brought it all about." And I explained it to him to the best of my ability. How do you think he reacted? He looked at me unable to believe that I, his former master, an army officer, now stood before him in so humble a condition and wearing such clothes. It brought tears into his eyes. "Why these tears?" I asked him, "why, you're a man I shall never forget. You should rather rejoice for me in your heart, my dear fellow, for my path is a joyous one!" He did not say much, but kept sighing and shaking his head over me with the greatest regard. "What has become of your wealth?" he asked. "I donated it to the monastery," I replied. "We live a communal life there." As I was taking leave of him after tea, he took out fifty copecks and gave them to me as an offering for the monastery, and I saw him thrusting another fifty copecks into my hand hurriedly. "That's for you, the pilgrim," he said. "You may find it useful in your travels, Father." I accepted his fifty copecks, bowed to him and to his wife and went away rejoicing, thinking on the way: "I suppose both of us are sighing now, he at home and I on the road, and yet we are smiling happily, in the gladness of our hearts, shaking our heads and remembering how God has brought us together." I never saw him again after that. I had been his master and he my servant, but now when we had embraced each other lovingly and in the joy of our spirits, a great human bond had grown up between us. I have given a great deal of thought to the matter, and here is what I think of it: is it so inconceivable that, in due course, the same kind of great and simple-hearted unity could also spring up everywhere among all our Russian people? I believe that it will, and that the time is near.

As for servants I will add this: as a young man, servants often aroused my anger. "The cook has served the meal too hot," or "The batman has not brushed my clothes." But something I heard my brother say when I was a child suddenly came back to me: "Do I, such as I am, deserve to be waited on by another and lord it over him just because he is poor and ignorant?" And I marvelled at the time why such very simple and, indeed, obvious ideas should come to our minds so late in life. Servants are of course essential in the world, but you must see to it that your servant should be freer in spirit than if he were not a servant. And why can't I be a servant to my servant, and in such a way that he will even see it, and without any pride on my part and no mistrust on his? Why should my servant not be like one of my kith and kin, so that I shall ultimately take him into my family and rejoice in doing so? That is achievable even now and may lead up to a grand unity of men in a future in which man will no longer seek servants for himself and will no longer desire to turn fellow-creatures into servants, as is done nowadays, but, on the contrary, will long with all his heart to become servant to all, as the Gospels teach. And is it a dream that man will ultimately find joy only in great deeds of enlightenment and mercy, and not in cruel pleasures as now—in gluttony, fornication, ostentation, boasting, and envious elevation of one over another? I firmly believe that it is not a dream, and that the time is drawing near. "When will that time come?" people ask laughingly. "And is it likely that it ever will?" But I believe that, with Christ's help, we shall accomplish that great task. And how numerous are the ideas that have appeared in the course of human history, which were unthinkable ten years earlier, and which, when their mysterious hour struck, suddenly emerged to spread all over the earth! So it will be with us too, and our people will shine forth throughout the world, and all will say: "The stone which the builders refused is become the head stone of the corner." And we shall ask the scoffers: if our idea is a dream, then when are you going to erect your building and order things justly through your reason alone, and without Christ? And if they declare to the contrary and claim that it is they who are advancing towards unity, that will be believed only by the most simple-minded among them, so that one cannot but marvel at such simplicity. Truly, their imagination is more prone to run riot than ours is. They think of ordering things justly, but, by rejecting Christ, they will end up by drowning the world in torrents of blood, for blood cries out for blood, for all they that have taken the sword shall perish with the sword. And had it not been for Christ's covenant, they would have slaughtered one another down to the last two men on earth. And, in their pride even those two would have been unable to restrain each other, so that the last man would have slain the other, and then done away with himself. And that would have come to pass but for Christ's promise that, for the sake of the meek and the humble, he hath shortened the days. When, after my duel, while I was still wearing my officer's uniform, I began to speak out in society about servants, that evoked general surprise, as I remember. "What do you expect us to do?" they asked. "Invite our servants to sit down on the sofa and serve them tea?" "Why not?" I would reply, "if only once in a while." They all laughed at the time. The question was frivolous and my reply vague, but I believe there was a certain truth in it.

(g) Of Prayer, Love, and Contact with Other Worlds

Young man, do not forget to pray. If your prayer is sincere, a new feeling will appear in it every time, and with that a new thought, one you were unaware of previously and it will imbue you with fresh courage; you will then understand that prayer is educative. Remember also: every day and whenever you can, repeat to yourself: "O Lord, have mercy upon all who appear before your throne today." For thousands of people depart this life hourly and at every moment, and their souls stand before God. How many of them pass on in solitude, unbeknown to anyone, in sadness and sorrow at having no one to feel sorry for them or even care whether they live or die. And so, from the furthermost end of the earth, your prayer, too, will perhaps ascend to the Lord for the repose of his soul, even if you had no knowledge of each other. How deeply will his soul be moved in the fearful presence of God, to feel at the moment that he has someone to utter a prayer for him and that there is a human being remaining on earth who loves him. And God, too, will look upon you both more graciously, for if you have had so much pity on that soul, how much greater will God's pity be on you both, for God is infinitely more merciful and more loving than you are. And He will forgive him for your sake.

Brothers, have no fear of men's sins. Even in his sin you should love man, for that is already a semblance of divine love and is the highest love on earth. Love all God's creation, the whole of it, and every grain of sand. Love every leaf, every ray of God's light. Love animals, love the plants, love everything. If you love everything, you will perceive the divine mystery in things. And once you have perceived it, you will begin to constantly comprehend it, more and more with every day. And you will at last come to love the entire world with an abiding and all-embracing love. Love animals: God has given them the rudiments of thought and untroubled joy. Therefore, do not disturb it, or torment them, do not deprive them of their joy, or go against God's intent. Man, do not exalt yourself above the animals: they are without sin, while you, in your grandeur, have defiled the earth by appearing on it, and leave your putrid traces behind you—alas, that is true, of almost every one of us! Love the children particularly, for they, too, like the angels, are without sin, and live to evoke mild emotions in us, purify our hearts, and give us a certain guidance. Woe unto him that offends a child! Father Anfim taught me to love children: in our wanderings he, that kind and silent man, would buy sweets and cakes for them on the small alms given to us; he could not pass a child without profound emotion: that is the kind of man he is.

Some ideas perplex you, especially at the sight of men's sins; you ask yourself: "Should it be countered with force or humble love?" Always decide to resort to humble love. If you resolve on that once and for all, you may subdue the whole world. A loving humility is a terrific force, the strongest of all, and there is nothing like it. Look at yourself, every day, and hour, and minute, and be on your guard to ensure that your image is a seemly one. You pass by a little child with spite, harsh words, and a wrathful heart; you may not have noticed the child, but it has seen you, and your image, unseemly and ignoble, may leave an impress on its defenceless heart. You may not know it, but you have perhaps sown a seed of evil in it, which may grow, and all because you did not exercise sufficient restraint towards a child, and because you failed to nurture discreet and active love in yourself. Brothers, love is a teacher, but one has to learn to acquire it, for it is hard to achieve, dearly bought, and calls for long labour and much time, for we must love, not fleetingly and occasionally but for ever. Anyone, even the wicked, can love occasionally. My young brother asked forgiveness of the birds: that may seem absurd, yet it is right, for everything, like the ocean, flows and mixes with everything else: touch it at one place and it is felt at the other end of the world. It may be senseless to beg forgiveness of the birds, but, then, it would be easier for the birds, for the child, and for every animal near you if you were yourself more kindly than you are now—just a little easier, anyhow. It's all like the ocean, I say. Then, moved by an all-embracing love, you would pray to the birds, too, in a kind of ecstasy, and pray that they, too, will forgive your sin. Prize that ecstasy, however absurd people may think it.

My friends, ask God to grant you joy. Be as joyous as children, as the birds of heaven. And let not men's sins trouble you in your work, fear not that they will stamp out your work and prevent it from being accomplished. Do not say: "Sin is mighty, wickedness is mighty, an evil environment is mighty, while we are lonely and helpless, the evil environment will wear us down and prevent the good work from being accomplished." Flee from that despondency, children! You have a single means of salvation: pull yourself together and make yourself answerable for all men's sins. Believe me, my friend, that is really so, for the moment you, in all sincerity, make yourself answerable for everyone and everything, you will at once see that it is really so and that you have, in fact, assumed responsibility for everyone and everything. But, by casting your own indolence and impotence onto others, you will end up by partaking of Satan's pride and murmuring against God. As for satanic pride, here is what I think of it: it is difficult for us here on earth to comprehend it, which is why it is so easy to slide into error and partake of it, even imagining that we are doing something fine and noble. Besides, many of the strongest feelings and urges of our nature cannot yet be comprehended on earth, but be not tempted by that, either, and do not think that it may serve as a justification for you in anything, for the Eternal Judge will call you to account for what you can comprehend, not for what you cannot. You will find that out for yourself, for you will then see everything in its true light and cease from disputing over it. Indeed, we seem to be wandering about blindly on earth and, but for the precious image of Christ before us, we should have lost our way altogether and perished, like the human race before the Flood. Much on earth lies concealed from us, but, to make up for that, we have been given a mysterious inner awareness of our living bond with another world, the higher world of heaven, so that the roots of our thoughts and feelings are not here, but in other worlds. That is why the philosophers say that the essence of things cannot be understood on earth. God took seeds from other worlds and sowed them on this earth, and made his garden grow, so that everything that could come up did so; yet, whatever has been grown lives and is alive only through a sense of contact with other mysterious worlds: if that feeling weakens or is destroyed in you, then what has grown up in you will also die. Then you will become indifferent to life, and even grow to hate it. That is what I think.

(h) *Should One Pass Judgement on One's Fellow-creatures? Of Consummate Faith*

Remember particularly that you can be no man's judge. No man on earth can pass judgement on a criminal until the judge himself learns that he is just as criminal as the man standing before him, and that he is perhaps more at fault than anyone else for the crime of the man on trial. When he has grasped that, he will be able to be a judge. That is true, however absurd it may sound, for had I been righteous myself, there might be no criminal standing before me. If you are able to take upon yourself the crime of the man standing before you and whom you are judging in your heart, then take it upon yourself at once, and suffer for him yourself, and let him go without reproach. And even if the law itself makes you his judge, then act in the same spirit as much as you can, for he will go away and condemn himself more bitterly than you have done. If, however, he goes away indifferent to your loving-kindness and scoffs at you, do not let that affect you, either: his time has not yet come, but will come in due course. If it does not come, that makes no difference: if not he, then another in his place will understand and suffer, and will judge and condemn himself, and truth will be done. Believe in that, believe it without any doubt, for therein lies all the hope and faith of the saints.

Carry on with your good work incessantly. If you recall, as you go to sleep at night, that you have not done all you should have, rise up at once and do it. If the people about you are spiteful and callous, and do not wish to give you ear, fall down before them and ask them for forgiveness, for in truth you are at fault for their reluctance to listen to you. And if you cannot speak to the embittered, serve them in silence and humility, without ever giving up hope. Even if they all abandon you and drive you away by force, fall down upon the earth when you remain alone, and kiss it, drenching it with your tears; the earth will produce fruit from your tears even if no one has heard or seen you in your solitude. Have faith to the end, even if it should so happen that all men on earth have been led astray and you are the only one to remain faithful: sacrifice yourself even then and give praise to God—you who are the only one left. And if two such should meet—then that will be an entire world, a world of living love; embrace each other with great tenderness and give praise to God, whose truth has been manifested if only through the two of you.

If you yourself have sinned and are grieved even unto death for your sins, or for your sudden sin, rejoice for others, rejoice for the righteous man, rejoice that, though you have sinned, he is righteous and has not sinned.

But if men's evil deeds were to arouse indignation and uncontrollable grief in you, and even to make you wish to revenge yourself upon the evil-doers, you should fear that feeling most of all; go at once and seek suffering for yourself just as if you were yourself guilty of that villainy. Accept that suffering and bear it, and your heart will be appeased, and you will understand that you, too, are guilty, for you could have given light to the evil-doers, even as one without sin, yet you have not given them light. Had you done so, you would have lit up their path too and he who committed the crime might not have done so if you had lit up his path. And even if you have done that but see that men have not been saved by your light, you must stand steadfast and without doubt of the power of the heavenly light; believe that, if they have not been saved now, they will be saved later. And if they are not saved later, their sons will be saved, for your light will not go out, even if you die yourself. The righteous man departs, but his light remains. People are always saved after the death of him who has come to save them. The human race do not accept their prophets and do them to death, but they love their martyrs and honour those they have committed to death. You are working for the whole, and acting for the future. Never seek reward, for your reward on earth is great as it is: that spiritual joy which is vouchsafed only to the righteous. Fear not the great or the powerful, but be wise and always serene. Know the right measure and the right time—learn how to do that. Pray when you remain in solitude. Love to fall down to the earth and kiss it. Kiss the earth and love it ceaselessly and insatiably. Love all men, love everything, seek that rapture and ecstasy. Water the earth with the tears of your joy, and love those tears. Be not ashamed of that ecstasy, and prize it, for it is a gift of God, a great gift, and not given to many, but only to the chosen few.

(i) *Of Hell and Hell Fire; a Mystical Discourse*

Fathers and teachers, I ask myself, "What is hell?" And I reason thus: "It lies in suffering from being unable to love any more." Once, in the infinitude of existence, which cannot be measured in time or space, the ability was granted to some spiritual being, on its appearance on earth, to say: "I am, and I love." Once and only once, he was granted a moment of active and *living* love, and for that he was given life on earth, and together with it, times and seasons. And what came about? That fortunate being rejected the priceless gift, prized it not, loved it not, scorned it and hardened his heart against it. Such a one, having departed from the earth, sees the bosom of Abraham and speaks to him, as we are told in the parable of the rich man and Lazarus, beholds Paradise, and can go up to the Lord, but what torments him so, however, is that he will ascend to God without ever having loved or come into contact with those who love and whose love he has ignored. For he clearly sees and says to himself: "I now have understanding and, though I thirst after love, there will be no great deed or sacrifice in my love, for my earthly life is over, and Abraham will not come even with a drop of living water (that is to say, again with the gift of former active life on earth) to cool the flame of the yearning for spiritual love which burns in me now and which I neglected on earth; there is no more life for me and there will be no more time! Though I would gladly give my life for others, I can do it no more, for the life is gone that I could have sacrificed for love and there is a great gulf fixed between that life and this existence." They speak of material hell fire: I do not go into that mystery and dread it, but I think that even if there were material fire, it would be welcome, for, I imagine, material agony would lead to the far more terrible spiritual agony being forgotten, even though for a moment. Moreover, that spiritual agony cannot be taken away, for it lies within, not without. Even if it could be taken away, I cannot help thinking that men's unhappiness would be more bitter because of it. For though contemplating their torment, the righteous in Paradise were to forgive them and call them up to heaven in their infinite love, they would multiply their torments by doing so, for they would arouse in them still more the flaming yearning for responsive, active, and grateful love, which is no longer possible. In the timidity of my heart, however, I cannot help thinking that the very consciousness of that impossibility would ultimately serve to alleviate their suffering, for, by accepting the love of the righteous without the possibility of repaying it, they will at last find in that submissiveness and in the effect of that humility, a certain semblance of that active love which they ignored on earth, and a kind of activity which is similar to it— I am sorry, my friends and brothers, that I cannot express it more clearly. But woe to those who have destroyed themselves on earth, woe to the suicides! I don't think there can be anyone more unhappy than they. We are told that it is a sin to pray to the Lord for them, and outwardly the Church seems to reject them, but in my heart of hearts I think that we may pray even for them. For love can never be an offence against Christ. All my life, I have prayed inwardly for such as these; I confess that to you, fathers and teachers, and I still pray for them every day.

Oh, there are some who remain fierce and proud even in Hell, despite their certain knowledge and contemplation of irrefutable truth; there are some fearsome ones who have given themselves completely to Satan and his proud spirit. For such, hell is voluntary and all-consuming; they are martyrs of their own free will. For they have cursed themselves by cursing God and life. They feed upon their wicked pride, like a starving man in the desert sucking blood from his own body. They can never be satiated and they reject forgiveness, and curse God when he calls them. They cannot behold the living God without hatred, and demand that there should be no God of life, and that God should destroy himself and all he has created. And they will burn eternally in the fire of their wrath, and yearn for death and non-existence. But they will not be granted death—

Here ends Alexei Fyodorovich Karamazov's manuscript. I repeat: it is incomplete and with gaps. The biographical data, for instance, cover only the early years of the *starets*. Selections from his homilies and his views, evidently uttered at different times and as a consequence of various motivations, have been brought together to form a single whole, as it were. What the *starets* said during the last hours of his life is not stated precisely, but the spirit and character of his last discourse can be gathered if compared with what has been quoted in Alexei Fyodorovich's record of his former teachings. The death of the *starets* came quite unexpectedly. For although those who had gathered in his room that last evening were fully aware that his death was at hand, they never imagined that it would come so suddenly; on the contrary, his friends, as I have already observed, seeing him apparently so cheerful and talkative that night, were sure that there had been a marked improvement in his health, for a short time at least. Even five minutes before his death, as they afterwards recounted with surprise, it was quite impossible to foresee it. He seemed suddenly to feel an acute pain in his chest, turned pale and pressed a hand to his heart. They all rose from their seats at once and rushed up to him, but, though in great pain, he gazed at them with a smile, sank slowly from his chair on to the floor, knelt, bowed his face towards the ground, stretched out his arms and, as though in joyful rapture, kissing the ground and praying (as he had bidden them), he quietly and joyfully gave up his soul to God. The news of his death spread immediately through the hermitage and reached the monastery. Those closest to the departed one, as well as those whose duty it was in accordance with their monastic rank, began laying out his body according to the ancient rites, and all the monks gathered in the cathedral church. And even before dawn, as was rumoured afterwards, the news of his death reached town. By the morning, the event was on almost all lips, and many citizens flocked to the monastery. But we shall deal with that in the next book; we shall only add here that before a day had passed, something so unexpected took place, and so strange in the impression it produced in the monastery and in the town, so disturbing and so confusing, that, even after so many years, that day, so upsetting to many people, is still clearly remembered in our town.

REQUEST TO READERS

Raduga Publishers would be glad to have your opinion of this book, its translation and design, and any suggestions you may have for future publications.
Please send all your comments to 17, Zubovsky Boulevard, Moscow, USSR.